Sophia Nash

Withdrawn

The Kiss

AVON

An Imprint of HarperCollinsPublishers

This is a work of fiction. Names, characters, places, and incidents are products of the author's imagination or are used fictitiously and are not to be construed as real. Any resemblance to actual events, locales, organizations, or persons, living or dead, is entirely coincidental.

AVON BOOKS
An Imprint of HarperCollins*Publishers*
10 East 53rd Street
New York, New York 10022-5299

Copyright © 2008 by Sophia Nash
ISBN: 978-0-06-123137-7
www.avonromance.com

First Avon Books paperback printing: March 2008

Avon Trademark Reg. U.S. Pat. Off. and in Other Countries, Marca Registrada, Hecho en U.S.A.
HarperCollins® is a registered trademark of HarperCollins Publishers.

Printed in the U.S.A.

10 9 8 7 6 5 4 3 2 1

To Grayson

Acknowledgments

Greatest thanks to agent Helen Breitwieser of Cornerstone Literary for her exceptional guidance and to Avon/HarperCollins Executive Editor Lyssa Keusch, Editor May Chen, and Cristine Grace for shepherding this book through publication with so much care. Much gratitude to Cybil Solyn for her terrific insight and support, Mike Odell at the Greenbrier Falconry School for his falconry lessons, and to Crystal Davis and Kelley Grasnow for providing the inspiration behind a strong heroine with a great heart and a desire to work hard—the type of person I most admire.

And special appreciation to several people who are always so encouraging: John Charles, Gregory W. Gingery, Kathryn Caskie, Elsie Hogarth, Louise Bergin, Candice Hern, Anna Campbell, Diana Peterfreund, Deborah Barnhardt, Diana Crosby, Hope Tarr, Ann Kane, Fairleigh Killen—and to www.RomanceNovel.TV's Maria Lokken, Marisa O'Neill, and Kim Castillo, as well as Michelle Buonfiglio at LifetimeTV.com.

Finally, as always, endless thanks to my beloved husband, children, mother, sisters, and parents-in-law, and to two very special cousins—Peter Nash and Count Arnaud d'Aurelle de Paladines—all of whom provide a well of love and support whenever I most need it.

The Kiss

Prologue

July 20—to do
- *review Penrose's ledgers*
- *distribute quarterly wages to all servants/laborers*
- *look to having carriages repainted/yokes replaced*
- *pack personal effects*

   - get married . . . <u>maybe</u>

"**M**oderation," Georgiana Wilde breathlessly cautioned her husband of several hours, "is the key to happiness."

The Marquis of Ellesmere's deep baritone chuckle filled the vast, elegantly appointed bedchamber that had served twelve generations of Fortesques very well. "Yes, but my dear, there are times when excess has its merits. And I do believe"—with a wolfish look Anthony swallowed the last of the brandy in his glass—"wedding nights fall into that category."

He turned her around like a recalcitrant child. "You'll have to stop gripping your arms if I'm to get this gown off you," he murmured, then nuzzled her neck.

Georgiana's insides roiled, yet she immediately released her elbows and stifled the urge to squirm under Anthony's tickling breath. This was every bit as embarrassing as she had imagined it would be. He was working the buttons at the back of her gown and she was precisely eight pieces of clothing away from utter embarrassment—one gown, one corset, one shift, two shoes, two stock—

Without warning her gown whooshed over her head and a button snagged her hair. "Ow!"

Anthony chuckled again and gently extricated the offending article. "It serves you right for dismissing poor Harris."

"Honestly, you didn't really expect me to undress in front of your mother's maid of forty years, did you?"

"Mmmm . . ." He had his face buried in her hair and she felt his fingers searching for pins.

"Why, when you asked for congratulations, Harris's lips became more pursed than the time you bit into an unripe persimmon." Now she was babbling and her voice sounded high and unnatural, even to her own ears. She was certain normal women did not bring up fruit on their wedding night.

She shivered but resisted the urge to wrap her arms about her shift-clad body again. Surely there was not one Ellesmere marchioness in the illustrious family tree who had had such a plain and frayed garment. And her serviceable corset with the yellowed whalebone sticking out . . . Well, Anthony had known what he was getting when he persisted in this ridiculous—

"Stay still." Anthony's arm snaked around her waist and he lifted her to stand in front of the bedpost. She grasped the finely turned rosewood and exhaled as her new husband—she still couldn't believe she had gone through with it—stroked a finger from her nape to the top of her corset. "You're not turning missish, are you? Most ladies of eight and twenty are over that sort of thing."

"Stop being ridiculous. I'm not . . ." she stammered, "I'm just a little . . ."

"Nervous?" he filled in, his lips nipping her earlobe. "I hope your mother hasn't been filling your head with nonsense about duty and pain."

"No, she only suggested the *rack* would give more pleasure." She felt his lips curl on her neck. "But I am to concentrate on the majesty of the Fortesque jewels."

Humor crawled into his voice. "Your mother is interested in the family jewels, is she?" He threw back his head and laughed before gathering her to his barrel-shaped chest. "You may tell her they were much *larger* than you expected."

"Well, if all else fails, I'm to put my mind to good use by planning my future role."

"As if you needed any inducement to make more of those confounded lists of yours." He slowly spun her around and wrapped his arms about her before lifting her to her toes and planting all-consuming kisses on her eyes, her nose, and finally her lips. She inhaled sharply and registered the smoky scent of his neck cloth. It was the sickly sweet aroma she had recently learned was the favored amusement of jaded gentlemen and worldly ladies . . . *opium*.

"Now, there'll be no more nonsense about duty

and torture." His fingers skimmed the top edges of her corset and shift, searching and finding the little bow. "But since you're so fond of plans, let me tell you what I plan to do to you. No, I see that look in your eye. I've spent *years and years* thinking about this night, and now I'll have the pleasure of telling you all about it, since we're properly married and you no longer have to pretend to be shocked."

Her nerves almost deserted her when the familiar dangerous glint appeared in his darkening eyes.

A short, piercing shriek echoed from the corridor on the other side of the locked bedchamber door. The unmistakable high-pitched voices of Anthony's mother, sisters, and Mrs. Harris whistled through the room's cracks.

"You're entirely mistaken, Harris," his mother's voice echoed. "Anthony gave me his word he wouldn't marry without my approval. He's merely enticed by that loose-moraled, scheming—"

"She was a-wearin' the ruby-and-diamond ring."

"Not Granny's," moaned a voice that sounded a lot like his younger sister's.

"I saw it wif me own eyes."

Harris never could hide her cockney roots when she was in a snit, thought Georgiana.

"Anthony," she whispered. "You said you'd informed your mother, and furthermore, she'd be away another three days. Oh, this is unbearable. What are we to do?"

"And I suppose when you say *we* you really mean *me*, if past history is any indication."

"You don't really expect *me* to go out there, do

you?" That was the thing about Tony. You never could really be sure.

"Well, if you just stick your hand out the door and show them the bloody ring, that'll quiet 'em right up. And then we can go straight back to my plans." His eyes were twinkling, but the odd look in the rest of his expression couldn't mask his concern. Facing judgement had never been one of Anthony's preferred activities. Beating a hasty retreat until everything boiled over was much more his style.

Anthony tugged at his neck cloth. "Oh, all right."

The rattle of the door handle rended the air. Georgiana grabbed her rumpled gown and threw it over her head, praying for something, anything, other than this awkward moment. "I'm not sure I'll forgive you for this—at least not in this century."

"My dear, cover your ears. Consider it my first husbandly order." He winked. "I think I could get used to that part of the vows." Hopping on one leg, he put on his breeches quickly and stuffed in the edges of his long linen shirt. His familiar lopsided smile worked far better than any wicked wink at tugging at her heart. She dutifully covered her ears upon hearing an explosion of very unladylike language on the other side of the door.

She loved the big imbecile, no matter how much she was tempted to wring his neck at times. It had been the way of things since they were three years old. Their nannies had been sisters from the village and had used every opportunity to join forces in attempting to corral their exuberant charges. Why, Tony's antics and hair-raising schemes to avoid his long-suffering string of tutors during adolescence were legendary.

And his actions as a man? Well, after one and a half very poorly executed years at Oxford, which were said to have been the cause of his father's apoplexy and early demise, ten mysterious years had followed in London. Georgiana knew there were some who whispered he was a thoroughly debauched, dissipated rake without a shred of a conscience or a lick of common sense. And they were right.

But only partially.

There was also a heart of gold half buried under those years of depravity, and also years of guilt. It was why she was willing to help him find his way back to a productive way of life.

And she'd do it because he was her best friend. Well . . .

Well.

If she couldn't have her ridiculous childhood dream—and she couldn't—then she could grab onto happiness with a man she could help. A man who needed her. A man who wanted her.

A man who loved her.

A loud crash intruded on her thoughts. She cautiously lifted her hands from her ears and realized Tony and his mother had boxed themselves up in the marchioness's rooms adjacent to this suite. The very rooms from which Lady Ellesmere would be forced to remove in order to give way to Georgiana. God preserve her.

"Anthony Edward Lawrence Fortesque, she is

a—a—a *peasant*. No, worse than that. She's the *deformed spawn of a nobody*. I will not share a house with that upstart—that conniving daughter of our *steward*. Think what your father would have said! Why, you must have this ridiculous union annulled right away. We shall call on our solicitor in town, and thank God I found this out in time before you consu—"

"Mamma," Anthony interjected. "Enough. It is done and I will not undo it. She is not a nobody. Our Mr. Wilde is a gentleman—merely impoverished. Wasn't his cousin the earl of some shire or other? You will just have to learn how to live with her. She really is a darling girl and . . . and I love her. I've always—"

"And her vile, common mother," the marchioness interrupted. "Clearly her parents helped her hatch this evil plan and somehow they worked on you in secret to soften your tender sensibilities. And to think I was on the point of arranging for the Duke of Eddington's daughter for you. She won't have you now. But then perhaps we could hush this up. Now there's an idea. I could prevail upon—"

"Mamma," Anthony said so quietly and tiredly that Georgiana could barely hear his voice through the wall. "Enough."

The sound of his footfalls came toward the connecting door before it opened and Georgiana could see the distraught form of Lady Ellesmere beyond. The virago's face was bright scarlet, which hid quite effectively the faded beauty that had once graced the older lady's countenance.

The marchioness shook a finger at her. "Don't you dare look at me—you scheming *interloper*. When I think of everything our family has done for yours. And this is how you repay us? Why, there is a special place in the devil's home for girls like you. I shall not rest until this sham of a marriage is—"

Anthony closed and bolted the door against his mother's ranting and took five long steps toward the second bottle of brandy on his bedside table. Not bothering to pour the amber-colored liquid into a glass, he pulled huge gulps of the spirits directly from the bottle for long moments.

Georgiana watched his Adam's apple bob below the shadow cast by the putrid green bottle and resisted the urge to caution him. She'd never seen Anthony exude anything but charm and good humor during their younger years. The Anthony who had returned to Penrose had a dark and tired sort of malaise coursing beneath his worn, thin, cheerful façade.

His mother still raged beyond; presumably her daughters and the housekeeper provided a more sympathetic audience. Georgiana heard something about London, a solicitor, and calling for a carriage while she crossed to Anthony and softly clasped his rigid back against the softness of her breasts. "Oh, Tony . . ."

There was nothing more she could say. She could only swallow her hurt feelings. There was no purpose to regret, no chance to unravel what they had done. They must go forward, make a life together.

At least she could promise a productive, useful life, even if she had to drag him to the point.

She turned him into her arms and took hold of the now half-empty bottle and gently forced it from his lips. He looked down at her from his great height, his slightly dazed sloping eyes glittering in pain and disillusionment.

"It's all right," she murmured, initiating for the first time an embrace with her new husband. "Everything will be right as rain in the morning, I promise. It always is. She'll get used to the idea. And even if she doesn't right away, I'll do my best to—"

He cut her off. "What have I done to you? I'm so sorry. I've always ruined everything. I should've thought how difficult this would be for you. But I only thought of myself. Georgiana, I was always selfish. I just wanted you for myself. You're my Georgie girl—my friend, my conscience, my love. I promise I shall protect you and I'll make this up to you. I will. See if I don't."

"Shhhh," she whispered as his lips came down to hers. The taste of the brandy wound 'round her senses and relaxed her slightly. It was strange how shared anxiety was binding her closer to her friend, more so than any of his overtly romantic tactics.

He pulled away distractedly and began rubbing his left shoulder and arm while muttering more apologies. She tugged his hand to her mouth and kissed it softly before releasing it to stroke his overly long burnished gold hair, which gleamed in the candlelight.

"Don't, Tony. Don't apologize. I'm glad we married. I know you love me."

He looked at her, a strange anxious look in his expression. "And you love me, don't you? Finally . . . you love me." He pushed a curl from her eyes. "Passionately? Ardently? At least devotedly?"

She swallowed. "I have loved you forever." She paused awkwardly and forced a smile to her lips. "Since the day you gave me Achilles."

He chuckled. "God, I'd forgotten that. He was the one with the back markings that looked like a map of Prussia, wasn't he?"

"Actually it was more like Italy," she replied with a small smile.

"It was very generous of me to give you that frog."

She thanked God the moment had passed. She hated to see his confidence waver. It made her feel very alone and unsafe.

"I know," she replied, making certain there was a hint of humor threading her voice. "In fact, I do believe I prefer that slimy creature over this ridiculous ring."

His lips twitched. "I knew we'd be back to jewelry eventually. But at least I'm prepared. Never say a Fortesque doesn't know how to please his wife. Hmmm . . . *wife*. I like that word. It fits you perfectly—as perfectly as this will." He slowly extracted a long rope of pearls from his pocket, all the while watching her face.

"Oh, Tony . . . you shouldn't. I mean, well, perhaps you should"—she smiled—"but really, all this is too much for one day."

"Shhhh . . . they'll serve a very good purpose. You're to bite them while I make love to you." He nipped at her neck and tickled her until she collapsed onto the bed in a gale of laughter.

Playfully holding her wrists in one hand, Anthony somehow managed to fully undress her and himself while he kissed her unmercifully. The last coherent thing she noted was the sound of the heavy front entryway door banging shut—presumably by the hands of the enraged marchioness—so forcefully that the very walls of Penrose seemed to shudder in pain, or perhaps relief.

Tangled within the heavy bedcovers, Anthony proceeded to demonstrate the difference between friendship and love. And buried as Georgiana had been in the simple, raw life of Cornwall, she had no idea such things went on between a man and his wife. None of it even vaguely resembled what her mother had described in simple country terms. She'd known there would be kisses but hadn't known he would remove every stitch of clothing. Hadn't known that it would be so terribly embarrassing. He was supposed to just raise her night rail and his night shirt and then couple with her—painfully the first time. And then—

"What is going on in that head of yours?" he asked, lifting his lips from the tip of her breast. His eyes were unnaturally glazed over as he pressed yet another kiss upon her. "If I can't hear your sighs of approval now, I fear what I'll hear later. Try to relax and enjoy this. You're mine now, and I intend to remind you of that every night in this bed."

A thread of discomfort unraveled within her. She wasn't sure how she was going to be able to repeat this every night for the rest of her life. It all just felt so awkward. She forced herself to run her fingers through his blond locks, which curled at the ends. At least his face was so very dear to her. It was only his amber eyes that had always given her discomfort. Eyes so much like . . . She shoved away the thought ruthlessly.

Perhaps it was the dimness of the light in the room, but he suddenly looked much older than his twenty-eight years, his face pale despite the fine sheen of sweat on his brow.

"I've always loved you, Georgiana. You always made me happy. You alone understood me. Well, Quinn understood me in a fashion too, I suppose." His lips twisted. "He always saw through me—unlike everyone else."

She removed her hand from his hair and pressed it against the bed. *Oh God. No, please don't let him continue.* She couldn't bear hearing the name that represented every lost dream.

"Enough." He dropped his gaze to her body and exhaled. "I want to kiss you everywhere. Ah, I'm a selfish beast, all right, but then you knew that when you married me." He smiled wickedly and ran his fingers down the side of her form all the way to her knee. His gaze trailed after his hand.

She stiffened. "You promised you wouldn't look at my legs."

His eyes returned to her own. "But I didn't promise not to touch."

"Please, Anthony," she implored softly. If only she could forget how ugly her limbs were tonight.

He touched the end of her nose with his finger. "I will, but only to please you. You know I will never torment you about your deformities. It was my fault, after all."

She closed her eyes in unbearable pain. "You promised not to mention it. And I've told you over and over it wasn't your fault."

His expression proved he had never forgiven himself, but that didn't stop him from resuming his exploration, touching, tasting, nipping her lips, her breasts, her fingers, until he tensed and covered her body all at once with his own. As he moved his body in alignment with hers, Georgiana realized this was the moment of truth.

She forced herself not to squirm and raised her eyes to meet his gaze. She dispassionately noticed the deep grooves on his damp forehead. Shockingly, she felt his fingers trail a path over her belly and touch her intimately. She wanted to clamp her legs together in shock. Oh God, how was she to let him do this? It was all too intimate. Too mortifying.

It was all wrong. All unbearably wrong.

He closed his eyes and shook his head slightly. "You're not . . ."

"I'm not what?" she whispered.

"You need some brandy. Could use more myself. Damn my mother . . . Damn them all to . . ." He stopped and his head swayed. His face was suddenly very flushed.

"Tony?" she whispered. "Are you all right?"

His eyes snapped open, but he seemed slightly confused. "Sorry," he muttered. "Hard to know how much is too much and how much is not 'nuf." With a dazed expression he looped the almost forgotten rope of pearls around her neck and teased her mouth by drawing the pebbled length against her lips. Tony sighed heavily and edged his weight onto her again. He was such a large man and Georgiana struggled slightly to breathe. Suddenly, his blunt flesh was against her most sensitive place and he was pressing into her.

And now it was not only embarrassing but also uncomfortable, and he was too stifling hot and clammy on top of her. And something else was wrong. She was dry and taut and unyielding and he was relentless and—

"Dearest," he said, straining. "Just think of . . . Just think of . . . of me. Always of me. Not of *him* . . ."

"What?" she said, her voice thin.

His eyes widened and then rolled back into his head before he slumped on top of her, his full weight pressing her down until she thought she might faint. The forgotten pearls slithered from her neck and mouth to the decadent silk sheets.

"Tony . . ." Something was terribly wrong. "Tony? Anthony!" She squeezed the massive shoulders that had collapsed against her own. She was shaking uncontrollably, and unable to budge him.

My God . . .

Oh please, Lord . . . Please help. Oh please, please help me . . .

Chapter 1

Twelve months later . . .

"Thank goodness you're returned, Quinn," the dowager marchioness said, rushing toward the thirteenth Marquis of Ellesmere. "I'd despaired of ever seeing you again. Why, my daughters and I were certain those pagan tribesmen would kill you off and then where would we all be?"

Quinn Fortesque resisted the urge to tell his aunt that if he were dead he probably wouldn't care a whit. He also knew any attempt to educate her on the civility of the Portuguese was futile. Instead, he slowly rose from the mandarin–style desk lodged in the library of Ellesmere House, Number Sixteen Portman Square, in the most important city in the world, and ruthlessly held in check his pagan desire to cut short the false welcome. "I hope I find you in good health, madam? And my cousins?"

"Henrietta and Margaret are well enough, but I fear my nerves will never recover." She sighed as if onstage and coyly offered her hand to him.

He took care to brush his lips on her fingers instead of kissing the air above as he was sure so many other gentlemen did. It brought a blush to the former beauty, just as he had known it would. Those who had had exquisite form only to watch it depart on aged feet were the ladies who appreciated attention more so than those who had never had any beauty to begin with. He offered this kiss, this laurel branch of peace, to the woman who hadn't spared him a thought until the moment of her son's death.

Lady Ellesmere sighed and sank into the low-slung Egyptian settee near the massive fireplace.

Quinn's aunt and uncle had always had a penchant for surrounding themselves with the most exotic, and most expensive furnishings. Upon his arrival two hours prior, Quinn had taken in the Italian silk draperies, the Chinese–influenced wall hangings, and the Grecian-themed carpeting. Why, the mansion was a veritable model for harmonious international diplomacy . . . among furniture merchants. Well, the Fortesque fortune could withstand the outrageous expense, and it was no doubt due to the machinations of the family's triumvirate comprised of a ham-handed solicitor, a stoic banker and a deceptively polite London steward.

His aunt tittered to break his prolonged silence. "Margaret and Hen are scouring the shops on Bond Street in preparation for the little season. If we'd known your ship was to arrive today, you can be sure they would've been here to greet you. We've so much to discuss." The marchioness withdrew an exquisitely embroidered handkerchief from her pocket and pressed the square of fine linen to her dry eyes. "To think the last time we were all together we were so blissfully happy and didn't even know it."

He raised one brow a fraction of an inch. Blissfully happy was not exactly the way he would have described his sentiments all those years ago when he had been lectured, whipped, and packed off to school on the back of his uncle's dogcart one cold, dark morning before the cock crowed. "I'm sorry you've been forced to suffer so, madam," he said quietly.

"Oh, you always—*well, for the most part at least*—behaved properly. Not that you shouldn't have, you understand. Nephews are always supposed to have impeccable manners."

Especially nephews who were *penniless orphans*.

"And I must thank you again for not getting yourself killed. I only wish you had come sooner to see to the marauder who has the audacity to call herself—"

"Madam, perhaps you didn't hear there was a minor problem of the colonies declaring *war* just after our diplomatic corps finished regrouping following the French withdrawal."

"Yes, yes, but you must remove that horrid gel from Penrose. I insist upon it. Why, she is running it to rack and ruin. The expenses are outrageous. Within a day of running us off the estate she shoved my dear, dear Anthony into a cold grave without telling us and then re-thatched the cottages of every petty laborer and tenant on the estate."

He would not interrupt her again. It would end all the sooner if he allowed her to have her say. Once.

"And she has the audacity to pass herself off as the new marchioness," she moaned. "As if someone who is intimately familiar with the barnyard has the right to sleep in my bed! The horror of it. Quinn, you must force the inquiry. It's moving much too slowly. The marriage wasn't valid. I'm certain of it. No one believes that half-cocked story she told of my dear Anthony choking during a late supper. And one of the maids hinted that the bed linens . . . well, I am too delicate to tell you more. You must question her yourself and you must see our solicitor and go before the House of Lords, and you must go to Penrose and toss that ungrateful Georgiana Wilde and her scheming family out of my room and off our land. I'll not set one foot there until every last trace of that family is removed from my home, ahem, *our* home." She finally paused for breath.

For a moment Quinn had feared she might expire from lack of air. He looked at her silently for a long moment until she finally recollected something.

"Quinn, you do have my deepest condolences. We were dreadfully sorry to hear about Cynthia a year and a half ago." Her expression changed. "I remember hearing how beautiful she was on your wedding day. I'm sorry I wasn't there to see it, your uncle was perhaps a bit unrelenting in your case—well . . . the columns said Cynthia wore a lovely pale blue gown with Valenciennes bobbin lace ruffles. I understand she was almost as pretty as your cousin Henrietta . . ." She had the good sense to stop when she glanced at him.

Quinn relaxed the features on his face to encourage her to prose on. It was always better to know the enemy's plans than to be caught unawares at a later date.

The marchioness giggled. "I know it's too soon to mention it, but Henrietta has never forgotten you, you know. She often speaks of you. And if my hunches are right, and they always are, I forsee—"

"Fine weather for my journey to Cornwall?" He quickly rose from his seat and offered an arm to escort her to the door. "I shall be leaving in a week to see to Penrose's affairs and the other estates. But first I must settle Fairleigh with Cynthia's parents."

"Your daughter is here? Oh, I must see her! Henrietta will be dying to meet her. I always thought Hen would make a very good mother. Is Fairleigh much grown—and does she have the Fortesque looks, or does she favor her mother?"

"An unusual combination." He must end this now. He would not allow a discussion about his nine-year-old daughter. He had almost forgotten how oppressive these scenes could be. "Forgive me, I must finish these ledgers and meet with Tilden before—"

"And that's another thing. You must tell that man he is not to countermand me. I've been on the point of sacking him several times this last year. Why, the very nerve of the man, suggesting I should economize. Well," she huffed, "as if I don't have the right to spend money the way I see fit, and all while that pretentious Georgiana Wilde is spending our fortune on God knows what. Why, when Anthony was alive—"

Quinn possessed the ability to turn off his hearing on command. It was a skill he had honed after years spent listening to diplomatic corps blowhards from every country in the civilized and not-so-civilized world. And Gwendolyn Fortesque, Lady Ellesmere, could blow with the best of them.

He allowed her to vent her grievances all the way to the doorway before he cut in, leaving her openmouthed. "Madam, if I am to remove to Penrose before Friday next, you must excuse me now." He doubted Lady Ellesmere had been interrupted more than once or twice in her lifetime, and surely never by anyone other than her husband.

Quinn glanced at Mr. Tilden on the other side of the doorway, standing patiently while suffering the withering glance of the marchioness as she huffed and swept away in a manner bearing a marchioness who had been born a mere miss and had used her beauty to claw her way up the social ladder the old-fashioned way, by marriage.

"Your ladyship." Mr. Tilden bowed.

Endurance, it seemed, thy name was Tilden.

Quinn invited the London steward into the study with a motion of his arm. "Mr. Tilden."

"May I be permitted to welcome you home, sir?"

"You may," Quinn replied, biting back a smile. The man hadn't changed a whit, bless his limited turns of phrase.

"And may I be permitted to offer my sincerest condolences on your losses, my lord?"

He nodded curtly, hating to be reminded yet again. "Tilden, I should warn you that I shall hunt you down and shoot you if you ever try to leave your post." He sat down and indicated for Mr. Tilden to do the same. "You're the only one I can trust in this madness."

The steward smiled slowly. "May I be permitted to thank you, my lord?"

"No. There's no need for thanks when I'm certain compliments have been far too few and far between these last years. Now let's get down to it, shall we? Before you explain the large increase in expenses at Penrose, what in heaven's name is a Russian sable liner and how did Lady Ellesmere manage to spend three hundred forty-seven pounds on it without my approval?"

"Well, sir, if you will permit me to explain, in the next ledger you'll find a correction. Returned it to the shop while the marchioness was at the lending library." He said the last under his breath.

"And . . ."

"And her ladyship thinks she left it at the Countess of Home's musical. Created quite a fuss about it. She had some, ahem, singularly unpleasant words with the countess."

"Send the countess some hothouse roses along with my apologies, Mr. Tilden."

"Very good, my lord," Tilden said, the gap in his front teeth making a merry appearance. "And may I be permitted to say again how good it is to see you here, my lord?"

Chapter 2

July 27—to do
- _oversee ricking of haycocks if sufficiently dry_
- _invite Ata and the Widows Club to lunch tomorrow_
- _resolve flooded field_
- _check bees_
- _check ledgers again in case he arrives . . ._

- _check pigsty—ugh_

The last chore of the day coincided with the last rays of the day. Georgiana could easily have put it off. But then with her gown already dirty from examining the new drainage ditch on the northeast corner, and from bits of wax and honey from the apiary, when would she ever find a better time? And there was no possible way she could leave this for Father. It was getting harder and harder for him to do anything other than check the ledgers.

Georgiana's shoulders sagged at the sight of the pigsty. They really were going to have to do something about that new man they'd hired. The reworked trough was an abomination. It was uneven; the bottom quite obviously had a gaping edge. Slops were piling under it and the pigs appeared underfed.

There was no use trying to find someone to help her. She had sent everyone home early as the wind was up, the barometer down, and an ugly storm brewed on the horizon.

There was nothing to do but manage it on her own. Wasn't that the way it usually went anyway? She refused to acknowledge that was the way she preferred it.

Grabbing the heavy tool basket, she stepped into the deep muck of the pen, her skirt catching and tearing on a rusted nail. She muttered her annoyance and slogged past the jumble of sleeping pigs half-buried in the mud. The gown was for the ragman now—not even the lowest scullery maid would want it. She shrugged. Her gowns seemed to have shorter and shorter lives these days.

Carefully, Georgiana balanced the tools on the end of the trough and reached for the hammer. She eased out the bent and poorly placed nails in the rotting wood and one side of the trough fell heavily, awakening all the swine. She had but a minute or two to reposition the wood and hammer it correctly in place before squeals of piggish delight heralded a small stampede toward her.

Inquisitive wet snouts searched all around— beneath the fixed trough, the edge of a bucket, even under her pinned-up skir—

Her last thought as she teetered and lost the battle to keep her balance was that even the ragman wouldn't want her gown after this. She looked down to find that almost every inch of her was covered in the delightfully greenish-brown sludge that smelled so strongly of porcine elements that it brought tears to her eyes.

And of course, to add to the final humiliation, Gwendolyn—Georgiana hadn't been able to resist giving her mother-in-law's name to the largest and most intimidating sow—used her prodigious snout to tip over the tool basket, sending the heavy, blunt end of an ax right onto Georgiana's leg. Her *bad* knee.

"Ohhh," she moaned, grabbing her limb. "Damn you, you, idiotic, pathetic excuse for a ham. I'm personally carving the bacon off your condemned sides today, Gwendolyn." Georgiana finished her rant with a blasphemous slew of words that had taken two decades to learn from the laborers on the estate. She was quite proud of her considerable skill at swearing a blue streak in private.

A sudden movement caught her attention. She looked up to find *him* standing right in front of her.

Quinn. *Quinn Fortesque.*

Good Lord. It was he. She opened her mouth to speak, but not a word came to her lips. She was sure he could see her heart pounding in her chest. She had typically acted like an imbecile when he was about, and it seemed fifteen years hadn't changed that. In fact, it was going to be far worse for her now, for he had fully grown into the impossibly handsome man she had known he would become.

He was looking as coolly collected, as perfect, as impeccably dressed as a Marquis of Ellesmere should look. Without a hair out of place he stood there, his shoulders ridiculously broad, his stance wide, his hands on his hips. He appeared as permanent and as ageless as the great oak on the front lawn of Penrose as he took in the full majesty of the mucky scene.

And yet there was something different about him. It was his eyes . . . or rather, his expression—the one thing about him she'd known she'd never be able to forget. Now there was none of the open warmth she remembered. Instead there was shadow.

"Well," he said, "that was an education. Although I'm not certain pigs can actually do what you suggested." His gaze never wavered from her own as a glimmer of amusement broke through his reserve at last.

"A person, a proper person at least, does not sneak up on a body," she muttered, hating to sound so defensive. She tore her gaze away from his before she made an utter fool of herself. "I'm completely justified—"

"It's good to see you too, Georgiana," he murmured.

She closed her eyes, the echo of his deep baritone warming her insides despite the clammy mud. His voice reminded her of hot brandy on a cold night. At least that hadn't changed.

Oh, this wasn't going at all like she had planned.

Would life ever unfold the way she envisioned? She made timetables, she outlined, she prepared, and it never, ever went the way it should. Just one time—

"Let's see. I think a plank will work, if you'll just wait one moment," he said, turning to a nearby pile of lumber.

She began to mutter to herself, a lifelong habit she had never been able to conquer. "I'm fine, really. I don't need any help, unless you want to fetch a nice, long, sharp knife for that" —she almost said a most unladylike word— "vile, horrid piece of pork."

"Such language." He seesawed one board away from the rest of the pile. "Didn't your father always say, 'You can take the swine out of the barnyard, but you can't take the barnyard out of the swine?'"

"That's not at all how the saying goes," she sputtered. "Did you just call me a *pig*?"

"Not at all. I was referring to that poor sow over there. You did just call her by my dear aunt's name, didn't you?" And then he finally relaxed his face fully and loosed that huge, deep, warm laugh that had always affected her breathing. Quinn shed his midnight blue coat and began unbuttoning the cuffs of his fine lawn shirt.

"No," she protested. "I won't be the cause of another ruined article of clothing." Georgiana rolled her hip to ease herself up, using her less-injured leg.

She had to stop staring at him; yet it was impossibly difficult to look away. It had been far too long, and she wished time would stand still so she could drink in the sight of him. Instead she forced herself to glance down and blow at a strand of hair caught in her mouth. No woman on earth could be less appealing than she at this moment. Thank goodness there were two undisturbed buckets of water nearby, and she quickly doused her arms, face and torso.

If she could just keep up the vaguely insulting banter the way good friends always did, he would never guess how much seeing him affected her. She had prayed so hard and for so long to be able to forget him, that the mesmerizing power he held over her would evaporate. Well, quite obviously the angels were having a good laugh right now.

She took a step toward the fence and forgot to do it with care. Her knee buckled and she grabbed onto the trough to avoid sliding back into the morass of slippery mud. She groaned before she could stifle the sound and closed her eyes against the pain radiating from her limb.

Suddenly she was hauled up by strong arms and she knew if she opened her eyes it would be Quinn. And she knew she would make a complete fool of herself if she allowed herself to drown in the depths of his gaze, his left eye slightly darker than his right, which had a wider band of mossy green surrounding the amber center. Oh, she had to collect herself, had to fortify herself against this. He had only ever held her once before, and at that time she had been almost unconscious from the pain and he—

"You smell—" he began.

"I know, I'm sorry," she interrupted, her head down, eyes firmly screwed shut.

"I was about to say that you smell *wonderful*. Rather like home," he said, breathing in the scent of her hair. "I'd forgotten Penrose's sage and honey. Of course the muck and delicate aroma of slops ruins the effect, but then one can't be too particular when returning home."

His strength and deep voice lulled her and she forgot to keep her eyes shut—his unbearably handsome face was now inches away. The perfect symmetry was more starkly evident now that his innocent boyishness had given way to the thirty-one-year-old man he had become. The flesh of youth had disappeared, leaving prominent cheekbones and a jaw which served to emphasize the hollows of his beard-darkened cheeks. Fine lines radiated from the corners of his eyes, as if they had seen too much and slept too little. Mysterious masculinity made him even more remote than he had been before. She longed to touch his brown hair, which was cropped shorter than the last time she had seen him.

Oh, the feelings he evoked were worse than she remembered. *Far, far worse.* She couldn't have said another word while he held her if her life had depended upon it.

Oh God. *It was Quinn.* And he was home after fifteen long years. And he was carrying her in his arms.

Before she could stop, her hands acted on their own volition, creeping up and around his neck while she rested her cheek on the crest of his shoulder. A shoulder that was so much larger than it had been when he had been a boy and she had been a young girl. She almost trembled as the warmth of his body wound its way past the mud and the linen between them.

She couldn't stop from burying her nose in his shoulder and inhaling the warm cedar and rosemary essence that was impossible to smell unless she was against him like this. She had pined for this scent, always searching the village shops for a hint of it. She became lightheaded when her body flushed from the remembrance of the aroma.

He gripped her more closely as he lengthened his stride. "How bad is it?"

"It's just fine, really. Barely hurts at all. Set me down. I can walk now that we're on firm ground."

"But the ax fell on the same leg as before."

"Oh, I'd forgotten." *Right.* As if he of all people would believe that. The entire situation released a flood of bad memories.

"If it's all the same, I think I'll carry you up to the house, *Lady Ellesmere*."

Her breath caught. "Don't call me that," she whispered.

He raised his brows.

Gusts of wind wrestled with leaves in the nearby trees, changing direction as a few fat raindrops landed on them. Within moments an avalanche of rain poured forth from the gray, rumbling clouds above. There was no point in hurrying the pace; they would be drenched to the bone by the time they reached the great house.

And suddenly it was too much—the banter, his closed expression and demeanor so unlike before, and yet all the while his poignant scent invading her senses. Worse, his arms around her meant nothing to him and everything to her.

"Put me down. I can continue on my own. I'm far too heavy. And I know why you're here. You really didn't need to bother." She had to almost shout to be heard above the rain shower. "I don't want a portion from the Fortesque coffers. I married Anthony because I loved him."

He paid no heed to her, only tightened his arms despite her squirming, and kept his thoughts to himself.

Georgiana finally wrenched herself from his grip and stumbled to the ground in front of the folly on the hill. A flash of lightning illuminated the dark sky and Quinn nearly fell trying to hold on to her.

Georgiana took the last few steps to the domed gray marble structure surrounded by Ionic columns, trying as hard as she could not to limp and failing abysmally. She swung around awkwardly and faced him.

Rain coursed down the harsh contours of his face, pausing at the hint of a cleft in his chin. His expression was murderously calm. He raked his fingers through his rain-slicked hair to comb it out of his eyes. "Look, Georgiana, you're hurt, and this is neither the time nor the place to discuss anything of importance."

"Actually, now that I think about it, perhaps this is the perfect time to discuss why you're here."

"Never let it be said that I would refuse a lady," he replied without a hint of ire. It was as if nothing could irritate him. "Why don't you tell me why I'm here, since you're certain you know."

"Lady Gwendolyn Ellesmere has sent you to toss the presumptuous marauder and her family of low connections from Penrose's hallowed grounds so that her ladyship can reassume her throne here."

She had to hand it to him. Not a muscle in his face twitched.

"No, no, Georgiana, you have it all wrong. I'm to kick you and your upstart family all the way to Wiltshire and have you tarred and feathered if at all possible. Yes, I do believe I will be given the honor of my dearest cousin Henrietta's hand in marriage if I manage it." As if to punctuate the ridiculous remark, a barn owl that had taken up residence in a nearby hollowed-out tree hooted its displeasure at the storm.

Georgiana's throat ached with a horrid combination of hurt and hollow humor. It was so unfair that he could almost make her laugh when she wanted to be annoyed. Henrietta was not only seven years Quinn's senior, but she was also the most mannish female alive and had the added attraction of being mean as well, which was ideal as it relieved everyone of having to like her.

"Well, since I seem to have lost the ability to make you laugh, shall I tell you the main reason I've come?"

He looked at her and tilted his head in that way Anthony also had used to do, and it made the ache in her throat triple in intensity. She nodded mutely.

"Mr. Tilden—I think you know the steward in London?" He continued without waiting for an answer. "During the course of reviewing all of the Fortesque holdings, he showed me the correspondence from Penrose for the last year. And—"

"And there is a considerable increase in the expenditures. I know, and I can explain—" She halted in mid-defense. There was something so calm in his expression, so patient and soothing, as if he could bear the weight of the world. He had always been like that, so unlike everyone else in that regard.

He said not a word, just looked at her, obviously thinking of something—of what, she had not a clue. She never could figure out what he was thinking. He had always been alone with his thoughts, letting others make fools of themselves by flapping their lips.

Oh, and all she could see was how deeply green the edges of his irises were in the mist left by the sudden rain. When had the rain ceased? "You were saying?" she said, trying to hold on to her shrinking dignity.

He cleared his throat. "I came here first and foremost to find out why the handwriting has changed on the reports from Penrose."

Her throat locked up.

". . . Why it became wobbly a year ago and then changed altogether to someone else's hand several months ago. Is your father well, Georgiana? And now that I'm here, I'd like to know why the apparent newest Marchioness of Ellesmere is fixing a trough in the pigsty."

She had wondered when he would bring that up. As usual he had lulled her into hoping he wouldn't ask. She sniffed, trying to draw up her form in the haughtiest pose a lady could assume, given the amount of slops, mud, and rain on her person, which precluded anything truly impressive. "Why, I like pigs. I hate to see them hungry."

"Georgiana . . . " He sighed heavily. "Look, I'm cold and more tired than I can say, and you're in pain and freezing as well, although a pack of wild dogs probably couldn't drag a complaint from you. But eventually—in the next twenty-four hours to be precise—I shall be paying a visit to your father."

She looked away.

He sighed. "You were correct on the other point. Before I leave next week to continue my tour of the family's properties to the north, we have *another* issue to discuss. That of your marriage to . . . my cousin. And the matter of a settlement. I shall leave it to you to pick the time and the place."

The reference to Anthony and his odd pause made her ill at ease. "There's remarkably little to discuss."

"We both know the validity of the marriage is in question. But we'll resolve this before I leave. And by the by" —he glanced away— "contrary to popular opinion, I was glad to hear you'd married him. The two of you had a very special bond. You always were inseparable."

"It wasn't just Anthony and I who were best friends. It was the *three* of us who were—"

He ruthlessly ignored her. "You were the only chance he had to turn himself around." He took a step closer. "If there was anyone who could have changed the direction he was taking himself, it was you. You usually had good sense. Why, there's not a silly, romantic notion in your body."

"I'm so glad you noticed," she said dryly, regaining her senses. "Everyone always underestimates the advantages of marrying a managing female."

His expression never wavered.

She had thought he would laugh. For the ten thousandth time she wondered what his wife had been like. He had supposedly fallen in love with and married a lady whose beautiful face and elegant grace had been the fodder of every gossip column Georgiana had chanced to see all those years ago. The news of his marriage had broken her pathetic heart irrevocably. Old dreams formed in youth were the hardest to die.

"You always did have a mind of your own, Georgiana. But I appreciate an organized mind. Well, I shall hope we can discuss this more rationally, in future. You have no reason to fear me. I, for one, am very willing to start anew. I never think of the past. Enough . . ." He looked up at the still gray sky and squinted. "It's starting to rain again. I can't force you to let me carry you. But if you move a muscle from this spot before I send someone with a cart, I'll—"

"Why do you never think of the past?" she whispered. "I think about it all the time."

He stared at her, and a drop of rain worked its way down his cropped hair to land on his broad shoulder. He turned and walked away, refusing to say another word.

"Oh!" Georgiana started. "Don't walk away from me. Oh, what is wrong with you? You've changed. You never used to walk away. Come back. I'll tell you what you want to know." She stopped when she realized he had strode away so quickly that there was no possible way he could hear her over the sudden surge of the returning rain. "Damn you, Quinn Fortesque," she whispered into the wind.

And the wicked wind carried it to his ears and he smiled despite himself. He'd forgotten what a hellion little Georgiana Wilde could be when she set her mind to it.

He was still mulling over the hellcat after dinner in the comfort of Penrose's library. *His* library.

But it didn't feel like his library. The ghosts of the two people who had held the title before him seemed to hover in the shadows, mocking him, forcing him to remember. Well, he'd be damned if he was going to give in to thinking about the past. He took a long pull from the cheroot he'd nearly forgotten, dangling from his fingers over the arm of the cushioned chair. Then he settled in to study the glowing embers at its tip—and ponder his dilemma . . . Georgiana Wilde, now Fortesque.

He was disgusted she'd almost made him forget

to hold on to the closed façade he carefully presented to the world. He usually measured every word before he allowed it to escape from his lips, and avoided messy scenes entirely. What could he have been thinking? He shook his head.

Georgiana had not changed. He smiled inwardly, remembering her amusing and original string of curses aimed at Gwendolyn, queen of the swine. Oh, Georgiana's angles had softened a little, but not her character. But then, he had never expected her to become a great beauty. In fact he wondered why he was thinking about her features at all. With her dark hair, dark eyes, and sun-darkened skin, Georgiana was the very opposite of refined elegance—the very opposite of Cynthia.

He stilled and closed his eyes when he thought of the ax butt that had fallen on Georgiana's knee. He wondered if the horrific injuries to her legs from so many years ago still pained her. They must. He shivered involuntarily when he remembered the accident that had almost cost her a limb. It was what had caused his immediate removal from Penrose, in fact. He forced his mind away from the incident. He had trained himself to keep all irrelevant thoughts of his childhood from cluttering his mind. He was only sorry she had suffered so.

A log shifted and sparks spewed out near the padded fire railing. He rose and brushed the embers back into the grate. Unbidden, like a creeping vine, Georgiana wound back into his thoughts. She had lost the innocent look of childhood. But then, he supposed he had too. Yet she had the same audacious temperament she had possessed at a very tender age, when he had first spied her shepherding an enormous flock of Southdown sheep with mischief on their minds.

It appeared she still had the inability to dampen her emotions—something he had learned how to do very well fifteen years ago. And if there was one thing he was certain of after seeing her today, it was that she was hiding something from him. Well, he would learn what it was, as methodically as he had uncovered state scandals and lies throughout his diplomatic career. Her reception of him proved yet again that the years he had spent here as a boy had been yet another transitory illusion of fellowship, permanence, and happiness.

Actually, he really didn't care very much what she was hiding. It was just that he didn't like secrets, and his methodical, disciplined roots would not let him rest until everything was examined, a solution found, and the lot of it settled in a proper fashion. Yet he would not shame her even if the marriage was questionable. She didn't understand that she had nothing to fear from him.

In the end, even if there was something dubious about the marriage, he would simply arrange a comfortable annuity for Georgiana and settle her far from Penrose so he wouldn't have another reminder of humanity's shortcomings.

He had sent a note to her father telling him to expect him early tomorrow morning. Quinn only prayed Mr. Wilde was not as ill as he suspected. He had always been a man Quinn respected, one of the few people who had always had time for him in his youth.

He turned his attention to a letter in his lap. His daughter had surreptitiously pressed the note into his hand when he had taken leave of her at the home of Cynthia's parents. He had read the note so many times on his journey south that the creases were worn. Large letters looped across the page, begging him between each line to return for her. He had no reason to feel guilty for leaving Fairleigh with his in-laws. She was much better off in London with Cynthia's mother and the governess they had found. Of course she was sad. She had left everyone she had ever known in Portugal, her mother had died the year before, and now he was away.

He closed his eyes for a long moment and remembered the day he had arrived at Penrose at the age of eleven, newly orphaned by the scourge of the pox that had invaded his parents' modest home in Dorchester.

He jumped up and grappled with the escritoire's drawer to find some writing paper.

They would be furious. He simply didn't care. He scribbled a note to Cynthia's parents, sanded it, sealed it with sizzling crimson wax, and stamped Penrose's symbol of a six-petaled rose—from the signet ring his aunt had given him, amid a public flood of tears on her part and none on his.

He hailed a footman and released the missive into the man's hands before he could change his mind. And then he realized he had taken another decision before he'd examined it in his normal, reflective fashion. He would not return to London at the end of the week as planned and then go on to the rest of the properties. He couldn't take his daughter willy-nilly across England for the next several months. She needed permanence after all the disruptions. Well, if anyone could banish ghosts, it would be his impish daughter. They would stay here in Cornwall, far, far away from the dazzling aristocratic and diplomatic circles of London. He shook his head. Who needed town bronze when one could have country dirt?

What had come over him? He made a point to never take decisions haphazardly. Any innocent spontaneity he might have possessed in his youth had been thoroughly expunged from him by experience.

It must be the mystical nature of the changeable Cornish air . . . or the fairies at mischief. He groaned. Fairies indeed. He stared at the untouched amber liquid in a glass the housekeeper, Mrs. Killen, had brought unbidden and then placed on the nearby desk before she had retired. He suddenly wondered if perhaps the muddy new Marchioness of Ellesmere was poisoning the firewater. He wouldn't put it past her. He wouldn't put it past any woman . . . especially a woman with a *plan*.

And Lord knew Georgiana Wilde always had plans . . .

Chapter 3

July 28—to do
- *tea with the Widows Club*
- *oversee spreading of hay to dry*
- *gamekeeper/traps*

  - *meet with His Highness*

"**B**ut my dear Georgiana," Ata St. Aubyn, the Dowager Duchess of Helston murmured with a little excited smile on her face, "you are too, too kind. Are you certain we wouldn't be an imposition?"

Georgiana smiled back at the tiny, old duchess, whom she had come to love with every beat of her heart. "Certain," she replied firmly.

"Oh, I know I should refuse. Know I should think twice before accepting your kind invitation to stay, but well, I'm too old to bother." She let out a peal of laughter and all the other ladies in the secret circle joined her.

Georgiana looked about Penrose's pretty blue

morning room and shook her head before joining in the laughter. In so many ways she was closer to the ladies in this intimate Widows Club that Ata had founded than she was to her own mother. They accepted her—despite her eccentricities—in a way that Georgiana had only felt before with her father, Anthony, and perhaps Quinn, when they were in the innocent bloom of youth. This deep friendship with the ladies surrounding her was the only reason she'd had the audacity to invite them all to stay at Penrose without consulting Quinn first.

Oh, to be honest, her impudent invitation was most likely *precisely* due to Quinn's arrival. She never would have presumed to have the authority until Quinn had shown a desire to question her and possibly control her future actions. Her perverseness when it came to people attempting to control her was the trait she tried hardest to change and the one she failed at most consistently. And yet she also knew if she searched her conscience the real reason she had invited her circle of friends to stay was that she needed a buffer. The sensations she harbored for him would be more easily hidden with Ata and the others here.

She was suddenly ashamed of the last notation on her list this morning. It was so hard to put into words the conflicting emotions she harbored in her breast for him . . . mostly disappointment and a terrible, constant yearning.

"I know exactly which rooms will suit each of you," Georgiana finally murmured. "Grace, you must have the rose room. It's very elegant, as it is the marchioness's chamber. Elizabeth, the green room will complement your eyes. Sarah, I think you would like the suite with the sunny front bedroom with the yellow-flowered wallpaper. And Ata,"—a bubble of mirth escaped her—"you shall enjoy the room with the Egyptian drawings. I do believe it is a gentleman's room, given the nature of the activities of the Egyptians."

"La! How can I refuse such an offer?" Ata chuckled. "Mind you, I always preferred the Greeks, but perhaps it's time I broadened my mind."

"But Georgiana," Grace Sheffey, the Countess of Sheffield said, her blonde beauty heartstopping in its perfection, "why aren't *you* inhabiting the marchioness's rooms?"

"The very question I've been asking myself," Quinn Fortesque said quietly as he stepped into the morning room unannounced.

All the ladies rose and he bowed, looking every bit as handsome and lord-of-the-manner-like as yesterday before Georgiana had escaped the folly and secretly spent the night at her retreat, the tiny lake house at Loe Pool.

"Ladies," he murmured.

They all curtsied and Ata tottered forward in her vibrant chartreuse gown and ridiculously tall high heels, which did nothing to conceal her minute stature. "Quinn Fortesque? Is that you?" When he nodded, she continued, "But Georgiana, why didn't you tell us? Never mind. We'd heard you were soon to arrive. I'm Merceditas St. Aubyn. Young man, I remember your father and mother quite well. They used to attend our affairs in town and were uniformly delightful. It is good to know their son is not only charming too, but a handsome devil to boot." The sly little dowager was obviously trying to outcharm a dyed-in-the-wool charmer.

Quinn reached for Ata's right hand but very smoothly changed direction when he noticed her withered, clenched fist, the one she refused to acknowledge or discuss. Quinn kissed the duchess's left fingers and his eyes twinkled. "Delighted to have the honor of your acquaintance, Your Grace."

"Oh please, since my friends and I are to be under your roof for at least the next month, couldn't you please address me as Ata, as all my intimates do?"

"I don't see why not, as we're sure to become *intimate*, madam."

Oh, he was just as charming as ever. Only a flicker of surprise had crossed his features. He had expertly hidden the certain shock he must have entertained at learning *four* heretofore unknown ladies had been invited to stay under his roof.

The duchess sighed and Georgiana guessed the dowager must be wishing she could slop four decades off her dish. It was vastly unfair of him to possess such poetic eyes. Eyes so like Tony's, only with something brewing in their depths. She fingered her brooch under the shawl.

"I'm delighted Georgiana extended the invitation as I asked her to," he said smoothly.

Why, he was lying through his teeth. And snatching away her giddy sensation of having overstepped her authority.

"I must thank you very kindly," Ata replied. "My grandson and his duchess have been ensconced nearby at Amberley since Rosamunde was delivered of twins a fortnight ago. I'm ashamed to admit that my friends and I are forever holding the babies and never allowing the papa and mama their turns. So I've taken it upon myself to remove—"

Grace Sheffey interrupted with a gurgle of laughter. "Oh, Ata, really, you must be honest with our host." The countess turned her lovely visage to Quinn and blinked, her lashes sweeping her porcelain cheeks. Grace was simply exquisite in a way that Georgiana would never, ever be. "My lord, Luc St. Aubyn suggested he and his wife needed a bit of privacy."

"Why, Grace," Elizabeth Ashburton added, "now you're the one telling bouncers. The duke had all our bags packed when we weren't looking and *kicked* us out. Not that I'm complaining, mind you." She glanced at Quinn and continued boldly, in her usual fashion. "He ordered the driver of his ducal coach to take us to his townhouse in London, my lord, which we can assure you is very nice indeed."

"But not as nice as Amberley," Ata said, her lip pouting in a ridiculous manner for someone so old.

"Ata prefers the country," Georgiana added, annoyed at appearing defensive.

"My dear lady," Quinn purred, looking at the dowager, "I do believe your grandson is in need of deportment lessons. If I had a grandmother such as you, I would never dream of sending her away. Shall I give him a good thrashing after I see you settled in your chambers?"

He chuckled when Ata seemed to seriously consider the idea.

Ata grasped his hand with her good hand. "We are going to get along just famously." She then smiled radiantly.

Lovely. Now Ata was fully entrenched under his spell—just as much as every other female who had ever met him.

"My lord," Sarah Winters said in her soft, melodic voice. "Thank you very kindly for inviting us into your home. It's extraordinarily generous of you, since I'm guessing you have never heard of any of us until now."

Leave it to Sarah, she of the older and wiser persuasion, to say the correct thing.

"Why, madam, that's not true a'tall. Georgiana and I went over a list of things to do today, and this invitation topped the agenda. Why, here it is."

If the floor could have swallowed her up whole, Georgiana would have gratefully eaten the splinters. That was her last thought as Quinn extracted her morning list she now realized she had left in the breakfast room as she often did when in a hurry.

The list that said, "meet with His Highness."

* * *

His Highness, indeed, thought Quinn with a smile a short time later. It was rare when a series of circumstances could be shuffled together to form a delicate house of cards that could be blown over with such satisfaction.

He waved away the footman's offer to have a horse readied for him. He would enjoy the walk to the cottage where the Wilde family resided.

The tang and salt of Penrose's Cornish air, made fresh by yesterday's storm, assailed his senses. He noted the overpowering jasmine and rose aromas from the formal gardens, then the eucalyptus tree and the more pungent, earthy scents from the hidden kitchen garden beyond. July had always been his favorite month here. The bees were droning about their business, and the laborers in the patchwork of fields beyond were moving about in the same efficient manner, spreading the hay to dry from the haycocks damaged in the storm. And just as he suspected, given Georgiana's list, there was the gamekeeper plundering a hedgerow in search of poachers' snares.

Well, it was no surprise Penrose was ever and always efficiently run. It was only for Quinn to find out precisely whom was to thank for the job. And he would eat his Portuguese barretina shako, the *Caçadores* hat his daughter loved so much, if it was Mr. Wilde alone. Clearly Wilde's son, Grayson—with help from his sister, to be more precise—was behind the position. But how Quinn was to rectify matters was an altogether different story.

It wouldn't work to have one Wilde as steward and another Wilde as the questionable marchioness of the same manor.

Quinn wrestled with the slightly rusted latch on the steward's residence and wended his way to the pretty rose-covered cottage. Its charm was slightly diminished as it needed a good whitewashing.

His knuckles hadn't even reached the door when it swung open and Mrs. Wilde was revealed.

"Quinn Fortesque!" the plump, graying lady exclaimed. "Mr. Wilde has been expecting you. My, how you've grown. Oh, you gave me a start. You always did have that look about you—like our dear Anthony. Such a pity." She tsked.

He stiffened.

"You simply must help my daughter. She won't listen to reason. Georgiana," she said without pausing to take a breath in her stream of conversation, "refuses to assume the role of marchioness. Refuses to take her rightful place."

He bowed and then breathed in a scent he had completely forgotten. The lemony aroma of Mrs. Wilde's poppy-seed cakes wafted from the kitchen and brought back an unwanted flood of childhood memories.

She preceded him down the cramped hall. "You were always such a good boy. I told my husband you would do the correct thing. The only fair thing. I know you will put a stop to that evil woman and her frightfully embarrassing inquiries. Georgiana is the rightful Marchioness of Ellesmere, don't you agree?"

She took up a tray handed to her by the maid at the kitchen door and presented it to him.

"Here, have a cake. I remember these were your favorite."

"You always made the very best cakes in all of Cornwall, Mrs. Wilde," he murmured before popping a tiny cake into his mouth.

"Oh, you're just being kind," she simpered. "But now that you mention it, they are better than anything Lady Gwendolyn Ellesmere served at Penrose. I keep telling Georgiana that we should all remove to the great house so her father and I can help her to manage everything."

Thank the Lord they were in front of Mr. Wilde's study. He knocked and edged around the door, somehow managing to escape without her trailing him. He turned to find the steward at his desk.

Oh God. It was much worse than he thought. It took every ounce of control not to jump to the man's side. He had grown gaunt and old since Quinn had last seen him. Why, the man must have lost three stone. Clearly, it was some sort of wasting illness.

"Mr. Wilde," he said coming around the man's desk to shake his hand. His grasp was more firm than Quinn would have thought possible. "Please don't trouble yourself to stand."

Mr. Wilde struggled to rise. "Nonsense, my lord."

"*Quinn.* Please, I insist," he said quietly, and then helped the man regain his seat.

"Well, well . . ." Mr. Wilde's eyes watered

slightly as he tried to hold on to some semblance of formality. "It looks as if you've gone ahead and grown into the man I knew you would become."

Quinn rested his hand on the frail gentleman's shoulder just as Mr. Wilde had used to do to him when he needed comfort or reassurance as a boy. A mere decade and a half had reversed their roles.

There was something about seeing this humble man that made Quinn want to run as far and as fast from this place as possible. He refused to consider why he would want to run from the potent illusion of honesty and kindness.

"I suspect," Wilde said, "you're thinking that I too have grown into the man you thought I'd become." He coughed once and gave a wry smile.

"Nothing of the sort. I suspect you're still the most slave-driving steward in all of Cornwall." He forced himself to maintain a light tone despite his sadness. "And if I may hazard a guess, probably with the same well-honed propensity toward terrible puns."

A light of humor filled the man's eyes. "It's always important to have a pun in the oven, you know." He chuckled. "I'm so glad you've finally come. I'm afraid there's been little humor here these days. Living like this, in such imbalance, has been a sore trial for Georgiana and Mrs. Wilde. But I knew you would come and sort it all out."

Quinn sat across from John Wilde in the old spindle chair he remembered from long ago. "You've great faith in my abilities, and I'm honored. But"—he paused—"I fear it will be some time before we can settle every matter. Most importantly, however, I've come to see to your immediate future."

John Wilde tried to sit up straighter in his chair. His expression, a combination of hope and thinly disguised despair, brought pain to Quinn's chest.

"You've served Penrose for what? Nearly four decades, have you not? I fear my uncle and Anthony were remiss in not arranging for the day you might eventually wish to retire your post as steward here."

He heard the door crack open behind him and assumed it was Mrs. Wilde with a tea tray. He continued, "The Fortesque family owes you a comfortable pension. It is your due for so many extraordinary years of excellent service."

"And here I was feeling grateful to you for your kindness to the dowager duchess." Georgiana's words were dangerously soft. She came in to stand at her father's side. "Little did I know it was probably done to distract me while you finessed my family's removal."

"Georgiana!" her father admonished. "Your manners!"

"No, Father. I, for one, desire to know the charges being leveled at us. Penrose is being kept in prime form. I would know what fault he finds with the stewardship."

"Georgiana," Quinn said softly, looking at her dark, flashing eyes. "There's no doubt in my mind that Penrose has been overseen with the greatest of care. This is a matter between your father and me." If she didn't let this go, he might not forgive her. He wanted to preserve Mr. Wilde's dignity. "Sir, I would be grateful if you would consider accepting a pension in the amount of four hundred pounds per annum as well as a deed to the cottage of your choosing. I would offer you this one, but Little Roses is entailed as you know."

"That is far too much," Mr. Wilde said quietly yet firmly. "There's not a steward in all the land who would receive a cottage and a pension such as the one you're offering."

"There is not a steward in the land with a daughter who has married the heir's predecessor, necessitating a quick removal to lessen the connection." Georgiana's words were so baldly honest that not one of them knew what to say in response.

Well, Quinn had to give credit where it was due. She'd never shrunk from the truth in her life. There were few who could make the same claim. But now, in front of her father, was not the time to—

"You'll forgive me for my lack of tact, but I will not play the passive, wilting female and let you wrest the stewardship—"

And then he did something he'd not known he was capable of doing. He grasped her arm and wordlessly forced her from the study, calling out to her father his promise of a return on the morrow, and a "Please consider my offer." He dragged Georgiana from the house, past the open-mouthed stare of her mother, and into the little bit of wilderness behind the hedgerow. He stopped when he realized with horror that she was limping slightly.

"Good God, Georgiana," he said regaining control of his emotions, something he never, ever, ever, lost. "Allow your father the peace he deserves and has earned at this point in his life. Perhaps since you see him every day, you've not realized how very altered he is."

Her eyes became turbulent with emotion. "You're not to bring his illness into this. We've done very well despite everything. And I'll not let you take the stewardship away from him. You can take the stupid Ellesmere title my mother loves so much, Lord knows I never use it, nor want it. But I will not—"

He roughly grabbed her into his embrace and held her so tightly he could have sworn that he could feel the fast beat of her heart against his own. She was deceptively smaller than he. Why, her head only reached the bottom of his chin. She had such a strong character that she appeared a half foot taller at arm's length. But what she lacked in height, she more than made up for in the strength he could feel emanating from her body.

She fought against the pull of his arms for but a moment before she stopped struggling against his breast.

"Listen to me," he said softly into her dark brown hair. "John Wilde is one of the best men I've ever known. I'm not trying to hurt your family. I'm trying to do the very opposite. I want to settle the matter of this pension as soon as possible since my life is the only thing separating your family from an uncertain future. I dare not leave your father to the mercy of some delightful fourth cousin I don't know how many times removed if something should happen to me."

She had stilled and Quinn was surprised she wasn't making any effort whatsoever to disengage from his embrace. She had suddenly gone very soft in his arms and he was finding it hard to ignore her lithe curves—especially when her fingers curled at the small of his back.

He swallowed harshly and tried to clear his mind. "Georgiana, what have I done to make you so determined to challenge me at every turn? Have I ever—"

"I'm sorry," she interrupted; her nose in his neck cloth muffled her words. "You're right, of course."

Well, that was a first. Ladies, in his experience, never, ever apologized unless a gentleman apologized first.

"Apology accepted," he said gruffly before she could change her mind. His body was becoming heated and he knew he should ease away from her but for some reason his body refused to obey his mind. Instead he found himself closing his eyes and leaning in to get closer to her warm soapscented skin.

"Shall we start over, Georgiana?" he whispered. "Shall we pretend I've just arrived, and you're happy to see me after my long absence? There was a time we were comrades, before we got on with our lives and went our separate ways as all children must."

She finally pulled away and he watched a veil draw over her usual open expression. He had forgotten the depth of her fathomless, large, dark eyes. She looked ready to speak for a moment, but then she stopped. Instead, she accepted his arm to walk along the hedgerow which secreted scores of birds determined to fill the air with a song of pleasure for a storm survived.

"Quinn," she said tentatively. "I'll allow Father is possibly unable to fulfill all the duties of a steward. But, if I can promise our family will keep Penrose in topmost working order, will you allow us to continue . . . please?"

He took a deep breath and turned to her, halting their progress. He shook his head slightly. "I realize you love it here. But this stewardship is too heavy a burden on your family. No, don't try to argue. Perhaps if your brother was a little older or had help . . . Where is Grayson, anyway? I've yet to see him or thank him for his obvious devotion to the estate."

A flurry of pain flooded her expression. "To sea. The Duke of Helston, Ata's grandson, secured a midshipman's berth for him two years ago, before Father became ill."

A ball of unease grew inside him. "Are you suggesting that you alone have overseen the estate? Georgiana, that is singularly appalling."

"Please, Quinn."

She said it so softly he had to lower his head to catch it. The intensity was such that he hated what he must do. "You can't think to continue on like this. It's impossible. Georgiana, I'm sorry, but I shall have to find a new man to—"

"I can do it," she insisted, the pleading in her face piercing his defenses.

"Georgiana, I know you can do it. But you simply *must not* do it. A marchioness—in truth or not—should not muck about in a pigsty. Even you must see the absurdity of it. Ladies are meant to undertake the feminine arts, oversee the female domestics, arrange entertainments, and that sort of thing."

She stared at him, a terrible combination of misery and disappointment etching her features. And then he knew he could not take this away from her altogether; it must be done more delicately, in degrees over time. "There must be a compromise. There's always a compromise, Georgiana."

"Not in this case," she said sadly. "You'll either flout convention or you won't."

His mind flowed about the locked channels, searching for ways around the problem. "I know," he said, taking one of her hands in his own. "You shall be given a share in the training and overseeing of a new man. And you shall have a say in who the man shall be."

He looked down to the smaller hand in his. He turned it over and saw long healed scars tracing a pattern under fresh scratches on her hands. He had never seen such a worn palm in his life. Why, his own broad, callused hands almost looked smooth in comparison, he thought with no small amount of disgust.

When she didn't answer immediately, he tilted his head to encounter her expression. To save her life, she couldn't have hidden her obvious thoughts to waylay the plan.

"No," he said before she could speak. "You,

in return, shall promise to help the man we choose."

She sighed. "As if I have a choice. I still don't see why I—"

"You do have a choice. You can either play a part in this or you can sit about the interior of Penrose arranging flowers, approving menus, and all other matters a marchioness should attend to."

"You don't really mean to formally end the inquiry and declare me the mistress of Penrose, do you?" She stared at him with an intensity rare to behold.

"You tell me what I should do, Georgiana." He stopped and grasped her chin carefully, very carefully, and peered into her glassy eyes. It was a dangerous moment. A critical, crucial moment during which he must determine the truth. "Are you the Marchioness of Ellesmere, in truth?" He kept his voice gentle, relaxed.

"You called me as much yesterday."

He stared at her. And for the first time he noticed she had the most expressive brows. They seemed to be constantly changing; one moment elegantly sloping up and around the edges of the quiet beauty of her dark eyes, the next moment angrily flattening into straight lines as impenetrable as a Cornish hedgerow.

"I should like to hear your opinion."

"*Now* you want my opinion?"

"Are you going to tell me the truth, Georgiana, or aren't you?" He honestly had no idea if she would have the nerve to tell him if she had consummated the marriage or not.

Her eyes hardened; her brows followed suit as he knew they would. "Well, let's see, shall we? My mother says I am. My father says nothing. Anthony's mother says I am not. The Fortesque solicitors also suggest I'm not if I understood their stupendously long and complicated correspondence. But to answer your question, I've chosen not to assume the title." She examined the edge of her worn apron. "I refuse to suffer the indignity of a doctor's examination."

So she would not tell him. But then hadn't his wife shown him the intricate workings of the feminine mind?

"What if I were not to press the point? What if I were to tell you that I should like to settle the matter now to cause the least amount of scandal possible to both families? What if I were to tell you that I intend to drop the matter of the inquiry and provide a generous widow's settlement that would keep you in the manner befitting a marchioness for the rest of your life?"

"I would call you foolish," she replied. "Obviously you have a well-hidden love for trouble, considering what your aunt's reaction would be."

"Georgiana . . . *what do you want*?" He tried mightily to keep the exasperation from his voice.

Oh, there was no question what she wanted. Had always wanted. Even now when he stood in front of her as coolly detached as a vicar at confession. She wanted to grab onto his lapels and pull him down to her and kiss him until he showed some sort of response that was not at all like the brotherly, reserved expression he exhibited. And for a moment, she teetered on the impulse, leaning toward him until her practical nature took control.

Now, looking into his cool green and amber eyes, she felt a sadness creep over her. The shell of the boy she had known—and maybe even what was beyond it—had hardened, making the man Quinn had become all the more unreachable. For some perverse reason the impenetrable armor he had built around himself made her now lash out at him, if only to see some form of emotion from him. And yet, another part of her yearned to protect him, comfort him. Why on earth she felt a need to comfort one of the most self-sufficient men she had ever known was a mystery.

"Well?" His expression was as emotionless as before. "What do you want, Georgiana?"

The real question was, What was her second choice? What was the best alternative, since she would never have what she really wanted? And this was where her ordered mind always found itself entangled in a quagmire of uncertainty.

"I want"—she hesitated and looked above his shoulder to the deepening mackerel sky—"I want to live as before."

"Well, I rather think you can't." He changed the subject. "Where are you living? The housekeeper says you are at Penrose, but you didn't come down for dinner."

She ignored his question with the only thing she was willing to admit. "My mother would not let me live at Little Roses."

"Then it's a good thing you invited the Dowager Duchess of Helston to stay as well as the other ladies. It wouldn't do for you to live at Penrose, alone with me there too. But we will have to come to an agreement about your future residence." He pursed his lips. "How did you come to meet the duchess and the others? They appear such an odd, little group."

"I suppose I should explain, since you're sure to figure it out during the month. Ata has a very generous heart, and I met her when she mysteriously attended Anthony's funeral here. After everyone had left, she introduced herself and invited, or rather, inducted me against my reservations into her circle of friends—all widows. The Widows Club is clandestine because Ata is convinced no one will ever want to include a gaggle of self-admitted, inseparable old crows in any amusing social gatherings."

He raised a brow. "I would never describe you as an old crow." Then he leaned forward, and for one heart-stopping moment, Georgiana thought he might kiss her. But of course she was wrong.

He brushed a lock of her hair out of her eyes. The moment his ungloved fingers touched her face, she felt the heat of a blush force its way to her skin. She turned and began the trek back to the cottage before he could see her reaction to him—all the while careful to hide the limp that appeared when she was inattentive.

"Georgiana . . . there's still much to—"

She waved her hand behind her, ending the interlude. She wasn't sure whether she wanted more for him to go away and never return or if she wanted to continue to suffer the sweet agony of seeing him and the occasional spark of *affection* in his expression when he looked at her. It was not at all like the darkening look of passion she dreamed about on those nights when she stared at the rolling mist coming across Loe Pool while she lay on her narrow pallet in the small glass-walled house on the island. She often slept there, away from her father's house, away from the Widows Club, away from Penrose, away from everything except her memories and her dreams.

Only now, Quinn's return was making her fondest wish appear even more fanciful than ever before.

Chapter 4

If Georgiana had known how awkward it would be to not own a name, she wouldn't have insisted after Anthony's death that everyone continue to address her as they had before her marriage.

Now everyone was confused. They didn't know whether to address her as "Miss Wilde," or to go against her wishes and use "Lady Ellesmere." The latter reminded Georgiana too much of her mother-in-law.

The housekeeper, servants, and laborers hedged their bets by sprinkling the bland "ma'am" in their responses or the more formal "madam" in the presence of others. The situation was worse than the endless stream of nicknames she had endured in childhood. She was Georgiana, Georgia, Miss G, and even George, to her younger brother when he was annoyed with her supervising ways. At least all the widows had adopted the use of her Christian name without hesitation. And she was grateful as she surveyed the powder keg of varying personalities assembled in Penrose's formal drawing room before dinner that evening.

The Duke of Helston, Luc St. Aubyn, paced before a raging fire in the massive fireplace. He had a sour look on his face as he addressed his host. "Well, I knew this was a monumentally bad idea. Is this the best you can do, Ellesmere?" He glanced in his wife's direction and shuttered his eyes. "Caroline and Henry will freeze in here, my dear."

His ravishing duchess, Rosamunde St. Aubyn, grasped his wrist to stay his incessant steps. A small bundle swaddled in lace and linen befitting a prince lay in the crook of her arm. The beautiful sleeping infant's tiny smile trembled in sweet dreamland. "Luc," she said softly, "Henry is perfectly content."

"Well," he responded, "perhaps. But Caro is chilled."

Ata cradled the other sleeping babe on her lap, a look of complete rapture on her wrinkled face. She appeared not to have heard a word. Indeed, she had stopped talking entirely when the duke and duchess had arrived with the twins.

"I said," Luc repeated, "Caro is *chilled*, Ata."

His duchess, silent, seemed to know better than to confront a lion protecting his pride of cubs.

Ata refused to meet her grandson's eye. "You can't have her. It's still my turn. I was to have fifteen minutes. And really, I think it should be thirty since I haven't seen her in so long."

The duke sighed heavily and took out his frustration by waving away a footman and then throwing a massive log on the burning timbers, which only served to send a dazzling amount of sparks up the flue. He grabbed the poker and began poking and muttering something about "infernal turns."

Georgiana smothered a laugh and glanced at Quinn under her lashes. He had the knowing look of a man well amused.

"It would seem," Quinn said without a glimmer of emotion, "Your Grace has not yet perceived the benefit of having a ready supply of arms. You might reconsider this shortly. There is nothing quite so exhausting as a new baby, or babies in your case."

"And it would seem you know little about the matter, Ellesmere," Luc said, frost emanating from his every pore. "But then I've always said that about diplomats. Always willing to advise, but never willing to *do*. The doing is always left to sailors or soldiers, true men willing to face death instead of—"

"Luc!" Rosamunde interrupted with horror and then directed her attention to her host. "Please excuse him, my lord."

The rest of the widows—Grace, Sarah, and Elizabeth—had retreated from such fireworks to admire the vast display of art gracing the walls surrounding them.

"That's quite all right, Your Grace. There must be some latitude given to new fathers," Quinn said with amusement to Rosamunde. "And I've always observed there is a reason God divides temperaments. There will always be those who lead by calm, rational, intelligent example and those who think fear and brute force inspire loyalty. And then there is the force of nature called fatherhood. Your husband displays that force—quite well, if I may be allowed to say."

Luc growled.

Ata looked up finally. "My dear Quinn, you simply must see Caro's face. She looks just like me."

Georgiana smiled to herself as she watched Quinn go to Ata's side. Surely that had to be the hundredth time Ata had uttered those words in the last few weeks. The baby woke with a start and began to cry. Luc St. Aubyn appeared as if he was going to snatch the baby from his grandmother and head for the hills of Amberley, eight miles distant.

"No, Luc," his wife said softly, catching his tightly clenched hand again. "I need your help with Henry." The twin had woken, hearing his sister's distress, and his tightly clenched little fists matched his father's. Luc clasped the infant to his shoulder and began the smooth pacing every parent seems to learn within minutes of their offspring's birth.

Tiny Caro cried most pitifully and Ata began to look a little frantic. Quinn interceded with his perpetual grace and calm. "Will you allow me the pleasure of holding her?"

Ata looked at him warily, very unwilling to give up her great-grandchild.

"I want to examine her likeness to you," he said.

"Oh yes, do. See how her eyes are wide apart, and she has the dearest widow's peak, and—"

Georgiana watched as Quinn expertly took the baby in both hands and rocked her while crooning into her tiny ear a lullaby about bunting and hunting. The baby immediately quieted and reached out to grab a lock of his shorn brown hair. He smoothly transferred her to his shoulder and stroked her head.

Was there anything more attractive than a man willing and able to soothe a crying infant? Georgiana realized that her yearning for Quinn had reached a new level. What she would give to have him stroke her head and whisper anything in her ear—even if it involved lambs and nappies. She glanced at the other widows and realized, by the looks on their faces, they were all thinking the same pathetic thought. Georgiana shook her head and made her way to the new duchess's side.

"Rosamunde," Georgiana whispered as the others continued to converse amongst themselves. "Shall we dine as we did at Amberley—in shifts?"

"He's very handsome, Georgiana," Rosamunde said softly, ignoring the question.

"Yes, I know."

"How long ago did his wife die?"

"Rosamunde!"

The beautiful duchess, her ethereal pale aquamarine eyes sparkling, smiled shrewdly. "You're in love with him," she said very quietly, knowingly.

Georgiana quickly glanced around to make sure no one had heard the outrageous statement.

"I absolutely am *not*."

She cocked a brow. "So it doesn't bother you

that Grace, as well as Elizabeth, and even shy Sarah are looking at him as if they would all be delighted by the chance to become a marchioness? Didn't Grace confide she's determined to arrange a marriage of convenience this year? Hmmm. He has such charm, such restraint, not at all like the fiery Helstons. In fact, if I wasn't already married" —and here she glanced at the darkly devilish duke and smiled, giving away her game—"why, I do believe I'd be very tempted to—"

"Stop," Georgiana said. "I'm well aware of his effect on our sex."

Rosamunde brushed aside Georgiana's lace fichu and stared hard at the small brooch all the widows had seen and commented on from time to time. Georgiana always wore the tiny Lover's Eye she had painted ages ago and framed in the jeweled brooch she had inherited from her father's family.

The duchess smiled slowly. "You mentioned Quinn is very much like your husband. I would say he looks almost *exactly* like him—or at least his eye—if this is any indication."

"Please, Rosamunde . . ." Georgiana begged softly. Oh God, Rosamunde always had been the most perceptive of all of them.

Rosamunde stroked her hand. "Come, help me up. I'm still embarrassingly weak. I only came to-night because I wanted to smooth over Ata's hurt feelings." She called out to her husband, "Luc, dear, shall we retreat to the other chamber with the infants while the others dine? And then we shall have our turn."

"How many, many, *many* times do I have to tell everyone that dukes do *not* take turns," he said more loudly than necessary.

The widows dared to giggle.

"I shall have a footman bring you plates, Your Grace," Georgiana insisted, forgetting, in the heat of his blast, the usual informality they shared.

Luc approached Quinn and with a single disdainful glance dared him to refuse to hand over the twin.

Quinn smiled. "Do you always get your wish, Helston? I find your ways singularly extraordinary."

Luc, he of the most devilish smile in all of Christendom, looked ready to do murder as he placed his other baby on the opposite shoulder. "Diplomats never can stand the heat of the cannon, Ellesmere. But if you can muster enough of your infamous charm to keep my grandmother and the gaggle of her friends away from Amberley for the next month or six, I shall pretend to think better of you than I do."

"I shudder to think of the alternative," Quinn replied with the hint of a smile.

With that, Luc St. Aubyn, better known as the Devil of Helston, exited before a footman ushered the other guests from the room, leaving Georgiana and Quinn momentarily alone.

"This is the gentleman under whose roof you stayed for a portion of the past year?" Quinn asked.

"When I was not needed here, yes. Ata and the other widows staying at the Helston estate were a great comfort to me after Anthony died," she murmured. "And the duke is actually a very good man. In fact, the best of men."

"Your ability to judge a man's character has deteriorated."

Georgiana stiffened. "No, not really." She gazed at him steadily. "If I have a flaw it is that once I form an acquaintance, there seems to be little the person can do or *not do* to shake me from my original opinion and feelings." She stopped suddenly, horrified at having had the audacity to admit something that cut so close to her heart. She searched his face in vain for the minutest indication of his understanding of the state of her heart, but his eyes were still mesmerizing pools of secrets and timeless mystery. She tried to ignore the discomforting silence.

Her gaze dropped to her dull gown and fingered the frayed edge of a pocket. The old silk mourning gown matched her mood—dark gray, and dreary to the very edges.

"Georgiana," he said quietly. "It's been a year. I think you might consider wearing colors again."

He was always so perceptive. Why couldn't he see her heart? But then again, and perhaps worse, he did and only pretended he didn't in order to allow her to save face. "I've never worn colors. Browns and grays are much more practical."

"It won't do for you to be beyond the fringes of fashion. I shall arrange for a dressmaker from town to attend to you." He cleared his throat. "You would do well to confer with the Countess of Sheffield on the style and colors that will suit you."

"But I'm not at all like Grace Sheffey, and never will be," she whispered.

"She seems very kind, and I'm certain she would be willing to help you."

"Yes, but—"

"How long has she been a member of your little circle?"

Oh . . . her heart plummeted. It was as Rosamunde had suggested. In less than a day some sort of interest had formed between Grace and Quinn. "Are you asking me how long the countess has been a widow?"

"Yes."

And with that one word all her dreams came crashing down around her *again*—somewhere in the vicinity of her ankles. Some perverse martyr within her insisted on twisting the pain to new heights. "Her husband died almost two years ago and left her a considerable fortune. Grace is simply the kindest, most dignified, and beautiful lady, and you could not find a bride more capable of becoming a prop"—she stuttered in hurt—"a *proper* Marchioness of Ellesmere." Her fists were so tightly curled that the nails almost pierced the worn fingers of her gloves.

He scrutinized her face and indicated for her to precede him to the doorway. "Come, we must join the others. And by the by, my daughter shall arrive some time in the next few days. I must tell you what to expect . . . or rather warn you about her rather, ahem, willful ways."

* * *

Would this evening never end? Quinn wondered as he escorted, or rather, dragged the uncivilized Duke of Helston out onto the balcony following dinner.

Quinn leaned against the railing and began trimming a cheroot, taking delight in the salty Cornish air he hadn't realized he'd missed so much.

Luc St. Aubyn continued his infernal pacing, muttering a curse Georgiana would probably have been delighted to add to her repertoire.

"Care for one?" Quinn casually offered the cigar to the duke. "It's from Portugal—very smooth."

"Absolutely not." The duke curled his lip in distaste. "For God's sakes, don't you have any brandy?"

"No."

"Whiskey?"

"No."

"Blue Ruin, then? Even complete barbarians have a little Ruin stashed away."

"Sorry, no. I don't imbibe—nor will anyone else until the wine merchant's delivery is made."

The Duke of Helston stopped dead in his tracks as if struck by lightning. "What?" His eyebrows rose so high they almost became part of his hairline. "I should've known. Never could trust a diplomat or a man who doesn't drink. I'm not surprised you're both."

Quinn smothered a laugh. The man was a complete blackguard, and uncouth to the nth degree.

How on earth the lovely duchess put up with him was something that boggled the mind.

"Care to reconsider my last offer?" Quinn asked again. He really didn't want to have to give up one of his Portuguese cheroots, but then he rather thought he might just make Ata and the other ladies friends for life if he kept this heathen from them for another half hour. And Quinn knew all the benefits of forming alliances.

"Oh, all right, if you've nothing else." Disgruntlement dripped from each word off the duke's tongue.

Quinn handed over the cheroot with disappointment and struck a flame from the tinderbox.

The duke inhaled and began choking in a most satisfactory manner, exactly how Quinn had known he would. These particular cheroots were powerful little devils, and only fools actually dared to inhale the pungent smoke. "Are you all right, Your Grace?" He pounded the duke on the back, careful to hide his amusement but all the while hoping the acrid fumes had singed his voice box, for all their sakes.

"Go to the devil, Ellesmere," the duke rasped out before another coughing fit engulfed him.

Quinn sighed and shook his head while calmly extracting another cheroot from his pocket and starting the trimming process again. He began to whistle.

"If your intention is to distract me, Ellesmere, from returning inside—you had best stop that infernal noise. Only imbeciles whistle."

"Well, I suppose I can take comfort that I've now risen in your estimation to the level above 'barbarian.'"

If Quinn had to swallow another smile he might just gag.

"What are your intentions, Ellesmere?" Helston growled suddenly.

"I beg your pardon?"

"I said," the duke almost shouted, "what are your intentions? Your plans. Your bloody devious goal."

"I'm sorry, Your Grace, I've no idea what you're suggesting."

"Georgiana Wilde. Georgiana Fortesque. Whatever you want to call the lady I've been coddling until you decided to drag your lazy diplomatic bones away from the delights of Portugal. She can't live here under the same roof with you after my grandmother sneaks back to Amberley with the rest of the crows."

The duke had not a clue how obvious his character was revealed with every contrary word he uttered. The man would have been an utter failure at the negotiating table.

"And what is she to you?" Quinn asked without a glimmer of emotion.

The duke sputtered. "Are you suggesting—"

"No. I make it a point to withhold judgment until I can fully make out a person's character," Quinn said with amusement. "And since the duchess appears .devoted to you, and I vaguely remember her from our childhood here, her good opinion forces me to reconsider my initial impression." He shook his head. "Although what she sees in you is hard to understand."

"Of course it would be . . . to a complete imbecile such as yourself," roared Helston.

Now he had him where he wanted him. "Actually, I'm glad you asked about Georgiana. She and her family are the main reasons I descended from town. I've a delicate situation to sort out and would be grateful for your aid."

"Why should I help you?" the duke asked darkly.

Quinn felt like strangling the man, but settled for flexing his hands behind his back. "Must I remind you of the excellent care I will be taking of your grandmother while you and Her Grace enjoy some time alone? Really, I hadn't wished to bring this matter up."

"What do you want?"

"I'm looking for a steward. A man I can trust to ease Georgiana away from the role she assumed when her father became ill."

"Going to give Georgiana and her family the boot, are you? I won't help you there."

Quinn sighed in exasperation. "No, you fool," he seethed, finally deciding on heat for heat as a last resort. "I'm trying to settle her in comfort— away from the damned pigsty. Now do you have a name for me or not?"

The Duke of Helston pursed his lips and broke out into a smile filled with deviltry. "Actually, yes. I have the very man for you. Brown is his name— John Brown. I think you and he will get along

verra well, laddie. In fact I *guarantee* it." The last
was said in a growling purr. "You must be riding
a Cornish wave of luck, as my former steward is
due to arrive for a visit any day now. I shall send
him directly to you. Of course, you'll have to offer
him a king's ransom to stay on. He retired to his
small Scottish property last year."

Quinn knew perverse pleasure when he saw
it, and he would bet his last farthing the Duke of
Helston was hatching a plan to confound him. He
sighed. Well, he would learn soon enough if this
Mr. Brown was a cheat, a drunk, a liar, or just plain
corrupt. He had had enough experience in those
arenas of humanity to render him an expert.

Hours later, long after the duke and his wife
had returned to Amberley with their raven-
haired cherubs, Quinn took pleasure in his evening ritual, which relieved the day's tension of
holding onto his every last emotion. He walked
from room to room on the lower level, checking
for lit candles, speaking to the servants, inspect-
ing every detail of the smoothly run great house.
"Putting the house to bed" was how he chose to
think of it.

He sighed.

A father missing a child was a wretched thing,
he thought ruefully. *Putting a house to bed, indeed.*

He continued his tour and took a lonely sort
of pride as the newest caretaker of this massive
estate, one of the largest in the British Isles. Penrose was the southernmost of five residences in
the Fortesque family portfolio of entailed proper-

ties. All of them were prosperous. It boggled the mind. How Cynthia would have reveled in all of it. If she had only shown restraint, only shown more . . . He ruthlessly forced the thought away.

He wasn't sure when he had taken the decision to walk to the opposite end of the house, where a small suite had been reserved for Mr. Wilde before the steward had married and been allowed the use of Little Roses cottage. But his unhurried step led him here. He slowed in front of the steward's rooms. Something was wrong, Quinn thought. The door to the spartan study was wide open, as was the connecting door to the small bedchamber beyond, and a fire burned in the tiny grate.

Georgiana, however, was nowhere to be seen.

Quinn lifted a candle to illuminate the small suite more clearly and stepped across the threshold. "Georgiana?" he asked to be sure. Opaque beeswax dripped onto his coat sleeve, and the familiar honey fragrance reminded him of the scent of Georgiana's hair when he had carried her to the folly.

He set the gleaming silver candlestick in the windowsill and opened the sash to breathe in the warm summer evening air. A thousand and one stars filled the night sky, all the way to the horizon.

A lone star lay lower than the rest, giving the illusion of resting its fiery head upon Loe Pool in the distance. And for a tiny flicker of a moment Quinn wished Georgiana was beside him. She was the one person, he instinctively knew, who would take joy in this magical illusion in nature. He blew out his candle to more fully enjoy the sight, only to find that the darkness brought naught but more melancholy.

Georgiana sat on the bench facing Penrose's great house, leaned her cheek against the cool windowpane in the glass lake house, and closed her eyes.

God. This was just too difficult. She wanted him with an intensity that bordered on the ridiculous. Was this obsession to never end? Would she always have to suffer such poignant longing without any possible chance of a return of his affection? It was so painfully obvious that he regarded her at best as nothing more than a quasi-relation to be dressed and then settled far away. Those long summer days of youth, when he had looked at her with a glint of amusement and affection and cross-my-heart-and-hope-to-die trust were gone. And yet, her perverse longing for him could not be doused.

And after tonight she realized her unquenchable thirst for him could indeed get worse. The morass of her pain would only intensify if she were forced to endure the possible budding attraction between Quinn and Grace Sheffey, one of the few people she not only admired but also liked immensely.

Grace had the sort of quiet dignity Georgiana would never have. And while the countess rarely confided in any of them, it had become obvious during their acquaintance that Grace had loved Luc St. Aubyn, the Duke of Helston, just as long

and as deeply as Georgiana had loved Quinn—
until the duke had married Rosamunde, a former
member of the club, last year. Yet Grace Sheffey had never uttered a whisper of hurt or pain
or anything but great happiness at the union.
The only sign of something amiss had been the
countess's sudden departure for a tour of Italy the
day following Rosamunde and Luc's wedding. To
her credit, Grace had returned refreshed and had
never shown any awkwardness when the duke
and Rosamunde were in her company.

Georgiana knew she did not possess that sort
of mettle or fortitude. If Quinn married Grace,
then she would simply go to pieces. Would have
to be locked away in one of the hay barns. She
shook her head in disgust and wondered if she
was the only female in the world who could con-
jure up a blissful marriage between two people
who had formed an acquaintance of less than a
week in duration.

She looked beyond the vast blackness of the
water surrounding the little glass house sitting
on the island of Loe Pool. And she imagined, as
she always did, Quinn rowing toward the magical
house. Toward her. *Only toward her*—with never-
ending love and longing in his eyes. The same
emotions he would behold in her eyes if he would
only care to find them beyond the façade she had
constructed soon after forming his acquaintance
at a ridiculously tender age.

She straightened her back in annoyance at her
maudlin frame of mind and suddenly noticed
a tiny flicker of light in her rooms far distant at

Penrose, dark in sleep. She took a deep breath and held it, trying to stifle her emotions again. She was being silly. It was most likely Mrs. Killen, the housekeeper, come to say good night. There was absolutely no pathetic reason Quinn would ever visit her rooms at moonset.

But that practical thought could not stop the prayer forming in her mind. The words she had whispered for as long as she could remember: *Come to me. Please, let him come to me.*

And suddenly the flicker of light in her room far away went out—just like her dreams should have done long ago.

Chapter 5

⸻ ⟨⟨ ⸻

July 30—to do
- _tour estate, check tenant cottages_
- _uncap honeycombs_
- _kitchen garden—meet new under gardener_
- _fit new hood and jesses on Oblige_

   - _try & try again to put away my dreams_

"Where were you last night?"

Georgiana did not need to look up to know that Quinn had entered the falcon mews. It was the last place she'd thought he would ever come. Lord knew it had taken her months to return here after the accident.

"Whatever do you mean? At Penrose, of course." She kept her gaze on the beautiful female falcon, who was bobbing her head and nervously pecking and restacking her tail feathers.

"You weren't in any of the chambers, nor were you in your father's old rooms."

She glanced briefly at him out of the corner of her eye and carefully fitted the feathered hood on the raptor. "Why do you ask?" she asked.

"Well, I was worried, naturally." He surveyed the chicken-wire wall of birdcage stalls.

"As you can see, I'm perfectly fine. I often tour the estate to check on the animals."

"So late at night?"

"The animals don't seem to mind. And"—she lowered her voice—"I find it soothing, actually, to tour the grounds before I sleep. I would hate for an animal to suffer or be hungry or thirsty all night." She secured the edges of her heavy glove. "Is there something you wanted? I've already arranged the menus. I'd thought you would dine with Ata and Grace and the others."

"I begged off after a long morning playing piquet with the lot of them. Had no idea a press gang of widows could cheat quite so much."

"The duke always encouraged poor sportsmanship."

"Why am I not surprised?"

She pursed her lips to keep from laughing. "How much did they fleece you for?"

"The Fortesque coffers won't suffer too much." He paused. "Actually, I arranged for picnic fare and came in search of you. I'd hoped to discuss a few things before Fairleigh arrives. Good Lord, is that Khubla?"

Georgiana raised her gloved arm to show off the falcon, her pinstripe markings tracing the pattern that had beguiled kings and emperors through the ages. "No. It's the daughter of the falcon I"—she hesitated and wondered if she dared refer to the awful past—"retrieved that day." She continued quietly, "That bird became the best hunter ever. Anthony named her Noblesse. And this is Oblige."

He stared at her until she looked down at the game bag resting on the table in front of them. He broke the stillness by reaching for the bag and casually hefting it to his shoulder before walking to the door and looking back at her. A sense of déjà vu enveloped her when he bowed and swept his arm indicating his wordless desire for her to precede him out the door.

They cleared the mews doorway, adjacent to the great shingle bar separating Loe Pool from the sea, and silently walked along the line of beeches and pine, favored aeries for all the raptors of Penrose. How many times had she been here with Tony and Quinn in her girlhood? How many times had they flown the falcons, fished, or swam themselves to exhaustion?

"I wondered if that nestling survived the fall," he said so softly behind her that it almost seemed she had imagined it. "And if you suffered for many months. I don't know how you bore it, Georgiana. How I admired your quiet strength that day. I never saw anyone before or since endure so much and complain so little. I always thought of you when people spoke of courage."

She unhooded Oblige and the falcon bent her knees and pushed off the glove in a great sweeping movement, her wings pumping the air to rise in fluid degrees to the tree limbs above. Georgiana was too moved to respond. *He had thought of her after all.*

She watched the raptor ascend the sky on an

updraft, the falcon's head twitching in an effort to detect movement below. "I use to wonder if you'd forgotten us. Anthony, me . . . Penrose."

"I'm sorry I never wrote. I could have at least written to your father."

"You don't have to explain." She walked into the undergrowth to flush out possible game. "You were very busy. School, your work, and then marriage—always moving between countries."

"I'm not asking for excuses. People's actions speak for themselves. In the end, words are fairly useless." His footfalls matched her own in the brush. "Don't you agree?"

"Actually, I don't." She stopped and faced him. "I always thought Anthony suffered the most from your silence. If there had been just one letter, one word . . ."

He abruptly turned away, his profile harsh in the sunlight. A striated muscle beat a tattoo along his firm jaw. "When I saw him in town years ago, words had very little effect on my cousin."

"Good Lord." The blood rushed to her fingertips. "I didn't know he'd seen you again."

The falcon dove for prey, the sleek body forming a perfect teardrop shape, astounding in speed. Faster than any other animal on God's green earth.

"Was that after he was sent down from Oxford?" She searched his face for answers.

"Yes. I saw him several times over the course of a year or so. It was inevitable. Unmarried gentlemen are in great demand at society events in London," he said, smiling oddly. "I last saw him after I married. Before I was dispatched to Portugal."

He was staring back at her and she couldn't figure why he appeared so remote. She was grateful for the occupation of collecting Oblige and refitting the hood before placing her on a tree branch they had always used as a perch.

"Well," she said evenly, "I'm glad you saw each other before he died. He changed somehow—actually, everything changed—after you left Penrose for school so suddenly. But then, I'm sure you saw that for yourself—his jaded outlook, his constant recklessness, most likely due to not having a father to corral him, or an older brother." She heard his footfalls come to a rest in front of her.

"Georgiana, when I left London I knew he wouldn't be able to negotiate and survive the ill effects of the dressed-up viper's dens in town." His pause begged her to look at him. "If I had been a better man, perhaps I could've found it within me to return at some point. To try and turn him around," Quinn continued, his eyes darkening. "But I am not a better man."

Earlier, she had attempted to provide false absolution for his ending all ties to her and to Anthony—his best friend. But it seemed he wanted more. Something she was hesitant to give. She was tired of pretending. This was the person she had loved with every ethereal pore of her soul for more than half her life. And so she would ask for the truth—something she'd never dared to do until now.

"Well, then, why didn't you return?" Her hands rose to her hips unconsciously. "Why did you forsake us? Why did you never write?"

He stared at her blankly, presumably shocked by her candor. Then his face became shuttered in a way that she had only witnessed since his return. It closed down to the blank canvas, which infuriated her.

"I can't even forgive myself for not saving him. You were his best friend, his cousin—really more like an older brother he worshipped. He would have done anything you asked." She hesitated. "Actually, I'm surprised you came back. All of us, even my father, said you'd forgotten us. And had never really even cared to begin—"

Strong hands grabbed her arms and shook her. She looked up to encounter his expression cracking to reveal intense emotion.

"I cared. You know that."

"Do I?"

His fingers bit into the bare flesh of her arms painfully. And his eyes burned into hers.

A rustle and small movement caught their attention and a young girl peeped out from behind a hemlock tree. The child giggled mischievously when she knew she'd been caught.

"Papa, when are you going to kiss her and apologize so I can come out?" A mischievous expression swept her features.

The blazing heat in Quinn's face changed in an instant, replaced by a look Georgiana had not seen since his return—unreserved happiness.

"Fairleigh!" He was walking to his daughter and picking her up to swing her about in a great circle. "And where is Miss Biddleworth?"

"Papa!" The little girl wrapped her arms around

his neck and hugged him fiercely. "Old Miss B is taking a lie down. Told me to do the same. Ha! As if I would do something so boring."

Georgiana watched Quinn in amazement. There was such joy radiating from him. Quinn open and fully happy was almost painful in its intensity. Actually, she admitted, she had *never* seen him like this.

"And by the look of your gown it appears you climbed out your window. I'll not ask how you managed not to kill yourself grappling down two stories if you promise to never, ever do it again. And by the by, how many times have I told you not to spy on people?"

"You do it," the girl said indignantly. "I overheard you talking about it to Mamma."

He sputtered. "Yes, well . . . during wartime sometimes people are forced to do things they wouldn't ordinarily do," he said, tweaking her nose. "It was part of my profession and I got paid for it."

"Perhaps then I should be paid for it too," she said, giggling. "Who is that lady, Papa? And why were you hurting her? You told me never to hurt anybody—even Timmy Bradford when he ripped off my doll's arm. That was much worse than whatever that lady could have said. I didn't see her ripping anything."

Quinn shook his head and then picked up the child before setting her in front of Georgiana with exaggerated pomp. "Madam, may I present my daughter, Fairleigh?" He turned to his daughter. "Darling, show her how well you curtsy."

The little girl's blonde curls bounced as she performed the worst curtsy Georgiana had ever seen. His daughter then proceeded to roll her eyes, the color of the bluebells that carpeted the Cornish countryside.

"Well, let's see if you can do it any better," the little girl dared in an outrageously funny manner after perceiving Georgiana's expression.

Georgiana thought she might just burst from withheld laughter. "Well, I think I can manage it a tad better than you, to be perfectly honest." And she did. But just barely.

"I like you." The little girl began to giggle. "What's your name?"

"Fairleigh! How many times do I have to tell you to wait for the person to be presented?" Quinn sighed in exasperation.

"Well Papa, I thought you'd forgotten to introduce her and I was covering up your rudeness by doing the asking myself."

Oh, Georgiana thought, where had this child come from? She possessed none of her father's formidable collected nature. She was all honesty and openness and exuberance. What she would give to have a daughter such as Fairleigh.

The girl fingered a blonde curl. "Papa, you still haven't made up to her. I'm apart from you less than a fortnight and your manners have gone all to pieces. I told you—you shouldn't have left me with Grandmamma and Pappy. You need me. Now, make up to her."

"Fairleigh—"

"No. In the usual fashion. You always said it

was unpardonable to hurt a lady and you were hurting her arms. I saw it."

"But Fairleigh, it isn't at all—"

"Now," the little girl said with such finality she surely had royal blood coursing her veins, Georgiana thought, enjoying the sight of a young girl bringing the oh-so-mysterious Quinn Fortesque to his knees.

Georgiana felt the brush of his hand along her arm and glanced up to find his unforgettable hazel-green eyes looking at her intently.

"Georgiana, pardon me if I hurt you in any way. It was done entirely unconsciously, I assure you. Please forgive me."

The little girl snorted. "I see you've even forgotten how to apologize properly, Papa. Where is the kiss? There *must* be a kiss."

Georgiana felt all the blood drain from her face. She had to put a stop to this. Now. "Fairleigh, I'm delighted to make your acquaintance and I'm so glad to have another lady here to help me show this brute of a papa of yours the error of his ways. But it's really not necessary for him to kiss—"

"Are you going to argue with me too?" Fairleigh asked, with all the majesty of a queen.

Surely she didn't really expect—

"Now," the miniature ruler harrumphed.

Oh dear God. Her mind froze as she glanced at Quinn. He wouldn't do it. She knew that. There wasn't a chance he would—

And suddenly he was leaning toward her, his firm lips meeting her cheek with a softness that was surprising given the chiseled harshness of his features. She couldn't breathe, couldn't move as his face pressed against hers near the tendrils below her temple. The momentary sound of his exhaled breath there teased her and made her slightly dizzy. It was so quick and yet his lips had felt like a warm brush with fate.

"Georgiana, again, allow me to apologize," he whispered. "I don't know what possessed me to—"

"You're supposed to kiss her on the lips, silly," his daughter chirped. "Everyone knows that, Papa. You only kiss *children* on the cheek. Ladies are kissed on the lips."

Georgiana stood stock-still in horror. The girl was some sort of devil child from Hades sent to torment her. Or at the very least a tyrant. An adorable, conniving tyrant.

"Fairleigh," Quinn said with embarrassment and not a little exasperation, but with no apparent reaction to having kissed her. "Gentlemen do not kiss *all* ladies on the lips when they apologize. Only"—he searched for the right word—"*certain* ladies. Ones with whom they have a special relationship. A longstanding bond."

"But you told me in London that you had known her a long, long time and that you had grown up with her and she was special."

Good God. There was no possible way he would—

"Fairleigh, how many times do I have to tell you not to refer to someone standing before you as *her*?"

The girl pouted. "But I don't know if I should call her Georgiana like you do, Papa, or Lady Something-ton or Other-ling. Or should I say Her Grace? Although she doesn't look like a Her Grace if you were to ask me."

Thank God the girl was off the subject of kissing. "Fairleigh, please use my given name. We are to be great friends. I am sure of it. Would you like to help me with the falcon? Did you see her? I've been very negligent and must return Oblige to the mews. I shall even let you carry her."

She seemed to consider it. "You're just as bad as Papa. You're trying to wiggle out of kissing him, too. He shouldn't have hurt you, but you have to pretend to accept his apology, and kiss him even if you don't feel like it. That's what Papa always forces me to do." The girl's eyes were slightly slanted, just like one of Beelzebub's minions.

Quinn made a long-suffering sound and rubbed his forehead. "Georgiana, you will confer with me before you ever decide to remarry and have children won't you? The grim reality is now before you."

He grasped his daughter's hand gently and looked down at her. "I should know better than to argue with you, Fairleigh. I have taught you how to negotiate too well, I fear, so the blame is all mine. But I have also taught you the art of compromise. So I shall promise to kiss Georgiana, for you are correct. We share a special bond—like a brother to a sister. But it won't be here or now, for apologies should be conducted in private—without an intermediary judging the performance."

Like a brother to a sister. Georgiana's heart shriveled a little more.

"Well, so far I think you've earned a very low score, Papa. But I do know how to compromise, as you say. I will just have to ask Georgiana to report your performance and you shall report hers to me after."

Georgiana was wrong about the child being the devil's minion. She was a dwarf-sized *Medusa*. A thousand snakes were surely lurking under those beguiling curls.

The little girl looked from one to the other of them and giggled. "I'm hungry. What's in the picnic basket, Papa? Oh, and Georgiana, you did say I could pet the bird, didn't you? Will she peck me?"

Georgiana rather felt like pecking her herself, but instead brushed one of those silvery-blonde locks from Fairleigh's face. The strands felt like warm spun silk, reminiscent of the downy brood patch on Oblige's breast when she was nesting.

The rest of the day was spent touring portions of the estate with Quinn and his daughter. The discussion about forgiveness and kissing was dropped as thoroughly as a stone thrown into the depths of the sea off Trewavas Cliff. As she watched Quinn with Fairleigh, she felt wholly isolated. Her memories of her youthful, carefree days with him would no longer bring her any comfort. He had gone out in life and lived—and he had forgotten her, despite his words to the contrary. He had formed a life so completely unconnected to hers, and had a beautiful daughter with whom to share love, and the memories of a beloved lost wife.

If she had been the sort to enjoy self-pity, she would have been touched by it now. Instead, she resolved to yet again fortify herself and put her feelings for Quinn in the past . . . where they belonged.

"Mr. Brown," Quinn murmured the next morning, still fairly suspicious of the older man sitting across from his desk. "Then we are agreed?"

The balding Scot chuckled amiably. "*Och.* Only a fool would say no to such a sum. But forgive me, my lord"—he shook his head, still laughing—"for saying that I'm thinking you're the fool to offer it. Are stewards such a rare commodity these days?"

The Duke of Helston stood propped against the fireplace mantel nearby, with an annoyingly smug expression. "Brownie, you can't say I didn't warn you that the man is a bloody imbecile. And he doesn't seem to trust a soul. It's as I always say—"

"Forgive me, Helston, if I ask you yet again to refrain from uttering one of those witticisms you're so fond of," Quinn interrupted. "I should like to get on with this."

John Brown coughed once or twice before he pulled out a handkerchief to swab his brow. Luc St. Aubyn looked ready to do murder.

Quinn wished he knew if this Scot would perform his duties as well as he hoped. And more to the point, if he would be able to manage the impossible feat of easing Georgiana away from the barnyard and into the drawing rooms.

A knock echoed from the study's door. "Yes?" he called out.

The dowager duchess's usually pleasant voice crackled in outrage beyond the closed door. "He wouldn't. Luc simply wouldn't. Mr. Brown was to stay with him at Amberley during his visit—not here. Why, there's no reason for him to be here with—"

Georgiana opened the door, her finger to her lips, her gaze on the dowager.

Quinn cleared his throat. "Ladies," he murmured as he drew himself up with the other two gentlemen to bow.

"I'm sorry to intrude," Georgiana said with a question lurking in her wide, alert eyes. "But the housekeeper mentioned Mr. Brown was visiting and I—or rather Ata and I—wanted to give him our best wishes before he returned to Amberley."

Georgiana bobbed a curtsy in Mr. Brown's direction and the older man leaned in and quickly pecked her cheek.

"Now lass, you're not going to begrudge an old friend a kiss are you? It's been far too long since last we met and you must take pity on me. Doddering old salts rarely receive kisses, you know. 'Tis a great pity. Old age is when we need them most."

Ata tottered up to Mr. Brown and stomped her cane on his boot.

Mr. Brown winced and was to be commended for keeping his ire to himself.

"Doddering, indeed. Why you're as doddering

as an old fox with an eye on the lambs. Don't trust him for a minute, my dear."

Georgiana's eyes glinted with amusement.

"And don't you dare look at me as if I should welcome your hide," Ata said. "You are a yellow-bellied coward, you are. The way you left after Luc's wedding last season, well, I should think—"

Mr. Brown effectively silenced the dowager with a very quick kiss on the lips. The duke's eyebrows rose to the edges of his pitch-black hairline.

"Well," Ata sputtered in complete shock. "Well, I never—"

"Thought I would return? I didn't either. But after your grandson's invitation, I changed my mind. I suppose I missed—"

Ata's eyes flared with something that looked like hope and she made a sound.

"—the balmy *Cornish air*," he finished with satisfaction.

"Why you are as ill-mannered as—"

Mr. Brown cut in softly, "And perhaps, just perhaps, I missed a certain feisty little bag of wind, too."

"Well!" Ata said in outrage.

The duke's laughter floated above them all. "I almost—I repeat almost—wish I could stay to witness more of this. But I must return to Amberley. Ellesmere, they're in your hands now. I trust you will sort it all out . . . eventually. The legendary charm"—he looked very pained—"you prize so highly should serve you well. But make sure you put a lock on my grandmother's door, will you?" He turned back from his retreat toward the door.

"Actually, I would install a lock on Mr. Brown's, too."

"Luc!" Ata shrieked.

"Come," Mr. Brown said to the tiny dowager. "Shall we escort Luc to the front hall? I must have a word with him about the importance of hiding keys."

Ata made a very unladylike snort and looked ready to recommence battle, but seemed to think the better of it after glancing at Georgiana. Instead, she sized up Mr. Brown and accepted his arm as they headed for the door, leaving Quinn alone with her.

Georgiana gave him a measured look. "You've invited Mr. Brown to stay?"

"Yes. Evens out the numbers a bit, don't you agree?"

"You invited him only to even out the numbers?"

"And as a favor to the Duchess of Helston, who deserves the peace every new mother craves."

"For no other reason?" A storm was rising in her turbulent expression. Her emotions were always so evident in her features.

"You know, Georgiana"—he edged closer to her and continued softly—"just because you've decided we're enemies doesn't mean we can't also be friends."

She looked away. "I never said we were enemies." Her face was flushed.

"I shan't lie to you, Georgiana. I would like for you to consider Brown as a possible solution. An aide to you . . . and to me."

"But—"

"We agreed we would search out a replacement."

"But—"

"And that you would train the person with grace and good humor."

She made an inelegant sound. "I never said I'd do it with grace and good humor. In fact, you know I'm incapable of the former."

He took another step closer to her and could see sparks of golden filaments radiating from the dark depths of her irises.

She shifted and appeared flustered by his proximity. He had never noticed until this instant that she became ill at ease whenever he stepped close to her. The same thing had happened at the folly the day he had arrived, and again yesterday when he had kissed her cheek.

The thought of that moment left a tightness in his chest. He had promised to kiss her properly. The way a man kisses a woman. He reached out to her and her eyes widened as she stared at his outstretched palm. "Georgiana" he said very quietly. "I do apologize again for losing my temper yesterday. Will you forgive me?"

"I've already forgiven you. You know that." She looked away.

He dropped his proffered hand, then grasped her arms and drew her closer. "Then may I kiss you? A kiss will wash away the awkwardness."

"I won't kiss you just because your daughter forced you to agree to some ridiculous notion."

Abruptly he wanted to kiss her.

"And if I told you my daughter has nothing to do with it?"

"I should not believe you."

In the moment of silence that followed, their eyes locked, and the air thrummed with tension.

And suddenly, quite inexplicably, there was something in Georgiana's eyes that made him want to crush her to him. *Protect her.* The rational part of his mind was screaming at him to turn the moment. God knew Georgiana had little need for anyone's protection.

"Is the idea so repugnant to you?" he whispered.

Something flickered in her expression. "This is ridiculous." She turned to go. "I've got to see to the honeycombs. They need to be uncapped today, and—"

At the last moment, he grasped her hand firmly and pulled her back toward him. A momentary flash of fierce longing glittered in her eyes before he lowered his lips to hers and was swept into a violent tempest . . . not unlike the last few knots of his storm-tossed passage through the English Channel. Only then he had been traveling to just another point on his eternal journey to a never-ending series of destinations. This time, this journey, *this kiss* felt like he had finally found shelter. Permanently.

It warmed his bones and . . . *and shocked the living hell out of him.*

And oh, what it did to her . . .

Chapter 6

List? What list?

Georgiana kissed him with every ounce of her being. She tried to steady the trembling she couldn't control while he teased the seam of her lips again and again until she opened to him. Sparks of yearning whirled deep within her, her skin aching with desire. *Oh God*. This was so much more than all her dreams over the years combined. Now she was allowing all the longing she had pinned down deep inside of her during the last two decades to escape the confines of her heart.

Georgiana unconsciously clung to his hands the way the falcons mated in the golden rays of twilight on the salty updrafts along Pentire Point, their feet joined in a spectacular sky dance, revolving in mesmerizing arcs as if to triumphantly show their devoted passion to the lesser world below. For when a falcon chose a mate, it was for life.

As that unbearable wish intruded upon her thoughts, she released his hands, released her hold on him.

His shuttered, mysterious eyes searched hers and darkened. "Oh no," he whispered. "We're not finished . . . not nearly."

And time slowed to a standstill as he again pulled her to him, this time wrapping her hands above his neck before he bound his own about her, enveloping her in his overpowering warmth as she melted into him. Her lips parted and he possessed her mouth, his tongue penetrating and sure. His breath thrummed against her cheek in time to her own harsh exhales as he tasted her, devoured her in shattering thoroughness while his hands gripped her back and then brushed against the sensitive sides of her breasts. And all the while his intangible, unforgettable scent captivated her senses and made her dizzy with an ache she couldn't define.

She was so very beyond her depth, her nerves soaring with unbearable longing for this to never end. Just when she realized the moan she had heard was coming from her throat not his, he eased his lips from hers and trailed a pattern of kisses past her cheek to nuzzle the sensitive jointure of her neck. His breathing became erratic against her throat and she froze . . . in horrified remembrance of Tony's uneven breathing on her wedding night . . . and of Tony's begging words to think of him always . . . not *Quinn*.

She tore herself away from him, never bothering to look back as she fled to lose herself in the security of her list of labors. Never bothering to search his expression for the very thing she had wished for, for so long: darkening desire.

It was there in his eyes, but only for a moment when she ran away—a very fleeting instant before he staggered backward and regained his senses.

But then, timing had never been Georgiana's forte. It had always been her downfall.

For the rest of the day and into the evening, Georgiana struggled to keep those moments with Quinn from invading her every thought.

And failed miserably.

His eyes, his embrace, his mouth on hers suffused every corner of her mind—while she took the early twilight air with the widows and through dinner, which tasted like the sawdust littering the chopping block.

Later that evening, as she watched the mist rising from the warm waters of Loe Pool into the cooler night air, she knew she would never be free of him. He had a grip on her that could not be unclasped from her heart.

Her mind was still fevered with thoughts of Quinn throughout a long chat the next morning with Mr. Brown, who seemed determined to humor her and help her no matter what. The ledgers, for the first time in her life, held little interest and much too much detail.

All the while she wondered where *he* had gone. Oh, at first she was glad he was nowhere in sight. Her emotions were too high, her shock at what had happened too new. She needed privacy to regain her sanity and to plan and ponder what would happen next.

Never in any of her dreams had she fully imagined the raw, desperate sensuality of kissing Quinn. Losing complete control of all her senses had never been at stake. His kiss was supposed to have felt like a romantic, dreamy state, not a violent, all-consuming desire to know more—a lot more.

By dinner, when Ata asked for the third time, "Where is dear Quinn?" Georgiana thought she would go mad with nervousness.

Did he know? Was he staying away because he had guessed her deepest secret—her great feelings for him? Obviously, he was embarrassed and trying to figure out a way to explain his actions.

That night, as she wrestled with the bedcovers in the steward's quarters she wished she were at Loe Pool. But with Mr. Brown's arrival she felt the need to guard the last vestiges of her father's domain at Penrose. Yet she longed to gaze at the stars, and lose herself in the familiar dreams of Quinn from long ago. Dreams that had now been wiped away by the raw reality of his kiss.

Quinn rubbed his jaw and moved the ledgers to the edge of his barreled walnut desk. He leveled a stare at John Brown.

The older man mopped his brow. "My initial impression?"

"If you please, sir."

"The lass is a better man than I."

"She's no man," he said quickly, without thinking.

"You've noticed, have you?" Mr. Brown chuckled the hearty laugh Quinn had warmed to a little too quickly, he thought with exasperation.

Living at Penrose was making him vulnerable. He, of all people, should know better than anyone the dangers of trusting someone.

Quinn forced himself to relax his clenched hands. "She can't continue on as before. She can't—"

He was interrupted by frenetic rapping on the study's door.

"Come."

The frazzled form of Fairleigh's governess entered, her hands shaking and clenched in front of her. "My lord, I regret to inform you that your daughter has led me on a merry chase again and I have searched everywhere for her." Two bright spots of color mounted Miss Biddleworth's cheeks.

The imp. "Hmmm. Did you try the stables?"

"No, sir. I assumed after your admonishment she would refrain."

He raised his eyebrows. "With my daughter it's better not to assume anything, Miss Biddleworth."

Mr. Brown chuckled again, his blue eyes twinkling.

"Sir—" the older governess began.

"What about the falcon mews?"

"Sir—"

"Or the hay barn? There's a rope swing tied to the rafters—"

Miss Biddleworth did the unthinkable and interrupted her employer. "Sir, I am trying to tell
you that I'm giving notice. I'm sorry, but I cannot
continue." She rose up to her most formidable
governess stance, which was somewhat comical
given that her knotted hair was losing its battle
with the pins. "I have the luxury of speaking
quite plainly to you, my lord, as I've decided to
retire to Somerset and live with my sister. Your
daughter is incorrigible. Never in my thirty years
have I seen a child so spoilt and so slow and unwilling to learn."

The governess, having allowed her rude
thoughts to escape, something she had obviously
never dared do in the last three decades, quickly
lost steam.

"Is there anything else you'd like to add, Miss
Biddleworth?" He kept his voice deceptively
measured.

"I would request someone to take me to the village for the next mail coach."

Quinn promised full payment of her quarterly
wages despite the circumstances and bid a polite
good-bye to the last in a series of six governesses
in as many years.

"Allow me to escort you, ma'am," Mr. Brown
said. "Say in one hour? Would that be sufficient?"

The governess nodded haughtily and departed,
closing the door none too lightly.

"You seem to enjoy feisty females, Mr. Brown."

"As do you, my lord."

"There you are wrong. I *endure* headstrong females. I do not enjoy them."

"Well, begging your pardon, but with a daughter such as yours, you might reconsider." The old man looked like he had more to say.

"Spit it out, Mr. Brown."

"Then there's the matter of Georgiana Wilde—or is it Fortesque?"

"Tread carefully, sir. I rather think you have your own worries, considering what Ata will think if you're seen escorting the governess about the countryside."

"Don't worry about me, sir. I've known the devil's grandmother for five decades. Nothing can frighten this old body of mine."

"You're a brave man, Mr. Brown. Braver than I."

"I don't know, my lord. I've faith in you to see the pleasure a woman of substance can—"

He didn't let the old man finish. "That'll be all, Mr. Brown."

A quarter of an hour later, Quinn's stride lengthened as he made his way past the barn doors, a few stray strands of hay on his clothes. He broke into a run as he allowed fear to curl around the edges of his mind. *Loe pool.* She wouldn't. Not after he had expressly prohibited Fairleigh to go there alone. She couldn't swim. She couldn't . . .

As he entered the downhill slope of a large stand of trees above the lake his gaze snagged on two figures in the far distance—one willowy and dark, the other petite and blonde.

He tried to regulate his breathing as he stopped and watched the pair, but residual fear for his daughter hampered the effort. At least that was what he told himself. He had resolutely kept Georgiana from his thoughts for the last day and a half.

That kiss . . .

Well, his reaction was to be expected. It had been years since he'd given in to his baser needs. Years since he'd sworn off females—including his wife, and even those women offering favors at very favorable rates at the best brothels in the worst parts of town.

They had been the last he had sworn off. The temporary corporal relief hadn't been worth the possible consequences, and he just couldn't bring himself to continue down that silken path.

Perhaps, he thought ruefully, it was why he had chosen on a whim to settle at Penrose for a while. He could more easily avoid the blatant invitations from the marriage-minded mothers and the wayward wives of his acquaintances in town.

He had thought every sort of female behind him. He had always taken pride in his ability to hold himself in check—ruthlessly—no matter what the issue. Celibacy had not been nearly as difficult as he had thought.

Until . . . *that kiss.*

The starkness in Georgiana's expression—a sort of abandoned yearning had been nearly unbearable to witness. If he only had the nerve to admit it, he likely feared the rawness he'd glimpsed because his soul was empty of everything save that same emotion. He mercilessly dismissed the odd feelings the thought brought.

He sighed and looked at Georgiana and his

daughter. It appeared they were painting, of all things—something he'd enjoyed doing many years ago. Well, at least they weren't in the pigsty. Or wading in the lake water.

He continued on his way toward them, noticing paint-stained aprons, their unbound hair, and exuberant laughter. With Miss Biddleworth's defection it was glaringly obvious he needed to find someone to take on the daunting role of supervising the proper education of his hoyden of a daughter. Someone who could provide a sterling example of femininity for Fairleigh while instilling in her a thirst for knowledge through the habit of reading, as well as a desire to learn embroidery, music, and the necessary household arts. Someone the very opposite of Georgiana.

"Fairleigh," he said when his daughter looked up. "You are to return to Penrose and remain in the schoolroom until you finish the work Miss Biddleworth set before you this morning."

"But Papa—"

"And then," he cut in, "you are to spend one hour on your needlework followed by one hour at the pianoforte." He hardened his heart to his daughter's pained expression. "And after, you are to pray for forgiveness for forcing Miss Biddleworth to hand in her notice."

His daughter smiled radiantly. "Well, Papa, I rather think you should be thanking me. She never taught me a thing. I will be saving you a good deal of money and I don't need a governess or tutor anymore. I haven't needed one for years."

He resisted the urge to throttle her. "Fairleigh," he warned. "You are to do exactly—"

"Georgiana and I," Fairleigh interrupted, "were just discussing your performance."

He started.

"Your apology to her," his daughter clarified when he couldn't make his mouth function. "She said that you kissed her quite—"

"Fairleigh, perhaps I can discuss with your father the idea of allowing you to paint again tomorrow if you do as he says right now." Georgiana stepped from behind her easel, her face a blaze of color despite her sun-darkened complexion.

He looked from one to the other and thought, not for the first time, that it was a quirk of nature that men ruled the world and not women.

"Fairleigh Fortesque, you have precisely to the count of three to start running toward the schoolroom. And if I don't find you there when I return, then I shall force you to select a fine birch switch with which to tan—"

"You would *never*, Papa." His daughter searched his face. "Well, you never did before. You're just annoyed old Beetleface quit. I'm certain—"

"One . . ." he said ominously.

"But Papa, really—"

"Two . . ."

His daughter glared at him imperiously and then turned and trotted away, her posture saying everything she dared not utter.

"What happens when you reach three?" Georgiana asked quietly.

"I'll answer that if you tell me what you told my daughter."

Georgiana tilted her head in such a way that the sunlight caught the bronze filaments in her eyes, which matched a few sun-bleached strands of hair near her temples he had never noticed before. Her skin was the color of honey and he found it oddly alluring. The pale, translucent faces of ladies he had known now seemed sickly in comparison. She cared not a whit for her complexion; her hat lay dangling from its ribbons along her back. Only the tattoo of an unseen vein beating erratically along her neck gave away her ill ease.

"She is very persistent," Georgiana replied.

"Really?" he drawled.

"Oh, bother. I was trying to be kind. I like her very much, despite the fact that she has more energy than I ever possessed. I'm sure you know she shows much artistic talent."

"Yet little inclination toward reading, writing, or anything requiring self-discipline to improve her mind or prepare her for her eventual duties in life."

"Children rarely enjoy applying themselves," she said with a smile. "Childhood is about escaping the schoolroom, going fishing, flying the falcons, racing horses, and climbing trees. Don't you remember?"

"I put behind me the follies of youth long ago." He watched as she gathered the brushes and stooped to place them in a small wooden box. Her knee appeared to buckle but she steadied herself before he could catch her arm. "You, of all people, know what inattention to studies and foolishness can lead to . . . lifelong regret."

Georgiana finally faced him then, a deep flush crawling up from the bodice of her drab, stained gown. "I actually have very few regrets. And I do not consider my deformity a permanent reminder of childhood folly. Quite the contrary. I consider it a shining example of my hen-heartedness."

"What?" he said incredulously. "You don't possess a cowardly bone in your body."

"Gentlemen always think bravery involves physical efforts. Sometimes cowardice stems from an inability to say something that needs to be said." She laughed oddly. "But never mind. I don't expect you to understand, especially when you no longer seem to possess the slightest interest in childish fun, or searching for adventure. It's all dreary duty to you now."

"That's not true at all."

"Hmmm," she murmured, a glimmer of amusement in her dark eyes. "Well, I dare you to organize some unbridled amusements for everyone—especially for your daughter, who will need some reward to entice her to stay in the schoolroom for all the hours you're suggesting."

"I shall consider it," he said, "if you'll answer my original question."

"Which one?"

Oh, he was certain she knew. Her glance away from him proved it. "What did you tell her? That I kissed you quite . . . what? Properly? Thoroughly? *Passionately?*"

"How ridiculous. I, of course, told her you kissed me quite *apologetically*."

He stepped closer and again that fleeting wildness appeared in her eyes. He spoke softly, "Is that really how you think I kissed you, Georgiana?"

"Of course," she whispered, looking aside.

He stroked one side of her face as lightly as he would a falcon's sleek wings. "Well then, it would appear you know as little about kisses as you seem to think I remember about adventure."

She looked at him sharply. "I know enough."

"Really?" He moved his head to better examine her face. "Allow me to beg to differ. If that kiss had involved a simple apology it would have been entirely different—more chaste, more proper. In fact, I'm glad of this chance to speak to you privately, Georgiana. I must apologize in earnest this time. I've no excuse for my behavior to you yesterday. I can only plead a momentary loss of sanity."

She paled visibly. "I know very well that only a loss of sanity would move a man to kiss me. I hardly need you to remind me."

He cursed his ill choice of words. "Georgiana, you've twisted my words completely. I'm begging your pardon for ruthlessly losing my head and dishonoring you in any way."

Without a word, she stared at him for so long, he thought she might turn to stone.

He knew it was a monumentally bad idea, but he couldn't bear to watch her another moment. With a rush, he gathered her stiff fingers in his hands. "It was wrong of me to press my attentions on you. Attentions you obviously found abhorrent. You ran away before I could apologize."

"I think I've had about as many apologies as I can stand, actually." There was such sadness in Georgiana's expression.

A goshan hawk keened in the distance.

"Listen to me, Georgiana. Please. You are a beautiful, vibrant young woman." Still the right words would not come forth. It was the first time he wasn't able to express himself with any fine precision.

"Oh, for both our sakes, stop. Aren't you the one who can't abide dishonesty? I just told you I don't require an apology." Her fingers were still cold in his hands.

He didn't care anymore about propriety, about being a gentleman. Her slender, sweeping brows framed her glittering hurt eyes, and nothing could have kept him from kissing her again. He refused to look deeper than the overwhelming desire to comfort her, to taste the raw essence of her.

He dipped down and captured her lips with his own, his body surging against hers and responding instantaneously to the remembered imprint of her body that had seared itself into his memory. She felt so slender in his arms and he took care when he enveloped her fragile form against his great hulking warmth. Within a heartbeat his blood heated and pulsed with desire.

Only this time the intensity was pushed to a higher plane—far beyond anything he had known. For now she had gotten past the shock that had frozen her the first time he had kissed her. This time, under the hot sun, blazing through the salty Cornish air, she gripped his body to hers with astonishing strength and purpose, and he hardened to painful intensity. He took possession of her mouth with unquenchable hunger, unparalleled heat and force, and all the while Georgiana's lithe muscles bent to answer his brutish demands.

Her dark hair felt like hot silk, heated by the sun and burning his palms. And for the first time in his life he completely unleashed the raw passion he had refused to acknowledge—the emotions that lay deep within the recesses of his being.

Perhaps it was the luxuriant honeyed essence of her invading his senses that pushed him over the edge. Perhaps it was when she slid her hands under the lapel of his coat for the long glide to his neck. He was quite certain that his last coherent thought was when she rose to her toes and instinctively cradled his heavy arousal within the sweet, warm juncture of her thighs.

He plundered the depths of her mouth, only taking, never giving, surrendering completely to his needs, feeling an overwhelming need to never let her go.

They wrestled—tasting, biting, gripping each other like two animals in the wild. He was so mindless with primal desire coursing through him that he was on the verge of laying her on the rocky soil amid the tall sea oats and taking her right there, all rational thought gone with the offshore ocean breeze.

Suddenly, the voices of Ata, Sarah Winters, and Elizabeth Ashburton reached through the fog of his drunken craving to force him to set aside Georgiana a moment before the three widows rounded the tall hedgerow nearby.

"Oh, there you are," Ata called out, waving to them. "We've been looking for you. Your daughter begged us to find you and tell you she has started her lesson and found her embroidery. Grace is with her, Quinn, in the morning room. They are darling together."

It took every inch of control to regulate his breathing, and gather in front of him Georgiana's easels and boxes to hide the evidence of his raging desire. He dared not look at her. "Delighted you found us," he said, his breathing uneven. "Will you accompany me to check my daughter's progress, or are you taking a tour?"

"Oh, please." Ata chortled. "Don't let our slow pace hold you back. I'm certain you'll want to see the pretty picture of Grace and Fairleigh together. And Georgiana promised to take us to the falcon mews. I've never seen a trained bird, and Fairleigh has quite whetted my appetite with her excitement."

He glanced at Georgiana and noted two high points of color cresting on her cheeks. He longed to speak to her alone. To settle matters between them. To find out what she was thinking. But it was not to be. And neither one of them was a good enough actor to stay in the other's company with an audience present and pretend indifference.

He bowed slightly to Georgiana. "Well then, Georgiana. Ata. Ladies, I bid you happy hunting." Quinn balanced the painting boxes and strode off, feeling a bit of cowardice for not insisting on speaking to Georgiana in private.

As he went through his evening ablutions, he thought back on the day's events and was amazed his goose hadn't been cooked but good. Why Providence had pushed Ata and her friends to find him just moments before he ravished Georgiana was something he would ponder for many nights.

Yet his body ached for release still. He stood before his bed—*Anthony's* bed, and his uncle's before him—and felt the weight of twelve generations of Fortesque marquises looking down on him. He fought off the feeling and stumbled into his breeches, and into the night mist, toward Loe Pool . . .

Quinn sliced his arms and shoulders through the cool waters of the lake, tasting the sweet water that had once been salty before the shingle bar had cut off the sea centuries before, and wished he could cut off the irrational emotions roiling in his body.

He would not open himself to feeling emotions for a woman again. Correction, for any person. But most especially not for Georgiana, someone who exuded emotion through every pore of her being. He had learned long ago that emotions were useless things, and that contentment had to be found within oneself, not with others, with the sole exception of one's children.

He stopped and treaded water halfway to the small island and shook the water from his eyes.

It was only then, he remembered, Georgiana had never explained why she had run away from his kisses in the study. In light of her actions today, it made absolutely no sense. But then, when had a woman ever made any sense to him?

The windows of the dark little lake house dimly reflected the moonlight. He wondered if anyone ever used the tiny retreat anymore. But of course they didn't. It had only ever been used by children—he, Georgiana, and Anthony—when they had desired an escape from the adult world.

Chapter 7

Georgiana had managed to avoid any chance meeting with Quinn the next morning by repairing directly to the first chore on her list: uncap honeycombs. She just couldn't face him until she had sorted out what, if anything, she should say to him. And she was certain she couldn't play the role of well-rested hostess to her friends when she had barely slept an hour, if one counted the endless half-conscious moments she had spent twisting the bedcovers.

Only her well-ordered list of things to do brought her any peace. She began the process of tending to the hive on the edge of the outer flower and herb gardens, cultivated for cutting. The rosemary and clover, nature's aphrodisiacs, were in bloom.

The bees hummed all about her, the sound calming her as she lit a chafing dish filled with coal and moist peat. The cycle of the hive suited her to perfection. It was a tidy life of purpose.

Since yesterday's kiss, they'd been forced to be in the same room only once, at dinner last night. And it had been appallingly easy to refrain from speaking to him since Ata and the rest of her friends could always be counted on to carry on no less than three conversations at any given moment. Quinn was at the head with Ata to his one side and Grace Sheffey to his other, while Georgiana sat at the foot with Mr. Brown to her left and Sarah and Elizabeth on her right.

It had not missed her notice that Quinn did not look at her once during the evening meal, and she had pleaded a headache soon after the ladies retired to the main salon before Quinn rejoined them. There seemed an unbreachable gap between them, and she imagined he was probably counting his lucky stars that the ladies of the club were proving to be such an effective diversion. But then again, Georgiana was too. It was just too painful to continue the madness.

Their passionate interlude on the shingle spit had left her ill with longing. Unfortunately, it was quite clear that what Quinn felt for her was most likely something entirely different. She was no fool. The male of their species was born with an unquenchable thirst for females. Hadn't Tony admitted that, and told her many times over that men's carnal needs often ruled their actions? And her father had often warned there were reasons the proprieties had to be observed and had never allowed her to oversee laborers or go about the estate without a trusted brawny groom or three.

What she had seen in Quinn's eyes was emotionless lust, not the love she held in her heart. He would never love her as she loved him. If he did, he would have shown restraint and courted her properly, and offered words of love. He was simply participating in what she had so blatantly offered. He would never dare do something so base with someone such as Grace Sheffey.

One particularly dark thought kept nudging her mind—that he had kissed her the second time in an attempt to prove she was pretty or desirable, which was a lie and they both knew it.

He pitied her.

It was warm and the smoke from the chafing dish billowed around her; the bees instinctively gorging themselves on honey with the threat of fire. Predictably, they soon became sweetly intoxicated, content, and almost harmless.

What must he think of her? She had very nearly bowled him over with her absurd, inelegant fashion. She had likely disgusted him with her wildly bold actions.

She would have to go away. She rearranged the folds of the veil covering her face. Oh, she had known when he'd first arrived that she would have to leave if he did not. And it appeared he was in for the duration. He was separating her and her family from Penrose as effectively as useless chaff from wheat.

And as if to prove the point, destiny intruded in the soft light of early morning, when Georgiana spied through the smoke haze a vision of the future coming toward her: Quinn and his daughter, her little hand locked and swinging in Grace Sheffey's.

"There you are, Georgiana," the countess said, the beautiful warmth of her smile spreading across her fine features. "We'd just about given up finding you, but I insisted we keep looking."

Georgiana rose and set aside the smoking pot and was grateful for the hat and veil that partially shielded her.

"What are you doing?" Fairleigh asked.

"Uncapping the hives, darling," Quinn said. "Georgiana is probably trying to keep up with that sweet tooth of yours." He turned his attention toward her finally, but Georgiana noticed he was actually gazing slightly beyond her shoulder in an awkward fashion.

"Georgiana," the countess continued, "Ata has had the mad notion that we hold a ball at Penrose. But, of course, we couldn't possibly consider it without your approval."

Quinn chuckled and looked down at his daughter. "Grace is being diplomatic. It was actually this one's idea."

"Well," Georgiana replied quietly, carefully removing her hat and veil. "You don't really need my approval, do you? If Quinn agrees, then of course we shall plan a ball. It's a lovely idea."

"I told you Georgiana would agree to it. She's always ready for anything fun," Fairleigh piped in generously while looking into the radiant expression of the countess. "She even dug worms for me and taught me how to fish."

"It will be very little work, Georgiana," Grace said stroking Fairleigh's curls. "I'm certain Rosamunde would be willing to arrange the flowers—you know her gorgeous creations. And I've a notion to import an orchestra from town, if you would like."

"It appears it's all arranged. There is nothing for me to do then," Georgiana said, forcing a smile to her lips. "I can't thank you enough, Grace."

There was an awkward silence as Quinn's eyes finally rose to hers and studied her. "Actually there is something more. We need you to organize the daytime activities."

"What activities, Papa?"

"Why, for Penrose's annual harvest festival."

"What?" Georgiana said, disbelief threading her voice.

"Don't tell me you've discontinued the tradition of the festival?" he replied.

"Well, yes. The last time was a decade or so ago, when Anthony's father was still alive."

"What activities?" Fairleigh said with excitement. "You never mentioned anything beyond a ball, Papa."

His eyes locked with Georgiana's, and discomfort knotted her stomach.

"Well, I'm thinking a little bit of *adventure* would do us all some good here. Don't you agree, Georgiana?"

"Adventure is always a good idea," she murmured, touched that he had remembered her advice.

He looked down at his pretty daughter. "Penrose was the seat of a festival at the start of the harvest. It was to celebrate the bounty of the summer months and apparently in ancient times to make an offering to the gods of wheat and corn. There's a huge bonfire, and contests of skill, and judging vegetables, and jams, and honey, and—"

"I should very much like to judge the honey making, Georgiana," Fairleigh cut in.

"And so you shall, if your father agrees."

"What do you think, Grace?" he said, smiling at the countess. "I think I shall allow it if you are able to wheedle Fairleigh into finishing that pretty embroidery the two of you started."

His daughter pulled a face.

Grace laughed. "My dearest Fairleigh, you are simply like any lady. You need a proper incentive. And I shall offer it." Grace lifted her impossibly long lashes and winked at Georgiana. "We shall just have to make sure there is an embroidery contest. And I shall offer the prize. Hmmm. How about that lovely strand of pearls from my collection you admired?"

Fairleigh's eyes widened and she grabbed the countess and began dragging her away. "Come on. We've got work to do. You said you'd show me how to do French knotting and . . . " The little girl's voice drifted and meshed with the countess's lovely laughter as Grace tried unsuccessfully to halt their hasty departure.

"Quinn and Georgiana, do forgive me," Grace called back. "I shall see you both at dinner to report our progress."

Only the hum of the bees filled the stillness.

"Well," Quinn began, "I suppose I should go after them before Fairleigh tries to talk Grace into throwing in the matching pearl ear bobs."

Georgiana ignored her veiled hat and quickly turned to pick up the chafing dish again. Her back was to him. "Of course." She was at least grateful he was not apologizing for yesterday's events. She didn't think she could bear it if he did.

But she heard not a single fading footfall. The air was as thick with tension as it was with the smoke emanating from the pot she stoked with more peat.

Georgiana lifted the top board from the box hive, dousing the bees again with pungent smoke and exposing the combs for her inspection. She lifted the first from its crusted slot, but it jammed at the top, most likely because she couldn't seem to make her limbs move gracefully when he was standing behind her, observing her.

A second pair of hands grasped the comb below her own and helped ease the board away. "Allow me to help you. Where is the scraper?"

"You'll get stung."

"Maybe," he said with a shrug. "But probably not, if they're anything like the bees in Portugal."

She finally looked up to meet the intense green of his gaze. The brown elements of his irises had retreated as his pupils enlarged.

"I let a cottage with Cynthia one summer to give Fairleigh a taste of the country. The one caveat was that we had to tend the gentleman's bees, his passion."

She handed him the scraper and set a pan underneath the comb. "And you were never stung?"

"Apparently the bees didn't mind my scent."

Of course not. He smelled of rosemary and everything bees loved. "You've not spoken of your wife before. I've been remiss in not telling you how sad we all were to hear of your bereavement. I understand she was a most beautiful lady, and very devoted to you." She bit her lower lip. "I—I'm very sorry, Quinn."

He finished scraping the honeycombs from the rack and replaced it. "How many more?"

His avoidance of her condolences said everything he did not. Clearly he still pined for his wife. "All but the last two," she replied while applying more smoke to the combs.

"The hives in Portugal were cylindrical, fashioned from the rinds of cork trees and covered with earthenware. Perhaps I could have some made for us to try."

"If you like," she said carefully. She was at least grateful they could converse with relative straightforwardness.

The strained atmosphere continued as they pilfered the honey from under the drowsy bees' notice. "And perhaps," he said, "you'll tell me more about beekeeping."

Thank God he had pushed forward a topic of conversation to fill the void. "Well, you probably already know about the division of labor in a colony," she replied.

"Didn't Shakespeare say, 'For so work the honeybees, creatures that by a rule in nature teach the act of order to a peopled kingdom.'?"

"It's a very self-sufficient life. There are the worker bees—all females, of course—who collect honey and pollen and nurse the young. The males—the drones—are altogether idle. All they do is—" She stopped abruptly and stifled an embarrassed laugh. When, oh when would she stop to think before blurting out everything?

"Oh no. You've obviously got to the best part. Spill it, or else." His eyes were full of the mirth she remembered from their days of youth.

"Well, I think your threat is fairly empty since even you know enough not to move quickly and raise the ire of thousands of bees. But I shall tell you, for"—she laughed here—"you deserve to hear it now. The drones do little but sit around getting drunk on nectar."

"That's it? Or are you just too shy to tell the truth of the matter?" He lowered the lids of his eyes and looked at her knowingly.

And suddenly she realized he knew everything about beekeeping. Probably more than she did. And she knew a lot. "Why don't you tell me then?" she said quietly.

"The drones accompany the queen on her *bridal tour*, shall we say? And in doing so they sacrifice their lives." His voice had become a whisper. "I think we can forgive them for drinking a bit too much, don't you agree?"

It was obvious he was now talking about something entirely different from bees. She straightened abruptly. He *knew*. Somehow he knew about Tony and what had happened on their wedding night.

She had to get away from him. Beekeeping etiquette forgotten, she tore off her gloves. A few bees rose up and clouded her vision.

Abruptly, she strode away without looking back, only to feel a sting on the tender flesh of the inside of her elbow. She broke into a run, vaguely hearing a clatter of boards behind her. And the voice of the man who had haunted her dreams for almost two decades calling after her.

Footsteps thrashing the tall grasses followed her. She knew she appeared foolish but could not gather the courage to stop and face him. She dog-legged to the left and entered the hay barn.

The scent of sweet, dry clover filled the air, and dust particles drifted in the single shaft of light from the double-wide doorway. His hand appeared on the edge of the entrance and he swung around to the inside, panting and resting his hands on his knees.

"What was that all about?" he asked, his breathing ragged.

"I think you know," she said, hurt still oozing 'round her mind.

"Well, the thought occurred that perhaps you misinterpreted my words. I hesitate to ask if this has something to do with your marriage. I don't want to pain you. Georgiana, let me see your arm."

She looked down to where she gripped her elbow. "I'm perfectly fine," she said.

"You're obviously not fine at all." He stretched out his hand and it hung in the space between them.

"I want you to leave," she whispered.

"Where?" Quinn asked slowly. "Here? This barn? Or is it Penrose?"

"Here. Obviously, I'm not in a position to ask you to leave Penrose," she said. "Oh, I told you I don't want the silly title. I just want you—every-one—to leave it alone." She stopped.

"How did Anthony die?" he asked quietly.

And God help her, she knew she would tell him. She would do the one thing she had sworn she would never do.

"In my arms," she answered, raw pain filling her eyes that were so dark they appeared black in the shadows of the barn. Her lips twisted in grief. "He drank to celebrate our marriage and prob-ably puffed on that horrid opium pipe and then he drank some more. And then we retired, and his mother intruded, and . . . and then she left, and we . . ." She closed her eyes and Quinn could see she was trying to collect herself. "And he died. *In my arms.* And I couldn't move, couldn't budge him off of me. And then I couldn't revive him. I think it was a weakness of his heart. There. Now you know. It's what you've wanted to know since you got here, isn't it? Now you can stop the bloody questions. And you could also try to stop being kind and concerned one moment and distant the next."

"I'm sorry, Georgiana." He felt wretched. "I don't want to cause you more pain—far from it. But I did need to know, if only to help you deflect scandal. No one believes the story you concocted about him choking and collapsing during a late supper."

"Did you really think I would allow him to be made a laughingstock in death? It would be intol-erable, having others think he died while making love to me." Her voice had become shrill with nervousness. "And then there was the possibility of becoming known as the Black Widow, as in *spider*. That's what someone—Augustine Phelps, do you remember her?—said behind my back after the funeral. 'An insect that mates and then kills' is what she said of me."

"I shall put an end to the inquiry," he said tightly. "Immediately."

She was rubbing the inside of her elbow.

He took a step toward her and she looked at him warily.

"You should have told me, Georgiana. Right from the start. Why didn't you trust me?"

"Why don't *you* trust *me*?" she whispered in return.

He stared hard at her and pulled her toward the light beam. A tiny barb was visible in the flushed, tender skin of her arm. He extracted it and looked up to encounter her dazed, exhausted expression. "Perhaps because I've learned that some women are also like their bee counterparts. They sting to protect themselves."

"And *die* trying," she countered.

He touched her cheek gently. "I think we both know that for the bee and beekeeper alike, to show fight is to court defeat."

Chapter 8

─────◦◦◦─────

August 14—to do
- cut hay in north field
- find new physician for Father
- write to Grayson
- ledgers—see Mr. Brown
- have lawns attended to for festival

   - last fitting of new gray silk ball gown—if time

A fortnight passed, with Georgiana taking every opportunity to be outdoors, working on the estate or at her father's bedside—anywhere but in the great house. She was intensely thankful the days had flown by without any more embarrassing incidents. Of course there was a reason for that. Both Quinn and she, in unspoken agreement, had kept all their interactions within the confines of the company of others.

She had known her time at Penrose was fast coming to an end the day Mr. Brown took up residence in one of Penrose's guest rooms. She just hadn't figured it would end so quickly or so smoothly.

Like so many others before her, she thought ruefully, she and her father were essentially expendable—as replaceable as the animals, the laborers, the tenants, even as disposable as the men who had borne the noble title of Marquis of Ellesmere.

She supposed it was just penance for someone who had taken too much pride in her ability to manage a vast estate almost single-handedly.

Glancing at the ledger—which was becoming increasingly filled with Mr. Brown's neat script, which slanted in a different direction from her own—she realized with sadness that she was truly no longer vital here.

"Lass, your presence has been requested in the morning room. Ata was very insistent," the older balding man said gently from the doorway of the steward's room. "I'm glad it's on your pretty head to organize the last few things before the ball tonight, and not on my balding pate. Nothing I hate more than discussions of flowers and lace." He widened his gummy smile and escorted her from the lair she was losing her grip on more and more with each passing day.

Tea trays appeared just as Georgiana entered the room. The maids placed them in front of the countess, whose natural regal bearing bespoke of steady hands when it came to pouring tea, something Georgiana managed to make a complete muck of time and again. Georgiana circled the group and sat beside Sarah, the quietest and kindest member of the group.

"My dears, the trick to widowhood is to stop thinking of it as permanent," Ata advised the ladies gathered around her in the blue room.

"The same could be said about marriage," a male voice said behind them.

Georgiana glanced quickly toward the doorway. Quinn stood poised at the entrance, drenched in the clear golden light of a fine Cornish morning. Like drab moths to light, all the widows turned their attention to him in a gale of giggles.

"Quinn, dear, you're not helping the cause," Ata said with a smile. "I was just explaining the necessity of broadening our experiences."

He raised an eyebrow. "Is that how you describe hunting husbands these days?"

Another peal of laughter and a chorus of denials echoed throughout the chamber.

"Well, I suppose"—and here he shook his head—"I could be accused of aiding and abetting your cause. Please excuse the intrusion, but I do believe you've all been waiting for these."

A footman and the harried form of the dressmaker Grace had arranged from town poured forth around him. They bore a kaleidoscope of beautiful gowns between them.

The fashionable silk dresses were distributed over the backs of assorted chaises and gilded chairs. Exclamations of excitement filled the air while the dressmaker ordered the footman to secure the drapes in the room.

The footman was then shooed out, leaving Quinn surrounded by members of the club and the mantua maker, who fussed over her creations in very poor, cockney-laced French.

"The Widows Club will make a grand showing tonight," Ata said, excitement and pride threading her voice.

"Of that there was never any doubt," Quinn said with a chuckle. "But I do believe, and actually I have been thinking this for a great while, that you might consider renaming your secret society."

Georgiana quietly retreated to a window seat, as she had been doing a great deal lately. It was better that way—to remove herself from the conversation when Quinn was among them.

"Why, Quinn, what a wonderful idea," Grace said with a smile, her animated expression radiant as she held her pale pink silk ball gown up to her form. That particular shade of rose had always been Grace's best color.

Ata giggled, wearing the silly girlish expression she adopted each time Quinn appeared. Why, he attracted ladies as easily as the last blooming flower of autumn tempted a horde of honeybees.

Ata grasped his hand with her good one; the withered one she hid beneath the ends of her shawl. "You are a rogue, I think, although you hide it altogether too well, Quinn. What name were you thinking of? I'm certain I speak for all of us when I say we're open to your excellent suggestions, as always."

"Hmmm," he murmured, a twinkle in his damnable eyes.

Georgiana was sure he knew precisely what he was going to say.

"'Barely Bereaving Beauties' would do quite adequately," he said, the hint of a smile about his lips.

Georgiana hated how everyone burst out laughing. She thought of Anthony and felt like crying. He deserved a better widow than she. Oh, she was being ridiculous. She really just grieved for the fact that she had not only lost Anthony but had also lost the ease of her past relationship with Quinn. In their youth she had at least had that. Now they had nothing—actually worse than nothing.

She felt a soft hand grasp hers and turned to find Sarah's very wise, kind eyes searching hers intently. "Come, Georgiana, will you help me with my gown? I can't seem to find it."

Georgiana glanced beyond Sarah and spied Quinn staring at her, above Ata and Grace's shoulders. Their eyes met for an instant before she looked away.

"I will leave you all for your fitting, then. Until tonight, ladies." Quinn bowed and exited amid a cloud of well-wishes.

The ladies eagerly went to the gowns and barely noticed several ladies' maids entering from another door. One of them approached Georgiana and bobbed a curtsy. "Ma'am. His lordship would have a word with you, if you please."

Sarah, still at her side, looked at her, a question in her eyes.

"It's all right. I'll be right back."

He was waiting for her on the other side of the door. "I beg your pardon, Georgiana, if I offended you in any way," he said, his voice deepening. "I hadn't meant to."

"I know."

"You do realize I was just teasing Ata and the others, don't you? I did it because Ata seems to enjoy it."

"Of course she does. I daresay you've thoroughly charmed her and very nearly replaced her own grandson in her heart," she replied softly.

He looked at her intently again. "Why do you look so sad, then?"

For once, her composure did not falter. "I miss the deep friendship we used to share—you, me, and Anthony. And I suppose I'm ill at ease because you and Ata and everyone else have formed such easy friendships, while our own rapport has altered so much." The last trailed into the silence on a whisper. She hated how half-truths and mistrust had eroded their private world.

"My dear, Georgiana, my feelings for you remain unchanged. I've always admired you greatly. I, too, have felt the strain." He hesitated before rushing on. "We both know it has to do with me taking liberties with you—kissing you. No—" He motioned for her to let him continue when she opened her mouth. "It's better to speak of it. My apologies must appear worthless to you, so I won't appease my guilt by empty words. I know you miss Anthony, Georgiana. And I will try to do a better job of remembering that. I'm glad for the chance to clear the air. Your good opinion and your friendship mean the world to me. More than anyone else's. And your happiness is one of my main concerns, Georgiana."

She was so overcome by his words she could not look at his face. "I'm sorry for this awkwardness too. And here I've failed to tell you how glad I am that you've come home." She did not make the mistake of looking at him. If they were to preserve this fragile overture of renewed fellowship, she must be on her guard.

"And I've been delighted to be in the company of my oldest friend again," he said simply.

"Well, then." She had to extricate herself before she wallowed further in this quagmire of raw sensations. Before she took a step closer and made a fool of herself. "I must go back. The others will wonder. I suppose I shall see you at the start of the ball, then?"

"You may depend upon it," he said, his hands gripped behind his back.

She fled to the comfort of her friends.

Ata held up a scarlet-colored silk robe with an overlay of very fine black lace and shook her head. "I'm certain I didn't agree to this color." She looked at the dressmaker with amusement. "Not that I don't like it, mind you. It reminds me of a gown I used to wear when I was much younger. It made me look like a Spanish dancer!"

"Yer Grace, I 'ope ye'll *forgivez-moi*," the dressmaker began in her atrocious mélange of accents and languages. "'is lordship insisted. 'e insisted on changin' all *lay cooleurs* o' yer frocks, 'cept the countess's."

Grace beamed and shook her head. "He kept saying something about it being another *adventure* for all of us."

Georgiana's heart leapt. She scanned the chamber for the gray silk she had requested to replace the frayed ball gown she owned, also in pale gray silk. Her gaze came to rest on the only unclaimed garment on a nearby chaise.

It was gold—a heavenly shade, with an ethereal sea-green pattern that was exposed when it caught the light. Seed pearls were embroidered onto the perilously tiny bodice. She turned the gown and gasped when she discovered ivory buttons shaped like bees. Whorls of stitching about the buttonholes gave the appearance of flight.

Oh . . . oh, it was the loveliest gown she had ever seen. And so unlike anything she had ever owned. Surely, it was not hers. She quickly glanced about, only to meet the bemused expression of Elizabeth Ashburton, who held up a deep-blue-and-white gown in fine gauze for inspection.

"Well, Georgiana," Elizabeth said, her dimples on full display, "I guess we shouldn't be surprised. You did tell us your husband loved practical jokes more than anything. I suppose that trait runs in the Fortesque family."

Grace giggled. "I do hope everyone doesn't mind. I'll admit that Quinn suggested it to me in private and I concurred wholeheartedly. None of you would have agreed if we'd asked you. But it really is time for all of us to stop hiding behind our widowhood."

"You're right of course, Grace," Ata said. "Sometimes I fear we have all become so content and at such ease with one another that we're retreating from the rest of the world. It was my intent when I formed the club to help each of you make a new start. Well . . ." She broke out into a huge smile. "I, for one, will be wearing this dress and I *order* you all to do the same."

Elizabeth Ashburton whispered archly to Georgiana, "Not that Ata ever did limit her color choices."

For the first time that day, Georgiana laughed. Ata's outrageous gowns and high heels were one of the club's favorite topics.

"What's that, Eliza?" Ata harrumphed. The petite dowager's hearing was excellent. "As I was saying, the *Barely Bereaving Beauties* are to mingle with the rest of the *beau monde* tonight. And I expect detailed reports tomorrow. I would like each of you to kiss at least one gentleman if you can manage it. And there'll be none of that watery ratafia for us tonight. We'll meet in here for a few glasses of my French Armagnac after supper. You'll find it quite *bracing*, I'm sure."

"Ata!" Sarah exclaimed in shock.

"No, Sarah. I expect both you and Georgiana, especially, to each kiss someone. Of all of us, you two are the most retiring and the most inclined to industriousness. I want you to enjoy yourselves. Grace, I assume you will accomplish this order with the least difficulty"—and here Ata winked— "I am very happy for you, my dear. No one is more deserving."

Georgiana felt slightly ill. But not as ill as she felt later that evening as she donned the most beautiful gown she had ever beheld.

And as she argued with the mantua maker over the impossibly low-cut, shimmering bodice, and lost the fight to retain her old gray shawl when the French-pretending dressmaker literally ripped it from her fingers, little did Georgiana know that of all of the widows, she would do much more than comply with the outrageous order the dowager duchess had made.

And she would do it *willingly*.

Of all the unholy ridiculousness of it, the club's new name had taken root. Ata had whispered it to Rosamunde while she made the last touches to the flower arrangements. And the dangerously beautiful duchess had whispered it to her devilish husband, who had barked with laughter. By the time it reached Mr. Brown's ears, the Barely Bereaving Beauties Club was forever etched upon the minds of its members. And it had suffused the widows with a sense of merriment that had been lacking for a long time, Georgiana admitted to herself while she wended her way from her father's old chambers to Ata's.

The name seemed to give the widows permission to enjoy themselves once again. After all, each of them had been widowed at least a year or two at a minimum. They *should* be searching for happiness, Georgiana rationalized.

But no amount of inner debate could remove her sense of dread.

She didn't like change. Never had, never would.

She brought a hand to her bare bosom again as she approached the dowager's door. This wisp of a gown was as fragile and delicate as a honeybee's gossamer wings and left her feeling altogether indecently exposed. She had always worn durable, heavy fabrics in dark colors—much more practical and made for longer wear.

"Psst . . . Georgiana." It was the Duchess of Helston, lurking in the shadows.

"Rosamunde?" she replied uncertainly.

"Shhh. Come along. I told Ata we would meet them at the top of the stair. The guests can't be counted on to arrive in the late fashion of town. But Ata refuses to observe country hours, as I'm sure you're aware." Rosamunde clutched her arm and pulled her along the corridors at a dizzying pace. "And by the by, you are ravishing. You should always wear light colors."

"Yes, well—"

"Georgiana, we don't have time to bandy about the bush. I wanted a moment alone with you." The duchess's magnificent jewels glittered in the dim candlelight emanating from the sconces. "What are you going to do about your sensibilities concerning Quinn?"

Georgiana stumbled to a stop, forcing Rosamunde to do the same. "I don't know what you mean. I—"

"Don't be ridiculous, Georgiana. We've known each other long enough to speak plainly. More so than sisters, even. And well, I can't watch this much longer. I have good reason. You know I do. I can't bear to see you suffer, and almost worse—to know that Grace might suffer all over again."

Georgiana held one of Rosamunde's slim gloved hands and studied the elegant lines of the duchess's fingers as opposed to her own chapped and callused hands effectively hidden by new gloves. "You haven't anything to fear. He's made clear his preference by his attentions to her. He holds Grace in highest regard, Rosamunde, as he should. He defers to her ideas, while I've never been more to him than a very dear childhood friend at best. Everyone knows that love cannot suddenly blossom between two old friends who used to splash mud at each other."

"Oh, Georgiana . . . I'd had such hopes for you and he."

She hated the sadness in Rosamunde's eyes. "Really. It's all right. I've grown used to it." She had to change the subject to force the tightness from her throat. "Actually, I'm glad for the opportunity to talk to you in private. Rosa, you would do me a great favor if you would speak to the duke and ask if he knows of a cottage my family could possibly consider purchasing near the sea, for my mother's happiness. It must be modest, but with land enough for a kitchen garden, small pasture and perhaps a small barn for one horse, one milking cow, and a few chickens, and—"

"Georgiana," Rosamunde's eyes searched her face, "don't say anymore. You have such courage."

"Not really. I'm just practical."

Rosamunde stroked her cheek. "But didn't the marquis say your family could stay in Little Roses for as long as he lives?" The duchess lowered her voice. "Your father is ill, dearest, and you don't need to remove at this time. It might be too much, too soon."

"I can't stay here much longer, Rosamunde." She stopped when she felt her voice might falter.

"Well," Rosamunde continued smoothly. "I happen to know he's arranged a very generous pension for your father as I'm certain he will do for you, so you'll be able to afford something much grander than you've described."

"No. I won't live off such generosity. We'll be very comfortable on the amount Quinn arranged for my father. But it feels wrong to accept huge sums of money simply because I was married to Anthony for less than a day."

"Pride is a very costly thing, dearest," Rosamunde said brushing a tendril of hair from Georgiana's face. "I spent a decade living off the effects of pride and I can tell you firsthand it can be a sad, sad business. Trust me on this." She paused and squeezed Georgiana's hand. "Well, I have another idea for your future happiness and security."

A gleam appeared in the young duchess's eye as she began to drag Georgiana to the reception area at the top of the second landing.

"But Rosamunde, really, if you would just speak to the duke, ask him if—"

"I will speak to Luc if you agree to dance with each of my brothers tonight."

"What? But you have *four* brothers. This is

truly—" She stopped when she noticed the implacable look Rosamunde had learned to use within a month of marrying His Grace. "Oh, all right. But I don't dance very well, you know that." Georgiana had always refused to talk about her bad leg. She had worked so hard for so long to correct the limp that had plagued her childhood that few knew of the frequent pain she suffered. Dancing had always been difficult and so she avoided it as much as possible, preferring conversation at all gatherings where there was dancing.

Georgiana saw a swirl of color out of the corner of her eye and noticed the other widows descending the stairs above her. But it was Quinn, resplendent in elegant evening dress, who fully occupied her attention when she spied him. His brown hair had always ever been tousled in an imperfect yet perfectly irresistible fashion—which was completely unfair, given the amount of time ladies endured to make their hair presentable. Yet tonight his hair was wet and ruthlessly tamed by severe combing. It made his impossibly elegant, sculpted features all the more evident. His stark hazel eyes appeared larger, more discerning, and his midnight-blue evening wear perfectly complemented Grace's pale pink ball gown.

At the bottom of the stair, Grace pinned a pink rosebud to Quinn's coat and he leaned down to whisper something, a smile playing at the corner of his lips.

He didn't appear to have even noticed Georgiana standing next to Rosamunde.

* * *

"You haven't forgotten, have you? You will honor me with the opening set?" Quinn asked Grace at the bottom of the stairs.

The pretty countess beamed. "Of course I haven't. I would be delighted, but what about Ata?"

"I had a word with Mr. Brown and I do believe he will make an effort in that corner."

"Quinn! You are becoming worse than Ata in your matchmaking efforts."

"Not at-at"—he stumbled over his words as he caught sight of Georgiana—"all. Matchmaking is much better left in the hands of women."

Grace giggled and it took all of his effort to resist the urge to look toward Georgiana again. *Why, she was virtually unrecognizable.* Quinn regained his senses and bowed to Grace before escorting Ata to Georgiana.

She appeared extraordinarily fragile in that flimsy ball gown with a bee theme he had asked Grace to design. He'd never seen Georgiana in anything except the shapeless, dark garb of every country miss. He now realized he had utterly failed to see behind the practical façade Georgiana wore so easily.

He noticed the tiny rosebuds in her lustrous brown hair, then glanced at her huge, dark eyes, which were like a caged lion's, wary and golden with the wisdom of the ages in their depths. He had opened his mouth to utter a nicety, when he chanced to observe the low cut of her gown. His mouth went dry.

"Georgiana, are . . . are you chilled? Surely you would like me to get you a shawl." Why, he could see every curve of her bosom and even a hint of the tightened tips of her breasts. He hadn't known she was so perfectly proportioned. Another half inch lower and he would be able to see the rosy edge of—his groin reacted in a thoroughly predictable manner and he smothered a groan. Of all the impossible things.

"Thank you, but no. The dressmaker hid every last one of them," she said archly. "I'm sorry. I know this gown is indecent. I told Grace—"

The lady in question leaned forward and tsked. "Botheration, Georgiana, my gown is much more daring than yours. I've told you the gown would be considered positively spinsterish in town. Enough of this foolishness. Tell her to stand straighter, Quinn." The countess made her way to the duchess as the first guests entered the great hall.

Quinn tore his eyes from Georgiana's form and tried to ignore the unbrotherly feelings she inspired. His body pulsed with desire and he hoped she didn't notice the heat radiating from him. He turned slightly, glad to give himself over to the endless tedium of being a charming host to the arriving hordes, kissing the air above the many gloved fingers and bowing and presenting Georgiana and the rest of the widows. Yet his body refused to forget the vision of Georgiana beside him in that revealing gown.

He swallowed.

He was determined to make a statement to all those in attendance tonight. Since every last member of nobility and gentry alike residing in Cornwall, and many from London too, were there, he knew his actions would have an impact. Everyone would see he had accepted Georgiana as a rightful member of the Fortesque family. She was the newest Marchioness of Ellesmere. And he could sense the relief in many guests' expressions when he presented Georgiana as such and they finally knew how to address her.

As the person of highest rank, the Duke of Helston had been asked to dance the opening minuet with Georgiana. Quinn only hoped she was up to the task. He wasn't even sure she could dance, but a discreet query to Ata had settled the matter. He worried about the pain it might cause her leg.

Oh, she hid it well. But Quinn knew how much it probably cost her. He also knew better than to discuss it with her. She would only lie and say she suffered not. But anyone who had been with her that fateful day when she had fallen from that pine tree next to the cliffs knew differently. He shoved away the unpleasant memory.

"Quinn?" Grace plucked at his sleeve.

"My dear?"

"That's the last of them, I think. Shall we open the ball, then?"

He nodded and glanced to his side to find the Duke of Helston at Georgiana's elbow, the damned gentleman giving her a head-to-toe survey. *Oh, absolutely not.* He stepped forward.

"Helston, I would thank you to stop leering," he said softly.

Rosamunde laughed, one of her endless supply of brothers at her side. "Luc?"

"I don't know what the devil you are inferring, Ellesmere, but if you treasure your cowardly, remarkably stupid hide I would suggest you stop before you make a fool of yourself." The duke's voice was strained.

Quinn was grateful the good Lord had given him an inch to tower over the blasted duke with the roving eye. "You know precisely what I'm talking about, and if you would like to discuss it more openly, let us repair to—" He chanced to notice Grace's expression, which was filled with sadness. He stopped abruptly.

"*Och* . . . what have we gotten into here?" John Brown appeared at Ata's side and his Scottish burr intruded. "Merceditas, there you are, lass. I understand you would like for me to dance with you. I am grateful to Quinn for—"

"I suggested nothing of the sort." Ata snorted. "Why, I would never condescend to dance with—"

"Come along, Ata," Luc St. Aubyn's tense voice cut in. "It seems that bloody diplomat has been at work in your corner as—"

"Why do you always feel it necessary to interrupt me?" Ata interrupted.

"Perhaps because you taught the lad well," Mr. Brown said to Ata, his eyes twinkling. "Care to make one last cutting remark in my direction before I escort you inside? I know you only do it because you're fond of me."

Ata sputtered and the tension of the moment eased despite the anger still brimming inside Quinn.

Rosamunde ushered everyone toward the double doors, where a vast crowd of guests mingled in the beautiful ballroom, which was rarely on display. Tonight flowers spilled from every table and the gold gilt of the molding gleamed from every corner. Bejeweled ladies eagerly awaited the dancing, while gentlemen resigned themselves to an evening of sore toes. At least there would be excellent wine and brandy to dull the pain.

Quinn noticed Helston gripping Georgiana's arm to lead her inside and it was all he could do not to fist his hands in anger. The vision of Grace's pretty bowed head stopped him. But it did not block out the voice of one of Rosamunde's brothers, asking Georgiana for the next set of dances. Quinn intervened abruptly before she could answer.

"Georgiana will be too fatigued to dance all evening, Miles. I daresay she will have better things to do."

Ata laughed. "Better things to do than dance at a ball? That's ridiculous, Quinn."

"Well, I was only trying to—"

Georgiana interrupted him, her voice laced with deadly calm. "I would *love* to dance the second set with you, Miles. It's been an age since I've seen you. How is your father?"

The melodic notes of a waltz began and Quinn tried to refocus his attention on the Countess of Sheffield and not on the vulturelike form of the duke. A waltz? He was certain Grace had arranged for a minuet to open the ball.

He looked at the five couples surrounding him: Mr. Brown and Ata, Rosamunde and her brother, each of the other widows paired with Rosamunde's other blond brothers, and finally the duke looming over Georgiana. And Quinn knew without a doubt that it was that ill-mannered blackguard Helston who had arranged this outrageous waltz.

"Are you all right, Quinn?"

He lowered his gaze to find a tremulous smile on Grace's lips, and he was mortified. "More than all right, Grace. How could I not be, with the loveliest lady in the room gracing my arms?"

"I hope you don't mind that I arranged for this waltz. I realize it's not quite the thing, but sometimes it's fun to be a touch audacious, is it not? I remember your fondness for daring and I'm afraid Ata has ordered us all to be a little outrageous tonight."

He laughed. "Why, Grace Sheffey, I wouldn't have guessed you to be so bold."

Her face flushed with shyness or the heat of the evening. "Sometimes it's tiring to be so proper all the time. You know, I'm only five and twenty . . . no, I shall not lie to you, Quinn. I am *seven* and twenty, but I feel like I've lived a very sheltered life, an only child, then married for such a short time, and now alone in the world . . . except for my friends here. Everyone says I should take comfort in the great wealth left to me, but I find it cold consolation." She paused. "Of course I would never admit as much to someone who did not share equal richesse—it just sounds too pathetic. I realize every day how very lucky I am, because I'm surrounded by other ladies who are not so fortunate. But then I suspect you know as well that riches do not guarantee happiness, do they?"

He looked down into Grace's eyes, which were glittering with emotion. "How very true, my dear."

And as he guided the pretty little countess into the measured whorls of the dance he realized not for the first time that a marriage to this lady could very well be the answer to so many of his dilemmas.

As a stepmother, Grace would set an excellent example for his hoydenish daughter, who had taken to the countess, if not to her twin passions of reading and embroidery. And unlike other ladies, Grace had nothing to gain by the marriage other than relief from her usually well-concealed loneliness. Why, she was nothing short of an heiress, and her character, integrity, and reputation were unblemished.

Most importantly, she was self-sufficient. She would understand the rules of a marriage of convenience. A marriage that would be very short on emotional entanglements and long on companionship.

Yes, she would do very well, he thought looking at her flawless face.

"Grace, I must thank you for spending so much time with my daughter. I know she can be a sore trial."

"Nonsense. She's a dear. Headstrong, yes, and so very animated."

He sighed. "She hates to read."

"Not as much as she loathes the pianoforte and needlework," Grace said, laughing. "But take comfort, she might very well change. She's still young."

Quinn heard the familiar low, lilting sound of Georgiana's laughter and turned. A devilish smile was carved into Helston's hooded expression, and Quinn felt like killing the man.

"Quinn?" Grace asked so softly he had to lean down to hear her.

"Yes?"

"I realize how very improper it is of me to ask you this. But I must know. What are your intentions toward Georgiana?"

"I'm impressed by the concern and deep friendship between all the ladies in Ata's club." He loosed his hold on Grace's waist. "After tonight my plans for Georgiana should be very clear. I've established her as a proper Ellesmere marchioness, and she will be provided for in the manner of all Fortesque widows."

"Where shall she live? With you and your daughter, here?"

"I don't know," he responded truthfully. "With her father ill, all must be decided later. I'm certain you understand. But enough about Georgiana. Tell me about your childhood, Grace."

He heard not a word she said, he realized, many minutes later when the set ended and he escorted Grace to her next dance partner, Mr. Brown. He bowed to her and turned to lead Ata into the minuet.

For the next hour and a half Quinn unconsciously performed all the functions of a host: paying compliments to the wallflowers, dancing whenever necessary—even a short jig with Georgiana that left everyone breathless with laughter, simple country dances with all the widows, and he even danced with Grace again. After the late supper, he circulated among the gentlemen in the card room and gave discreet orders to the servants during the last dance to fully open all the windows to ease the discomfort of the heated ballroom. But suddenly, he realized something was off.

Something was very wrong.

Georgiana was missing.

At first he thought that perhaps she had repaired to the ladies' withdrawing room. But she'd been gone much longer than necessary, even if the entire hem of her gown had come unraveled.

He swung around and a cold chill hardened his spine. Helston was nowhere to be seen either, yet his duchess was surrounded by two of her brothers, her sister and the vicar.

A blinding fury swept through him, an emotion unlike any he had known before. How dare that blackguard sailor lure Georgiana away from the event that was to ease her back into society?

Beyond the doors leading to the terrace, he slipped into the heat of the inky blackness of the summer night. The air was so thick and still, surely a storm was in the making. After a few moments his eyes adjusted to the darkness and he discerned a few couples leisurely strolling through the gardens, illuminated by lanterns in the lower limbs of the trees.

He rushed down the marble stairs, heedless to everyone around him, and refused to gather his wits.

Where was she?

With long strides he descended the *parterre* gardens, perfumed by late summer's roses. On the lowest level he spied a couple, half hidden by a massive oak. A large man, clearly Helston, was locked in a heated embrace with a woman who had rosebuds entwined among the locks of her hair.

His blood ran cold as his fists balled so tightly he couldn't feel his fingers. He might just have Helston drawn and quartered after he disemboweled the adulterous swine.

Without another thought, he strode up to the man's back and grabbed his collar to pull him off her. The gentleman grunted in surprise and mumbled an oath. Quinn slammed his fist into the man's jaw and a satisfying crack echoed in the night.

The next sounds were decidedly less satisfying.

The distinctive voice of Elizabeth Ashburton sent a cool trickle of reason into his disordered thoughts.

"Quinn? Is that you? What on earth? Oh, Mr. Langdon . . . are you all right? Your poor face."

Quinn's horror was complete when the bulky form of Fitzhugh Langdon, one of Rosamunde's brothers, recovered its balance and bore down on him. *Damn Langdons.* They were all country-bred brawn, but he prayed they had none of famed pugilist Gentleman Jackson's town-taught finesse.

Fitz's head rammed into Quinn's stomach and the two of them wrestled on the ground like two adolescents.

"Fitz . . ." Quinn panted with exertion. "Look, I'm sorry. Thought you were someone else." Finally he flipped Fitz onto his stomach and pushed one of the younger man's arms to the middle of his back.

"Let me up, Ellesmere," Fitz muttered, his mouth buried in the grass. "Who the hell did you think I was? Miss Ashburton, you could have told me you had another admirer. Dash it all, what is a fellow to think? You led me out here, for God's sakes."

Elizabeth Ashburton, wide-eyed and blushing to the roots of her hair, looked at the two of them and laughed in horror, which made Quinn all the more embarrassed by his absurd actions.

"Eliza, have you seen Georgiana?" Quinn muttered. "Or Helston?"

That made her stop her infernal laughter. "Georgiana and Luc? Why, of course not. Whatever are you sug—"

Fitz stepped forward and growled, "You don't mean to infer that my brother-in-law is . . . is . . . and not with Georgiana? Georgiana *Wilde*?"

"Don't be ridiculous," Elizabeth said. "I mean, really. Whatever can you—"

"I'll kill him," growled Fitz. "I'll kill him and then I'll . . ."

Quinn didn't wait to hear Fitz's plan to search the chambers in the mansion. He was making his way toward Loe Pool. It was the most isolated spot on the estate and one that Georgiana had favored during their childhood. The sharp saw grass cut his thin silk stockings below his knee breeches to ribbons as he crossed through a pasture in the moonlight.

By the time he rounded the last stand of trees, still far from the lake, he was completely winded. The sight before him made his heart stall in his tight chest.

Oh, this was worse. *Far worse.*

Chapter 9

❧

They waded past the shallows and Georgiana lowered herself into the cool water. "Come, Fairleigh. That's it. I have you. Doesn't this feel heavenly?" The dreadfully hot evening had been considered a great success by everyone, although, thought Georgiana, it had been an unmitigated disaster for her heart. She had been so glad when Fairleigh had appeared and provided the much wished for excuse to escape the ball.

"Oh, Georgiana . . . you are the very bestest," the little girl moaned in pleasure as the water reached high above her waist. "You won't tell Papa, will you? You did promise."

"I thought we had a bargain. We would take a secret swim to cool off and then you'll go to bed without another minute of lurking and spying on the poor guests. Why, old Mrs. Hotchkiss nearly died of apoplexy when she saw your hand come out from under the settee."

"Oh, pooh. It wasn't as if it was a viper."

"Shall we float on our backs and look at the stars? If you're lucky you might be able to make out a shadow of geese cutting across the sky, and if we're really lucky we'll even see Oscar."

"Who's Oscar?"

"An otter with the curiosity of a cat. He loves to come out at night and scare me to death. I'm certain he does it on purpose."

Well, if she had had to endure the torture of watching Quinn dance twice with Grace Sheffey, at least this delightful little midnight swim with Fairleigh would cheer her up. It had been stifling in the ballroom and the tension of maintaining an air of cool refinement for so long had taken its toll. She had only fully relaxed during one dance with Rosamunde's brother, Miles Langdon, a male she had known her entire life. He had acquired an air of maturity since returning from his grand tour this summer.

But her leg ached from dancing and the cool waters felt wonderful.

"Will Oscar hurt me?"

"No, but his whiskers tickle when he swims under you."

"Ohhh . . . I hope he comes. But I don't know how to float."

"But of course you do. If you can swim, then you can float."

"Um . . . I don't *precisely* know how to swim. Well, what I mean is, I know I must kick my feet and paddle with my arms, and—"

"Fairleigh," Georgiana interrupted, "I would never have taken you here if I'd known you couldn't swim. It's too dangerous at night. Why, your father—"

"Show me how to float—please?"

"You're impossible." Georgiana sighed in exasperation.

"I know. Old Beetleface used to call me that at least once a day." She said more quietly, "The other governesses called me dim-witted, unmanageable, stupid, and untamed."

Cold mud oozed between Georgiana's toes and she pulled the little girl into her arms. She just couldn't stand hearing those words. They were too reminiscent of the phrases the village teacher had used to describe Georgiana.

"It isn't true. You mustn't believe those things. I haven't known you long but you are as far from being unintelligent as they come. Now you might try to be a little less hoydenish . . . for example, you could try climbing trees only on Thursdays instead of every day. That's what I do."

"You do *not* climb trees!"

"No. You've just never *seen* me climb a tree. You must be unobservant on Thursdays alone, since you are the most perceptive girl I know."

Without Fairleigh even realizing it, Georgiana had taken her in her arms and was positioning her to float. "Lay your head back now."

Georgiana looked down onto the moonlit silhouette of the little girl and saw wonder written on her every feature. Within moments the girl was floating on her own, although Georgiana didn't dare remove her arms. Fairleigh was a natural-born fish.

A loud masculine shout followed by a splash alerted Georgiana they weren't alone.

For not a moment did she doubt it was Quinn bearing down on them, in smooth, long strokes cutting the surface of the lake. *Lovely*. And she was very nearly naked in her thin shift.

And then he was upon them and jerking Fairleigh into his arms. The moonlight played havoc with the harsh shadows slicing the furious expression he gave Georgiana as he dragged his daughter to his chest. "What on earth are you doing? Georgiana, you might have thought it fun and games when we were young to go swimming at night. But my daughter is only nine years old. She cannot swim and could easily drown."

He hauled his daughter out of the water and ignored the girl's squeals of protest and explanations. "No, Fairleigh. I've long forbidden you to swim and while I might have relented, you coming here expressly against my wishes . . . well, you shall never be allowed within the vicinity of Loe Pool ever again. Do you understand me?" He spoke softly, with only the hint of a hard edge to his voice. It was almost worse than hearing him bark at his daughter. Not that Quinn would ever bark at anyone.

"But Papa, I wouldn't drown like Mamma. I know better than that."

Drown? *His wife had drowned?* The obituary notice had said she had succumbed after a brief illness.

"It was so hot, Papa, I couldn't sleep. The music was so loud. And I wanted to see all the gowns. I—" Fairleigh stopped abruptly. It seemed her father's silence scared her more than any scolding.

Georgiana, mindless with embarrassment over her own near nakedness, strode over to the ball gown and tossed it over her head. The thin fabric immediately adhered to her wet shift and when she looked down she noticed that the pale gold fabric appeared the same color as her skin.

And just when she thought the moment could not get any worse, Georgiana heard the muffled sound of footsteps in the sea grasses. Rosamunde and Luc soon appeared, running toward them, Fitz Langdon not far behind.

"Ellesmere," the duke said breathlessly, "you had better have a bloody good explanation or I shall be slicing your kidneys for breakfast tomorrow morning."

As he closed the gap, Georgiana noticed that one of the duke's eyes appeared slightly closed, the skin puffy around it.

"Dibs on his giblets," muttered Fitz, who stood with a cut on his chin, looking embarrassed beside his brother-in-law.

A very faint smile lurked at the corners of Rosamunde's lovely mouth. "Quinn, I'm certain you've a very good reason for all the nonsense my brother's been spouting. Are you all right? Why, they're all dripping wet, Luc."

"I don't care if he's bloody drowning. An idiot like Ellesmere can't just go about sullying—"

"Luc, darling," Rosamunde looked pointedly toward Fairleigh. "Perhaps this would be better discussed in private?"

"Oh, it'll be in private, all right. It'll be so damned private no one will know where to find his bones."

"I'll help," muttered Fitz.

"I realize an apology won't suffice, but I feel honor bound to offer it," Quinn said stiffly, "to you both."

"Why are there bruises on your faces?" Georgiana was completely mystified by the swellings on the duke and Fitz Langdon, and also hoped this line of questioning would deflect attention from her revealing silhouette.

"While I'm certain the *diplomat* will invent numerous excuses for his far-fetched notions, they're certain to bore me to tears," Luc said dryly. "If you'll forgive me for ending this delightful tête-à-tête, I shall await Ellesmere's *brilliant* resolution to this tragedy of errors in the next twenty-four hours. And if it doesn't bloody well include at least five cases of the very best French brandy then I will stuff every damned one of his Portuguese *throat torches* down his gullet and light his toes. Now if you'll excuse me . . ." He turned and walked away, absolute black fury dripping from his stiff posture. Fitz turned and followed him, murmuring a coarse Cornish proverb under his breath.

Rosamunde glanced from Quinn to Georgiana knowingly. "Hmmm. Perhaps it would be best if Fairleigh returns to Penrose with me? By the look of it, I feel certain you have some things to discuss . . . and by the by, my lord, you might want to ask Ata about the brandy. I think she's made friends with a reliable smuggler in the area."

Fairleigh appeared so grateful for the diversion,

she went along with Rosamunde with nary a peep of protest after quickly kissing her father on the cheek.

Soon only the crickets could be heard breaking the tension of this late summer night. Georgiana turned away from his view and plucked at her gown, attempting to detach it from her wet underclothes. "Did you strike Luc and Fitz?"

"This is a matter best left alone. I shall make the necessary reparations."

"Well, I'm guessing you struck Fitz, because if you had punched Luc he would have pulled a pistol on you without hesitation. But why would you hurt Fitz?" Before he could answer she continued, "And who struck Luc?"

"Probably Fitz."

"Why would he do that?"

"You're changing the subject. I require your word that you'll never again take my daughter anywhere without my express permission." He picked up his evening shoes and coat, the only items he'd shucked before going into the lake.

"I'd never have suggested swimming if I'd known you'd forbidden it. Or if I'd known she couldn't swim." She was hurt. "You know that."

He slowly perused her form.

There was something about his cold silence that unnerved her. She couldn't stop herself from forcing the issue. "But I do think if you're going to live here, so close to the sea and Loe Pool, it might be a good idea if Fairleigh learns how to swim."

"Ah," he said with a terrible tone. "You know what is best for a young girl, do you?"

"I know what is harmful. Your governesses used humiliation and hurt her tender sensibilities with such nonsense. They insisted she was stupid and lazy—all because she wouldn't read Fordyce's sermons, play the pianoforte with skill, or make lace."

"Religion and needlework and music were always wasted on you, Georgiana. But perhaps you're wrong. If a lady is to make her way in life, knowledge of feminine skills is an asset, not a detriment."

"Not if the lady in question will never reach any sort of impressive proficiency in those arts. Quinn, don't you see she needs to succeed in at least one endeavor so she can gain the confidence to succeed in others?"

He shook his head. "Are you suggesting that if she learns how to swim she will also develop a sudden taste for philosophy?"

"Don't be ridiculous . . . I won't argue with you. You always could win any dispute—but this isn't a debate. This is about your daughter. You can't make someone into something they are not. You can't force someone to like something they cannot."

You can't force someone to love someone they do not.

She suppressed a sigh. "Look, I'm sorry I took her swimming and I shall never again distract her without your express permission. In any case, I won't be here for many more weeks. I've decided to begin the search for a cottage for my family."

In the vacuum of silence that followed, Georgiana's skin prickled with nervousness despite the heat in the air. She was clammy from the wet garments and the heated conversation and she became even more discomfited when Quinn advanced toward her.

"Georgiana," he said sadly, as he grasped her hands. "This is a fine renewal of our friendship. And I'm wholly to blame. Will you accept my apology? I let fear for Fairleigh's safety cloud my judgment." He shook his head. "I seem to do nothing right where it concerns you these days. Well, I intend to defer to your good judgment from now on.

"What?" she said in disbelief.

"For the first time someone has said something of sense concerning my daughter, and I must thank you. You are entirely right. I know better than most that you can't change someone."

"Well . . . I don't know what to say. It's so rare when anyone agrees with me." She looked into his eyes. "Especially you. Especially recently," she said, so quietly he leaned in to catch her words.

Her heart hammered in her breast and a chill ran up her damp arms. "I'm sorry, Quinn, about your wife. I didn't know she'd drowned. I know you were very much in love with her and of course you were worried when you saw your daughter . . . " She stopped when she dared to glance at his expression.

He raised her chin and she met his dark, mysterious gaze. She swallowed.

"You're entirely wrong." He released her and moved away. "Cynthia was bedazzled by the diplomatic circles in town and was convinced I would rise far and fast when we married. Soon after she went through my meager earnings, she discovered drink and *other distractions* to soften her disappointments. She drowned while boating on a lake with one of her long string of lovers late one night."

Georgiana stood stock still, horrified beyond words.

"Yes, well . . . now you know the truth, so you can stop consoling me for my loss. The effort is completely wasted on me."

For the first time in her life Georgiana did not rush to fill the void with words. There was absolutely nothing she could think of to say—nothing she could do.

Oh, but there was.

She stepped so close to him she could see the shadow of the line of his beard on his taut face in the moonlight.

She stretched her arms up high and around his neck and laid her head over his pounding heart. He remained motionless, his arms at his sides.

She gently stroked the skin above his shirt collar and breathed in his scent that left her melancholy with longing.

And then she took her decision. A decision that would unbind the secret she had bound tightly to her soul for so very long that it had seemed impossible to reveal.

She would do it for him—unselfishly, expecting

nothing in return, because she loved him and he needed to understand that someone loved him for who he was, and had always been. He deserved to hear it. It was painfully obvious he needed to feel love. *Anyone's* love. Even someone who hid hideous deformities under many layers of shifts and gowns.

She tried to speak three times, opening her mouth in the darkness, her arms still gripping his impossibly broad and motionless form.

The fourth time she succeeded in making a strangled sound.

"What is it, Georgiana?" he asked quietly. "I told you I won't have your pity. We've known each other too long for the niceties."

"I-I don't pity you. My heart aches for you, that's all. I'm allowed, for I've known you forever and I hate that you've suffered."

His arms moved to encircle her like iron bands. "Now is the moment for you to disentangle yourself from me, Georgiana," he said into the top of her head. "Do it. Do it before I make an ass of myself and something happens you're sure to regret."

She damned her cowardly silence and stroked the damp cloth on his tense back, unable to bring a word to her lips. Unable to tell him of her great love. Yet also unable to let go of him.

But it seemed Quinn had a stronger sense of propriety than she. He finally pushed away, allowing the heavy night air between them. "Come, I shall walk you back. Perhaps not everyone has left, although most were departing when I went out in search of you." He tugged on her arm and she reluctantly stepped away from the sandy spit. At the last moment she stopped and he turned to her, a question in his eyes.

Without a word she laced her fingers through his and pulled him toward the nearby thicket, which only a very few knew secreted a small mossy clearing in its center. At the perimeter she dropped his hand and glanced at him again before turning to enter the leafy enclosure. She was very unsure if he would follow. For long moments she heard only the threshing sound of her own body moving past the branches.

She entered the private domain, her heart in her throat as she realized he had not followed her. Then suddenly, he was beside her.

It had been the place where Anthony, Quinn, and she had gone when they chose to hide themselves from the outside world. Where they had dared each other to perform outrageous feats. It was here the trio had met as friends the morning of the very last day they were together—before disaster had struck.

Right now, she wished with all her heart he would just swoop in and take her into his arms. But she knew instinctively that he was probably ever too much the gentleman to do it. He had always possessed an uncompromising moral compass. It was one of the reasons she loved him.

"Quinn," she said quietly. "I—" But words were useless. Had he not said so himself? She would show him her love, she thought, all the while knowing she was as craven as a person facing a tribunal.

She moved forward and slipped her hands under the folds of his damp coat, the wet had seeped from the fine shirt underneath. And suddenly his arms were surrounding her, enveloping her. She was unnerved by his strength, unnerved by the desperation she sensed.

"Georgiana," he said roughly, "this is madness."

"No," she replied, "you're very wrong. This is everything right."

His mouth found hers and he pushed past her lips to taste what lay beyond. All the while her heart raced with longing.

A maelstrom of potent desire swept from her fingertips to the core of her body and then reversed direction. Emotions tumbled inside of her—wonder, the rightness of it, and above all an unquenchable wanting—all while his strong hands gripped her and brought her hard against his body. His ragged breathing echoed in her ears, begging her to take him, comfort him.

Yet he pulled back, her face in the cradle of his hands. "Oh God, Georgiana," he rasped. "Tell me to stop. Please."

She cupped the harsh plane of his cheek. "No. I want to hold you," she whispered. "Be with you."

She was still shocked that he had opened his utterly impenetrable façade and let her in. Perhaps she had been wrong before. This was not lust—this was a long-denied need for comfort, for reassurance that someone truly cared for him.

His lips never left her face for a moment after her passionate benediction. His hands explored her arms, her sides, face—and stroked her hair, brushing it away from her eyes.

Not another word passed between them. Oh, but what she saw in his eyes when he looked down at her through the night shadows.

Desperation combined with vulnerability.

There was never any question where this was leading. If anything, she was impatient. She pulled at his coat and damp linen shirt, slipping her hands underneath to feel the heat of his skin and the sleek power of the muscles on his back when they bunched and released. He tore at his articles of clothing as well as her damp gown in his desire to meet her skin to skin.

His ardor brought a secret smile to her lips and she knelt on the discarded clothing, ignoring the pain in her knee. The heat of a blush chased along her skin and she was grateful for the darkness and her overly long shift that hid her gross deformities from him.

She would somehow keep his hands from her lower limbs and perhaps he would not notice. But all rational thought disappeared when he knelt before her to untie the lace tapes of the shift. He eased the bodice from her shoulders and lowered his head to her breast. Her back arched in wordless supplication at the first silken swirl of his tongue on the sensitive tip of her breast. Like a falcon guarding its sustenance, his hulking shoulders and long arms swept around her.

God. *This was Quinn.* She was alone, on a hot

August night with the man she had loved for as long as she could remember. She felt as if she were in a dream.

He suckled and nipped her flesh, then traced an unbearably erotic pattern on the side of her breast. Something was building way down deep inside of her, in the nurturing, feminine place—her womb. A place she had never been aware of until now. It seemed to ache for him—for his essence, which should bond with her own.

In the veil of moonlight, she drew her trembling hands down the vault of his ribs. She marveled at his strength and then shivered uncontrollably when his scent invaded her senses. Rosemary and sage melded with moss and his heated skin still damp from the lake waters. The combination overwhelmed her.

His fingers peeled her shift down further, his mouth trailing behind—down the sensitive path to her navel. He moved aside and arranged her body in the nest of clothes.

She wished for the hundredth time that she wouldn't ultimately have to fully disrobe. He seemed to sense her thoughts, because a moment later he was bunching her shift and moving it past her hips and limbs. She fought the urge to stop him. Now she was completely bare before his gaze. She turned her head away, humiliated. She couldn't face the disgust she was sure to find in his eyes.

She sensed rather than saw him removing the last of his own clothing and thanked the Lord he had not been so revolted by her ghastly scarred limbs as to actually stop what had begun. His elbow dragged past the side of her head and he leaned toward her.

"Georgiana, your femininity takes my breath away," he murmured.

She turned her head quickly into the comfort of his shoulder. "Please, no lies between us. I couldn't bear it."

"I would never lie to you. But I see words will not prove the beauty I see in you."

Before she could catch his beautiful broad hands with her own he stroked the top of one of her scarred legs. She knew she was as stiff as the planks in the barnyard, and as cold. She moaned, "Please don't touch there."

"Georgiana, it's what I want to do most. I must touch you. All of you. Especially here"—he dipped down and kissed the length of the most hideous gash, from her hip to the inside of her thigh—"and here"—he stroked her swollen knee and bent to lovingly kiss it over and over again.

She inhaled in shock and felt tears coursing past her temples. "You don't have to do that," she whispered.

"I want to," he said in his hauntingly familiar voice, now gravelly. "And it would be unfair of you to deprive me."

And suddenly he slipped his wide shoulders between her legs and framed her hips with his large hands.

Oh God. This was her worst nightmare and fondest dream all balled into one impossibly tense moment. He was starkly staring at all the ugliness, inches from his face, and she was trapped, unable to move.

His fingers slipped under her knees and he drew them farther apart gently.

She refused to resist him. *Let him see me then*, she thought in sadness. *Let him see every last terrible detail.*

For long moments he traced his fingers over the myriad silvery lines that mapped out the horrors of the accident that had disfigured her. He massaged her knee, and the last of her resistance melted. No one had ever bothered to try and ease the stiffness from the permanently swollen joint—not her mother or her father—and it felt simply heavenly.

He kissed every scar, and each time she thought he would retreat, he returned his fingers and his lips to her knee, murmuring his desire. And here, she thought, she had meant to comfort *him*.

She closed her eyes at the wonder of the loving way he addressed every reminder of her disgrace, erasing momentarily her immense mortification.

Until he . . .

Until his tongue moved too high along her inner thigh and almost brushed against . . .

She inhaled sharply and opened her eyes, simultaneously trying to close her legs despite his great bulk between them.

"No, Georgiana, stay still." He refused to ease away from her.

"But, you can't mean to . . ."

"Yes—if you'll allow me the privilege."

"But—"

"Trust me," he whispered, staring at her through the darkness.

She would trust him with her life; she'd already entrusted her heart to him. She relaxed her limbs and stopped squirming against him. Her cheeks felt hot and swollen from the dried tears and a flush she knew was upon her. She was certain that when he touched her she would burst from all the emotions and sensations pouring through her body.

And suddenly she sensed the heated brush of his breath on her trembling thighs and his mouth descended, his tongue tentatively tasting her. She arched off the mossy bed.

What began as soft and soothing soon changed to hot and demanding as he patiently yet ruthlessly held her in place and stroked the tender folds at her jointure deep and deeper until a thin, high line of pleasure bordering on pain began to keen within her. His fingers caressed her breasts and lightly pinched the tender ruched buds, and she tried mightily to stay still under the onslaught.

He slipped a hand between her legs and probed the entrance to her. At the same agonizing moment his tongue sought and found the peak of her sex and paused. She thought she might burst from wanting.

He then suckled her deep within his mouth, sweeping against that sweetly sensitive spot and pulsing his finger within her. Her mind instantly shattered into whiteness and her body involuntarily clenched and released, seizing something she could not name. Rapture flooded her, sending pulsing waves throughout her body, unfurling a spiral of lush pleasure.

She went utterly still to experience every last moment of this unknown ecstasy. "Oh . . ." she breathed, in complete awe. "Oh, Quinn . . ." She exhaled and closed her eyes against the shock of returning to reality. She knew she could never feel like this ever again.

She forced herself up on her elbows and saw his head bowed to her navel in rest. She reached a hand to entangle her fingers in his soft, cropped hair. "Quinn," she murmured, "I never knew . . ." She was too shy to continue. "Please." She tugged gently on his shoulder, urging him to cover her body fully with his own. The gentle roar of ocean waves crashing echoed in the distance.

His eyes were hooded and glazed as he moved up the length of her; his heavy arousal brushed along the inside of her thigh. He kissed her breasts one last, long instant, and Georgiana felt protected in his hawkish embrace.

He drew face-to-face with her and his darkened, mysterious eyes looked into hers. "Are you certain you want this?" he asked quietly, belying the rock-hard tenseness she felt surrounding her.

She nodded her response, for she couldn't speak.

The world receded around them as he gently hooked an arm under her less injured leg, raised her to him and opened her further. He stroked her plush slickness with the blunt end of himself.

Unexpectedly he stopped, lowering his forehead again to hers.

"Take me," she whispered, trembling. "Please, Quinn. Now."

Her communion buoyed him and in one long motion he drove his thickness into her depths with sundering force.

Her breath caught in her throat. The immense, thick hardness was such an invasion and shock—nothing at all like her wedding night, she realized with blinding clarity. This was nothing like before.

This was burning *possession*.

And while the smoldering pain should have scared her, it didn't. She welcomed it. She had wanted him her whole life. The pain was nothing to her—for he was everything. And he made her feel almost beautiful and desirable. She only prayed that by giving herself she would ease for a moment in time his essential loneliness.

Chapter 10

G od, what was happening?

This was *Georgiana*, for Christ's sake.

He knew it with crystal clarity. And he was enraptured.

After tasting and touching every soft inch of her, he was overwhelmed by the desire to possess her fully. His mind was as coldly aware as his body was drunk with a primitive desire to mark her as his own. And now she was crooning encouragement for him to enter her and possess her fully.

He couldn't have torn himself away from her at this point even if his conscience had demanded it. All of his bodily desires would have bound and gagged his scruples, without question.

Her skin was so soft. He hadn't guessed it. Even in the pitch of night he could see she was very bronzed from the sun and her body was supple and strong. And yet touching her arms, her breasts, and the flesh between her thighs, he had felt sleek femininity and downy softness. The taste of her flesh and the scent emanating from her skin was as intoxicating and fragile as a wild rose after a spring shower—equal parts sweetness, rain, and earth. He couldn't get enough of it.

As his painfully intense arousal demanded knowledge of her, he prayed he had at least proved to her that her scars did not make her ugly to him. Just the reverse. God, she was so womanly, and yes, *beautiful*, and he wept for the agony she had endured. He cursed himself inwardly for never having fully seen her magnificent splendor until tonight.

She was Venus's muse. Her scars, if anything, added to her allure. They were harsh proof of a bravery few women, few people, possessed.

He caressed her for long moments, ignoring the raw desire coursing in his veins as best he could. It was nearly impossible to hold off.

The sweet plea and the sound of his name on her lips drove away the last of his reservations. He settled his weight fully between her slender thighs, pressing her deeply into the moss carpet.

His last thought before he plunged his entire length into the depths of her tender body was that he could at least be grateful she wasn't an innocent.

The whisper of her shocked intake of breath pierced his conscious at the same fraction of a moment as he registered a barrier callously breached. He stopped, dropping his head forward until his hair brushed the tops of her beautiful breasts.

My God.

It was impossible. Perhaps he had imagined it. Perhaps she was just nervous and her body had clenched against his, protesting against the invasion.

The rationalizations stopped. He had never been any good at rationalizing. Every fiber of his being revolted against it.

His body strained against his mind. He needed to move, but he refused to move a muscle for fear of hurting her further. A fine sheen of perspiration escaped his skin. She was impossibly tight and his body reacted by lengthening and pulsing dangerously.

"Georgiana, I've hurt you," he said his voice almost gone from strain. "Don't move. We should stop."

"No,"—her voice thin—"*please.*"

His body won the war over his mind and he gripped her tightly to him, thrusting involuntarily into her exquisitely taut well, trying valiantly to control the tide of passion.

Oh God. His usual cast-iron control was slipping. It had just been too long and her pulsing internal caress was irresistible. She made a small movement that only served to wedge him more deeply inside her, if that were possible. A bead of sweat trickled down his temple.

"Don't move," he gritted out. "Georgiana, please."

"I'm so sorry . . ." Her voice was unnaturally high-pitched. She tried to rise up and his control broke like a dam before a flood-swollen body of water.

He involuntarily rooted himself deeper still and held at the edge, teetering on rapture. He felt her trembling hand stroke the fine hairs at the base of his spine and he couldn't stop the heavy rolling of his body, instinctively plunging forward like the unstoppable incoming tide.

Her sighs lured him deeper into her heat and she widened her knees to accept more of him.

He groaned. He'd never experienced a woman so intimately or exquisitely, and holding back was killing him.

When he finally heard her keening cry of pleasure, he let himself go, pumping fiercely into her. He stretched his muscles to the limit, and his seed exploded into her body in endless pulses.

A feeling of peaceful lethargy enveloped him. Yet, the corporal sensation was fleeting as he absorbed the fact that they now had complete and irreversible knowledge of each other.

Undeniably, she had been a virgin.

Oddly, for one of the very few times in his life, he didn't question for a moment her honesty. He wasn't sure what had happened on her wedding night with Anthony, but it most certainly had not been this.

He'd been the first to take her—widow or not—and that made all the difference in his turbulent mind. He must do his duty by her. For some reason his mind didn't rebel against the notion. It wouldn't be a burden. Not in the least.

She was his dearest and most beautiful friend. His Georgiana.

A cascade of emotions tumbled through her—the intense pleasure—pain of possession, the joy of holding him to her breast, his loving response when faced with her great deformities, the unforgettable bond they shared. She had never felt so close to anyone in her life—or so supremely happy. It freed her from the grip of earthly worries. Quinn had given this immense gift to her.

Joy radiated around her and she gloried in the weight of his body, which soon relaxed in slumber on top of hers. He had tried to move off of her but she had not let him. Instead she had pressed his head against her shoulder and gently twined her fingers in his dark hair while she listened to his breathing grow slower and deeper. He had been fast asleep for many minutes.

"I love . . ." She swallowed awkwardly. "I love you," she said on a quiet exhale.

His breathing changed and she fought a feeling of panic. He had been asleep—she was certain.

Suddenly he lifted and turned his head, resting it near her ear. "Oh my dear," he said quietly. He gently brushed her hair from her face. "My dearest Georgiana."

She held her breath and prayed with all her heart that he would tell her what she most longed to hear.

The silence that followed nearly killed her. He uttered not another word—no murmurings of love, no mention of sweet affection. The air was filled with the unrelenting whir of crickets and an odd string of calls from a night-loving mockingbird, which seemed to take pleasure in laughing at her in its scornful fashion.

She swallowed hard against the lump growing

in the back of her throat. She would not cry. She wouldn't.

With each swallow, her heart shriveled inside its shell a little more and it took every ounce of self-will not to curl from under him and run away so she could feel sorry for herself in private.

God, how could he explain himself to her? He had no heart to give. Not to her, not to anyone. If he did have a vessel within him at all, that withered organ perhaps was best known to his daughter. Even with Fairleigh he tried to tell himself he was not overly attached. Everyone knew the grim reaper claimed a fair portion of children via illness more than anything else. Hadn't his brother and sister and his own parents all died within a week of one another when he was but eleven?

Lying there in the darkness, surrounded by the whispers from the sea and the rustle of leaves, a memory washed over him—something so deeply buried he wasn't even certain it was true. It was the voice of Molly, his parents' maid of all work, exhausted from caring for the family, now all dead save he. On the other side of his chamber door, Molly was weeping and moaning her worries to the vicar.

"Perhaps 'tis for the best, sir. Master Tom was the favorite of 'is mum, and Miss Agatha of 'er pa. It fair near broke Mr. Fortesque and his lady when those two little angels died. I swear 'twas heartbreak that killed them—simple heartache. God have mercy on poor little Quinn—his Ma and Pa didn't have enough love left over to try and live on for him."

Quinn's heart pounded in his chest. The vicar had told Molly she was speaking nonsense and had tried to comfort the weeping woman.

But Quinn knew Molly had been right. Oh, his parents had showered affection on him, but never as freely as his father did for his sister or his pretty mother had done for his older brother. Well, at least he had been the second favorite of each parent.

He had always been alone in the world—as a child, as a young husband, and now as a man. Just as much as he would be when he departed it. He was only glad he had stopped long ago his damned eternal search for something that didn't exist in this temporal plane—permanence and . . . love.

A perfect love. It was simply an illusion—a silly notion found in Banbury tales. Yet he didn't have the heart to disabuse Georgiana of her thinking.

"Quinn . . ." Her voice, devoid of emotion, woke him from his reverie. "I'm sorry, but I think I should get up."

"Oh my dear, I'm completely squashing you. I'm so, so sorry." He clenched his eyes closed, refusing to look in her face as he withdrew that part of himself that was still hard due to his long celibacy. He rolled off of her and immediately tried to gather her in his arms but wasn't fast enough. She had sat up and quickly grasped her shift to cover herself.

"Don't get up, Georgiana," he said quietly. "Don't go yet. Please." He grasped her free hand and held it tightly. "I'm sorry I hurt you. You must be very sore. I would . . . Well, I would have been more careful, more gentle, if I had known you were untouched."

"I wasn't," she said firmly. "And I'm fine. I told you Anthony died in my arms. He did much the same as you did, but perhaps, I realize now, we did not fully complete what we started. I suppose I never was in truth his marchioness. But then, I kept telling everyone I didn't want the title. Now you can take comfort that you owe me absolutely nothing. Oh, this is completely mortifying. Do we have to—"

"No. We'll never speak of it again. You will ever and always be a Marchioness of Ellesmere. Everything else is irrelevant."

She was about to argue, but he placed a finger to her lips to stop her, and then dropped it to grasp her chilled fingers.

"No—there'll be no argument on that point. Georgiana, I won't trifle with your tender sensibilities tonight. Especially after you've given me such a gift. You need rest. In fact, I'm grieving about the idea of the harvest festival starting at first light. We shall find a way to excuse you if—"

"No," she interrupted, rising quietly to redress, forcing him to do the same. "I told you I'm perfectly fine."

A nervous sensation seized his mind. "I know I just said I wouldn't trifle with your feelings now, but Georgiana, I find I cannot wait until tomorrow. I don't want this left unsaid." He stopped her as she edged nearer to the exit of their old secret spot. "What I am trying to say, quite inelegantly, is that I am begging you to honor me with your hand in marriage, my dear."

"What?"

He got down on his knee and grasped again her hand, and would not let her retrieve it. He felt irrationally calm. "Will you make me the happiest of men by marrying me?"

She slowly removed her hand from his and said not a word for many long moments. Even the crickets seemed to halt their night song.

"You do me a great honor," she whispered. "But I'm sorry, I cannot. While I have the greatest affection for you and hold you in the highest regard, there are two reasons I can never marry you," she said very evenly. "I should've told you I decided after Anthony died that I would never remarry. You see, I cared very deeply for him."

A feeling of dread and repressed anger coursed through him at the mention of his cousin's name. "That would be understood. Ours would be a marriage of convenience."

"No. I'm sorry but I prefer to honor his memory always. *He loved me.*" She paused. "He was *first* in my heart and I shall always be loyal to him. It would not be right even if it was convenient."

First in her heart. Anthony was first.

A cold blast rushed through him and he became lightheaded. Her words weren't surprising. He had always known Anthony was more important to her than *he* had ever been. He shook his head several times as if to clear the dizziness. He rose slowly. "Perhaps you've forgotten our actions might have consequences. I'm sorry if it causes you more pain but I can't allow you to face the censure of the world, and what's more, a child needs a father. We made an unspoken promise to bind ourselves to each other before the church when we lay together." He crushed her fingers within his own. "And I will never, let me repeat, never live apart from a child of mine. Or worse, allow another man to raise my child—even your own father."

She stared up at him, her eyes deep pools of regret. "Well, then, we shall just have to pray that a child has not been conceived. At the very least you are absolved of any responsibility until we know if there are consequences." She flexed her hand away and turned, walking quickly through the overgrown brush.

"Georgiana . . ." But she was already gone. And he didn't have it within him to go after her.

It was only many minutes later when he broke free of the thicket, his outer clothes in hand, that he remembered she had said there were *two* reasons she wouldn't marry him but had only mentioned one reason—her great love for Anthony.

Then he did the very thing he had forbidden his daughter. He dove into the dark water of Loe Pool and swam toward the island in the center, the cold numbing his senses. His lungs heaved with exhaustion and his mind ached with misery.

It seemed every major event in his life would end in tragedy. Each time he offered himself, he was unacceptable, rejected, and usually with a double dose of disaster on the side.

After his family died, his aunt and uncle had taken him in with some reluctance and many admonitions. He was two years older than Anthony, the heir, and he was instructed to remember his place, his subservience, his unimportance. But his two immediate friends, Anthony and Georgiana, were very successful in making him forget his uncle's unwelcoming words.

It was only when he had tried to protect his best friend, scrape-grace Anthony, during that awful afternoon when disaster struck, that he was awakened to his cousin's true character. He learned yet again the grand illusion of fellowship. Anthony, without knowing that Quinn could hear every word on the other side of his uncle's study door, wrongly faulted Quinn for the accident, lying to the marquis that Quinn had goaded them to climb the half-dead pine next to the cliff, all to retrieve a nestling Quinn supposedly wanted from a falcon's scrape in the cliff face.

In his shock, Quinn had accepted the blame without a word. His uncle caned him brutally, and promptly removed him from the family by enrolling him in the notoriously grim and barbaric Collager program at Eton.

"It's where you'll fit in best—with the other forgotten boys," his uncle had said sternly. "Perhaps it will finally teach you your place. At the very least you will learn how it feels to be bullied, as you have done to your cousin and my poor steward's daughter, who will bear the scars of your impudence for the rest of her life. No man will ever marry her. I shall pray for your soul."

His uncle would have been pleased to know that Quinn had learned his lessons well. Semi-starvation and being locked in at night with the other Eton Collagers had given him bitter food for thought on his value in this world. Poor Cynthia had taught him the rest.

It was paramount to close oneself off to humanity and not trust a soul. The reverse only bred disappointment or worse. And the very best method to face life was to remain detached. Charming, witty, and detached.

The most amazing part about adopting this attitude was that others seemed drawn to people possessing these traits. There was something about a reserved, remote character with occasional doses of kindness and wit that lent an air of mystery, thereby ensuring curiosity. It had worked wonders in diplomatic circles and with the feminine sex.

As he dragged himself onto the tiny island and the glass-walled lake house, he felt more alone in the world than at any other time in his life. Georgiana had refused him, and Anthony would always be first in her heart.

He was within an inch of sealing himself from the rest of humanity when he went to open the door and realized it was locked. Since when had this door had a lock? And suddenly this bolted entrance, for which he should possess the key—since he was the owner—represented everything that had been locked away from him in his life: familial security, connubial fidelity and devotion, fellowship, and . . . love.

Something long simmering possessed him in that moment and he gripped a nearby rock and heaved it against a small pane beside the lock on the glass door, shattering it.

He reached through the gap and unlocked the door. Stepping past the shards, he struck a flame from a tinderbox to light a candle. He'd never been here at night and was almost instantly calmed by the solitude. The sounds from the sea—Neptune's gentle roaring—on the other side of the sand spit slowly eased the pain from his chest and he took in his surroundings.

It seemed someone visited the place often, given the neatly made pallet without a trace of dust. There was little else, save for a stack of blankets he well remembered from his youth. He lowered himself onto the hard cot. Before giving in to his desire to lie down, he noticed the glimmer of a small bauble on the cool slate floor. He picked it up and turned the brooch over. It was a piece of ladies' jewelry, one of those unusual mourning brooches featuring the eye of a lost loved one, a Lover's Eye.

In the faint, flickering candlelight, he realized it was very familiar. Why, it was obviously a miniature of Anthony's eye, with the distinctive Fortesque slant. He remembered seeing Georgiana wearing it on occasion, half hidden by shawls or fichus.

He dropped it on the cot's pillow suddenly, as if it had burned his hand. Was he to be always surrounded with memories of his deceitful cousin? Yet he told himself resolutely again that he would never dare blacken Anthony's image in Georgiana's eyes. Why deprive her of illusions that gave her comfort? She should be allowed every tiny portion of happiness she could find in her harsh life.

She had given herself to him, and he would do the best he could by her—only interfering in her life if fate decided to intrude in the form of a tiny infant. It was simply unfortunate that fate had a way of being extraordinarily fickle in its attentions when one was adrift in the pickling air of Cornwall.

Chapter 11

August 15—to do
- *arrange corner for Father at the festivities*
- *sacks for sack races*
- *archery targets*
- *corn dollies*
- *check cider and food, roasting spit*

   - *begin anew after today*

Georgiana awoke in her tiny bedchamber at her parents' cottage full of newfound resolve and energy despite having slept in the most patchy fashion. She had tiptoed into Little Roses since it was the only place she knew she wouldn't encounter Quinn. As she sipped the tea the maid had brought to her chamber and reviewed her list, she wished for the day she could go to bed each night in a room she could call her own.

As the blackness of night had given way to the smallest glimmers of a new day, Georgiana had felt a peace she had never known wash over her.

Something had changed. The heavy weight of her obsession had finally lifted, leaving her strangely calm. She had spent three quarters of her life thinking about Quinn Fortesque and it was a relief to put her dreams on the shelf.

He did not love her.

He never had and he never would.

She was his great friend and that was all. If she had but known how immense her relief would be with the absolute knowledge, she would have forced herself to reveal her feelings long ago. But wasn't hindsight always annoyingly insightful?

Well, she was leaving Penrose—and she would do it with her parents—even if it meant dragging her mother away, kicking and screaming. It shouldn't be that hard, really. Her mother might be mollified by the promise of a beautiful dwelling overlooking the sea—her long-held dream. And her father's health appeared to have taken a slight turn for the better.

It was hard to admit, but Quinn had been right. With the strain of Penrose's stewardship removed from his frail shoulders, her father had improved, his face taking on better color, and he had appeared to regain a little of the weight he had lost.

She would talk to the Duke of Helston today about finding a cottage, and she would put the word out elsewhere.

But before everything else, she must get through today, the day of the festival. And she would enjoy every moment of it. It had been so long since the people in this corner of Cornwall had celebrated the ancient tradition.

She squirmed in her hard wooden chair against the sting of her loss of innocence. It had been a great shock. She had thought when Anthony had entered her body on their wedding night that the discomfort had meant they had well and fully consummated the union. Oh, but how wrong she had been. Last night . . . She hadn't known a man could penetrate a woman so profoundly. Well, she had suffered far, far greater pain in her life. This was nothing. She would heal and get on with her life, as it were. And fate would not be so cruel as to punish her further with a child.

What had happened with Quinn in the hidden dell was pure possession, the most intimate experience of her life. It was as if he had touched her soul, known the very essence of her. And now she felt horribly exposed, for she had revealed all, only to find not a single corner of his heart engaged.

She could never hate him. He had shown too much compassion for her, for her deformities, and she in return had proved to him he was loved. She tried to feel altruistic about her unrequited love, but she had never possessed a martyr's bone in her body. She abruptly forced herself to stop these thoughts, the thoughts that had been sweeping 'round and 'round her head all night.

She cleared her throat and brought the delicate teacup to her lips, glad no one was in her bed-chamber to see her trembling hand.

She would live through this. She would.

She turned in her chair at the sound of a light tapping at the door. Well, at least she wouldn't have to face him today without a festive crowd to hide behind.

"Grace," she said with surprise. "I thought you were my mother. You're up early."

The Countess of Sheffield smiled her warm, sunny smile and arched a brow. "I was awakened by a little girl unwilling to wait a moment longer for the big day to begin. Your mother, bless her heart, is occupying Fairleigh below stairs with an amazing assortment of cakes. But be warned, Fairleigh was quite determined to find you to get permission to clang the bell to start the events." Grace's face turned serious. "Ata and the others were very worried about you last night. And then we couldn't find you this morning."

Georgiana looked at her hands. "I won't hide anything from you. Quinn and I had a row last night because I took Fairleigh swimming without his permission. And then, well, I came here after I . . ." She didn't know how to go on so she stopped.

Grace grasped Georgiana's calloused fingers in her petite, gloved hands and squeezed. "Rosamunde and I spoke last night. You're in love with him, aren't you, Georgiana?" Her voice was very soft.

"No," she said firmly. "Grace, whatever else you believe, please know that I am not. Perhaps," she said swallowing, "I was in love with him at one time. But now I find I can only care for him very deeply as my husband's cousin." She squeezed Grace's fingers. "And I can assure you *he* does not love *me*. It might have appeared that way because my late husband and Quinn and I knew one another in childhood. But we grew up, and we each of us went our separate ways. And I have found that now we are adults and would not suit each other at all."

"I can see you're telling me the truth, Georgiana, even if it pains you. Rosamunde must have been mistaken. Dearest, since you've been so kind as to take me into your confidence I will tell you my thoughts too. And then we will never speak of this again." Grace's radiant blue eyes searched hers and she continued in her dulcet, cultured voice. "You see, I think I could be happy with him. He told me recently he misses town—the varied amusements—just as I do. He enjoys traveling, too, which I adore. And I could help him with his daughter. Help her to become a refined young lady." She smoothed her dress with wide-stretched fingers. "I'm not looking for a love match, you know, just companionship."

"Grace, I wish you every happiness. You, above everyone else, deserve happiness." A curlew in the fragrant honeysuckle beyond Georgiana's bedchamber window sent up its song.

Grace touched her cheek, and her eyes darkened with sadness. "We shan't have any secrets from one another, shall we?" She appeared greatly embarrassed by her frankness. "I've never spoken of last year, or of Luc." She examined her hands. "There is nothing quite as painful as unrequited love, I think. But I do know that time and distance has effected healing. And mutual admiration and companionship—a marriage of convenience—

will allow me to be content. But my happiness will only be complete when you and the other ladies find it too."

"I should tell you my family will remove from Little Roses in near future, Grace. I'm looking into possible cottages." She glanced at the clock on the mantel, carved from green-veined serpentine rock from the Lizard Peninsula nearby. She forced a smile. "I do believe it's time to start the festival. Let's collect Fairleigh before my mother allows her more cakes than she ought. I predict Fairleigh will regret her visit to my mother's kitchen after several rounds of judging pies, honey, and jam."

The entire grounds of Penrose were awash with activity. Every class of Englishman was well represented—be it peasant, servant, merchant, gentry, or aristocrat. Penrose had opened its famed golden doors once again to revel in the cornucopia of the season.

It was a chance to give over to a pagan ritual that begged for a bountiful harvest. And the Cornish knew how to celebrate and offer up thanks properly.

Sir Rawleigh, the handsome blond vicar who had sailed and fought bravely alongside the Duke of Helston, and who had parted with one of his arms in the process, presided over the commencement of the event by giving one of his popular, brief benedictions before the throngs of people. His wife, Rosamunde's sister, obviously with child, was at his side, gazing at him adoringly.

In the lull of the prayer, the calls of summer songbirds came from every direction. It was as if the flocks had come to look down their beaks at man's foolishness; the reed-thin voice of the wren from the yellow gorse, the trumpet of the linnet in the apple grove heavy with fruit, the sweet cooing of the mourning doves pecking for forgotten grain. The prayer ended and, as if on cue, hundreds of starlings swooped above, their maneuverings a study in perfect mass symmetry in the crisp, azure sky.

Georgiana looked down at the touch of fingers on her own. Fairleigh's shining cornflower-blue eyes stared up at her in excitement.

"Oh, Georgiana," she said breathlessly, "I have the list you approved yesterday. May I begin the announcements?"

She touched her shoulder. "Of course. Here, let me help you onto the mounting block and you shall open the festival."

Georgiana reached for the little girl but a pair of strong arms beat her to the job. Quinn lifted his daughter to the platform.

"Fairleigh," he said quietly, "you may stand beside Georgiana and help judge, but it is the Marchioness of Ellesmere who makes the announcements." He looked directly into Georgiana's eyes. "That has always been the way."

Oh, he was insisting she was still the marchioness. She felt very shy suddenly, facing him, remembering vividly what had happened last night.

"Come," he said, grasping her hand.

She hated speaking before a crowd. It unnerved her, almost as much as Quinn's hand helping her up the steps. She clamped down on her feelings. He clapped his hands to gather everyone's attention.

She felt the weight of hundreds of eyes staring at her, but then she noticed everyone was smiling at her, accepting her, and she smiled back, her nervousness in check.

Fairleigh handed her the list the girl had carefully written in her childish hand. "All right, then. Sack races and more on the south lawn in five minutes—I shall judge. Awards for best of stock—sheep, chicken, pigs, cows, bulls, mares, and stallions at the stable block in one hour. The judges shall be Mr. Wilde and Mr. Brown. Household arts, embroidery, and corn dollies at the same time, near the folly—judged by the Dowager Duchess of Helston"—Georgiana heard Ata's exclamations of delight—"and then preserves, honey, and pie judging by Lady Fairleigh Fortesque and the Countess of Sheffield under the old oak tree. There will be archery after, on the north lawn, judged by His Grace, the Duke of Helston. And a special demonstration will be held during the picnic supper to follow. After, the lighting of the bonfire by the Marquis of Ellesmere."

In the silence that greeted her announcements, a boisterous voice called out, "Let's hear it for the marchioness and the marquis. Welcome home, sir, and thank you for arranging all of this." Thunderous applause and whistles pierced the air, and Georgiana turned to see tenants and gentry alike vigorously shaking Quinn's hands and gripping his shoulder in a heartwarming display. Quinn appeared overwhelmed until Grace appeared at his side and he took her arm within his and walked toward the south lawn. Georgiana turned in the other direction and carefully descended the mounting block, Fairleigh tugging her arm in impatience.

Thirty-odd children and good-humored adults lined up for the sack race, which was handily won by the limber youth of the nearest tenant family. Georgiana spied disappointment on Fairleigh's face.

"Come, dearest, there's the entire day before you. Perhaps you'll do better in the three-legged race next."

"No, I won't. Everyone already has a partner. I don't know any of the other children."

"Is it Saturday?"

"Saturday? What does it matter if it's Saturday?"

"That's the only day I accept invitations to race."

"Oh, Georgiana!" Fairleigh's eyes shone. "It is indeed Saturday."

"Well, then. Are you asking?"

As the little girl chattered with excitement, Georgiana glanced behind her and encountered Grace and Quinn. He looked at her steadily.

Thank God, he said not a word at her unlady-like behavior, nor did he try to stop her as he had when he tried to limit her dancing at the ball last night. But then, last night's ball seemed a very long time ago.

Georgiana repaired to the starting line and tied a length of heavy string around one of Fairleigh's slim ankles and her own. She appealed to Miles, who had just arrived, a pretty bouquet of flowers in hand, to start the race. His sister, Rosamunde, had escorted him to watch.

Miles looked at her helplessly and chuckled. "But I have something to give you." He winked and darted a glance at the flowers.

She felt very flustered. No one had ever given her posies. But there wasn't time to think, for Quinn suddenly signaled to Miles that he would do the honors himself.

Quinn shouted, "Take your mark, and go!"

Georgiana gripped Fairleigh tightly to her hip and urged her to march with a "left, right, left, right." Ah, they almost made it, despite the horrid jarring and ache in her knee. But as the finish line loomed, Fairleigh became too heavy to hold back, and they both tumbled awkwardly a few lengths from the end.

Georgiana came up laughing, only to find Fairleigh's horrified face, staring at her exposed limbs. Before she could move to cover herself, everyone pressed closer and whispers snaked through the crowd.

She quickly pulled her gown into place and looked up again to see Miles's shocked expression and Rosamunde's pale visage beside him. Someone lifted her to her feet abruptly.

"Well, madam, it appears you and my daughter have been soundly beaten by Tom Paine and his partner," Quinn said. "Master Paine, if you keep winning each race I wager you'll be the richest boy in Cornwall. Grace, will you award the prizes?" He chuckled and the tension of the moment dissipated. The gathering's attention was soon swayed to preparing for the next event.

"Are you all right?" He asked softly when the crowd had turned away.

"Yes." She'd die before admitting to any pain. "Perfectly fine."

Miles eased forward, a stricken look of pity in his brown eyes. "Georgiana . . . shall I carry you back to Penrose?"

"Lord, no. Thank you, though."

"I didn't know your injuries were quite so . . . What I mean to say is that, are you certain I can't . . . No, I can see—" He stopped abruptly, mid-stutter. "These are for you." He handed her the beautiful bouquet.

Georgiana glanced at Rosamunde, who shook her head and smiled. "I know absolutely nothing about this," she insisted. "Well, almost nothing."

"Why everyone seems to think my sister is the only one who knows the language of flowers, I'll never understand," Miles said, his head cocked knowingly.

"I'm very impressed," Georgiana replied, burying her nose in the pretty arrangement.

"I shall prove it," Miles said, chuckling again. "The white jasmine symbolizes your amiability, gloxinia is for your proud spirit, Mercury reflects your goodness, and the amethyst is a symbol of my admiration."

"And the celandine?" Georgiana asked, delighted beyond measure.

Rosamunde sighed. "You don't miss much, do you?"

"Why, I'm glad you asked," Miles addressed Georgiana. "It signifies joys to come."

"And the throatwort?" Grace Sheffey asked quietly.

Miles paused. "That I can't tell you."

"Why ever not?" Georgiana asked.

"My sister insisted on adding it at the last moment."

The four of them turned expectantly to Rosamunde.

"Oh, for heaven's sake," Rosamunde muttered. "This is between my brother and Georgiana. We should allow them a bit of privacy."

Quinn answered the question with deceptive calm. "I believe throatwort refers to neglected beauty."

Her eyes met Quinn's and melancholy curled within her before she returned her gaze to the posies. "Thank you, Miles. And you too, Rosamunde. They're lovely. I shall always remember this moment, and shall press some of the blooms. I've never received flowers before." She wished she could withdraw the sentence. It sounded so pathetic. It was just that her sensibilities had overwhelmed her.

"It was my pleasure," Miles replied, a grin finally making its appearance. "Perhaps I shall simply have to bring you flowers every day, since this deficiency should be corrected."

She smiled. "Absolutely not. Everyone knows too many flowers will turn a lady into a spoiled creature who lies abed at every opportunity to order people about."

"Perhaps"—Miles offered his arm—"you're right. That would explain the change in my sister. Ever since she married Luc and gained access to his vast gardens, she's become ridiculously overbearing."

"Miles!" Rosamunde laughed and punched her brother in the arm. "By the by, are you putting on weight? I do believe you should lay off the sausage."

"What?" he sputtered.

While the brother and sister traded well-honed barbs, Georgiana finally dared to glance at Quinn.

And oh, what she encountered. A granite wall. As she looked at the firm contoured lines of his mouth and remembered the coarseness of his cheek brushing against her breast last night, she forced herself to glance away.

Ata was coming toward them, waving a handkerchief. "Georgiana, Quinn, come quick. There is such a to-do. One of the stallions escaped and no one can catch him. Oh, and the housekeeper asked me to convey that Fairleigh is already sampling the sweets."

Georgiana turned quickly and realized that indeed Fairleigh had disappeared.

Grace's melodic laugh intruded. "Come, Quinn, let's go refresh your daughter's memory as to the importance of adhering to the schedule. And, I think it's only fair we allow Georgiana a moment to thank Miles properly." Grace winked at her.

Ata's eyes rounded. "Oh, yes, let's all go. Luc and Mr. Brown will do just fine catching the horse, with Mr. Wilde's excellent direction."

"I'm certain I'm needed in the nursery," Rosamunde added, smiling.

They were all conspiring to allow her time with Miles. Quinn was silent, his expression devoid of emotion as he walked away with Grace.

Miles scratched his head as the rest disappeared.

Georgiana forced a smile to her lips. "Is there anything like good friends and family to make one feel embarrassed beyond measure?"

"No." Miles chuckled. "And sisters are positively the worst of all—always trying to control and arrange your life."

"I'm sad to say my brother would probably agree with you. In fact, he told me he joined the Royal Navy because he was tired of being ordered about by, ahem, me," she replied, with a laugh. "I, however, should have liked a sister."

"Hmmm," he replied and offered his arm. "I always thought you much more at ease with gentlemen. Anthony and Quinn were your favored companions when we were growing up—never saw you with any of the girls in the neighborhood."

"I rather think that was a matter of my station more than anything else. My mother wouldn't allow me to play with the tenants' children, and no one of high birth in the area allowed me to play with their daughters. Luckily, the late marquis rarely cared enough to take note of the where-abouts of his son and nephew."

"To your everlasting detriment. It's a crime what happened to you."

"No, Miles, you're very wrong. It was no one's fault but my own. I was a foolish, headstrong girl determined to retrieve a falcon to give as a gift."

"To Anthony," Miles said. "He always *was* lucky. Well, until he—what I mean to say . . ." Miles blundered along in his usual fashion. "Oh, hang it all. I'm not much good at conversation, Georgiana. I'm sorry."

She smiled. "That makes two of us. I think that's why I've always liked you."

A radiant smile appeared on his face and he barked in laughter. "Come on, Georgie, let's go watch the judging at the stable block. I'll wager you ten quid that my mare will win as best all-around. She's a prime goer."

They walked up the rise, Georgiana praying her knee would not give out on her. "I don't know. Rosamunde's stallion is going to be hard to beat."

"Damn sisters," he muttered.

Georgiana laughed.

The stable was filled to the rafters with every barnyard animal conceivable. Georgiana could have cried for the joy of seeing her father sitting in a place of honor, his thin gray hair wetted and carefully combed into place.

"Georgiana," he called out in his dearly famil-iar, deep voice, "come sit beside me. Mr. Brown and I are having a difference of opinion on these sheep. He prefers this Cheviot to that Southdown over here. What do you think? We need you to break the tie."

Moments later, her mother bustled her way and suggested she go to the kitchens to see to more lemonade and ale for the thirsty crowds. "Georgiana, His Grace spoke to your father not a half hour ago—just for a moment, you understand— about locating a cottage for us. He said you had asked for his assistance. What are you thinking? We were all to move into the great house."

"No, Mama. That is what *you* wanted. But I've been thinking that Papa and I—and you, I hope— will be much happier away from all the memories and strain of overseeing Penrose. Look how much Papa has already benefited by the rest Quinn arranged for him. And you've always wanted to live in a cottage overlooking the sea. And . . ." Her words slowed to a stop. She was so surprised her mother hadn't yet interrupted her with an argument.

"You've grown up, Georgiana," her mother said in a tone Georgiana had never heard from her parent. "I'm so glad. I only wanted to remove to the great house to firmly ensure your rights as Anthony's widow. But now that Quinn is here, he's made it obvious he intends to do right by you, not to mention his excessive generosity toward us all. Well, the only thing holding your father and me back from leaving here has been, quite frankly, you."

"Oh, Mama . . ." Georgiana rushed into her mother's arms.

"There, there, child. Come along now, that'll do. That awful Augustine Phelps is demanding champagne, for goodness sakes. Whoever thought to invite her? You remember what she's like. If I don't find the housekeeper and return with a bottle right away, she's sure to begin that screeching again. Sounds just like a peacock in season!"

Georgiana burst out laughing and was grateful to her mother for her silly banter.

She left her mother at the stairs to the cellar and returned to find Augustine Phelps, an embroidered cushion in one hand, in a standoff with Ata, who had Elizabeth on one side of her and Sarah on the other.

"Well," Auggie huffed, her nose in the air. "If I had known this wasn't a true contest, I wouldn't have bothered to enter my beautiful embroidery. The very idea of giving a child the top pri—"

"I've *always* said she wasn't one of us," Ata muttered to Elizabeth.

"Pardon me, madam, did you just sug—"

"Perhaps you don't know the proper way to address a duchess, Baroness?"

Elizabeth was doing a terrible job of keeping a straight face.

"Why, I—" the baroness began.

"I've never liked many baronesses, actually." Ata sniffed and turned to Sarah. "Too far down the peerage's social ladder to be of any importance really, yet ironically, usually too filled with self-importance to be of any use to the gentry."

"I would have you know that my father was a—"

"Madam," Ata interrupted again, "I've always wondered why ladies feel the need to discuss their breeding lines. Makes me always think of horses and dogs for some reason. By the by, is the baron here?" Ata's studied look of innocence caused Georgiana's stomach to ache with repressed laughter.

Elizabeth looked to be in the same condition, if the mirth in her eyes was any indication, while Sarah maintained the same serene expression for which she was universally beloved.

Everyone for miles around knew that Auggie's awful husband was terrified of encountering the Duke of Helston after the baron had behaved abominably toward Rosamunde last year and Luc had promised death and dismemberment, in the reverse order.

Auggie turned her glittering eyes toward Georgiana. "As hostess, I would think you would try to enforce civility among the guests, Georgiana."

All the widows gathered about her. And Georgiana suddenly realized she had actually gotten her wish for sisters long ago. All the widows hovered, as if some signal had passed among them, to protect her as true sisters would protect one another.

"Well, here comes the *servant* with my champagne. Finally," Auggie said, looking at Georgiana's mother, who had just arrived with a glass and bottle.

"I beg your pardon," a deceptively calm, deep voice said.

All of them, Ata included, had been too shocked to form a retort and none of them had seen Quinn's approach behind them.

"Oh, my lord," Auggie purred. "The champagne has arrived. Do let me send for a glass for you."

Quinn looked at Augustine Phelps. His gaze never wavered as it slowly trailed from the top of her overly ornate hat, dripping with fake birds, all the way down to her tiny pale yellow striped slippers.

All the ladies save Auggie, held their breath.

"Madam, I've asked a footman to bring 'round your carriage."

"I beg your pardon?"

"You have precisely until the count of three to apologize to the marchioness and Mrs. Wilde and find your way out."

It was obvious she struggled to remain in control, her voice shaking. "And if I refuse?" Auggie wore a pout remarkably like Fairleigh's when she was denied a treat.

"I'll set the dogs on you."

As Auggie gasped in outrage, Ata positively beamed in rapture and then sighed. "He's even better than Luc."

"Now, then. One . . ."

Auggie shrieked a string of invectives, betraying her shop origins.

"Two . . ."

Augustine abruptly closed her mouth and began walking very inelegantly toward the side of the great house.

Ata giggled. "Sorry, I can't resist." The tiny dowager called out, "Three," and pressed two fingers to her lips to whistle like a dockside sailor.

A most satisfying screech came from the side of the house. It was the last anyone saw of Augustine Phelps for the rest of the day.

"And here I thought you a diplomat, Quinn. Forgive me for saying that I do believe you're sorely out of practice." Ata laughed. "And it agrees with you."

"I beg you not to tell your grandson," he replied with a twinkle in his eye. "He might be forced to take a liking to me. And then where would we all be? Cats and dogs living together."

For a moment Quinn glanced directly at Georgiana, and the light of humor was in his eyes as his mouth relaxed into a smile, making him appear like he had used to in their youth.

Little did she know, it would be a long time before she would see that light again.

Chapter 12

~~ ∽○∽ ~~

Georgiana didn't see Quinn again until the end of the long and exhausting day. All afternoon his daughter had twirled the pearl necklace she won from Grace, and then became ill on Georgiana after judging the honey, preserves, and pies. Georgiana had led the little girl to her chamber and tried to cheer her up by showing her how to make a traditional corn dolly while she rested on the bed.

By the time Georgiana returned to the gardens, the picnic supper and archery contest were nearly at an end. Rosamunde had trounced everyone, including her four brothers, quite soundly.

A plume of happiness bloomed in Georgiana's heart as she glanced at the gathering. Her father was comfortably settled in a chair Quinn had arranged for him, her mother urging him to eat "just a little more." All the many, many dearly familiar tenants, villagers, and gentry from the surrounding countryside sat on blankets, their children making merry and playing games of tag and cricket in the lower meadow. Beyond them the golden rays of late afternoon illuminated the pinkish-gold patchwork of fertile fields filled with hay, rye, and stripped cornstalks all the way to the dark blue sea and the horizon. It was a little slice of heaven here, and it never failed to move Georgiana.

She heard the call of a peregrine falcon and turned to see the raptor swoop to land on Quinn's gloved arm. Oblige pecked at the raw food Quinn had lured him with. Grace stood beside him, while Mr. Brown carried Georgiana's old hunting pouch. Georgiana was supposed to have given the demonstration with Quinn.

But this was how it was meant to be. They were beautiful together—Grace so blonde and so elegant, and Quinn starkly handsome. He wore his refined garments so easily, naturally. Georgiana looked down at her stained gown. It was her Sunday best—something that could never even be the countess's Monday worst.

And suddenly she was mortally tired of playing the plain, practical list maker.

Quinn bowed slightly at the smattering of applause while adjusting the hood on the peregrine falcon, and then handed the bird to John Brown.

He leaned in and whispered in the older man's ear, "Have the small pane of glass next to the door of the lake house repaired as soon as possible, will you, Mr. Brown?"

The older man scratched his head. "And what, pray tell, happened to the glass?"

"I'll double your first-quarter wages if you do it by first light."

The older man raised his thick, gray eyebrows. "Fisticuffs, breaking windows . . . what will be next? I thought you were a fancy-word diplomat." He shook his head. "Are you certain you're not a sailor?"

Quinn rolled his eyes before grasping Grace's arm and escorting her to a table filled with refreshments.

A quarter of an hour later, they made their way toward Georgiana.

"Fairleigh refuses to stay in bed, Quinn. Mrs. Killen is rebraiding her hair, and she's to rejoin us in a few moments," Georgiana said when they walked up to her.

"Somehow I'm not surprised." Quinn shifted his gaze between the two ladies. There was no doubt who was deficient in appearance. Georgiana had a bit of straw in her hair, and her petticoat was slightly torn from the earlier race. There was a stain of something that looked like cherry pie on her gray gown, and there was a bit of dirt, too, on the other side, no doubt due to checking horse's hooves during judging. Grace had not a flaw on her person. The day had brought a pretty glow to her.

"Georgiana?" Grace asked, "Shall we go refresh ourselves? Do allow me to remove that bit of—"

"No," he said before he could stop himself. "She's lovely just the way she is. Reminds me of past festivals, when all the young girls and their mothers made corn dollies, and bits of straw were everywhere." He'd forgotten all about it until now.

"Why, you're exactly right. Georgiana is lovely—straw and all," Grace demurred.

"I believe it's time to start the bonfire, in any case," he announced.

"What happens after?" the countess asked.

"Everyone is free to walk about looking at the prize-winning articles and animals," he replied. "Some tour the estate or go to Loe Pool for boating. Others toast cheese at the fire. Everyone is at liberty until the fire burns out and the vicar sends up a final prayerful plea to the harvest gods for good weather and bountiful crops."

"I think I'd fancy a short row on the lake, Quinn," Grace said, with a smile. "And Georgiana could go with Miles. Shall we?"

He *loathed* the idea, of course. But he didn't want to disappoint Grace. Georgiana refused to meet his eye.

"It would be my pleasure," he replied.

"That would be lovely," Georgiana said at the precise same moment and became flustered.

"It's agreed, then." A smile lit Grace's face.

He bowed and extended an arm toward each lady, escorting them to a mock arrangement of druid stones, set in an ancient circular pattern. Enormous logs and sticks clogged the center, piled to the height of a small cottage. It was the one part of the festival he had seen to himself. He wanted it to be a sight everyone would remember—a fire so immense it would dwarf all previous harvest-festival bonfires.

And so it would be.

Grace's arm lightly rested atop his, her pale-pink-gloved fingers on the lace extending beyond his coat sleeve. He glanced at Georgiana's bronzed bare arm, which rested heavily on top of his other arm, her fingers grazing his, skin to skin. Her legs, or her knee, were obviously paining her. She of course said not a word.

He signaled to a footman to ring a peal to announce the lighting while he extended the small torch to Georgiana.

"Absolutely not," Georgiana said. "It's your duty."

"It's always been the task of the marquis and marchioness."

"No, it's the task of the marquis and *his wife*," she insisted.

He stared at her, remembering what had passed between them late last night in the dell.

"I'm sorry to intrude, my lord." A red-faced footman trotted up, very embarrassed. "But the Dowager Marchioness of Ellesmere has arriv—"

"There is no need to introduce me, you dolt," Lady Gwendolyn Fortesque barked as she made her way to Quinn's side. "What in heaven's name is going on here? Never say it's a harvest festival. I didn't believe Mrs. Killen. Why ever didn't you write to me of this, Quinn?"

The dowager marchioness suddenly noticed the torch in his outstretched hand and Georgiana beside him. His aunt snatched it from his grasp before he could stop her.

"You weren't going to let her light the bonfire, were you?" Gwendolyn said, shock lacing her words. "I'm glad I got here in time. Why terrible luck and misfortune would have befallen the countryside if—"

"Are you related to Augustine Phelps?" Quinn muttered under his breath.

She obviously heard him. "Why, yes, indeed. Lovely girl. She's my goddaughter. Is she here? Oh, I long to see her."

Quinn glanced at Georgiana out of the corner of his eye. She was very pale.

His aunt seemed to recollect herself. "Come along, Quinn. Let's get on with the lighting before I greet Augustine and everyone else. Then I have a matter of the utmost importance to discuss with you. It's the reason I'm here. Traveled in a most uncomfortable fashion, day and night." Gwendolyn turned her glare on Georgiana. "Are you still here? Well, you, miss, had better go pack your bags. You've outstayed your welcome."

A slew of shocked gasps erupted all around. There was not a proper Cornishman, woman, or child who was not thoroughly versed in the fine art of eavesdropping. And the echoes of whispers coiling through the mass of people gathered proved that gossip was their next most beloved sport.

"I beg your pardon, madam," Quinn said stiffly. "Would you care to reconsider and rephrase your words more carefully? I'm certain the marchioness"—he glanced at Georgiana—"who has always been extraordinarily forgiving, will consider favorably your apology." Quinn grasped his relative's arm. "And then we'll retire to my study."

The older lady dug in her heels and refused to budge. "I absolutely will not apologize to that scheming girl. She must have some sort of mysterious pull on your sex—women like her often do. Although what her allure is, I've never understood. She has had the audacity to insinuate herself here and—"

He hated to make a scene. Hated scandal. He'd had enough scandal with Cynthia to last him all his days. "Madam," he interrupted her loudly, and then dropped his voice, the ironlike force tightening around each syllable. "You have apparently forgotten who is the head of this family—perhaps from the fatigue of your long journey." He heard her shocked intake of breath. "Now, if you would kindly repair to the house immediately, I shall be delighted to continue this discussion in my study—after *Lady Ellesmere* and I light the bonfire." He strengthened his grasp on Gwendolyn's arm to encourage her retreat.

"Impossible! Georgiana Wilde was never legally married to my Anthony," the grand dame nearly shouted in her vexation. "And I have the proof of it right here. Mr. Tilden, finally proving of some use, made an inspired discovery—after you agreed to continue the inquiry."

"I never agreed to—"

"I always said you were bright. I told my husband you were. And Henrietta always thought you showed poten—" She finally stopped.

With each word the crowd had eased closer, silently, suffocating them. Quinn noticed Grace had drifted to Georgiana's side and was gripping her waist with one hand and her fingers with the other. Georgiana appeared rooted to the spot, like a fawn caught in the mesmerizing glow of a fire at nightfall.

And he felt equally caught in this god-awful nightmare. He moved to within inches of his aunt's face and stared at her, daring her to utter another word. He leaned down slowly and whispered, "I shall cut your annual portion in half if you utter one more wretched word. I told you I would hear you out—if only because Tilden is involved—but not now, not here. You shall turn around and repair to the house—to my study, to be precise—or go back to London. But there is one thing you will *not* do, and that is to remain here for one more bloody moment."

His aunt opened her mouth and then closed it quickly. Money always had been her soft, fleshy vulnerability. He resisted the urge to begin counting.

The dowager backed away slowly, absolute fury building on her sallow, aged face.

Quinn moved to Georgiana's side to say quietly, "I realize ordering you to do something is tantamount to ensuring a refusal. So I'm begging you to take this torch and light the bonfire. If you do not, in the eyes of every person here, she will be proved right and you wrong."

"How does she know?" She asked the question so hollowly he barely heard her.

"I beg your pardon?"

"Why did you continue the inquiry? I thought you said you weren't going to. You said—"

"I said I would end it. Now please, please take this torch. If not for me, then for *Anthony*." His stomach clenched in pain, but he forced himself to continue. "He would have wanted you to."

He noticed the growing buzz of conversation all around him. Snatches of phrases reached his ears.

"Maybe she shouldn't light it" . . . "Bad luck" . . . "Wouldn't take the chance" . . . "It's our livelihoods" . . .

"Well, that was a bloody poor display of your infamous diplomatic skills, old boy," Luc St. Aubyn said, leaning in closer from the skirts of the crowd. "But then I expected no less of you after last night's farce, for which you will *never* be forgiven no matter how prettily you ask."

"You're such a comfort, Helston. I don't know how I managed without you before."

Quinn turned to the crowd. "Your attention, please, everyone. I fear the dowager marchioness has been ill advised and is under a great misapprehension. I ask you all to have patience while this misunderstanding is sorted out. And . . ." Quinn paused when he felt sticky little fingers worm their way into his tight fist, and he glanced down, surprised to encounter the questioning expression of his daughter. An idea captured his mind. ". . . And I've a new tradition to begin today. I've long thought the harvest gods have been having their way with us—actually laughing at us mere mortals below—while an ancient stream of Ellesmere lords and ladies lit the bonfires through the generations. Yet, in all the tales I've read, the gods have always preferred the offerings of innocent young girls."

He heard Fairleigh giggle beside him. He looked down at her and stroked her soft, blonde curls, so unlike her mother's auburn hair.

"You're not going to sacrifice me in the fire are you, Papa?"

Bellows of laughter resonated in the late-afternoon light.

"I won't if you promise not to eat any more sweets tonight."

"Oh, Papa, I think I can promise to never eat another sweet my entire life."

He handed Fairleigh the torch and directed her toward the pyre. "Careful, my darling," he whispered in her ear. "There now, light the nearest branch."

Firelight danced along a thin, dry reed, feasting on the material before racing to the branches above. Within a few moments a shower of sparks erupted, licking the larger timber.

Quinn glanced at all the hundreds of people surrounding the blaze. Firelight glowed on the awed faces of humanity. Quinn's cursed cynical outlook on life—something he tried to keep in check always—enveloped him. It served them all right, these lemmings, willing to believe an old harridan's rantings against one of their own. Georgiana was worth more than the lot of them any day of the week.

As he gazed down at Georgiana, who was instructing Fairleigh to toss in the torch, he wondered what all these ridiculous, superstitious folk would think if they discovered there was not a drop of his blood in his daughter's veins.

Not one drop.

He ruthlessly pushed back the thought— surprised he had dared to examine something he had buried so long ago. She was his daughter and he would kill anyone who dared to say a word otherwise. It was the very reason he had accepted the post so far away from London, away from the past—away from the extraordinary, ugly truths he'd been forced to face in his marriage.

"Fairleigh," he said, kneeling down to his beautiful child, "I want you to stay with Mrs. Winters and Mrs. Ashburton, here." He nodded to the two widows, who bobbed their acquiescence to his request.

He looked at Georgiana, who had drawn a shroud over her usually open expression. "I won't allow her to insult you."

Before she could reply, the tiny, wizened form of Ata appeared beside Georgiana. "Well, I won't let her face that woman without me."

"Nor without me," Grace said softly.

"This is ridiculous," Georgiana said.

"Luc?" Ata poked her grandson.

"Bloody hell. This is Ellesmere's problem, not mine. The man is nothing but problems, if you ask me."

Ata stamped her cane on his foot.

Quinn was amused to note how well Helston hid his discomfort.

"*Delighted to help, Grandmamma.* Always enjoy a

good debate. And Lady Gwendolyn should provide much entertainment, if recent history is any indication."

Quinn wasn't sure why he allowed the large group to accompany him and Georgiana. He typically preferred to sort out problems by himself. A prickle of uncertainty had pounded in his chest at the idea, and he held back a demand not to intercede.

It was quiet as the group walked toward the house in the lengthening shadows of twilight. Only the *en-onk, en-onk* of a *V* of geese above drew their attention. They appeared like skeins of brown and black wool unraveling across the rose-tinted sky. A drift of sapphire dragonflies skimmed along in the air currents in front of them, searching, always searching for less-fortunate creatures to capture.

Lady Gwendolyn sat beside the fire in the study, directing two footmen to use bellows on the blaze, as she was chilled.

"I suppose you've brought in your friends to argue against me." His aunt sniffed. She extracted a sheaf of papers from an old leather portfolio next to her. "But I'm actually grateful for the audience, for the sooner everyone knows the truth, the better.

"Georgiana Wilde left this parish for ten days to attend a fair during the critical period before the purported wedding ceremony." She shifted in her seat. "If one takes the time to carefully read the rules governing a Common License—"

Quinn interrupted. "Anthony and Georgiana were married by Special License, which would render your argument useless."

"No," Georgiana said quietly, all eyes on her. "We were married by Common License."

"As I was saying, before I was so rudely interrupted," Lady Ellesmere continued, "Lord Hardwicke's Act requires that at least *one* of the parties 'live' in the parish for at least four weeks immediately before the granting of the license. There is to be not one single interruption of residency. Mr. Wilde and his daughter attended an *agricultural*"—she said the word with great disdain—"fair in Devon." She turned to Georgiana and tilted her nose in an arrogant manner. "Did you, or did you not attend this event for six days during the month prior to securing the license and the purported union? And remember, missy, that I have witnesses to the fact that you were there." She paused and hissed, "You were looking over the *pigs*, I understand."

Quinn felt the chill of fear rise along his spine. He couldn't move and he damned the feeling of inadequacy that was forever to torment his soul at the most important moments. "Georgiana, you are not to answer," he said.

"Why ever not?" she replied. "I have nothing to hide. Nothing to fear."

Ata clasped her hand with her good one, gaining her attention. "Everyone has something to hide, my dear. You wouldn't be interesting unless you had something to hide."

That broke the tension for a moment.

"And your son?" Luc said slowly. "Was he not here during those four weeks? That would have satisfied the—"

"My Anthony went up to London during the same period the two Wildes were in Devon." She handed the thick sheaf of legal documents to Quinn with a flourish.

He quickly scanned a few of the pages until his eyes came to rest on a paragraph. "It does say in Canon One hundred two that one of the parties must live in the diocese for four weeks prior. But really, madam, the word 'live' is open to interpretation, as I see it. One could easily argue that to live in a parish means to reside, or to maintain lodging, not necessarily to be present there for every moment of the four weeks."

The old lady tilted her head in an odd angle. "That's not how the Archbishop of Canterbury's assistant, Lord Thornley, saw it when he condescended to grant me an audience last Thursday. Perhaps you would like to discuss it with him."

An awful silence wended around the occupants of the room before Georgiana broke it. "How many times must I say it? I've never had any use for the title."

"You might be able to fool everyone else with your noble performance, but not me. Of course you want the title. Everyone wants to better themselves. And if you don't want it, then why did you stay here?"

The color in Georgiana's face drained away.

Luc leaned toward Quinn and quietly drawled,

"Ahem, now would be an excellent time to unshackle yourself from that namby-pamby diplomacy of yours and unleash some good old-fashioned shouting."

Quinn maintained an iron grip on his control—refraining from the intense desire to throttle someone: Helston, Gwendolyn, or his own blasted inability to protect the one person he knew deserved his protection—had earned his protection—but did not want it or him.

Ata's eyes narrowed, glaring at him in expectation. He turned and saw expectation in Grace's eyes as well. In Georgiana's eyes, there was no expectation—only blankness, and it chilled him to the core, nearly blinding him with a desire to take her in his arms and shield her from everything.

"Madam," he said finally into the stillness, a surge of something forcing him to say the unutterable. "There is a certain brand of ugly selfishness and questionable morals that abides in the hearts of many. Most are capable of suppressing their true natures. Unfortunately, you, and *your son* were incapable of doing so."

Georgiana inhaled sharply. "This has absolutely nothing to do with Anthony. I'm certain he had no idea about the laws pertaining to—"

"Wait, Georgiana," Ata interrupted. "I, for one, want to hear what he has to say."

"I will not allow you to say one single word against Anthony. He was everything you are not," Gwendolyn Fortesque shrieked. "He was the best of sons, the best of men. He—"

"—is not under discussion," Quinn finished. "But, then, neither is Georgiana. I will not allow you to discuss your daughter-in-law or your odd notions regarding the legality of her marriage to anyone beyond this circle. If you dare breathe a word of this ridiculous theory to anyone, I will transfer every last unentailed farthing to Georgiana in my will. Have I made myself perfectly clear, madam?"

"Bravo," Ata said softly.

Georgiana cleared her throat. "You know, all of this is really unnecessary. Lady Ellesmere," she said, "my family and I had already decided to remove from here, now that my father is no longer steward of Penrose. There is no need for—"

Quinn interrupted her with sadness. "You do not have to answer to anyone, Georgiana. You may choose to live wherever your heart desires."

"Well, I never—" began Gwendolyn Fortesque.

"—know when to stop," interrupted Ata.

His aunt's instincts were clearly at war within her. On one side was the obvious desire to humiliate Georgiana and on the other the need to impress the woman who outranked her: the tiny yet powerful Dowager Duchess of Helston. The latter won out.

"Your Grace," Gwendolyn said, "I do beg your pardon for having to witness this sad business. I have always been a great admirer of yours, and have always hoped a friendship would bloom between us. I was much honored to learn from our housekeeper that you and your friends are staying with us. Do allow me to escort you to see the rest of the activities tonight. The harvest festival here is the most famed in all of Cornwall. But I'm sure you know that, Your Grace."

Quinn had not taken his eyes off of Georgiana for a moment. She wore a mask, yet he knew with all his heart that she would not be able to take another moment of this insanity. "I've decided to end the festival early," he said. "I'm going outside to make an announcement. I'll have the vicar offer up the final prayer immediately. There will be no further festivities."

Georgiana looked at him. "That's not the way of it, Quinn. Everyone will be so disappointed. Please don't. Don't do this. I, for one, will be disappointed."

Georgiana Wilde—no, *Fortesque*—damnation— was the greatest liar he'd ever encountered. He was a fool to have never known it before now. He'd always thought her as transparent as the water in Loe Pool. But then, hadn't he proven to be the poorest judge of character the world had ever known?

Chapter 13

〜ⓒ〜

August 28—to do
- *review ledgers—again*
- *visit with ladies at Penrose—again*
- *organize menus—again*
- *ask Mrs. Killen to hire an additional personal maid—again*
- *write to Grayson—again*

> - *look at properties Luc has proposed . . . yet again*

Georgiana twirled a single fragrant stem of dog rose between her fingers while she reviewed the stack of ledgers Mr. Brown had left for her. The last two weeks, someone, probably Miles, had ridden by Little Roses and mysteriously left on the doorstep each morning a different bloom—always a rose—for her, sans note. Georgiana supposed it was because, at heart, he was a gentleman, and felt it his duty to supply an admitted wallflower with posies. It had been so silly to mention that she'd never received any bouquets. It was just unfortunate she wasn't as well versed in the language of flowers as Rosamunde and her kindhearted brother.

Most mornings she had carried the bloom up the short hill to the great house, forcing herself to pretend everything was fine and normal while she visited with all the ladies within Penrose's hallowed halls. And every day, a footman had interrupted her visit after five or ten minutes to inform her that her presence was kindly requested by Mr. Brown. And again, every morning, she had gratefully escaped to the steward's chambers, which had slowly but surely become Mr. Brown's. Even his soothing bay rum scent had seeped into the walls.

She wasn't a fool. She knew Mr. Brown was trying to divert her, spare her as much as possible from the indignities she endured when forced to spend time with Gwendolyn Fortesque.

Oh, it was awful. Ata had no idea how much her constant defense, and that of the rest of the widows, pained her.

"My dear Georgiana," the tiny dowager duchess said to her this morning, "since you, Rosamunde, Grace, and I are the four highest-ranking ladies in Cornwall, I think we should have our likenesses taken, don't you? Grace knows a wonderful portraitist in London." She continued without waiting for Grace's support. "Oh, do let's have a painting commissioned. Sarah and Elizabeth must be part of it too, of course."

And Gwendolyn Fortesque had spent the next fifteen minutes attempting to insinuate herself.

"Perhaps Your Grace might consider including my daughters? Henrietta and Margaret are visiting my sister, but I could send a letter to them. They would make a lovely addition . . . or even I might . . ." She lost her nerve after encountering Ata's sour expression.

Gwendolyn's newest tactic toward Georgiana was to ignore her completely, going so far as to stare at a point on the floor when forced to converse with her. Never meeting her eye, yet never, ever daring to insult her.

And Georgiana's misery had been complete, when Ata sent the marchioness on some ridiculous errand to afford the rest of them some privacy. "My dear Georgiana, there are only two reasons I endure her. I'm resolved not to remove to Amberley until you are settled away from that horrid woman. And I'll stay here until then to make sure she behaves toward you in the proper manner."

"No matter what she says," Grace had added, "all of us know you were properly married to her son. You are a marchioness and all of us will stand by you."

Elizabeth and Sarah had touched her hands and murmured their support. And Georgiana had felt as little like a marchioness as ever.

"And," Ata had added, with a smile toward Grace, "I shall wager my black pearls that there will be another lady among us who will share the title with you before the year is out. Then the two of you will be almost sisters in truth—and you'll have no need for any of the rest of us."

Grace had then cradled Georgiana's calloused fingers in her own and kissed the top of her hair. "I should very much like to have you for a sister, Georgiana," she whispered, and squeezed her fingers.

Georgiana had been unable to make her mouth function properly.

And then, thankfully, a footman had come to get her.

She sighed and looked down at the new stack of ledgers Mr. Brown had left for her. Well, she would take comfort in the familiarity of her old tasks, and look again at the information the Duke of Helston had sent regarding several properties within fifty miles of Penrose.

She suddenly noticed that a new property had been added to the bottom of the stack. She glanced at the specifics and was immediately intrigued. It was located on a hill not five hundred yards from the sea. It was quite a find, considering the overall size and price. Hmmm . . . quite promising.

The door cracked and Fairleigh Fortesque peeked inside. Her eyes were so like her father's—not the color, but the shape. The slope of the lid and the straight brow. She wondered suddenly if Quinn was ever haunted by having to see glimpses of his wife's features in his daughter.

"Have you finished your pianoforte lesson, dearest?"

Fairleigh nodded with a pained expression. "Mr. Tyler said I only ruptured *one* of his eardrums today."

Georgiana forced her lips not to twitch. "Well, that is saying a lot, for I am certain he told me I ruptured his entire *brain* on one occasion almost twenty years ago."

Fairleigh giggled and skipped toward her. "And I spent one half hour on the needlework Mrs. Killen set out for me."

"A full thirty minutes?"

"Maybe it was twenty-nine minutes," the little girl murmured.

"Was it at least longer than a quarter hour?" She lifted the girl's little chin with the palm of her hand.

"You're tougher than old Beetleface ever was."

Georgiana laughed. "It's only because I want the very best life has to offer for you, dearest. And all refined ladies play an instrument, or sing—"

"I think everyone knows I can't sing." She rolled her blue eyes.

"And they embroider, and—"

Fairleigh interrupted her again. "I'd settle for less than the best life as long as it doesn't include embroidery."

"And they most certainly do not interrupt—"

"Ata does."

"—their friends," Georgiana finished with a smile.

"I'm sorry, Georgiana."

"That's all right. I've been slipping on that rule myself lately."

Fairleigh looked at the ledgers with an eager expression. "Oh, do say we can start. You said I could write that note to the mill near Penzance.

Has the post arrived? I hope that man you sent a letter to in Scotland will sell us his sheep. And you promised I could watch a lamb being born this winter. You won't forget, will you? Can I add the figures in the ledger today?"

"*May I.*"

"May I add the figures in the ledger?"

She passed the top leather-bound book to the child as well as a scrap of paper and the inkwell. "Trim the quill first, dearest. And I never forget a promise. I've already told Mr. Brown our agreement and will tell your father when I leave."

The little girl's eyes became very wide. "But you're not going to leave any time soon. It will take a long time to find a place. Oh, why does everyone always have to leave? Why can't people live in one place all their lives?"

Georgiana refused to lie to her—refused to suggest she might visit often. She very much doubted she would be able to tolerate visits. It would not be fair to Grace or Quinn, or to her own fragile heart. "Perhaps you'll be happy to see me go, after I tell you I'm leaving you my paints and new canvases when I take my leave. But not a moment before," she added when she saw the little girl's face bloom with joy.

Fairleigh clapped her hands but then stopped. "Oh, but it won't be nearly as much fun painting without you."

"Perhaps your father will paint with you. As I remember, he used to enjoy it when we were growing up."

"Papa? He likes to paint?"

Georgiana handed her the paring knife. "Yes, but no more discussion. It is time to get to work if we are ever to finish."

Quinn peered past the edge of the door to see two heads bent earnestly to their tasks—one small and blonde, the other glossy and dark brown. Two hands gripped plumes that moved in unison. Two brows furrowed in concentration on the task before them. And two right feet tapped in deliberation.

He swallowed.

He didn't dare interrupt them. Georgiana didn't know, but he had observed them on numerous occasions the past two weeks or so. And it was always the same. Georgiana had accomplished what scores of governesses and tutors had failed to do.

Fairleigh was reading and writing and actually adding and subtracting figures.

It boggled the mind.

And warmed the depths of his soul.

One of his deepest fears was that his daughter possessed her mother's unstable character and would never endeavor to improve her mind. Would never care a whit for anything other than life's little amusements—fashion, cards, and gossip.

And here Fairleigh was, writing letters. He pursed his lips in amusement. Letters to a sheep farmer, if he had to hazard a guess. But they were letters nonetheless.

He gazed at Georgiana's dark head, a flood of

warmth invading his breast. Her hair was so soft to the touch, he remembered, and had gleamed in the moonlight. His body tightened in remembrance, and as if on cue he wondered if she nurtured his child within her. It was a thought that reoccurred as frequently as the chiming of the clock in the front salon. He longed to protect her, comfort her, tell her not to worry, that he would always watch over her. And yet he knew she was the only woman who didn't need or want protection or comfort. He shook his head.

Her quill stilled and she looked up.

Large, dark eyes met his, and his breath caught in his throat. She was so dearly familiar to him. He realized he had known her longer than any other person in his life. He had at least known and seen goodness—only goodness—in one person. And she loved him in a fashion—although not as she had loved Anthony. He was forced to admit that he had unconsciously known she had cared deeply for his person for a very long time. He had been lucky, after all.

And the evil he had endured became less important.

He cleared his throat. "It's my understanding you two ladies have been slaving in here for nearly two hours."

Fairleigh jumped up and ran to him. "Papa! Oh, this is ever so much more fun than those horrid primers old Beetleface used to make me study."

"I daresay it must be. Just how many sheep have you decided to add to our flock?"

"Silly. Georgiana and I discuss everything

with Mr. Brown before we decide on numbers. But did you know a Southdown's wool is softer than the new Leicester's? But if you breed the two together—"

"So you're discussing breeding now?" He shook his head.

"Only a little," Georgiana said quickly. "A very little."

"Hmmm. Well, perhaps it's a good thing I stuck my head in here."

"Why did you come, Papa? Georgiana and I do not like to be interrupted during our afternoon duties." Fairleigh had an imperious look on her face. "At least that's what Georgiana always says."

"Then I suppose I shall just have to go out in the garden and eat worms all by myself," he replied.

A huge smile broke out on Georgiana's face. A smile he hadn't seen in a long while.

"I see." Georgiana winked at his daughter, "That was always our secret signal around adults to suggest we go fishing."

"Oh, well then, I want to go and eat worms too," Fairleigh said. "But I won't really have to eat them, will I? I mean, I will if you do, but I don't think I'll like it."

Quinn laughed and picked up his daughter in his arms and kissed the end of her nose. "Only the one who catches the least fish is forced to eat the worm."

She shrieked with laughter. "It won't be me, Papa, or Georgiana." She bolted from his arms and ran to the door. "I'm going to get a head start."

He looked at Georgiana after Fairleigh's footsteps echoed from the hallway. He bowed and extended his arm. "You will join us, won't you?"

She shrugged helplessly and looked over her shoulder at an unfinished letter. "Perhaps I'd better not. These letters should go out today."

"When did you decide to take the weight of the world on your shoulders?"

She laughed. "Funny. I could ask you the same thing."

"And probably receive the same answer. Come, Georgiana, you did suggest diversions and adventure on occasion, did you not? And"—he leaned in and said with a conspiratorial air—"Gwendolyn was last seen headed this way. The lady, not the sow."

Georgiana smiled ruefully. "You know how to work on me too well."

"No. I just don't want to eat the worm, since my daughter's had too great a head start now."

"Oh," she replied, quickly stepping in front of him toward the door. "Don't you dare suggest I won't catch more fish than you."

It proved too hot for fishing. The tiny gnats were biting instead of the fish. And to add insult to injury, Oscar the otter made an appearance and seemed to snicker at them, his whiskers twitching, as he wiggled to the edge of the dark, cool depths of the pool and dove in expertly.

Fairleigh looked at her father expectantly and slapped at an insect on her red neck.

"Papa?"

"Yes, my love?"

"I have a proposition."

"Hmmm . . ."

"I might be willing to admit defeat and eat the tiniest bit of a worm if you'll allow me to go wading." She rushed on. "Not swimming, mind you, just walking near the reeds. It's really very shallow there. Oh Papa, it's so hot," she wailed.

He felt Georgiana's eyes on him. "And what would you be willing to do if I allowed you to go swimming instead of just wading?" He looked away from his daughter to encounter Georgiana's expression.

She was smiling at him.

"Oh, Papa, I'd do anything!" Fairleigh shouted with excitement, and bent to the task of untying her small boots.

"Be careful, dearest," Georgiana warned. "It's better to hear the conditions first. Your father sometimes had a way of offering people, me and his cousin Anthony especially, the very thing one most wants in exchange for things one doesn't want to do at all."

His hands clenched instinctively at the mention of Anthony's name and he frowned. What on earth did she mean? But there wasn't time to think. Fairleigh was already down to her shift, having wiggled free from her dress, and was now tossing her stockings willy-nilly over her shoulder and racing to the edge.

"Ohhh . . . the mud is cool and feels like heaven, Papa."

"Wait," he admonished, while struggling with his boots. "Don't go any deeper." He shucked off everything except his breeches and shirt and then dove into the lake. He surfaced and shook water from his hair and eyes.

A moment later, Georgiana came up for air nearby. She was laughing, and her coronet of braids had fallen, leaving her with childlike braids on each side of her head.

Drops of water clung to her long eyelashes and her thick concealing shift floated all around her. She tilted her face toward the sun, and a huge, innocent smile spread across her golden face. She rose up on her toes and revealed her willowy torso. The linen of her shift molded itself to her uptilted breasts and her small rib cage down to her sleek waist and the smooth slope of her abdomen—such an astonishingly fragile feminine form for someone he knew to be so strong.

My God. She looked almost exactly as she had used to look so long ago. Only now she was quite obviously no longer a girl. She had become a sleek, tantalizing woman.

She turned more fully toward him and he was struck by her beauty.

His groin constricted and he was grateful for the secrecy the water allowed, and the coolness of it.

"Papa, look—I can float." His daughter attempted the feat while Georgiana sunk back into the water and moved beside her. He waded over to them. His daughter's eyes were open, her expression one of complete bliss. A slight curl of happiness lurked in her lips.

And he vowed at that moment to make sure he

put that look on his daughter's face at least once a day from now on.

"You can see the birds so much better from here," Fairleigh said loudly, water clogging her ears. "Hold my hand, Papa. You too, Georgiana. I don't need you to hold me up."

They each held one of her hands and looked upward. Gazing at the deepening color of the afternoon sky, he remembered how they had used to escape the great house and do this almost every day in summer. Only then it had been Georgiana between the two boys—until Anthony would drag Georgiana under the surface and tickle her until she resurfaced and shrieked with glee.

His cousin had always been in love with her. Well, as in love as his reckless cousin could be.

And Georgiana had always preferred Anthony. She'd always laughed a little louder and a little longer with Anthony than with him.

Those childhood years were perhaps the only reason he hadn't challenged his cousin in London a decade ago when he'd last seen Anthony and had been on the verge of killing him.

At the time, it had appeared the only option to maintain his sanity.

Chapter 14

Georgiana looked disbelievingly at the tiny drops of blood on her shift and squeezed her eyes shut. She should be relieved, and yet she was not. She should be delirious. She was not. It was the shock, she supposed.

She had been late. But then that always happened when she was overly worried. So it should have been expected, but it had not been. She had convinced herself she was with child, and had taken a perverse amount of joy in it. If she couldn't have Quinn's love, then at least she would have a part of him, tangible proof that at one single moment in time they had shared passion. She'd tried to keep at bay her deep longing for a child, something she had not dreamed of ever having after Anthony died.

Well. It was not to be.

She should be glad.

But she was not.

And now she would be forced to find a moment of privacy with him and suffer the extraordinary embarrassment of having to inform him that their actions had not produced a child, thereby reminding him of what had happened between them.

Something he clearly regretted, given the amount of time he spent escorting her beautiful friend Grace Sheffey and the other widows about the countryside to various amusements.

She closed her eyes and hoped his relief would not be too obvious when she told him.

Well, those who dabbled with letting loose their tightly bound secrets and long-held desires always suffered the consequences.

She avoided him most of the day, until her emotions were as taut as a child's when facing the tooth drawer.

Quinn had taken all the widows, or Beauties, as he still insisted on calling them, on a long tour of ancient druid burial grounds. Georgiana had declined, pleading some excuse, and then she had had to suffer watching her friends return two by two, each pair laughing as they arrived, explaining their plan of leaving Quinn and Grace alone together.

Ata was the last to return, with Rosamunde, who glanced at Georgiana with a knowing expression while Ata prattled on about her plan.

Rosamunde surreptitiously stole to Georgiana's side while Ata dismounted and gave an enormous apple to her mount. "If Grace ends up hurt again, I won't forgive you," Rosamunde whispered to her.

"I'm certain we already had this conversation," Georgiana replied quietly.

Rosamunde pulled her to the other side of her

own horse. "When are you going to force the issue?"

"I did. I told him."

"What? Wait a minute, I have to hear this. Ata," Rosamunde called out to her grandmother-in-law, "I swear I can hear Caro and Henry crying up at the great house. Would you be so good as to see to them for a moment while I take a peek at these two horses Georgiana is so intent on purchasing?" Rosamunde winked at her.

"Take your time, Rosamunde," Ata replied out of sight, not waiting for another invitation to spend time with her beloved great-grandchildren. "Oh, I do so love babies. I hope Grace and Quinn have a child by next summer. It would be so delightful for Caro and Henry to have a friend. And just think, maybe in another two decades we could plan a wedding between the two families . . . finally."

Rosamunde rolled her eyes. And Georgiana couldn't help but laugh in the agony of the moment.

Ata left a moment later, humming a wedding march.

"You know you can't listen to Ata, dearest," Rosamunde said. "I love her and I would never let anyone say a word against her, but she is wrong in this case. You know it and I know it. And if no one else can see it, then they are blind fools. Now what on earth did you tell him?"

"What you never had the courage to tell Luc last year."

"You didn't . . ." Rosamunde said, wide-eyed.

"I did. And he didn't return the favor."

"What?" Rosamunde said, disbelieving.

"Not everyone is allowed a fairy-tale ending, Rosamunde."

"I don't believe it. You told him *you love him* and he said nothing?"

"No. He called me his 'dear, dear, Georgiana' when I said it, and *then* he said nothing."

"I'll kill him." Rosamunde pulled her down the long aisle of horse stalls when a stable hand appeared nearby. "Or better yet, I'll let Luc kill him. He's been dying for any excuse to do it. When we returned home the night of the ball he cursed a blue streak and immediately began sharpening two dueling swords, a medieval saber and a nasty-looking little dagger." She shook her head.

Georgiana suppressed a sigh.

"Georgiana?"

"Yes?"

"He hasn't taken any . . . well, any *liberties* with you, has he?"

She refused to look away from Rosamunde's beautiful, pale aquamarine eyes.

"I'll kill him myself, after all."

"We're not talking about this, Rosamunde. It was my choice."

"With that little dagger, in his sleep."

"Tell me you didn't do the very same thing with Luc St. Aubyn last summer, when you—"

"That was different," Rosamunde interrupted, then stopped. A soft smile appeared at the edges of her mouth. "Oh, perhaps it isn't different. But—"

A clatter of hooves sounded from the outside,

and within moments the silhouetted forms of Quinn and Grace appeared at the stable entrance.

Georgiana pulled Rosamunde close. "I beg of you to find an excuse to escort Grace to the hall. I need a word with Quinn."

Rosamunde's eyebrows rose.

"Please . . ."

"I will, if only to allow you a chance to strangle him in private. If you don't, I'll return this week to do the job myself."

Georgiana entered the nearest stall, to ostensibly look over the big-boned gray hunter that had arrived that morning from the famed Godolphin stables nearby. The sweet smell of alfalfa assailed her. She loved the scent. It reminded her of springtime and racing across meadows and along the beaches. She looked at the horse's intelligent eyes and ran her hands down his deeply sloping shoulders, down his front legs, and then to the rear legs. She examined a swelling on one of the haunches.

Feminine voices drifted away from the stable, leaving only the calming munching sounds of the horses and an occasional pawing of a hoof.

The stall darkened and she knew Quinn stood at its entrance. "Do you think it will heal?"

"I don't know. I doubt it . . . It's such a shame. I first saw him not three months ago," she said, "and at the time I wished there was an excuse to purchase him for Penrose. He had the smoothest gaits."

"He was kicked by another horse?" Quinn entered the stall.

"Yes," she said, "in a pasture at Godolphin."

Quinn's long, tapered fingers stroked the gelding's flank, stopping at the inflammation.

"The stable master was debating what to do with him when I went by last week to find a hunter for you," she explained.

"Mr. Brown told me." He came to stand beside her and leaned in to capture her attention. "Georgiana . . . you have always placed the needs of others and this estate above your own. And you do it without ever drawing attention to the fact. I suspect no one has ever thanked you." He grasped her hands. "I would thank you."

She was so filled with embarrassment and anxiety over what she had to tell him that she released his hands and ignored the compliment as she always did. "I found a lovely bay mare. She's in the next stall for you to look over."

"Yes, I know. I tried her earlier and told the man I would take her."

"I'll arrange for this one to be returned, then."

"No—"

"You don't have to keep him just because I had him brought here. It makes no sense. I had thought maybe he wasn't as badly injured as I originally thought, but clearly . . ." She stopped when their hands accidentally brushed on the horse's flank and Georgiana dropped hers.

"I already paid the man, Georgiana," he said, his deep voice soothing her. "He's staying here. I will personally see to him. I'd forgotten the peace I'd always found tending the animals here."

"I have to tell you something," she said in a

rush before her courage failed her. "I'm . . . I'm not with child. I, well, I . . . am certain."

During the long pause that followed, Georgiana didn't have the courage to look at him. Instead she stroked the length of the gelding's leg and urged the animal to raise it so she could examine the frog of the hoof. "Well, at least his hooves are sound. Perhaps if we applied compresses to—"

"Georgiana," he interrupted her.

She ignored him. ". . . to the swelling twice a day, he might recover in time."

A shadow passed over her and his arm tugged at hers to release the animal.

"Georgiana, look at me."

She did.

"I'm sorry," he said quietly.

"What?" .

"I'm sorry you're not with child."

His expression was so remote, she couldn't tell if he was telling the truth or not. He couldn't possibly really want a child with her.

"I can see you don't believe me," he murmured. "But you see, the truth of the matter is that I'd hoped to have a child of my body one day."

"I don't understand. Fairleigh—"

"—is my daughter," he said fiercely. "Always has been, and always will be. I love her with every fiber of my being and would kill anyone who brought her an ounce of harm. But, she is not . . ."

Georgiana stood stock-still.

"I know you will not say a word of this to anyone, Georgiana. I only tell you this so you understand I was telling you the truth. And I still implore you to marry me. What we did . . . What I did to you . . . It makes no difference that there is no child."

"No," she said. "We already discussed this. And I'm begging you to drop it." She circled to the other side of the horse. She looked over the gelding's back and met his gaze. "Please," she begged.

"Because of Anthony," he said. "It's always because of Anthony, isn't it?"

She concentrated on her hand stroking the horse's withers. "Yes. I won't settle for a marriage of convenience—not when I had so much more with *Anthony*." The horse snorted and stomped one hoof. And Georgiana had the nearly irresistible urge to laugh or cry hysterically. Well, at least she had had Anthony's love. It might not keep her warm at night, but at least she knew one man had loved her. And he provided a convenient excuse for not marrying a man who wanted her solely out of a misplaced sense of duty. But it would surely haunt her the rest of her days. She had to take one last chance. Rosamunde would have. "Quinn, I—"

Grace Sheffey's lilting voice sounded from the stable aisle. "Georgiana? Quinn? Oh dear. Excuse me, sir, can you tell me if his lordship left the stable? Or Miss Wilde, or rather Lady Ellesmere— Lady Georgiana?"

Oh God. Even Grace didn't know how to address her. What was she doing here? She didn't belong here. She was the steward's daughter, and disfigured, and everything wrong. She turned suddenly to Quinn. "I won't keep you. Thank you for taking the horse. You always were kindhearted, always taking pity on injured creatures. I thank you." She bobbed a curtsy and exited the stall.

Exited his life.

Anthony. . . . "Not when I had so much more with Anthony."

Would he never be rid of him? Even in death Anthony was determined to take everything he possibly could. Quinn flexed his hands convulsively and tried to ignore the pounding in his head. The pain had come suddenly and was nearly blinding. This headache was no different from the others he occasionally had suffered. Threads of pain needled their way into the radius of his vision while he escorted Grace Sheffey back to the great house.

"Would you mind if we rested for a moment, here?" Grace asked. A very old, crumbling stone bench, overlooking the lower gardens, was in front of them. "It's so hot today."

"Of course not," he replied, grateful for the shade of the beech tree beside them.

She looked off into the distance, unconsciously exhibiting her elegant profile. "Quinn . . ." she murmured shyly, "I've received a letter from a dear friend in town—the Duchess of Kendale."

He breathed in as slowly and evenly as possible to ease the ache blistering his mind.

"And she has invited me to a house party at the

duke's magnificent estate just twenty miles past the outskirts of London."

"Kendale Hall?"

"Yes, that's the one." She smoothed a wrinkle in her gown. "And Christina mentioned that she would be sending an invitation to you as well. The invitation is for five weeks from today."

"And you would like to go." It was not a question.

"Why, yes, I would." She hesitated and continued softly, "With you."

His head was ready to explode and he closed his eyes to lean against the coarse bark of the tree. A vision of Anthony's face rose up, his innocent grin taunting him. And suddenly all Quinn wanted to do was forget. Really forget the past. Start anew. With someone who was not in any way connected—someone who was dignified and untouched by complication, someone who could truly offer a life of friendship and quiet companionship.

"Grace," he said, "I would be honored to accompany you. I will arrange for two carriages. Will Ata and the others join the party?"

"Actually, no." A flush bloomed on her cheeks. "I was thinking we might take only one carriage."

What?

Her smile was forced. "Quinn, I know we've not known each other a long time. But since the day we met I sensed we were very much alike—of one mind, so to speak. We, both of us, might enjoy the quiet contentment an arranged union could bring." Her small hands were fidgeting in her lap.

"But then I should not presume you feel the same way I do. It's just that in the past year or so, I've decided that life is too short to waste time waiting and wondering."

"My dear Countess," he replied. "Are you honoring me with a proposal of marriage?"

"No." She laughed. "I'm not so bold. But I will go so far as to say that I would not reject you if *you* were to ask."

She was so pretty, sitting there, patiently waiting for him to ask her to marry him.

"My dear," he said gently, lowering himself from the bench and reaching for her slim hand. The pain slammed back into his head as soon as his knee dropped to the ground. "You do me a great honor, Grace. And I would be the happiest of men if you would, indeed, agree to consider becoming my bride. But to be fair, I feel it necessary to remind you that it would include taking on the role of stepmother to my, ahem, scrape-grace daughter."

Grace was smiling, the flush of embarrassment gone. "Well, I suppose I should also tell you that I am an only child and do not have any living relatives. I would hate for your daughter to be as alone as I was as a child. I would hope to provide her with a sibling, if you agree." She hurried on. "And there is just one last thing . . ."

"Whatever you desire."

"I would prefer that we not announce our engagement until we depart for the house party."

"Why ever not?"

"Because I have also learned not to make hasty decisions. I admit I wanted to know if you desired to remarry one day. But now that we've been honest with each other, there is no rush."

She was everything rational and good. "Grace, I'm not certain I deserve you, but I shall endeavor to always ensure your happiness, my dear."

She fingered her pearls and smiled. "I feel precisely the same way," she murmured.

"We shall do very well together," he said, and then kissed her fingers. They were so soft, so unlike Georgiana's in every possible way.

His head pounded viciously, and he was irritated that he had thought of Georgiana at this moment.

His head continued to pound intermittently for the next week. The pain finally receded at dinner one evening while he watched Grace radiating with happiness to his left and Ata needling his aunt to his right. Georgiana always sat at the opposite end of the long table, obscured by a large arrangement of flowers.

Tonight the Duke of Helston was at table and kept staring at him as though he wanted to debone Quinn with the silver carving knife. His bride appeared ready to follow up with tar and feathers. Thank the Lord for Mr. Brown and Sarah Winters. The former ensured joviality at every turn, while the latter added a measure of civility.

When he could stand it no further, Quinn rose and dropped his napkin on the table. "If you will excuse us, ladies, His Grace and Mr. Brown are invited to retire for a few moments to my study. If you agree, Georgiana, we shall rejoin all of you in the front salon shortly."

Luc St. Aubyn didn't wait for her answer. Instead he growled and removed from the room. Mr. Brown followed suit after a wink at Ata, who pretended not to notice.

"What the bloody hell are you doing, Ellesmere?" Luc St. Aubyn seethed with ill humor while he prowled around the edges of the book-lined study.

Mr. Brown laughed. "This is all so familiar, I feel like I'm watching a Shakespearean comedy."

"This is no comedy, old man," Luc muttered. "It's a bloody tragedy of epic proportions, and he's playing the villain to perfection. Well, Ellesmere?"

"I believe I owe you a formal apology, Helston." Quinn moved next to his desk and looked down at the floor. A large number of bottles stood there. "We agreed on French brandy. Five cases. I secured ten. And a case of Armagnac for your grandmother."

Mr. Brown rubbed his hands together. "Oh, well done, my lord."

"Don't you dare show him an inch of gratitude, Brownie," Helston said, still frowning. "I'm sorry for the day I suggested you for his employ."

"That's all right, Luc," Mr. Brown replied. "It was worth it—monetarily and for the diversion. Lord Ellesmere is proving even more entertaining than you were."

Quinn stiffened. "I don't know what you find so amusing, Mr. Brown. Would you care for some brandy?"

"Armagnac, if you please."

Quinn raised his brows. "I'm sorry, but I only have the brandy. Ata hid all the Armagnac, for some odd reason."

He poured two glasses of brandy and then turned to the gentlemen—one tall and menacing, the other portly and bald. He lit a cheroot for himself and raised it in mock salute. "To your health, gentlemen."

"We certainly won't drink to yours," the duke muttered, while John Brown's lips twitched.

"Come now, Luc, I've never seen you so unforgiving," Mr. Brown said. "But then I've always found that when one encounters one's mirror image, absolute disgust is inevitable."

Luc sputtered. "If you dare to suggest I'm anything like this, this dandified diplomat, I might have to kill you. After I kill him." The duke unleashed his obvious fury and crossed the space that separated them to stand toe-to-toe with Quinn. "Ellesmere, what makes you think I'll stand by and watch you toy with Grace Sheffey's affections while you dishonor your cousin's widow? You are nothing but a damned dog dressed up in finery." Luc retrieved his gloves from a pocket. "And since Anthony Fortesque isn't here to protect his wife's honor, I shall just have to stand in for him."

Every muscle froze within Quinn.

Mr. Brown had stopped laughing. "Luc?"

"Do you deny it, Ellesmere?"

"No."

"Well?"

Honor compelled Quinn to remain silent.

Helston slapped his gloves across his face. "Pistols or swords?"

Mr. Brown cleared his throat and looked at Quinn. "So, lad, it appears congratulations are in order. Which lass will you be escorting down the aisle before getting yourself killed?"

"Swords," Quinn said, quietly.

"Answer Brownie's blasted question, you bastard."

He resisted the urge to punch Helston, if only because the desire to maim himself was greater. "Grace—but I'm honoring her request to remain undeclared for the next few weeks."

"And Georgiana?" Helston barked.

Quinn paused, his hands clenched behind him. "I would ask for your aid."

"What?" Helston appeared ready to explode. "Do you think anything could tempt me to help you?"

"Now, Luc. Hear him out," pleaded Mr. Brown. "There's clearly something more at stake here than you know."

"I don't care if all the stakes in China are involved. The only question is how to dispose of his body when we're through, old man."

Quinn had considered every option and hadn't been able to think of another plan that didn't involve the duke. "She won't accept what I've arranged," he said quietly.

Finally, blessed silence.

"I've found a suitable property for her—one overlooking the sea in Godrey Towans. A second, smaller property adjoins it. I know she was intrigued by the smaller property, for I observed her perusing the documents describing it. This morning I purchased the larger estate for her and the adjoining property for her parents. The properties combined contain several hundred acres of pasture and farmland and a few acres of woodland. There is a good mill—Trehallow mill—nearby, and—"

"Good Lord," whispered Mr. Brown. "He's gone and purchased Trehallow for her. Why, it was once the most prosperous estate in all of St. Ives. Granted, the great house might need a bit of refurbishing—it hasn't been inhabited for many years, I don't think, since the Earl of Crowden died without issue. This is extraordinary—"

"I told you not to condescend to him, Brownie," Helston said gruffly.

"As I was saying, she would never accept it from me. I want you"—Quinn forced himself to relax his fists and expression—"to tell her you've arranged it all. I'm certain you can think of a suitable excuse, Helston. Frankly, I don't care what you tell her and her father. I was able to overcome the legal barriers, and managed to have her name listed on the deed. The smaller property, which will eventually devolve to Georgiana's brother, Grayson Wilde, is in Mr. Wilde's name."

Helston looked at Mr. Brown with disgust. "Observe the man before you, Brownie. Here stands a man willing to pay through the nose to save his neck."

The duke then turned toward him. "I suppose you think this relieves you of ingesting metal before breakfast tomorrow?"

"I find I cannot deprive you of enjoying the reality of your great imagination, Helston."

"Now, now, lads," Mr. Brown murmured. "If you think I'll allow either of you near a sword or a pistol, you're out of your minds. You may be hotheaded young bloods fueled by a misguided sense of honor, but I'm a practical old man who always thinks of the consequences." He scratched his bald head. "Luc, your grandmother would fry my liver for supper if I let either of you near a dueling ground."

"Brownie, you're a bigger coward than he is."

"You're absolutely right."

Helston turned his black gaze on Quinn. "If either Grace or Georgiana ends up hurt, I will hunt you down and—"

Quinn held up his hand wearily. "Look, are you willing to meet Mr. Wilde and Georgiana to discuss the transfer of the property or not?"

"It appears I have little choice in the matter." Helston held out his hand for the documents. "I'll see to reviewing these and meeting the Wildes tomorrow morning."

"They should not consider removing before the end of the month," Quinn continued. "I've arranged to have some improvements made before then."

"Come along, Brownie," Luc said, crossing to the door. "Perhaps my grandmother will allow you to strain her tea if you ask nicely enough. Shall I fetch you a mobcap and an apron?"

"Laugh all you like, lad. It's taken four decades to learn the proper way to court your grandmother and I don't have another forty in me to win back her favor should I lose it again." Brownie grinned. "And perhaps you've forgotten that if I get her in the proper mood, she might even offer up a bit of her Armagnac."

"Don't hold your breath, old man."

Quinn stubbed out the forgotten cheroot, and hoped Luc St. Aubyn was a man who knew how to lie convincingly when necessity demanded it. Grudgingly, he thought he might be able to count on the barbarian. In fact, Luc St. Aubyn might just be one of the few people he could trust in this damned world. And wasn't that just one more ironic proof that there was no sense of order in the universe?

Chapter 15

"Georgiana, you know there's really no need for you to be seeing to these sorts of things now," her mother said a fortnight later. She picked a remnant of cornstalk from her daughter's hair.

"I love working on the estate. It helps calm my mind. It's the only thing familiar amid all these changes." Georgiana buried her nose in the Carolina rose she had found on the cottage doorstep upon her return from the fields.

"I realize that, dearest. I can barely contain myself at times."

Her mother stroked her hair distractedly and then drew a letter from her apron. "A footman delivered a letter from Grayson this morning. He's finally been granted leave. His ship is due in at Portsmouth—Lord knows when, precisely, but he's coming."

Georgiana's heart swelled with relief. This was the small answer to her prayers. She added the rose to the vase filled with an assortment of roses now always present in her chamber.

Her mother touched her fingers on the vase.

"Miles Langdon has been a most considerate and constant friend lately, hasn't he?"

"Mama," Georgiana said. "You're not to read anything into it. I've known him my entire life and he was always very kind."

"Well, I do believe he's taken a fancy to you, my dear." Her mother moved the vase to the small, plain dressing table and indicated the bench. "Come, allow me to redo your hair."

Georgiana acquiesced. "There's no need, really."

"I would disagree. You must make a haughty impression on the potential servants we're to interview."

"Mama, it's all so ridiculous. I still can't feel comfortable with Papa's arrangements with the duke. I'm certain Luc St. Aubyn has laid out an absurd amount in addition to Father's portion from Quinn. And it's all because of my friendship with Rosamunde and Ata."

"And well he can afford it, my dear. These great men gamble amounts some nights that would take a family such as ours three lifetimes to acquire. You needn't feel guilty, you know. The duke will receive the vast majority of Trehallow's tenant rents as repayment, don't forget. If your father accepted the settlement, you, above anyone, know that it was all fair and good."

And she did know that. Father possessed more scruples than she. But that didn't mean she couldn't feel ill at ease.

"For once, all is falling into place as it should for us. Your father has finally been able to rest properly—and the benefit shows. And you shall be settled in a place befitting a proper marchioness—and everyone will forget everything Gwendolyn Fortesque said." Her mother brushed the tangles from her plain, dark brown hair. "With time and encouragement, Miles Langdon might even offer for you. With an estate such as Trehallow—well, it would be hard for a gentleman to do better. Especially a gentleman who is not the heir and one who is determined to stay in Cornwall, such as he."

Georgiana swallowed.

Her mother lowered her voice. "And you'll face none of the awkwardness of having to explain your deformities. He's shown he's willing to accept you as you are, my dearest Georgiana. And so handsome. You are a very lucky girl, indeed."

"Very lucky," Georgiana whispered, looking down at her scratched and sunburned arms.

"With a modicum more of luck, perhaps you'll even make me a grandmother by next year's harvest festival. I should like having a tiny, blond-haired Langdon for a grandchild." Her mother smiled. "And think of all the proper young ladies of the neighborhood who will take an interest in Grayson now. We shall just have to work on him during his leave to give up this hard life at sea. I can't bear the months of worry I suffer while he's away."

"Mama, but he loves it so."

"It's an impossibly cruel life. And when you have a child of your own, you'll see just how awful it is for a mother to watch her children leave. I feel so grateful you will always be near us, Georgiana. It will be such a comfort."

"Mama . . . just promise me you won't raise your hopes too high. You know I am happy just now. I'm not certain I will ever want to remarry. And now there will be no need. I am very lucky indeed."

Her mother tsked. "Come along. Let's see to the candidates. I understand from your father that Helston saw to them personally, also. I don't think this will take us long. It will be so nice to have a full complement of servants!"

Several hours and interviews later, Georgiana was grateful to Miles for saving her from additional exaltations of joy from her beloved mother. Mama was taking to her soon-to-be life of leisure as quickly and as loudly as the martins were taking to the enormous new triple-stacked house Georgiana had erected near the gardens to dispatch some of the insects that plagued every picnic.

"Are you certain riding won't cause you too much pain?" Miles asked gently as he escorted her to the mounting block.

Georgiana eased into the sidesaddle, hooking her bad right knee around the upright horn. "I've told you before that I ride all the time. There's no need to worry." She wished Miles would stop constantly mentioning her ugly limbs. He had no idea how much it irritated her. Would he ever understand that she pretended it never ailed her because she wanted desperately to be normal? Sometimes, but only very rarely, it worked.

"I've always liked that you don't complain, Georgiana," he murmured.

"Maybe you just don't know me well enough." She laughed. "I only complain on Saturdays."

"And why is that?"

"So I'll have something to repent on Sundays."

He grinned. "If that is all you have to repent, then you are nothing like my family." He swung up on his horse. "Where to?"

"The beach? For a race? But let's set a good wager."

His face lit up. "Racing and wagering? Clearly you've been spending too much time with my family, Georgiana."

"Perhaps I'm trying to become more like your family." She clucked at her mount.

He abruptly stopped his horse and looked at her shyly. "I should like it very much—or rather, I'm certain I would like it if . . . if, well, if you were part of my family." His face flushed beet red, the color clashing with his fair complexion.

She had never had the opportunity to flirt with gentlemen, and she became tongue-tied for a moment. Apparently Miles was as awkward at flirting as she. And she liked him all the better for it. "Miles Langdon, are you suggesting you would like me for a sister?"

"Lord, no. Got enough sisters to ensure a place for me in Bedlam." He continued on, their horses trotting behind the stables toward the path to the beach. "Nothing but trouble, sisters. But I was referring to—Hey, ho, wait up."

Georgiana broke into a canter to ease the jarring to her knee and to escape his suggestion. She called back over her shoulder to him. "Since I happen to adore your sisters, sir, your penalty if—or rather, *when*—I beat you will be high."

He caught up to her, laughing, and they both halted. "I beg of you—"

"No. You're in it but good now. If I win, you shall pick roses for Rosamunde every day for a fortnight—roses like the lovely ones you leave for me."

"What roses?" He wore a comical, owlish expression.

"You know very well which roses, but play the innocent if you wish."

"I'll never understand females." He rolled his eyes. "More importantly, let's discuss what I will receive when *I* win."

"One could never accuse you of modesty." She grinned. "Well, then. Name what you would like."

"Maybe I will. Blast it. Georgiana, I . . . oh, hang it all. Maybe I should like permission to talk to your father about what I would like." He didn't look like he wanted to do anything of the sort.

Oh, she thought faintly, she should know better than to dabble with flirtation. She dug the edge of her heel into her mount and burst forward into a gallop as soon as her horse's hooves touched Porthleven Sands. Flocks of coot and shoveler together with yellowlegs tangled into the sky above her, nearly obliterating her view for a moment.

She urged her horse on. Like a tight winch, she scissored her legs in the sidesaddle; her bad leg clenched around the upright horn, the other less injured limb pushed against the leaping horn. Her damaged, sinuous muscles screamed against the pain, and knotted.

"Georgiana! Georgiana!" She could barely make out his voice as the wind whistled past her ears.

The devil was in her now, and she would be damned forever if she didn't beat Miles.

Perverse. That was what she was. Perverse in the extreme. As she ignored the pain and drank in the sparkling beauty and tang of the sea, she wondered for an instant what was wrong with her. What made her run from every possible promise of happiness? What made her run from a chance to forget and begin anew, something she'd promised herself? It was all so unfair. She had a rut in her mind and couldn't deviate from it.

Well, she would—if it killed her. She gently eased back on the bit in her horse's mouth, and a moment later the other horse shot in front of her. Miles shouted with glee.

At the end of the crescent-shaped beach, he whirled around, his mount crow hopping to avoid the bubbling foam at the water's edge.

"I won! I won!" He shouted, unable to contain himself.

Georgiana laughed. "Careful. I'm not your sister, and I think you're supposed to be a bit more contrite when you best a lady, sir."

"But I *never* win." He appeared chagrined by his rash comment. "That is, I almost never win. I beat Fitz and sometimes even Phinn, but, well, what I mean to say is . . ."

He really didn't want to admit the obvious, so she did it for him. "What you mean to say is that you've never beaten a *girl*."

"That's it precisely—oh, hang it, Georgiana. You're supposed to let me play the knight in shining armor. Well, at least that's what my sisters do with their husbands."

Georgiana burst into laughter.

He jumped off his horse and eased her from the sidesaddle. She crumpled when her feet touched the sand, a cramp seizing her right leg.

"Oh!" she said, desperately trying to muffle the sound. She grabbed her thigh and knee and tried to push against the pain.

Miles dropped both horses' reins and dipped down beside her. "What is it?"

"I'm fine. Really. It's just a tiny cramp."

His face blanched as his gaze lowered. "Can I do anything? Shall I carry you to that log?"

"No. No. Just give me a minute." She discreetly rubbed the painful muscles, trying to appear collected while the stinging ache retreated bit by bit. She wished he wouldn't watch while she dug her fingers deeply into the muscles lying below the folds of her dark brown riding habit.

After long moments, the cramp released its hold on her.

"Does that happen often?" Miles's face was still pale.

"No." She should tell him the truth. "Only occasionally when I ride."

"Perhaps we should walk back, then?"

She nodded and he stood up to offer her his

hand. She looked up into his whiskey-colored eyes framed by dark blond brows, his pale hair ruffled by the breeze.

It was such a gorgeous day, not a cloud shadowed the sparkling perfection of the sea. Only the call of the numerous gulls and other birds disturbed their privacy. She placed her hand in his broader one and he helped her up.

"Georgiana?" He looked at her bashfully, his face just inches from her own. "May I kiss you?"

She blinked. "I suppose so."

Georgiana closed her eyes and tilted her head toward the sun. She felt a shadow fall over her face and then the light pressure of his lips against hers.

He didn't dare touch any other part of her. He didn't embrace her or rest his form against hers. He simply touched her lips tenderly for several long moments.

He kissed her quite properly—gently, never daring to part his lips as Quinn had so shockingly done to her. It was a proper kiss. A kiss that showed the respect he held for her. There was really only one problem with his kiss.

It felt like she was kissing her brother.

She stepped back and looked at him. His Adam's apple bobbed.

"Dash it all, Georgiana," he said in wonder. "That was lovely. Shall we have another go?"

She smiled but shook her head. "I really think we should return to the house. A physician is to come for Father and I want to hear what he has to say."

"Hang it, Georgie. The doctor can wait a few more minutes. Do say you'll allow me to kiss you again." He was gripping her shoulders now, but she wasn't worried at all.

Indeed, his excitement left her with a quiet joy welling within her. She was about to protest when he went ahead and kissed her again. Even if it was all a bit foolish, it felt good to know someone desired her, truly.

Suddenly Georgiana felt a hand on her shoulder and Miles was pulled away from her harshly.

"What on earth are you doing?" Quinn asked Miles, his eyes dark. "Step away from her if you know what's good for you. And by the by, when a lady shakes her head, it means *no*."

"Quinn!" Her heart churned. "You're supposed to be in London."

"Well, I rather think it's a good thing I'm not," he barked. "And you both have precisely half a minute before Ata, *Fairleigh*, and the rest of your friends"—he looked pointedly at her—"join us. However, you were not so fortunate with Grace. She didn't miss a moment of the display."

Georgiana looked over Miles's shoulder to see Grace, half turned and determinedly looking at a stand of trees. She couldn't bear to return her gaze to him. What must he think of her?

She was supposed to be so true to Anthony's love and memory that she would not ever consider anyone else. And yet she had repeatedly kissed Quinn—had *made love* to him even—and had refused him. And here she was with Miles Langdon a month later, kissing him on Perran Sands for the whole world to see. He must think her completely lacking in morals—or worse.

"Look lively, Miles," Quinn ordered. "Collect the horses. You have but a moment."

Georgiana stood there, unable to raise her eyes from the sand. "It's not what you think," she whispered.

"Really?"

"It was awkward. I know you'll think I'm foolish, but I couldn't hurt his feelings by refusing."

He raised a brow.

"Look, you above all people know how I feel—what my choice is. It's just that in this instance I made a mistake."

He looked closely at her and she resisted the urge to squirm.

"Unlike you," she breathed, "I seem to have a penchant for making mistakes."

"Don't fool yourself. I'm very capable of making mistakes."

Oh, he was always so kind to her. But then, since he didn't love her, of course, he wouldn't rail against her actions, wouldn't be jealous. He would just think badly of her, but never say it aloud.

A chorus of greetings floated to her ears and she finally looked up to find Ata, Elizabeth, Sarah, Fairleigh, and now Grace coming toward her.

"Georgiana!" Ata said waving. "Oh, I'm so glad we found you. Your mother asked us to tell you the doctor has arrived."

She took a few steps toward them, and the cramp returned to grip her leg with a vengeance.

She stumbled and closed her eyes against the pain before she righted herself. She would not let anyone see her discomfort.

She would not.

She breathed in slowly through her nose and reopened her eyes to wave at the ladies. "Oh, thank you, Ata! Is it not a beautiful day to take the air? You must walk along the beach. There are so many birds, and Fairleigh will enjoy it so."

She took a tentative step forward and the cramp ripped through her thigh down to her twisted knee, and she thought she might just lose consciousness. If she could just reach the log or the earthen berm that fronted the sand. She took another step or two and her slipper caught on some half-hidden seaweed.

Large hands gripped her waist before she fell. "Lean on me," Quinn commanded while wrapping an arm around her. He half carried her to the berm.

Thankfully, Ata's party was distracted by Fairleigh's interest in a lesser yellowlegs nest she had discovered.

"A cramp?" His voice was low, concerned.

She nodded.

"Can you ride?"

"I don't think so." A fresh wave of tight pain crawled along the corded muscle when she attempted to flex her foot. "No, I can't," she admitted, barely able to breathe.

"Well, then, I'll send them all away and help you back to Little Roses," he said, his eyes hooded. "Or would you prefer Miles?"

She wanted to cry. He should be raging at her. He should be chastising her. He should be disgusted.

But he was not. He was as kind and patient as always. Only now the veil she had sensed upon his return to Penrose two months ago had fallen over his emotions again.

Miles appeared with the horses in hand.

"Georgiana?" Quinn asked softly.

"You," she whispered. "I want *you* . . . to help me." She just couldn't deny herself.

"Take the horse back to the stable, Miles," Quinn ordered. "Georgiana and I must confer on estate business."

"What?" Miles asked, confused. "But I was—"

"And I would ask you to tell Mr. Brown to send down the architectural drawings I've forgotten. We've much to discuss about the proposed new boathouse here."

Miles stared at him and then at her. "What the devil—"

"What's this about a boathouse?" Ata stumbled in the sand in the high-heeled half boots she favored. "Grace, you didn't tell me Quinn was planning a boathouse. Oh, I long for a sail. It's been an age since Luc took us out on *Caro's Heart*."

"Quinn?" Grace looked so pretty, tendrils of her pale blonde hair dancing in the breeze. Her blue eyes were so trusting.

"I've ordered the yacht out of drydock and the boathouse is to be reconstructed."

The ladies chattered amongst themselves with excitement while he stepped closer to Grace and whispered something to her. Grace nodded and turned to rejoin Ata and the others.

"Come, Ata. Let's go back and find the plans ourselves." Grace added, "And this new hat is useless against the sun. I need my parasol."

"Of course, my dear. Come along Elizabeth, Sarah. Will you collect Fairleigh, Grace?" A mischievous light appeared in Ata's eyes. "Oh, Miles. Do wait a moment. I fancy the idea of riding that lovely animal."

"Ata," Quinn said with a smile. "That horse is not safe for you."

"Nonsense," she replied. "I'm an accomplished horsewoman."

"I don't doubt it," he replied. "But you see, I'm afraid I won't be able to face your grandson or Mr. Brown if they see you on that horse."

"What?" she fumed. "Luc has absolutely no say in what I do or don't do. And that other man you mentioned has even less say."

"Understood. But I'm rather attached to my internal organs, and I'd hoped you'd developed a certain fondness for them as well."

She began to giggle. "And pray, what do your intestines have to do with my riding this horse, Quinn?"

"They've indicated they will tie me to a tree with them if I allow you anywhere near my horses."

"This is abominable," she sputtered. "Utterly outrageous. Just because I, perhaps, just perhaps, mind you, have had the misfortune to become unseated on occasion due to several unrelated, unfortunate circumstances, doesn't mean I am not an outstanding horsewoman."

Georgiana made the mistake of shifting her weight and a blaze of pain shot through her again. Her whole body convulsed. Quinn glanced at her out of the corner of his eye.

"I have a hogshead of very good French wine, which will be yours if you do not get on that horse," he said in a placating tone.

"And the use of your phaeton?"

"And my best driver, Ata."

A huge grin broke out on her face. "Oh, Quinn! You are very kind! I adore driving as much as riding. I'm holding you to your promise, you know." Ata left with the others in her wake.

"You're in for it now," Georgiana murmured despite the pain.

"What?"

"She's wrecked every single one of Luc's carriages," Georgiana replied.

"Christ," he said under his breath. "I shall have Mr. Brown put locks on the carriage house."

The moments dragged while Miles remounted and the widows and Quinn's daughter threaded their way back up the short hill, out of their view.

"Is it the calf muscle or the thigh? Or is it the knee joint? Let me ease you."

"Absolutely not," she said, trying not to be so obvious with her desire to clench and release her muscles repeatedly.

"Can you stand?"

She stood up and then immediately sat back down, her lips tightened against the twisting pain.

"Come," he said, "let me help you."

She couldn't stand it anymore. She dug the heels of her hands along the length of her knotted thigh and closed her eyes. A burst of white-hot pain seared her leg. Oh God, she'd never felt anything like this. She should have known better than to race.

He brushed her fingers away and placed his large hands over her riding habit. His wide finger span bracketed her limb. She tried not to bend over in agony. He firmly gripped her and steadily applied more pressure. Amazingly, the force of his hands, while painful, released the deeper ache beyond and she prayed he wouldn't let go.

"Oh God." She sighed. "Please don't move."

"Do you trust me, Georgiana?"

"You know I do," she whispered.

He released her and quickly moved his hands under the hem of her heavy riding habit. His hands glided up her ankles and calves, past the ribbon tied to hold up her stockings, along her knee and beyond, all the way to the source of her agony. He worked her limb with his deft, strong fingers, always kneading deeply the bunched, rigid muscle.

And each time she thought he was going to stop and the cramp would return—for now it seemed it would never recede—she would nearly faint with longing for him not to stop.

But he did not. He seemed to sense the horrid, raw pain, and for once she couldn't pretend she was all right. His hands moved higher and higher, trying to find the end of the knotted muscle, until they were closing in on the most intimate place on her body. And she simply didn't care what he did to her at that point, as long as he didn't stop.

Her fingers dug into the sandy soil behind her as she leaned back. Who was she fooling? She would never be free from pain. She would never be free from wanting him. She would never be able to fully put the past behind her. She was disfigured forever because of wanting him. And he had claimed her forever as his when he had lain with her.

She felt something soft on her thickly scarred knee and opened her eyes. He was kissing her leg in broad daylight while his fingers worked their magic on her thigh. He stopped and stared at the vivid ugliness. And then lowered his mouth again and caressed her limb with his beautiful lips. And suddenly she felt a drop of water. A tear had fallen on her knee.

"Don't worry, darling," he said hoarsely, not looking up. "I won't stop until the pain is gone. I promise I will make it go away."

His words and kisses were more tortuous than the pain, for they were a reminder of everything she craved and would never have after she left. And the meaning behind the tear—pity—burned a trail of hurt deep within her. She shuddered.

At some point the pain became intertwined with rolling waves of relief. And many minutes later the waves of relief began to change into waves of pleasure. He continued to murmur promises as he rested his hollowed cheek against her knee and slowly ratcheted back the pressure in his hands.

She gripped a large bunch of tall grasses to stop herself from reaching forward and burying her fingers in his hair, which had grown longer. The many dark layers glinted in the lengthening rays of the sun. His hair would be soft, and if she leaned just a little closer she would be able to catch the scent of him. She held onto the grass even more tightly and swallowed against the burn of gathering tears.

He finally glanced up at her. "Georgiana," he whispered. "It's all right. Cry if you have to."

"I'm not crying." She angrily brushed at her eyes and cheeks with the heel of one of her hands.

"I know," he said. "You never did when we were young. Even when you fell from that tree. I've never seen you cry. You—"

"I've cried," she interrupted, detesting his pity. "You've just never seen it. I cried at Anthony's funeral."

"Of course," he replied, suddenly distant.

"Oh, why do you do that whenever I say his name? Why do you hate Anthony so?" She couldn't stop the words from slipping out. "He never did anything to hurt you."

His hands stilled and she wondered why for one time in her life she just couldn't refrain from saying something the instant it entered her mind.

He dropped his hands away from her and now she really did feel like crying.

"I don't hate him." He paused. "It's just that I wish I could have everything I have in my life now with the exception of having known him. But that," he said cryptically, "would be impossible. I know you don't understand."

"Explain it to me." She watched as her hand, of its own accord, reached out and stroked his head. "Please."

The sunlight caught the deep green edge of one of his eyes, and his pupil became smaller. "I've debated for so long the merits and disadvantages of relating the facts surrounding . . ."

"Surrounding what?" she prompted when he stopped.

"I had thought I should leave it in a letter to be opened upon my death. But then it might be better left unsaid, for it would not change anything. It's just that I have lived my entire life paying homage to the notion of the importance of truth. And yet I am living a lie."

A sense of calm blanketed her and for once she didn't urge him to speak. She wasn't sure she wanted to know what he might say.

"And I had promised myself I wouldn't tell you. I don't want to sully the memories you hold so dear. But, this part of his life did not concern you, had nothing to do with you, so it cannot hurt you."

"Quinn . . . what is it?" She insisted faintly. "Now you must tell me."

"You see, I love Fairleigh and I don't want her to be raised by Cynthia's parents or Gwendolyn if something should happen to me."

Oh God. This was going to be very bad. "Fairleigh? What has she to do with Gwendolyn?"

He stared at her for a moment and then his gaze drifted to the sky as the shadow of a wild falcon passed over his harsh features. "Gwendolyn is Fairleigh's true grandmother."

Georgiana jumped up. She had to move. She limped a few paces toward the sea and stopped, a deep ache invading her heart as she gazed at the dark, swirling undulations of the churning sea beyond the shoreline.

It couldn't be true. She closed her eyes against the pain.

But of course it was true. She clenched her hands. "Did he get her with child while you were married to her?" She would not turn around to look at him.

"I want you to promise me that if anything should happen to me that you will be Fairleigh's guardian. I shall have a solicitor draw up the documents."

She turned to him slowly. "Did he? Did he get her with child before or after your marriage?"

He ignored her question. "You will care for her, love her, as if she was your own, won't you, Georgiana? For you loved him, you said you did. And she would at least be a reminder of the man you loved."

She closed her eyes again. She had been blind. She, the artist . . . the one who knew the Fortesque eyes so well. She unconsciously touched the outside of her pocket, which hid the Lover's Eye brooch she had finally found on her pillow in her sanctuary at Loe Pool. The shape and slope of Fairleigh's eyes were like both Fortesque men but her blonde hair was exactly like Anthony's. She even knew Quinn's wife had had auburn hair. She felt so foolish, so blind.

"And because you know the truth, I won't have to tell anyone else. I don't want to leave Fairleigh at the mercy of Gwendolyn or Cynthia's parents or some unknown cousin next in line."

"It was after you were married, wasn't it?" she whispered, thinking of Fairleigh's age. "My God. Anthony had an affair with your wife right after your marriage."

"It doesn't matter."

"It does matter." In her mind, she guessed the truth. Anthony had always been jealous of Quinn because he had known how much she loved Quinn. But until now she hadn't realized how much Anthony had been secretly tortured by that jealousy. Quinn had always been a little bit better at everything than Anthony and she. And her love of Quinn had probably been the last thing to bring Anthony's jealousy to the boiling point.

He came up behind her but did not touch her. She could feel a hint of the warmth of his body radiating along her back.

"Will you, then? Will you promise to care for her if I die?"

"What about Grace? If you marry her, she would be Fairleigh's stepmother."

"You know it would be a marriage of convenience. The child of a former wife might not be something Grace would wish for should I die. I hate the idea of my beautiful daughter being considered a burden. I want her to feel love every day of her life." He touched her waist gently and kissed the top of her head. "Grace will most likely bear her own children. And no matter how many times you suggest she would never show preferential treatment to children of her own body, you will not convince me. You have said you will never marry . . . although I am wondering if perhaps this revelation changes things in your mind. I'm sorry to have hurt you. It was never my intention." He rested his hands on her shoulders. "Georgiana, it's obvious my cousin loved you deeply. There was no ulterior motive to his love for you. It was pure. But perhaps you will reconsider Miles now that you know the truth."

She thought she just might be ill, and was grateful he could not see her face. "Miles is a good friend. But I will never marry him." She followed the path of a flock of swallows soaring inland. "And I've always known the flaws in Anthony's character. I just hadn't realized they were as terrible as the rumors from town suggested at the time. I married him despite his faults just as he married me despite mine. And no, don't try to be kind and say I don't have any. We all have faults. But as you said, Anthony loved me without an ulterior motive—as I loved him. I'm only sorry— horribly sorry—for what he did to you. It was unforgivable," she whispered.

"Well, then, will you answer my question?" He turned her so she was facing him, her back now to the sea. "You are the only one who would love Fairleigh as much as I do."

"I love her already." She held her hands behind her back to stop herself from reaching for him. "I would consider her the daughter of my heart."

He kissed the top of her head and she felt it all the way down to her boots.

And in Quinn's heart?

Well . . .

Her words still echoed in his mind.

"Anthony loved me . . . as I loved him."

Chapter 16

Quinn's List

October 7—to do
- *arrange for pond to be dug at Trehallow*
- *inspect new greenhouse*
- *construct Portuguese beehives*
- *see to falcon mews*
- *last tour of house with carpenters*

- *meet with the devil*

It was amazing what money could do very quickly when it was offered in nearly obscene amounts, Quinn thought, while gazing at the gleaming panes of the enormous greenhouse now winging out from the south side of Trehallow. A swarm of workers crawled over the last remaining details of the beautiful addition.

He turned to the far north and with great satisfaction watched another group of men hammering in the distance at the last of the two revitalized barns and new falcon mews. A brood of raptors would bring Georgiana much delight.

"Confound it," Luc St. Aubyn muttered as he walked up to him from the direction of the stable. "And how precisely am I to explain away all this new construction to Georgiana? You said it was a *small* greenhouse. This looks like bloody Versailles." The two gentlemen began a tour of the property, walking toward the barns.

"I'm certain, with your superior way with words, you'll find a suitable explanation."

"I've about stretched the limits of my imagination, Ellesmere," Helston said. "Her father's hangdog, knowing eyes are upon me already to such a degree I'm afraid I will confess everything in a moment of weakness. He's like a damned Catholic priest."

"Actually, I think it's pretty fair." Quinn smiled. "If I have to face Brown's annoying looks each time I hand him a new demand for payment, I don't see why you shouldn't have to face Mr. Wilde. If you remember, you were the one who sent Mr. Brown to me—*and* your grandmother—*and* the other beauties in her club."

Luc sputtered. "I don't know what you're talking about. I did you a favor."

"A convenient favor." A few moments later they entered the new mews, empty of falcons still. Quinn wasn't sure yet how he would acquire the raptors. It would take time.

"And what is this?" Helston asked with no small amount of disgust. "An enormous chicken coop? I'll never be able to account for it."

"It's for birds of prey. Georgiana is fond of them."

The duke shook his head and muttered something about "complete pushovers" while he marched past him. They made their way to the adjacent barn, which was wholly completed.

At the entry, something touched Quinn's boot and he looked down to find a marmalade-colored cat rubbing against his ankles.

"I see you've even acquired a barn cat," Helston said, biting back a smile.

The cat began purring.

"No." Quinn sneezed. "I don't like cats."

"Well, my friend, it appears the feeling is not entirely mutual." Luc bit back a smile. "At least a cat will be easier to explain than if you had ordered a stable full of horses and a pasture full of oxen."

"The animals arrive tomorrow."

Luc shook his head and uttered an oath.

The cat stretched up to find Quinn's hand and when he leaned down, it practically jumped into his arms. Its purr was like a tiger's.

"By the by," Quinn said, "perhaps now would be a good time to warn you that your grandmother has been seen trying to pick the lock to my carriage house."

"I told you that under no circumstances was she allowed to be near any set of reins."

"No. You said that under no circumstance was she to be allowed access to a horse."

"I warn you, Ellesmere—"

"*Quinn.*"

Luc St. Aubyn stared at him for a long moment before using his Christian name. "Quinn...I won't pay for any damages to your bloody carriages. After all I've done for you—"

"Agreed," Quinn interrupted, and then suppressed a smile. "You know, I was wrong about you."

Luc blinked. "I beg your pardon?"

"Georgiana said you were a great man."

"Georgiana's observations are always brilliantly spot-on."

Quinn tried not to laugh. "But she was wrong in your case."

Luc raised his looking glass to his eye.

"You're not a great man. You are one of the *greatest* men . . . no, the greatest *friend* I have had the honor to know."

Helston's discomfort was palpable, which pleased Quinn enormously.

"Well . . ." Luc said, "this is very inconvenient."

"Why?"

"It's so much more amusing to hate you."

"Perhaps," Quinn admitted, holding back his laughter.

"But then," Luc said thoughtfully, "I'd be willing to consider friendship if it will take up less of my time."

"That's doubtful. One always has to watch a friend even more closely than an enemy, don't you think?" Quinn pushed back the memory of his friendship with Anthony as a young boy. He took a step forward and Luc held up his hands to keep space between them.

"You're not going to try and embrace me, are you?" Luc's eyes were black with horror. "Well, it would explain your idiotic actions toward Georgiana." Luc barked with laughter and moved to slap him so hard on the back that Quinn almost lost his balance.

"You know," Quinn said, slapping Luc's back even more soundly, sending the duke sprawling forward into a pile of wood shavings. "I do believe I preferred you as an enemy."

"Too late," Luc said, regaining his feet and brushing his breeches.

"Well, then, perhaps we should continue the tour." Quinn crossed the length of the empty barn and went out into the sunshine. Beyond the stand of trees in the distance, three dozen men labored with shovels.

Luc came up beside him—and whistled. "Good Lord. What have you done?"

"The estate needed a body of water. It will be just a pond. Or . . . maybe a very small lake."

"You've lost your mind." He waved his arms at the barn, the greenhouse, the lake. "This is absolute insanity. It'll cost you a bloody fortune."

He ignored him and pointed to the center of the pit. "There's to be a small island, too. All this is a much smaller version of Loe Pool."

The duke rolled his eyes. "Well, it's time for your lecture. I promised Rosamunde I would lecture you. And it's the least I can do, for a *friend*."

"Don't bother. I'm certain I've already had this conversation with Mr. Brown at least ten times in the last ten days."

Luc arched a brow and ignored him. "Now then. How are you going to extricate everyone from this absurd situation? Start with Grace Sheffey, if you please."

"For God's sake. Don't you know she's still in love with her husband?"

"Grace? Grace Sheffey never loved the Earl of Sheffield," Luc said.

"No. *Georgiana*. Georgiana will never remarry. She's made her wishes very clear."

"I thought we were going to discuss Grace. You do realize that if we're going to be friends, you'll have to be able to take direction from me."

Quinn rubbed his forehead in exasperation.

"Oh, all right." Luc waved his arm. "Start with Georgiana. She's the one you want anyway. But don't think I'm allowing you out of your obligation regarding Grace. If she still wants you, I'll tie you up with a pretty ribbon on top and present you to her on a platter with an apple in your mouth."

Quinn turned on his heel toward the great house and Luc followed him.

"You're wrong." Quinn finally replied. "I do not want to marry Georgiana. I want her to be happy, to live out her life very comfortably—in a place that will remind her of everything she has known. But I do not want to live the rest of my life with a woman who is in love with my *estimable* cousin." He'd be damned if he'd explain his interactions with his blasted relation. And he just couldn't abide the thought of lying next to a woman who would be dreaming of Anthony Fortesque—and worse, feeling pity for a man who had been a cuckold.

"Brownie was right. You *are* a bigger fool than I ever was. If you're not willing to have her any way you can get her, then you deserve all the misery you're headed for . . . and more." Luc shook his head. "Anthony Fortesque is *dead*, you ass."

In the distance, the *cree-cree-cree* of a peregrine falcon sounded, and Quinn looked up into the sky and changed his course to find the source.

Luc leaned in and whispered, "And you're not . . . although you fool just about everybody with that corpselike air that decorates your face."

Bloody dukes. Always had to get the last word.

Georgiana had hoped Quinn's second sudden trip to London a fortnight ago would have at least afforded her some peace at heart. But as she looked down at Fairleigh's small blonde form surrounded by all the members of Ata's Widows Club sitting on the hill in front of Loe Pool, Georgiana realized his absence actually made everything much worse.

"Georgiana?" Fairleigh whispered. "How much longer is Monsieur Latoque going to make us stay in this position?"

Georgiana glanced at the diminutive Gallic portraitist, half hidden by his massive canvas. "If you don't ask me that question again, I'll go riding with you tomorrow."

The little girl bit her lip. "Georgiana?"

"Yes?" she returned.

"At what time?"

Georgiana hid her smile. "Dawn?"

There were five seconds of blessed silence.

"Which horse?"

"Don't you mean which *pony*?"

Fairleigh sighed and Georgiana almost laughed as it was an exact imitation of her own exasperated sound.

"Oh, all right." Georgiana relented. "You may ride Lady, the small gray mare in the last stall. But only if you stop talking. Monsieur Latoque might paint a mustache like his own on both of us if you don't."

"It's ever so much more fun to do the painting instead of the sitting."

Sarah Winters leaned in. "But all those who gaze upon the painting will be very grateful that you made the effort to sit still, dearest. Look."

Sarah handed Fairleigh a locket and the little girl worked the latch to open it. Georgiana glanced over her shoulder to see a likeness of a gentleman in a military uniform. Of all the widows, Sarah was the one who had mourned the most faithfully a beloved husband lost in the war against the French.

"Was this your husband?" Fairleigh asked.

"Yes." Sarah stroked her hand through Fairleigh's hair and Georgiana noticed how beautifully fragile Sarah's hands were. "And I am forever grateful to him for having made the effort to sit for this. If he had not, I would have nothing to remember him by, other than my memories."

"Oh," Fairleigh interjected, "have you seen the eye Georgiana painted of her husband?"

Sarah glanced at the edge of Georgiana's shawl and nodded.

They were all silent for a moment before she heard a sniff from Fairleigh's direction.

"What is it, dearest?"

"I don't want to have my likeness taken. It could be bad luck."

"And why is that?" Sarah asked gently.

"Because everyone seems to *die* after it's done," Fairleigh wailed.

"*Et alors?*" Monsieur Latoque waved his paintbrush in the air. "This is impossible. I cannot create *un chef d'oeuvre* unless you remain in position. You must make mademoiselle sit still."

"Monsieur," Georgiana said, standing to stretch her stiff joints. "I'm so sorry, but I do believe the light is fading and mademoiselle has been very good the last hour and a half. I think we should recommence tomorrow. Don't you agree?"

Ata murmured her accord. But Gwendolyn Fortesque, who had stayed on at Penrose despite the obvious wave of dislike from all the other ladies, disagreed. She'd arrived on the hill a few minutes ago with an expression more sour than the lemonade a beleaguered-looking footman bore in his hands.

"*You* would allow a child to dictate to everyone?" Gwendolyn snorted in disgust. "She needs better guidance. You are not fit to oversee her. She's coddled and spoiled to the core—without a shred of feminine talent or proper education."

Georgiana had never dared to stand up to the marchioness. But the thought of anyone saying something hurtful about Fairleigh made her lash out. "What did you say?" Georgiana walked over to Gwendolyn Fortesque. "Take it back."

Gwendolyn sputtered, "I beg your pardon?" She lowered her voice. "I do not answer to the daughter of a *steward*."

"You will take it all back or I shall—"

"You shall what?" Gwendolyn's arched smile held all the satisfaction of a woman who had been a marchioness for four decades. "Throw me off my own estate?"

Out of the corner of her eye, Georgiana saw Ata marching toward them. She put up a staying hand. "No, Ata. I thank you, but I shall not allow you to fight my battles any longer."

Ata stopped and motioned to the other widows to stand beside her.

Georgiana turned back to Gwendolyn. "Take it back or I shall make your life a misery."

Gwendolyn laughed. "I fail to see how it could get any worse. My life is wretched anytime I'm forced to endure your presence."

There was the shocked intake of breath from the widows nearby. And Ata's visage was purple.

"I don't care what you think of me but I won't allow you to utter a word against Fairleigh. Do you really consider yourself a model for bringing up children after the way you stood by and did nothing to curb Anthony's sad way of life in town?"

"You put him in the grave, not I," the dowager replied. It was clear Gwendolyn had completely given up every hope of becoming part of Ata's circle of influential friends in town.

A blast of coldness invaded her lungs. Georgiana had never been any good at putting people in their places. Had never been any good at the quick rejoinder. And she had only been able to get laborers and servants on the estate to do her bidding because they were embarrassed to see her trying to do the work herself.

She felt a slim hand grasp hers and looked up to see Grace's petite form beside her.

"Lady Ellesmere?" Grace said. "I for one will not let you forget you are here because Georgiana allows it. No, let me state it more clearly, for I fear you misunderstand. None of us cares about your inquiry or your meeting with the archbishop's assistant. And furthermore, none of the Dowager Duchess of Helston's friends, or *my* friends in town will care about it either. So you have a choice before you. You may either show Georgiana the respect she is due here and now or you shall face social ruin in London."

"Well, the very idea—" Gwendolyn sputtered.

"It's your choice, of course. And really, all of us"—she indicated the rest of the ladies—"are unfortunately not as civilized as we ought to be. I suppose it is due to the combined influence of living with the Devil of Helston and, lately, living under the roof of the *daughter of a steward*—a woman who has more grace in her calloused hands than you do in your rather"—Grace lifted her nose and surveyed every inch of Lady Ellesmere—"*inelegant* form."

It was the ultimate insult to a lady who prided herself on her dress and deportment. It was the only reason for her existence, Georgiana thought. But while she was extraordinarily grateful to Grace for standing up to Gwendolyn in such a superior fashion, at the same time it reinforced how very much she was out of her element.

She simply wished the entire encounter had never occurred. She was so close to leaving Penrose anyway—and would never have to see Gwendolyn Fortesque again. Suddenly the scene was just too much.

"Gwendolyn," she whispered, addressing her mother-in-law by her Christian name for the first time. "I know why you hate me. I remind you of where you came from. But you see, I don't care what you think of me. I've never cared. But if you ever say another unkind word about Fairleigh I shall—"

"Go running to Quinn?" Lady Ellesmere interrupted. "I don't doubt it. You always did run to him—or to my darling Anthony."

Georgiana closed her eyes tightly then reopened them. "No, I won't look to others to solve my own problems. If you don't apologize I shall come to London and haunt your every step, much as I loathe town. I shall accept Ata's invitation and go to every entertainment, every soiree, every fete or dinner, every musical, every ball and you shall be forced to endure my presence. And if you push me too far, I might even secretly arrange for a particular sow to be delivered to your chambers."

There was the sound of a forced cough. Georgiana turned to see Quinn leaning against a tree behind all her friends, half hidden by the foliage. Lord knew how long he had been standing there.

"Quinn!" Gwendolyn Fortesque said. "When did you arrive?"

He pushed off of the tree and crossed toward them. "Georgiana and Grace neglected to inform you of one additional point, madam. Before you take your leave *tonight*"—he was extracting something from a leather portfolio—"you should know that if Georgiana does decide to visit Grace or Ata in town she will be properly introduced as the true Marchioness of Ellesmere—or," he said, looking toward Grace, "the newest dowager marchioness, for I have a document in hand which states as much."

"That's impossible. Lord Thornley, the archbishop's assistant said—" Gwendolyn interjected.

"Perhaps. But the Archbishop of Canterbury saw it differently when I met him last week. *Very differently.* Georgiana's marriage to Anthony is valid and always shall be." He placed several sheets of heavy vellum in Georgiana's hand.

"You did not . . ." Gwendolyn said faintly.

"Indeed, I did, madam. And by the by, while I was in town I took the liberty of arranging for your daughters and all of your affairs to be removed to Ellesmere Abbey in Cheshire. You shall join them, as I shall arrange a carriage for you tonight. You will all be very comfortable there."

Georgiana heard Ata whisper, "Oh, but that's not nearly far enough away . . ."

Georgiana glanced at Quinn and his eyes met hers just as Grace grasped his shoulder and leaned up to whisper something in his ear. He shifted his gaze to the countess and smiled.

Quinn held a tiny rosebud in his hand and Grace grasped it and twirled it in her elegant fingers.

Chapter 17

October 12th—to do
- see to the last of the trunks and valises
- bid farewell to Mrs. Killen, Cook, maids, footmen, the stable master and hands, and the gardeners, the dairy-maids, the shepherd, the gamekeeper—everyone
- 1 o'clock—Luc arrives with carriage for Father

-try to leave without breaking down

The lovely early autumn day was at odds with Georgiana's melancholy mood. It should be raining. Heavily. But it was not. The air was crisp and the sun shone high overhead as the Duke of Helston, showing great condescension to a man far beneath him, personally drove the ducal carriage to the front of Little Roses and handed the reins to the groom as he sprang from the seat.

He bowed to her slightly. "Are you ready, Georgiana? Shall I assist Mr. Wilde?"

"There's a footman to help. We're ready. Father

is very excited. He's been up since dawn. My mother, too."

Luc tilted his head and looked at her oddly. "And you, Georgiana? You are excited, happy, too?"

She glanced at the carriage. "Oh, very much." The lie came so easily to her tongue. "I'm so grateful—"

"No," he interrupted. "No more thanks. Didn't Rosamunde warn what I might do if I have to suffer one more inch of gratitude? Can't abide it. Besides, I think I made out very well in the bargain. Ata and the other ladies will be delighted to stay with you this coming year."

Georgiana smiled. "It is I who am grateful to them." She moved aside as a footman exited the cottage, carrying several bandboxes. With a nod, Luc went past her and disappeared into the cottage, leaving her momentarily alone for the first time this morning.

She knew she should follow the duke back inside. There were a few last things to attend to and she wanted to make sure her father was settled into the carriage properly, but she had to see Loe Pool one last time.

She quickly made her way up the small hill and stared down past the stand of trees to Loe Pool. She hadn't been able to bring herself to remove everything from the glass lake house. She'd left the cot made up and all the blankets. One day, perhaps, Fairleigh would convince her father to swim there and it would be ready for them.

Last night she had stared at the tiny locked chest

in the glass house for a long time before opening it. This was where she kept Anthony's few letters to her as well as a small, half-completed painting of Loe Pool that Quinn had painted. She had asked for it when he was about to discard it all those years ago in their youth.

Then she'd taken off the Lover's Eye brooch that everyone—except Rosamunde—assumed was of Anthony's eye. She'd worked open the tiny secret catch behind it and touched the dark strands of hair inside one last time before shutting her eyes against the tears and placing the brooch on top of the painting. She'd locked the chest and put it inside the cabinet under the bench, all the way in the back corner beneath yet another pile of blankets. She doubted anyone even remembered that the bench opened.

It was a good place to secret away dreams unfulfilled.

Now Georgiana stood looking down at the lake house for many long minutes, the breeze playing with locks of her hair that had come undone.

Good-bye, Penrose.

Good-bye, Quinn.

She would not come back. She had consciously made the decision to never return, not even for future harvest festivals or any other entertainment. She would see all her acquaintances in the neighboring countryside, but she would never set foot on Penrose property again. It was for her sanity.

And so she'd said all her formal good-byes last night to Mrs. Killen and all the servants who worked in the great house. And she had tucked Fairleigh into her huge bed in the chamber adjacent to her father's. That had been the very worst of all. She'd braided Fairleigh's angel-like hair and kissed her cheek before the child had tugged her to lie on top of the bed with her. Fairleigh's head had fit perfectly in the crook of her arm and her little form had snuggled against her. Georgiana had told her stories about Penrose until she fell asleep.

And then Georgiana had said good-night to Ata and the other widows in the formal drawing room after dinner. It had been ridiculous, really. They all agreed it was not really good-bye. After all, they would remove to join her at Trehallow next week. Quinn had said not a word as he sat beside Grace.

When she took her leave, he had merely escorted her to the terrace along with the rest of the ladies and brushed his lips against the back of her hand in good-bye. "I wish you much happiness, Georgiana," he had said gently.

"I must thank you again for your generosity in providing for my parents and me," she had said, and bobbed a curtsy.

"You know it's Helston whom you should thank. He's the one who found the properties and secured everything for your family," he had said.

"Well, then. I wish you safe journey."

She had nodded and all the ladies reached forward to embrace her, some of them giggling and murmuring good night.

She hadn't dared to look at Quinn again. She hadn't been sure she could keep her careful façade in place. This was it. She would not see him again. She had reached behind her for the railing and once finding it, steadied herself and turned to dash down the steps into the evening, calling out a good night one last time.

When she got past the arc of lantern light from the torches on the terrace garden, she had leaned against a hickory tree to catch her breath.

Emotion had burned the back of her eyes as she looked back toward the terrace, only to find that all but two of the figures had returned indoors. Quinn and Grace were silhouetted against the bright candlelight past the glass-paneled French doors.

Grace had reached up and stroked Quinn's head, her fingers lingering on the back of his neck. Georgiana had a vivid memory of how soft his hair was near his collar. A moment later, the two figures had merged into one in the shadows. Georgiana had swallowed a sob and run blindly back to Little Roses, her leg aching.

A tear threatened to cross the edge of her lower lashes as she remembered. She brushed at it with annoyance. It wasn't as if she didn't know what was going to happen. She was so very foolish. So foolish she had not truly prepared for this good-bye or for her future, she realized, looking at Loe Pool one last time.

She'd not once gone to Trehallow since the day the duke handed her the deed. He had insisted she not go and he'd been so serious when he'd said it that she had not thought about going against his wishes. In truth, she had little curiosity.

Trehallow was near St. Ives, well beyond the neighboring estates she had known all her life. Georgiana knew it would require a bit of work to restore it. And she knew the duke had already started some of the work. He had probably wanted to present her with a challenge to occupy her mind. But what the duke did not know was that she was tired of challenges.

She was mortally tired, period.

She just wanted peace.

Deep down inside, she knew Trehallow would give it to her. And she was grateful. Every time she saw Luc St. Aubyn it was all she could do not to throw her arms around his dark, gruff figure and kiss him. She would be forever grateful to him and Rosamunde and Ata, if her hunch was correct. All of them had done this for her, and she had no way to repay them for their endless kindnesses. Kindnesses she did not deserve.

Several hours later, the gratitude she felt for the duke and his family was increased tenfold.

The carriage took a turn from the main road and someone—Luc, probably—rapped a cane from above—to draw their attention to the scene.

"Papa," Georgiana whispered, leaning forward in the plush carriage to touch her father's knee while her mother dozed in the corner. "Look."

At the end of a very long drive, shaded by enormous, evenly spaced poplar trees, rested an ancient stone four-story great house. Two turrets, one crumbling, flanked the main portion.

Georgiana swallowed. It was beyond anything she had imagined.

It was so very beautiful.

"What do you think?" her father asked thoughtfully.

"I had no idea," she whispered. "It's too much."

"Yes," he said, "but, then again, Helston warned that half is unlivable. It stood empty for so long because no one was willing to take on the time and expense to restore it." Her father touched her hand. "Will you be up to the task?"

"It's a bit too late to back out now, don't you think?" She laughed nervously.

"That's my girl," her father said.

Her mother's eyes fluttered open. She looked out the window and was speechless for the first time in her life. "Oh Lordy. Why, 'tis almost as grand as Penrose."

The carriage lurched to a stop, and suddenly the small door opened and Luc's dark face was peering in. "Come along now," he said gruffly.

"But," Georgiana said, "shouldn't we settle my parents at—"

"No," Luc said abruptly.

Something was wrong.

"Blast," Luc said under his breath. "Look, I've never been any good at these sorts of things, and I can tell you're about to ask a lot of questions, which I won't answer. So, here it is. There is a group of ladies and gentlemen in the rear gardens and they are all waiting to surprise you." He removed his hat and scratched his head before returning it to his head. "So act surprised, will you?"

Georgiana turned to her parents. "Did you know about this?"

Her father chuckled. "Quinn told me yesterday because he feared I would ruin it by suffering a seizure during the critical moment."

"Quinn?" She rearranged the folds of her gown. "He's here?"

"Yes." Luc's dark blue eyes bore into hers.

"He arranged this?"

"No, my dear," Luc replied. "Grace arranged it. She and Ata invited your closest neighbors to come for tea and cakes for a welcoming party. You are to do nothing but enjoy yourselves and meet everyone for the next hour or so, and then I promise to make them all go away so you can get settled."

"But Father"—she turned to him—"you must be too tired for all of this. Perhaps you should—"

"No, Daughter. I've had enough coddling. I want to meet Mr. Washburton. He's our closest neighbor and I understand he has bred a new type of sheep that produces very fine wool."

She looked from her parents to Luc. "And Fairleigh is here?"

"Quinn had the devil of a time getting her to keep the secret." Luc smiled. "Come along, then."

Georgiana played her part very admirably. And in the end she was very glad for the opportunity to meet all her neighbors. Ata, Grace, and Fairleigh graciously took on the roles of hostesses, ensuring everyone's needs were tended to.

No one knew how much it cost her to face Quinn again after she had made her proper goodbyes and thought she would not have to see him again. Or worse, see Grace and Quinn together. But there they were, strolling the gardens arm in arm, stopping every so often to chat with guests. An orange tabby cat followed Quinn's steps, threading itself between his boots each time he stopped. They were a mere few feet away now.

Georgiana smiled despite herself. Quinn had always loved cats. Cats, on the other hand, had never appeared to like him—the only animal on this earth who did not seem to immediately take to him. He had suffered numerous scratches during their childhood to attest to that sad fact. At twelve, Quinn had renounced all felines. But it seemed this cat had not received the announcement.

"What are you smiling about?" Miles Langdon accepted two glasses of lemonade from a footman and passed one to her.

"That cat."

"Hmmm. I thought you were smiling because of your good fortune. Luc is a dashed good fellow for arranging all this for you. A fine brother-in-law indeed. Although I'm thinking you're so grand now, I won't ever be able to persuade you to elope to Gretna Green with me."

Georgiana smiled and noticed the strange expression that crossed Quinn's features when she chanced to glance at him over Miles's shoulder.

"I don't know," she teased. "If you were willing to bring a large-enough fortune into the equation, or maybe if you would just promise to rebuild the turrets single-handedly, I'd consider it," she said with a twitch to her lips.

Miles was so busy choosing from a selection of cakes on the second footman's tray that he ignored her comments.

He turned and placed a delectable morsel in her gloved hand before popping two in quick succession into his mouth. "I understand these are your mother's recipes. They're absolutely divine."

"Careful, brother mine," Rosamunde said, sidling up to Miles with Luc by her side. Each of them carried an infant. "I warned you earlier— you're looking a bit thick about the middle."

Miles sputtered. "I most certainly am *not*!"

"You know," Rosamunde added, "I don't think Georgiana fancies portly suitors."

"What did I tell you?" Miles turned to Georgiana and muttered, "Sisters . . . the bane of every gentleman's existence. And I'm not allowed to retaliate if I want to still be considered a gentleman."

Luc smiled. "Unless you're a duke. Dukes are allowed to do and say anything they please. They only answer—"

"To the Prince Regent?" Miles interrupted.

Georgiana giggled.

Luc glared at Miles. "I was about to say that dukes only answer to *duchesses*." He glanced at Rosamunde as his lips dropped to the top of Caro's head. For a moment the duke's eyes flared with a love so potent that it was almost painful to witness.

What would it be like to have someone so devoted? Georgiana turned to Rosamunde just in time to catch the answering passionate glimmer in her expression.

Miles sighed with exasperation. "Whatever happened to the sexes presenting a united front? Luc, you're ruining everything."

Luc chuckled. "Perhaps you'll see things differently when you marry."

A footman passed by with another tray of cakes and Miles looked after the tray longingly. "I suppose I will if my wife provides cakes such as these." He winked at Georgiana. "I'll be right back." Miles trailed after the footman carrying the cakes.

"Well," Rosamunde said, switching Harry to her other shoulder, "if there was any doubt as to Miles's soft spot, I think those cakes put it to rest."

Georgiana changed the subject. "Luc, I realize you don't want my thanks, but I beg you to suffer through this. I had no idea Trehallow was quite this . . . this beautiful, or immense. Surely, the generous portion Quinn provided did not—"

"As I told your father, Georgiana, you'll be forced to give over the vast majority of the rents. That should more than make up the difference."

"But, the repairs. The enormous greenhouse, and I can see the new wood on the barns in the distance. Frankly, I'm terrified to see what you've done inside. We'll never be able to repay you." She bowed her head.

"Ah," he said, his expression darkening. "But you've forgotten to mention the new falcon mews, the horses, the oxen, chickens, the sheep, and the"— he cleared his throat—"*bloody ocean* that is being dug as we speak." His eyes were half hooded.

Her jaw had dropped. "What?" she whispered.

"It should be done in the next month or so. I hope you won't mind that there will be a small island in the center, much like a miniature Loe Pool." He swore under his breath. "I was able to talk him out of the glass house in the center he was so intent on building. I hope you don't mind."

"Darling," Rosamunde said to Luc softly, "I don't think she can take much more."

"I'm sorry. You know gratitude always brings out the worst in me."

Rosamunde stroked his cheek. "And that is why I love you."

Luc cursed again under his breath and refused to look at Georgiana. "They need larger brimmed hats. The sun is too bright for Caro and Henry." He sighed and then lifted his other child from his wife's shoulder. "I'm going inside. I shall leave you to rectify this mess, Rosamunde. I'm done with it. Never should have agreed to this farce."

As Georgiana looked at Luc's retreating back she caught sight of Quinn again, the cat at his heels just like a dog. Grace stood beside him, a smile on her lips, within a small circle of new friends. Quinn leaned down to scratch the cat's ears and the orange tabby jumped into his arms.

"He did it all," Georgiana whispered to Rosamunde. "Oh God."

"I'm sorry I didn't tell you." Rosamunde gently touched her shoulder. "He was determined to do it and Luc forbade me to tell you. Quinn was certain you would refuse it all if you knew. It appears he likes gratitude even less than my husband."

Georgiana's throat closed and she couldn't say a word—couldn't move.

"Oh, my dearest friend," Rosamunde whispered sadly as she looked at her. "Come, take my arm. We'll go to the greenhouse where there's privacy. Can you walk? It's only a little way. Shall I get Luc? You're very pale. You're not going to faint, are you? Oh, please don't."

She forced herself to speak when panic laced Rosamunde's words. "No, no. I'm perfectly fine." She grasped Rosamunde's arm and they walked very carefully toward the huge glass-paned greenhouse, which was more like a French-style giant orangerie.

The beautiful space was empty save for the beginnings of a foundation of the plants Georgiana knew would take years to find. This would be her refuge. It was different from anything at Penrose—unlike the lake and mews he had arranged.

Georgiana sank onto the nearest bench. She retrieved a handkerchief from her pocket and twisted it. "He's always been so unbearably generous and kind. It's what makes everything so difficult. I've never known a more honorable man, Rosamunde. And I fear"—she gulped—"no . . . I *know* I will never encounter another like him. No, you are not to say a word. I do not feel sorry for myself. It is a rare person who does not suffer unrequited love at least once in their life. And I am the luckiest woman alive. I will be living in the lap of luxury, and I have projects in front of me that will take up the rest of my life and longer."

When Rosamunde did not argue with her, Georgiana knew. She knew that even her best friend had given up hope of Georgiana ever securing Quinn's love.

"I am determined to make this estate the most profitable in all of Cornwall—if only to pay him back every last farthing. And I will work day and night to do it." She retrieved the stub of a pencil and a list from her other pocket and tried hard to force back her emotions. She would not burden Rosamunde any longer.

In the long pause that followed, Rosamunde laid her hand on Georgiana's shoulder and patted it. "And you will do it too."

She felt her friend's fingers trail around her waist and then tug her into an embrace. "Georgiana, I hate to tell you this now, but there might not be another moment of privacy between us," she whispered into her ear. "Grace told me last night that Quinn has agreed to accompany her to the Duchess of Kendale's house party the week after next."

The list fluttered from her fingers.

She was so numb she barely felt Rosamunde tugging her closer. "You must prepare yourself. It is certain he will make a betrothal announcement before they leave."

Georgiana withdrew from Rosamunde's embrace and forced a smile to her face. "It's all right, you know. It will be a relief almost. I've been waiting for it."

"I'm glad Ata, Sarah, and Elizabeth are coming to stay here. And Fairleigh will want to come too, when Quinn and Grace go to Kendale."

"I should be very happy to have her with me," Georgiana whispered and looked down at her hands.

"Georgiana, you are not to pretend with me. I am guessing you would prefer not to see Quinn. But fear not on that point. I don't know how or when, but a miracle occurred sometime during the last month. Luc and Quinn have formed a friendship. And I will make sure it's Luc who brings Fairleigh to you since Amberley is so close by."

"I'm so glad Trehallow is such an easy distance," Georgiana returned. "You are the very best friend in the world, Rosamunde. I hope I will always deserve your friendship."

Rosamunde smiled lovingly. "The feeling is entirely mutual, dearest. I'm very grateful to you for inviting Ata and everyone else to stay with you." She looked at her closely for a long moment. "But you must promise me you will not cut yourself off from future chances of happiness. My brother, Miles, much as I tease him, admires you greatly. Perhaps, with time, things might—"

"No, Rosamunde. I respect him and appreciate his attentions of late. But if I ever sensed for a moment that his heart was seriously engaged, that would be the end of it. I even went so far as to tell him that, several days ago. And he seemed relieved. Now we flirt with great ease, since we both know there is nothing behind it." She grasped her friend's hand. "I just can't tolerate the idea of a marriage of convenience, much as I might desire the promise of companionship."

"I thought not," Rosamunde said, sadly. "Well, I know you'll forgive me for trying to make you my sister in law."

Georgiana smiled. "Considering how poorly I

fared with my in-laws, I shall be delighted simply to remain your best friend."

A half hour later found Georgiana standing beside her father and mother, bobbing curtsies to each of the departing neighbors. She wasn't sure how she managed to contain all the emotions running through her.

He had done this all for her.

All of it.

And yet, it was simply because he was a man of great character, bound to adhere to the strictest of principles, which included providing for the widow of a man who had cuckolded him.

And suddenly he was before her. Quinn thrust an interesting object between them. "A small gift for you, Georgiana. Fairleigh and I made several of them."

She looked at it, careful not to meet his eye. "It's a beehive, isn't it?"

"Yes. I'm not sure if we constructed them properly. It was from memory."

"This is the design you described—the corkbottomed ones from Portugal."

"The very one."

Grace was beside Quinn and she placed a beautifully embroidered cushion into Georgiana's other arm. "And this is from me. I hope you like it."

"Oh, Grace. It's exquisite. I shall cherish it always. It's the most lovely thing I've ever possessed.

A hand was tugging at her arm. "Georgiana, Papa told me the bestest news ever, this morning. He said that when he goes to visit his friends I can come and stay with you and Ata and the other ladies if you'll have me. And I told him that was ridiculous. Of course you would have me—"

"Fairleigh," Quinn broke in with his exasperated-father voice. "I told you I would have to discuss it with Georgiana first. It isn't proper to invite yourself."

Georgiana dropped to her knees and put all the gifts to one side to take Fairleigh in her arms. "You must listen to your father, dearest. He is always right, you know. But I will tell you a secret. There will always be a chamber next to mine with a bed and a painting box next to it. And it will always be reserved for you, and you alone."

She finally raised her eyes. Grace was conversing with departing guests and Quinn was looking down at Fairleigh, wrapped in her arms.

"Thank you," he whispered.

"It is I who should be thanking you," she whispered back.

He looked at her for a long moment, his eyes glimmering with unspoken emotion.

The feelings it engendered in her breast were so powerful, she had to glance away. Beyond his shoulder, she saw the familiar form of a lone rider coming over the rise to the east, and a tremor of hope flickered.

And then, all hell broke loose.

Chapter 18

Ata's List

October 12th—to do
- transport hidden cache of Armagnac to Trehallow
- discuss marriage plans with Grace
- figure out a way to see Caro and Henry more often

- take out Quinn's carriage!

"**L**ord Ellesmere!" Mr. Brown shouted while running from the stables as fast as his spindly old legs would allow. "Lord almighty! She's taken your phaeton."

Quinn grasped the arm of the new Trehallow footman. "Four horses, man. Have four horses saddled immediately." His voice held the authority of a king. The footman ran so fast that his white wig flew off his head, revealing the dark queue beneath.

"Bloody hell." Dark horror streaked Luc's face as he came running. The gaggle of remaining guests said hurried good-byes and flew away.

"Luc, circle St. Ives. I'll take the road to Penzance," Quinn said quickly. "Brownie, you go toward Penrose; Miles, take the north road, and"—he looked at Georgiana—"tell whoever is coming through the gardens to take the eastern route to the opposite coast."

Without another word they scattered.

Georgiana ran as fast as her damaged limbs would allow. She had another reason to run.

He was silhouetted against the brightness of the sun but she would know him anywhere.

Grayson. Her brother.

He was returned and she thought her heart might burst from the joy. She had no idea how he had known to come here. But she had never been so grateful to see someone in her life.

Brownie cursed the number of cakes rattling around his insides as he rode hell for leather toward Penrose. Lord almighty, he would strangle that thin, little wrinkled neck of hers when he caught up with her in that bloody death trap of Quinn's. He tried not to think what he would do to himself if he was too late.

How could she have done it? How many times had he warned her? How many locks had he installed over the years? And yet here he was again, racing to save her stubborn, brittle bones.

He silently cursed again the good Lord above for arranging his life so that he would only ever fall in love with one woman. A four-foot, eleven-inch ball of fire. An Armagnac-loving goddess from hell with the generous soul of an angel. Tears streaked past his age-spot-riddled temples as he urged his horse to new speeds and tried to ignore a hundred different aches in his old body.

He spied a small stile off the sandy lane and guided the gelding over it at a full gallop. Cutting through the string of meadows would give him a chance. A half mile later he jumped back onto the road and was now certain someone was up ahead.

His heart hammered in his chest as he tore Ata's ridiculous, fruit-laden hat from a low tree branch as he galloped past it. Around the next corner he saw her.

Just then, the phaeton skidded wildly around another bend, and Ata's shriek sent a bolt of pure terror through him. His horse must have sensed it, for the bay leaped ahead. He leaned forward in the saddle and raced along, spitting out dust and praying for a miracle.

Just when it seemed he would never overtake them, his horse surged past the vehicle's absurdly large wheels and he leaned in to grab the dangling rein of the horse galloping beside him. He straightened and tugged evenly, hoping all the while that he would not pull them all into the ditch. "Whoa," he said deeply. "Hold up, boys. There now. There now. Whoa." He kept up the calming stream of words, managing the trick of alternating between a slow release and a regathering of the single rein, thereby edging his mount past the two carriage horses.

The phaeton finally came to a halt, the horses stamping and snorting their displeasure.

John unglued himself from the saddle. Without a word he tied his horse's reins to the back of the carriage, and noticed a missing spoke on one wheel, a partially ripped-away groom's stand in back, and deep scratches in the paint. He shook his head and mounted the treacherous side of the tall phaeton. Och, a damned ridiculous modern notion for a carriage, this was.

All the while he could hear the she-devil muttering. He slid his frame onto the small bench and sat there, hoping he would not have a heart seizure now that it was all over. A sweat broke out on him, and propriety be damned, he removed his wool coat and rolled up his shirtsleeves to his elbows. He couldn't bring himself to look at her. "Give me the reins."

"No," she said petulantly.

"Give me the reins this very second, *lassie.*"

There was a long pause before Ata whimpered, "I can't."

"Can't or won't, lass?"

"Look at me, John," she murmured.

That got his attention. She hadn't uttered his Christian name in almost five decades. There were tears in her eyes when he glanced at her. He covered her one good hand and her other withered one with his own. "Let go, Merceditas."

"I can't," she wailed. "They won't open."

He carefully turned her working hand over and pried the three remaining reins from her clenched fingers.

One of the horses whinnied its desire to walk on.

Reins collected, he urged the horses forward into a slow trot, all the while hoping the damaged wheel would hold till they reached Penrose, where he could recover his sanity in the relative quiet of the study—provided a pint of brandy could be found.

"John," she said again. "It wasn't my fault. It wasn't. I was driving them perfectly well. I know everyone thinks I'm an abominable horsewoman, but I'm not. My one hand works perfectly well. And Quinn did invite me to use his carriages whenever I wanted. You see, I was going along at an acceptable spanking pace when three deer popped out of a hedgerow and nearly collided with us. But I steadied the horses, quite expertly, I might add. And everything would have been just fine. I would have arrived at Penrose and I would have shown everyone that they were wrong. But then I turned a tight corner and a branch caught the near horse's outside rein and tore it from my grasp. And the silly horses bolted, and . . ." Her high-pitched voice finally trailed off.

"And?" he said.

"And . . . why won't you say something? Go ahead. I know you're dying to say it. Tell me I'm an old, stubborn fool."

"That's no' what I would say."

"Well, then, say whatever you have to say and be done with it. At least I'll be able to tell Luc you've already lectured me. And Quinn would never say a word. He . . ." She stopped talking when she realized he wasn't going to interrupt her.

For a quarter of an hour only the clop of the horses' hooves against the packed ground could be heard.

"Stop the horses," Ata finally said forlornly. "Please."

He complied and pulled the pair to the side of the lane, where the shade of fall foliage beckoned. He looked at her. "Well, lassie?"

"Talk to me. Go ahead. Rail against me. Just, please . . . Talk. To. Me. I can't stand your silence."

He stroked her wrinkled cheek. "Really? For all the silence I've endured the last five decades, I'd begun to think you liked it."

"John, I'm so sorry. I'll never take another horse or carriage again without someone with me." She chewed her lower lip. "But I will still be able to drive as long as someone goes with me, right?"

She nearly broke his heart. He could so easily see beyond the wrinkles and the thick, gray locks of her hair half tumbled from her head. She was still the sixteen-year-old lass he had lost his heart to five decades ago.

He eased her hair away from her face. "The problem is that you've always felt the need to prove everyone wrong. There never was any need."

"But of course there was," she replied.

"And why is that?"

"Because no one takes me seriously," she said. "Oh, all the mushrooms of society and sycophants condescend to me to elevate themselves. But everyone else, from the time I was fully grown, has treated me like a child, because I'm so small and

I'm female. It's ridiculous. For goodness sakes, you would think people would begin to take me seriously at this point, at my age."

"No," John replied sadly. "This need to prove everyone wrong started long before now. It started that summer you came to Scotland with your family and we met for the first time."

"No," she begged. "We will not speak of this."

He grasped her pointed chin and tugged it toward his gaze. "We will speak of it. I'm tired of waiting for you to come around. And I'm not sure these old bones of mine will be able to keep running after you."

Her eyes were full, but he knew pride wouldn't allow the tears to flow past the lashes.

"Are you ever going to forgive me?" he asked quietly. "Are you ever going to admit that perhaps, just perhaps, lass, you were wrong too?"

"Wrong?" Her eyes flared. "Wrong? You dare to suggest I was wrong? I was the one willing to leave everything behind for you. I was the one who arranged it all. You were the one who didn't love me enough to go through with it. And I was the one who suffered the consequences, not you." She looked down at her withered hand and winced in silent remembrance of a mysterious event she refused to reveal to anyone, including him.

He wiped his hand over his face. "Och, lass. If you only knew . . . I suffered every day of my life since the day you married that terrible man. I know you did it to spite me. If you had only waited. Waited until I could earn enough to keep you."

"You asked me to wait too long," she replied.

"I couldna do it to you, lass." He knew his Scottish burr riddled his speech when he became overly passionate. "I had so little to offer. Your parents would ha' disowned you and you were but sixteen and I couldna be sure you wouldna regret marrying a lad with nothing to his name."

"Oh," she said, her anger in full bloom. "You're like everyone else, so sure I was too stupid to know my own mind. It was your fault, not mine. You were and still are hen-hearted, and I loathe everything cowardly."

He dropped her hands because he knew his own were shaking. "Och, you're an unforgiving lass. I'd hoped time and everything else would soften you. But I see I've been a fool again."

"I won't forgive you for standing me up at the altar—"

"It was a bloody anvil at the smithy—"

"I waited two hours before I realized you weren't coming—"

"I told you before, I didn't come because I knew you'd talk me into ruining your life, what with those big, dark pussycat eyes o' yourn."

"The only reason I tolerate you is because you watched over Luc at sea."

"I stood by your grandson in every battle he fought for more than half a decade, and I did it for you. But I see you've hardened your heart against me."

That petulant set to her mouth did not bode well for him. He knew it all too well. "Merceditas . . . please. This might just be our last chance. Marry me, lass. Let me take you back to Scotland, back to where we first met. Back to the anvil."

"I said it before, John Brown, and I'll say it again. You had your chance. And after experiencing decades of something other than marital bliss, I've no taste for gentlemen ordering me about. I'm lucky to be in a position where I don't ever have to be under someone's thumb again." She shifted her knees away from him. "Now, if you please, I would like to return to Penrose. I'm leaving for Trehallow in a few days to help Georgiana, and I must arrange many things before I go."

There was a long pause before he spoke. "The problem with old age is that we become inflexible . . . and prone to giving orders. But then, lass, you always did like to give orders."

She lashed around to face him again, fury in her dark eyes. "I think I rather earned the right to give a few orders after being *forced* to obey so many during twenty-four years, three months, two weeks, and one day of marriage."

He looked at her sadly and clucked at the horses to move forward in their traces. "And that's why I follow your orders and have been for forty-nine years and I don't know how many months, weeks, and days. But now that I know you won't ever change your mind I won't bother you again." His burr disappeared. "I shall return to Scotland as soon as I can arrange for someone to assume my duties at Penrose."

It was too bad John Brown did not, in that moment, chance to gaze into Ata's eyes. If he had, even his old and blurry eyes would have been able to discern her heartbreak.

But as it stood, Ata told herself later, it was much better that way. And all so achingly familiar.

Timing was a funny thing in life, Quinn thought, as he sat at his desk at Penrose a few days later. Mr. Brown was seated across from him, hat in hand. It was either perfect or it was a disaster, but timing was never in between the two extremes. It was unfortunate that in this instance, like the vast majority of the events in his life, timing was a disaster. With his departure imminent, who could Quinn find on short notice to oversee Penrose?

"It's quite all right, Mr. Brown," he assured the older gentleman. "We agreed when you accepted my offer that it was most likely temporary in nature. I would, of course, prefer you to stay, now that I have come to admire you so much. Can I not convince you to remain here after all? Perhaps if I offered you more—"

Mr. Brown held up his hands. "Och, no. You pay me too much as it is and what with those horrendous bills from Trehallow, you must keep a closer eye on your income. Besides, I was never in it for the money, but I think you know that." He scratched his gray hair. "I must return to my small bit of property in Scotland. But I wouldna leave you in a bind, my lord."

"*Quinn*. I insist. You should address me as Quinn if you're no longer going to be in my employ. I would be honored. It has been a pleasure to know you." He wouldn't try any harder to get the older gentleman to stay. He knew Ata was behind the misery that dogged the older Scot ever since the dowager duchess had almost turned his phaeton into kindling. "And you are not to worry about Penrose. Grayson Wilde might be persuaded to consider the position, if not permanently, then at least temporarily, I'm certain of it."

"She'll no' forgive me," Mr. Brown said under his breath. "I must leave because she'll never forgive me."

"If my words can ease your despair," Quinn said quietly, "I can assure you that Ata loves you."

"Perhaps. But you see, love and forgiveness must go hand and hand. You cannot have one without the other."

"I assume you've asked for forgiveness?" He wouldn't embarrass the man by asking him what he'd done to raise Ata's ire in the past.

"She's so stubborn."

"Keep trying."

"Begging your pardon, but I don't see you trying."

"I've done nothing for which to seek forgiveness."

Mr. Brown looked at him with those razor-sharp intelligent eyes. "Perhaps you haven't, but I shall warn you that you won't much like spending the next fifty years such as I have, waiting for the love of your life to come around and regretting your actions in the past."

"Love of my life?"

"You don't really think you'll be happy with Grace Sheffey, do you? I mean, she's rich and a countess and all, as gentle and sweet and as beautiful as they come—but she's not at all like Ata or Rosamunde— or *your* Georgiana, for that matter."

"I fail to see how—"

"Listen to me. You won't find happiness through convenience and quiet living. Look at Luc, for God's sake. You and he might not share the same temperament, but other than that, you're as alike as two peas in a pod. You both need an exuberant woman full of life, but more importantly a woman who has a heart full of love and a willingness to accept the avalanche of love you are withholding from the world." Mr. Brown took a deep breath. "There, now I've gone and said it. I figured I might as well, since I'm taking my leave. I hope you will not take offense at my presumption."

"I appreciate your advice, sir. But I, like you, seem to be much better at giving advice than receiving it." Quinn stroked his roughened jaw. "Suffice it to say that there are some things that can never be altered, and I'm afraid Georgiana's heart is one of them."

A flicker of something appeared in Mr. Brown's eyes. "That, sir, is the first bit of sense you've uttered this last half hour. And the last thing I'll dare to say is that you're going about it all wrong. Forget those posies you left at Little Roses. That might have worked for Rosamunde. No—don't worry, I'm the only one who saw you." He shook his head and leaned in. "It's the birdies she likes. Did you never think about that? The gamekeeper told me he has always been in awe of Georgiana.

He said he'd never known a little girl who loved animals so much or had such a way with them—almost as much as *you* once did apparently, but *your cousin* did not."

Quinn rose quickly. "I would ask you not to bring my cousin into this."

"But he's already in it. I've no' figured out what he did to you, but he sits on your shoulder guiding your actions every hour of every day. Pardon me, I would leave you now. I've overstepped and really perhaps you shouldna take too seriously advice from an old man who has wasted his life chasing an impossible dream."

A quiet wellspring of happiness bloomed in Georgiana's breast just short of a fortnight after removing to Trehallow. She gazed at the handsome profile of her brother, and the identical yet aged profile of her father as two of the three of them worked the soil in her new kitchen garden. Their father sat in the cool sunshine of autumn, watching them toil.

She was content, happier than she'd been in months, and she knew why. She was no longer stuck in a place where she did not belong, in a house pretending to be a proper marchioness. And she no longer had to worry about running into Quinn, or worse—Quinn arm in arm with Grace.

Joy had seeped back into her as she worked with the farm animals. She had helped the shepherd gather the new flock of sheep. She had overseen the activities in the dairy barn, where the calming clouds of fogged breath of the animals on a cold

morning greeted her. And she even enjoyed the
little grunts of welcome from the pigs when the
slops arrived, the nickers from the horses when
she brought grain, and the head butts of the goats
seeking her out. She felt at home and at ease again.
Her confidence returned, and she was . . . happy.

She sat back on her heels.

"I see I worried for no reason," Grayson said
quietly. "And for that I'm so thankful."

"I beg your pardon?"

"You. Father. Everyone. Georgie, it's so good to
see you happy." He stopped digging. "Your letters
terrified me more than the cannon."

"I'm sorry. But, I was so concerned about Father.
I wanted you to come before he . . . but miracu-
lously, he is better. I tried not to alarm you, but
obviously I failed."

"It was the rational, collected nature of your
letters that put the fear of God in me. You can't
imagine how much I prayed for strong winds to
carry me home."

"I'm so glad you're here." She would not tell him
how much she wished him never to leave again.
She knew how much he loved the sea and his new
life. She watched as he resumed expertly planting
a line of spinach.

"It's funny, Georgiana. When the ship set sail
eighteen months ago, I was delighted to remove
the dirt from my fingernails. And now, here with
you and Father, I have never been so content to
see dirt on my hands again." He was looking at
his palms and smiling. "And by setting sail, I also
learned two other important things."

"Yes?"

"First, I will never like fish."

She smiled.

"And second, there is nothing worth seeing beyond here." He shook his head. "I learned that I'm just like you, Georgiana, much to my chagrin. I was mistaken in thinking there was something important I was missing beyond the edge of nowhere."

"I know that feeling, Grayson."

"Well, let me spare you the trouble of finding out that there is nothing beyond Cornwall that will truly make you happier than you already are."

"Such a change of heart," Georgiana said. "I've heard sailors say that they are never so happy to return home as well as to return to sea."

"Well, perhaps you're right, but this midshipman has decided that only the first part of that sentiment holds any truth." Grayson picked a large stone from the earth and tossed it into a nearby rock pile. "I'm not returning to sea, Georgie. I have to face the uncomfortable task of speaking to His Grace, who was so kind to secure the berth for me."

"You might change your mind . . . or Luc might change it for you."

He laughed. "Are you trying to get rid of me already? And here I thought you wanted me to never—"

He couldn't finish his sentence because she had moved quickly to tackle him sideways with an embrace. "I'll never let you leave now. God, how I missed you," she whispered.

"I love you too, Georgie." He chuckled and his warm brown eyes gazed into hers. "And I've discovered something quite delightful since my return."

"What is that?"

"I've finally grown taller than my older sister and gained the advantage."

"Don't you dare—" she began, and then was lost in a hail of giggles as he tickled her.

"I've many years retribution due," he warned.

Grayson's laughter and her shrieks brought a warm, secret smile to their father's face. "Georgiana and Grayson, come sit beside me."

They immediately stood up, brushed the dirt from their clothes, and went to him.

"Did I hear rightly?" A smile decorated his thin face. "Are you quitting the Royal Navy, my son?"

Grayson hesitated and they all watched the orange tabby cat prowl in the nearby hedgerow.

"What?" Their father prodded. "Cat got your tongue?"

"Father," Georgiana said laughing. "Don't you dare. You know how much he hates puns. And if you start he might change his mind."

Grayson smiled. "I see you're still living under the cat's paw, Papa."

Their father smiled broadly and extracted a rumpled list from his pocket. "Now then, since Grayson has decided to stay on, I have a short list of things to do before—"

"Oh God," Grayson said, shaking his head, "not the list. Please, no lists. I'd forgotten all about—"

Georgiana pulled another list from her own pocket. "Actually, Father, I had wanted to discuss the ditch in the—" She burst out laughing when she looked at her brother's expression of horror.

Their father scratched his head. "You'd best start trimming quills yourself, Grayson. If my hunch is correct, you'll be making lists of your own in short order. Don't be surprised if Quinn Fortesque comes scratching on our door with a fine offer to keep you in catnip and cream if you'll consider taking on Penrose."

Georgiana darted a glance at her father and frowned. "But Grayson's only just returned. Surely he won't—"

"Just as long as there are no fish involved, I'd very much consider it," Grayson interrupted. He glanced sidelong at her. "Well, you didn't think I'd stay here and take orders from you, did you?"

She forced a smile to her lips. "I see you really can teach an old dog new tricks."

"When pigs fly," her father added thoughtfully.

Both his children groaned.

Chapter 19

Fairleigh's List

Late Octoberish—to do
- *go riding*
- *figure out a better way to escape my chamber when needed*
- *bribe stable master so I can ride Lady whenever I want*
- *do not leave Penrose*

> *- figure out a way for everyone to live at Penrose forever, especially Papa . . . and Georgiana*

Luck. It was amazing how poor Georgiana's blasted luck was on occasion. She'd never heeded all the superstitious advice Rosamunde's sister Sylvia, who was married to the handsome vicar in the village, had told her to follow. And Rosamunde was forever telling her that her own negligence in observing the old Cornish proverbs had led to a former decade of misery. And so

Georgiana could only blame herself for being in the unfortunate position of having to return to Penrose unexpectedly.

Georgiana looked at the grains of salt she had spilled on the table in Penrose's elegant dining room, threw them over her left shoulder, and said a prayer for good measure.

"Fairleigh," she muttered, "are you certain Grace isn't feeling well enough to join us?"

"No. She said her head felt like a huge pumpkin." The little girl piled three muffins onto her plate, unperturbed by Georgiana's ill ease. "And Papa said it would be better for her to wait one more day before they leave."

Quinn and Grace were supposed to have been gone by the time Georgiana arrived to collect Fairleigh. Georgiana would have sent a carriage for Fairleigh, but her father had given her a long list of things to do at Penrose—from retrieving an endless number of books Quinn was lending him to arranging several cartloads of hay, a bin of corn, three sacks of grain . . . and the list went on.

She was to do it all and return the next morning with Fairleigh. She sighed. So much for her overly dramatic recent good-bye to Penrose. Would she never be free of the place?

"Are the babies any better?" Fairleigh asked, while slathering an inordinately large amount of butter on one of the muffins.

"I saw Ata yesterday and she said the fevers had broken." She didn't add that the dowager had also suggested it was actually the duke who required the most care. He had been beside himself since the moment Caro and Henry had first sneezed a week ago.

"Will Ata and Sarah and Elizabeth be at Trehallow when we arrive tomorrow?"

"I don't know, dearest. Ata's note said she might come here, now that the babies are better. She wants to see how Grace fares."

"Well, she better come very early tomorrow morning, because Grace said she and Papa were going to leave no matter how ill she was." The little girl's lip suddenly quivered.

"What is it, sweetheart?"

"Oh, Georgiana, I don't want him to go away." She burst into tears. "Why won't he allow me to come with him? Grace said I could come, but Papa won't allow it. Said it was a house party for adults."

Georgiana rose and gathered Fairleigh in her arms. "Come, I have a long list of things to do and I need your help," she whispered in Fairleigh's soft curls. An idea popped into her head. "And I have a present for you."

Fairleigh lifted her tear-streaked face from Georgiana's soggy shoulder. "A present? What kind of present?"

"So much for being patient."

"It's not that. It's just that Grace has given me so many presents—pretty gowns, and pearl earrings, and embroidered cushions, and a pearl bracelet. Well, your present isn't pearls, is it?"

"Hmmm. No, there are no pearls."

"Oh, it's a horse, isn't it?" Her blue eyes were large and round.

Georgiana grasped her hand and hid a smile. "No, it's not a horse. But I shan't tell you now and ruin it." She just had to leave the house before Quinn appeared. Perhaps she could accomplish everything she needed to do without seeing him again. Perhaps this wouldn't be as unbearable as she had thought. "Come, I have something I've always wanted to show you. Then we have to get to work if we are ever to get everything done today."

They made their way to Loe Pool, and Georgiana dragged a small boat to the edge of the lake. After several false starts, Fairleigh learned all the basics and they slowly rowed to the island.

"Oh, I've always wanted to come here, but Father said it was too far for me to swim and he doesn't like rowboats."

Georgiana could guess why, and changed the subject. "Have you seen Oscar lately?" She had missed the otter.

"No. Father and I swim when it's warm enough, but we haven't seen him since you left." The little girl rested her oar on the edge of the boat. "Oh, I do wish you still lived here, Georgiana. It's so inconvenient. And it's not nearly as much fun without you here. Grace doesn't like to go fishing as often as you do."

The bottom of the boat hit the sandy beach of the tiny island and Georgiana carefully lifted her stiff limbs over the rim of the small vessel. "Hurry now," she urged. "The gift is inside."

Her eyes sparkling with excitement, Fairleigh was completely taken with the glass house. "Oh, this is the most beautiful place on Penrose. I shall ask Father if I can have this as my room next summer instead of those stuffy chambers next to his. This place is magical. I'm certain fairies must live here. Lake fairies." Fairleigh twirled, and light glinted from the myriad windows and illuminated the white blondeness of her hair. Georgiana had never seen the little girl so happy. She quickly retrieved the gift she had rashly decided to give her.

"Fairleigh, this is for you." She forced herself to place in Fairleigh's slender hands the poignant remnant from her past. The golden edges of the Lover's Eye brooch gleamed in the sunlight.

"Oh, Georgiana. Why, this is your beautiful brooch. The one you painted." The little girl looked at it in awe. "I'm not sure I'll be allowed to accept it. It's too . . ." She didn't appear able to find the right words.

"You are growing up," Georgiana said softly. "I am so proud of you, dearest. But I want you to have this. Perhaps it will help you miss your father less while he is traveling. But this is a secret between us. And you are only to wear it when he is away. The rest of the time you must hide it."

The little girl stared at the brooch and then at Georgiana. "It's Papa's eye, isn't it?" She stroked the tiny brooch reverently.

"Yes."

"But everyone thinks it is someone else's eye."

"Yes," Georgiana replied.

"Why did you paint it?"

"Because your Papa and I were very good friends and I missed him when he went away. But now I am all grown up and I want you to have it in case you miss him when you are apart. And the brooch setting is from my family, so you'll also have something to remember me."

Fairleigh's innocent, wide blue eyes gazed at her for a long moment. And Georgiana could have sworn that a glimmer of some ancient female calculating expression crossed her face before the little girl squelched it.

"Thank you, Georgiana. You are the very best. Now then, what is on your list of things to do today? We should get started, like you said. My list includes riding," Fairleigh said, drawing a rumpled paper from her pocket. "I will be allowed to bring Lady with me tomorrow, right? She would get lonely if I left her here."

Georgiana stroked Fairleigh's hair. "Of course, she can come. Oh, oh, look." She pointed at a whiskered snout breaking the rippling surface of the water. "Oscar is just there. Let's find him a treat."

"Does he like worms, Georgiana?"

Georgiana laughed. "I don't think so. But he *loves* that which eats worms. "

Fairleigh rushed out of the glass house to get a better look at the otter, her list dropped and forgotten. Georgiana knelt down to examine it, her heart heavy as she read the last notation: figure out a way for *everyone* to live at Penrose forever, especially Papa . . . and Georgiana.

* * *

Grace's drawn face filled Quinn with ill ease. "My dear, I know how much you long to leave, but I really don't think you'll be well enough to go tomorrow. There's no rush, you know. I shall write a note to the duchess explaining our delay."

"No," Grace replied, sitting up straighter on the long settee in her chamber. "I'm feeling much, much better. Ata's note mentioned the babies are recovering too." She took a sip of tea and Quinn noticed a slight quiver of the teacup as she brought it to her lips.

Quinn directed Mrs. Killen, who was hovering at the doorway, to bring a fresh pot of tea.

"And Georgiana has come all this way to collect Fairleigh. She will not feel right taking her tomorrow if we are still here. And I'm certain she has much to do at Trehallow."

Quinn stiffened at the mention of Georgiana's name.

"Are you certain Fairleigh should not come with us?" Grace asked gently. "You'll miss her so much—as will I."

"We won't be gone long. I'd thought you might enjoy the entertainments of a house party devoid of children." Quinn stood up and paced. God, how he wanted to get away from here. He needed time and space away from Penrose to resume his life. To form a new life with Grace. It wouldn't take long, he was sure of it. A few weeks away from here would do the trick. Then he would collect Fairleigh and the three of them could spend the season in London. After Parliament finished its sessions in late spring they'd tour the other Ellesmere estates.

There was a knock and Fairleigh's face appeared around the door.

Grace beckoned to the child. "Oh Fairleigh, do come and help me eat all these biscuits. Your father has been no help at all."

Fairleigh hopped onto the pale green settee, settling herself between the two of them. She bit into a chocolate biscuit, her face filled with delight. "Thank you, Grace."

Oh God, he was going to miss her too much. He kissed the top of her head. "Here, let me get that bit of chocolate on your cheek." He picked up a napkin and urged her to sit on his lap. "Ouch. What is that?"

Her eyes became very large as she jumped up and gripped the side of her gown. "Nothing."

"Fairleigh, what are you hiding in your pocket?"

She shook her head and looked at the carpet. "It's really nothing."

He put his hand, palm up, in front of her. "Give it to me right now. It's dangerous to carry fish hooks in your pocket."

She stood very still and he was forced to search her pocket himself. He withdrew a small piece of jewelry and leaned in to examine it more closely. He blinked. "Where did you get this brooch?"

"It was to be a secret. Georgiana gave it to me." Her large, innocent eyes filled with ill ease. "She said it was to remember *my Papa*."

Grace glanced at it and quickly looked away without a word.

"You may not keep it." He felt the marrow curdling in his bones.

Fairleigh burst into tears and he quickly hugged her fiercely to his breast.

"Oh, Papa, I wouldn't have accepted it if I'd known it would make you so mad."

"I'm sorry, sweetheart. I'm not angry with you. You're the dearest thing to me in the world. You are my daughter and I won't ever let anything or *anyone* come between us."

"But Papa, you don't understand. It's—"

"No, Fairleigh, no explanations. Now, have you seen to packing your dollies?" It took every effort to appear collected when every muscle screamed to destroy the damned brooch in as violent a fashion as possible. It represented every evil in his past.

Fairleigh murmured that she hadn't gathered her dolls and so he used the opportunity to escape both Grace and Fairleigh. At the doorway he turned to find Grace rearranging the skirt of her gown. He could only see the countess's lovely pale profile, but he had the distinct impression that a tear was balanced on her lower lashes.

Something stronger than compassion drove him from Grace and Fairleigh. Fear and anger twisted into a thin wire of pain that snaked through his body. He didn't stop to think. Didn't stop to plan. He acted on instinct alone and flew out of the room.

He would find Georgiana. And when he did he would end this thing that was between them. He had given her everything—had even given her his trust, just as he had been foolish enough to give his trust to Anthony and again to Cynthia. Fire raged in his palm. He released his grip on the brooch and saw a smear of blood in the center of his hand where the pin had pricked his skin.

He cursed both Anthony and Georgiana to hell and back as he stalked down the path to Little Roses, his fury growing with every step.

He found her among several stacks of books, a roll of twine in hand.

"Quinn!"

He stared at her through a shaft of light cutting across her father's study. And in that instant a thousand images sped through his mind: Anthony and Georgiana climbing trees, swimming, fishing, running, racing, eating cakes, and always falling all over each other with laughter in their eyes. The identical look in Fairleigh's eyes. His heart contracted in pain.

"Why did you do it?" His voice cracked with the strain.

"What are you talking—"

"Why would you give Fairleigh a likeness of your *husband*?" He couldn't even say Anthony's name, his hatred was so deeply embedded.

She lowered her eyes to a book she held and said not a word.

"Oh no. You will explain yourself. There'll be none of the shrinking violet here. How could you do it? How could you give my daughter a painting of the man who ruined my chance of happiness at every turn? Were you going to reveal the truth of her parentage, to boot?"

She would not look up.

"You refuse to answer. Even you cannot defend your audacious action. But isn't that the way you have always lived your life, Georgiana? You and Anthony always managed to avoid unpleasantness by not answering to anyone."

He ran his hand through his hair and realized it was shaking. "When I confided to you the secret that has plagued me for a decade, I was fool enough to think you wouldn't reveal what I told you to anyone."

She raised her eyes to his. A blaze of pain streaked through them. "A decade? You've been plagued with a secret for a mere decade?" She whispered, her voice quavering with emotion.

He ignored her. "Can't you see that by revealing I'm not her true father, it would only cause Fairleigh confusion and pain? I want her to live in a cocoon of security and love her entire life—unlike my own."

And she ignored him. "Let me assure you a decade is a trifle. Now, two decades is a bit more impressive. But I'm guessing that even that will seem like a drop in time when I'm staring at sixty years in my dish."

She wasn't making any sense at all, and her voice had grown in strength and was now bordering on hysteria. And suddenly his infamous control snapped.

A fire crackled in the grate. In his mind's eye he saw the brooch in the fire, the metal sizzling and dripping while Anthony's miniature painted eye burned into ash and only the tiny glittering jewels remained on the hearth.

With two long strides he was before the fire his arm drawn back.

"No!" She sobbed. "No. Don't you dare!" She was beside him, her fingers working his tightly clenched fist. "Oh God, Quinn. Please don't."

He immediately opened his fist and she took possession of it and gripped the ugly thing to her breast.

He was now numb to every emotion. Even anger had melted away in the face of her devotion to the man who had tormented him. "Fairleigh will be leaving with me tomorrow. You may take your leave of us now as I'm certain you've no wish to remain here."

Her eyes were closed tightly. "It's of you," she said barely above a whisper.

A log in the grate broke in two and a spray of sparks swirled.

Her lids parted to reveal dark, almost black eyes. Her breath rattled. "I painted it fifteen years ago—while I lay in bed the week after you left. It's *your* eye, not *his*." She paused and then rushed on. "Perhaps you're right. Perhaps I should burn it, since both you and Anthony hated it."

Now it was he who could not make his mouth open to save his life.

"I gave it to Fairleigh so she could have a part of you near while you went away with Grace. I'm certain she will be very excited about having Grace as a mother. I'm not sure she has told you or Grace this, but I did want to make sure you knew. And she can't wait to go to London and see the sites—especially the Tower. Grace and Fairleigh are so beautiful together, with their blonde hair and matching pale pink gowns and pearls. Soon no one will even remember that Grace is not her real mother." She spoke swiftly and without pause, like the ever-moving tide. "But I only beg of you not to forget to always propose adventures for her: riding and fishing and an amusement every day. She will not be happy only doing lessons and embroidery. But what am I saying? You know that now very well. You've changed back to the man I used to know and are the perfect father for a high-spirited girl such as Fairleigh. She is a very, very lucky child to have a father such as you and a mother such as Grace."

He held out his hand and she placed the brooch in it. A tiny eye stared back at him, slanted, arresting. He drew it closer. The barest hint of green edged the outer edge of the amber iris.

His heart slammed into his chest.

He looked up to find Georgiana gone.

He searched everywhere for her—he had to apologize. Her team and carriage were still in the stable. She could not have gone far, and her old injuries would prevent her from going anywhere very fast without a horse. But she held the advantage of knowing every corner of the estate even better than he did. There were miles of hedgerows, acres of long grasses along the beachhead, and no end to the number of trees. Three hours later, he wanted to keep going, but his lathered horse could not. Quinn negotiated a steep, winding path to the beach and then rode a short distance toward the rocky cliffs. He dismounted and climbed to a berm of sandy soil and the blessed shade of several wind-whipped pine trees.

Exhausted, he leaned against the rough bark of the tallest tree, the cliffs behind him. A cool, salty wind blew from the swirling morass of the dark blue ocean. The scent of wild gorse and pine teased his senses as despair filtered through every pore.

God. Nothing made any sense. It was *his* image? He retrieved the brooch from his pocket and looked at it again. His thumb felt a tiny indentation along the edge and he noticed a tiny catch. He released it to find a few strands of dark hair. A gust of wind carried the strands away before he could catch them; but he knew they were his own. They were certainly not Anthony's blond. He cursed his stupidity and returned the brooch to his pocket.

The familiar *cree-cree-cree* of a peregrine falcon caught his attention and he looked up to see the raptor fly onto a ledge. He turned quickly and realized he was very close to the place where Georgiana had fallen all those years ago.

Yes. There was the tree, almost impossible to recognize for it was denuded of all its greenery now, completely dead, unlike before. He swallowed convulsively when he saw the jagged remains of a limb many feet above. That was the one that had given way. He hadn't seen it break, had only come upon her as she was falling.

He could still remember the sickening sound of her body hitting branches in its descent, her petticoat and gown catching and tearing, only to leave her limbs exposed to such terrible injury. He even heard the awful whoosh of her breath as she hit the ground inches from his outstretched hands. And he could remember Anthony's panicked, high-pitched voice from the tree.

Unconsciously, Quinn gripped the strong, living trunk of a pine growing in the shadow of the tree that had caused her so much anguish and changed her life forever. He gazed upward and saw light filtering through the pine needles.

The falcon's scrape was high above and he was suddenly certain he would find a nestling despite the lateness of the season. He had never been so sure of anything in his life. He would retrieve a chick for her barren mews at Trehallow and then leave to fulfill his commitment to Grace.

It was the least he could do for Georgiana. She was so good that he was certain she would accept this peace offering, even if she could never bear to see him again after the awful things he had said to her. It would be a final gift to someone who had given so much of herself to him.

As he climbed the sap-smeared branches of the enormous pine, his mind sifted through his memories. His heart swelled again at the thought that she had cared enough that she had painted his eye to remember him after he had been sent away. *She had missed him.* Deeply.

And he had missed her.

Quinn repositioned his grip on a branch. Then stilled. Memories from so long ago poured over him, pounding the floodgates to his soul.

When he'd been sent away, been locked away, really, with all the other miserable Collager students at Eton, he had used to dream about her. Yet he'd tried to forget those sweet memories because Anthony had always been in those dreams as well.

He'd dreamed about smashing those damned windows in the fourth floor of the dormitory and flying back to Penrose to find her. And she was always waiting for him at the top of some far-flung cliff, her arms wide in greeting, her smile as dazzling as the happiness in her earthy brown eyes. He would capture her in his arms and swing her 'round and 'round until they were dizzy and they fell off the cliff embracing each other. Quinn had felt such happiness gazing into her eyes that he hadn't cared that they were falling, until they crashed to the sand and waves washed over them. Anthony would be waiting to pick up her crumpled form and walk away, leaving Quinn to be pulled out to sea.

But now Quinn realized he didn't care that Anthony had been in the dream. He'd always found happiness when he was with her, Anthony be damned.

While he had been away, he'd missed her innocent goodness, her laughter, and their shared love of nature, and adventure, and animals, and, yes, even painting. He'd forgotten they had used to paint together. They'd shared such a passion for life . . . for living.

He reached the level of the ledge in the cliff face and peered through the pungent pine needles. An angry-looking adult female guarded three downy white chicks in a scrape made of rough-hewn sticks.

He bit the corner of his lip. Perhaps the falcon would fly away at his approach. He inched along the branch and she screeched in outrage.

He stopped. In that instant, a piece of his spirit fell into place. A piece he'd been denying in order to avoid any chance of repeating the past, where broken trust had plagued his every connection—and scarred his soul as effectively as the accident had scarred Georgiana's body.

He loved her.

No, it was something so much stronger than that. Something he couldn't put into words. She owned his heart and always would. He had been so numb to every emotion that he had been blind.

He had little warning before the tiercel, obviously the mate of the female in front of him, struck, its sharp talons scoring his sleeves and throwing him off balance.

Chapter 20

Mr. Brown's List

October 26—to do
- *finish packing*
- *good-byes to Mrs. Killen and others*
- *a pint with the gamekeeper*
- *last look at ledgers*
- *new lock on carriage house—key to Quinn*

    - arrange a carriage seat for . . . a lass if she accepts my offer

One could only stay in hiding for so long. And one could only walk for so long—especially with an aching knee.

And she was freezing.

Besides, Georgiana knew she was being ridiculous. It was not as if he didn't already know the state of her pathetic heart. It was just that she didn't particularly like acting the fool twice over.

As she limped toward Penrose's kitchen entrance, she hoped she would not have to face Quinn again before she left. And she prayed she was making the right decision.

The housekeeper was conferring with Cook in hurried tones. "Pardon me, Mrs. Killen, but has his lordship returned?"

"No, Lady Ellesmere—" the housekeeper said. "But—"

"I'm so sorry, Mrs. Killen, but I must see to something immediately." She quickly made her way to the upper floors, unable to stay another moment.

Georgiana leaned heavily against the railing. How she had once loved this house. The wide, polished mahogany railings were so familiar. She had helped Mrs. Killen polish them as a child. She had even slid down them with Anthony when no one was looking. Her fingers traced the pattern of the newel post at the top while she stared at the door that was supposed to have been her chamber as Anthony's wife—the one she had specifically designated for the countess.

She forced herself to walk to the door. She must have a word with Grace, make certain she was recovering, and then gently insist that it would be better if Fairleigh went to the house party. She had no idea if Grace had been present when Quinn had discovered the brooch. She would smooth things over as best she could if that was true. And finally, she would tell Grace that pressing matters required her return to Trehallow.

She knocked on the door.

Silence.

"Grace? Grace, may I come in?"

Silence.

She knocked again and when there was no response, Georgiana eased the door open.

The chamber was in complete disarray, the bed coverings twisted in a heap on the floor. An abandoned, open trunk yawned before the bed, a drift of white frothy linen exposed. On a table, a vase of flowers lay on its side, water dripping from the lip of the marble tabletop onto a darkening spot of carpet below. A single yellow rose rested on a pillow in the middle of the bed.

A note lay under it.

Georgiana peered toward the adjoining sitting room and then crossed the room. Water from the rose's stem had pooled on the black ink lettering, making her name barely visible. Heart pounding, she quickly blotted the drops before breaking the seal.

My dear Georgiana,

When we spoke about love and marriage at Little Roses, there was something I did not fully understand. We agreed that a marriage where one loves and the other doesn't is intolerable. Experiencing unrequited love makes that point very clear in a person's mind. The only difference of opinion we had was of the happiness I am certain two people can find in a marriage of convenience for the mutual goal of simple companionship. You suggested nothing could induce you to marry again except a love match.

I have come to realize there is something possibly worse than unrequited love. It is when a man says he is looking for a marriage of convenience yet refuses to see he might indeed be in love with someone else. Marriage to such a man would be worse than intolerable.

And so I must leave. Mr. Brown has been kind enough to offer me a seat in his carriage.

You are so good I know you and Ata and everyone will grieve for me. But please don't. You see, my heart is not engaged, so I do not suffer. And please don't think you owe me some sort of apology.

Georgiana, he is in love with you. I don't know why he can't grasp what is in front of him. But I think if you have the courage to tell him what I now believe you might still feel for him, all will fall into place. And I wish you both every happiness.

My dearest friend, I am not sad. I am not angry with anyone. I am only discomforted to stay in a place where I do not belong.

Your devoted sister of the heart,
Grace

Georgiana scanned the pages three times before the words became so blurry she couldn't go on. At some point her knees gave out and she sank to the carpet.

What had she done?

She should never have painted his eye. She should never have returned here. She should never have entrusted that brooch to Fairleigh.

She would never take pride in her supposed good sense again.

Georgiana crumpled the note and leaned against the slender tooled bedpost. She would shake and shake Grace if her friend were before her. She would tell Grace how wrong she was, how Quinn was not in love with her and how he did indeed desire a marriage of convenience—with Grace. And she would tell Grace how very foolish she was being.

An odd yet familiar three-beat gait sounded from the corridor beyond. Georgiana looked up to find Ata at the door, cane in hand. She was never so grateful to see that sallow, wrinkled face.

"What's this?" The tiny dowager's penciled-in eyebrows were raised in concern. "What is going on here? I just arrived from Amberley. The babies are much recovered, by the by. But everyone is at sixes and sevens below. Can't get a clear answer from anyone, even that nice Mrs. Killen."

"Grace is gone," Georgiana whispered.

"Eh? What did you say? My hearing is usually excellent."

"Grace has left," she said louder.

"Ah . . . so I've missed them? Hmmm. I'd thought they would wait till morning to get a full day's start. It's too bad, but I couldn't leave the babies before now. Oh, I wanted so much to kiss Quinn and my beautiful girl good-bye, and to give her a special bridal present. I'd wanted to—" Ata stopped and Georgiana could feel her scrutiny.

"Why is this room in such a sorry state? Looks like the French army passed through . . . What's that you've got?"

Georgiana looked at her hand as if it weren't part of her body. The crushed missive was still in her fingers. "I've ruined everything," she said faintly.

"Nonsense," Ata said firmly and turned and shut the door before walking to her and leaning down to grasp the note.

Georgiana made no move to stop her. She simply closed her eyes, unable to witness the unbearable sadness that would wash over the dowager duchess she loved like the grandmother she'd never known. She hated to disappoint her. Ill ease and guilt thickened the lengthening shadows in the chamber until Georgiana was numb to everything.

She became aware that Ata was kneeling beside her, and a warmth covered her ice-cold fingers. It was Ata's own withered hand.

"My God. She left with Mr. Brown? I hadn't known he was leaving so soon." Ata's sad voice held something more than concern. "And is all the rest of this true? Is there something between you and Quinn?"

"No. I wish she were here so I could tell her she is entirely wrong. She would have found peace and companionship with Quinn, and he with her. I'm certain of it. I would only be miserable with him and could only serve as a constant reminder of his horrid past."

"You're willing to give up the man you love?"

"You don't understand."

"So you do love him," she said in wonder.

"Ata. That's not the point. He doesn't love me."

"Really?"

"Really."

"You know, Georgiana, it is a little unnerving to listen to you."

"Why is that?"

"Because I recall having a similar conversation fifty years ago with my godmother." Ata tried to caress Georgiana's arm, but her damaged hand was bent in an unnatural state. "And now, my dear, I understand why my godmother was so impatient with me—although I shall try, very hard, mind you, not to make the mistake she made with me. You see, I've recently learned that I'm always wrong when it comes to matters of the heart. No—you are not to disagree with me. It might be the only time you hear me admit I'm wrong, so you might as well enjoy it. Although you will give me your word before we leave this room that you will never repeat that I admitted to ever being wrong."

Georgiana couldn't help but smile at Ata's words. She couldn't stop herself from embracing the woman and then bursting into tears.

"There, there," Ata murmured against her hair. "I've never known you to cry. We are both too practical to give in to tears. Take my handkerchief."

Georgiana almost smiled when she saw Ata's ridiculously impractical chartreuse lace handkerchief.

"Now then, what are we to do about all this? I have an idea. Let's try the very opposite of what I would do. Let's follow Grace's advice, shall we?"

Georgiana dabbed at her face and then carefully refolded the handkerchief. "You're not suggesting I—"

"That's precisely what I'm—"

"I already have. Twice. *In a fashion*."

"And what does that mean?"

"I told him I loved him . . . after the ball, and then today he realized my brooch held a miniature of *his* eye, not my husband's."

"And he said nothing?" Ata replied, eyes huge.

"Correct."

"I'll string him up by his toes."

A hysterical gurgle of emotion was stuck in her throat. "If you and Rosamunde were not already related I would swear you should be. Oh Ata, I'm so, so sorry. I've made a mess of everything and ruined the happiness of so many people. You would think that someone who plans every waking moment of her life would be better at avoiding disaster."

A hint of a smile appeared in Ata's face. "Perhaps, but I've learned that sometimes good can come from disaster. It was true with Luc and Rosamunde, you know—although, in my case, it has never been true." She glanced at her withered hand and then rested it on Georgiana's injured knee. "We both have had to endure pain and the harsher realities of life—something most people do not. I'm too old to go back and change the direction of my life. But please, Georgiana, I beg

you not to do as I have done. Follow Grace's advice
and bare your heart yet again. Even though you
are the least cowardly person I know, I am guessing you were craven in very clearly expressing
yourself to Quinn. And remember, selflessness—
a very necessary ingredient for mothers—has its
place, but it has no place here. You grab that Quinn
Fortesque by his neck cloth and tell him you love
him, will always love him, and will not let him go
whether he likes it or not. And then you kiss him
within an inch of his life. You do know how to
kiss him properly, don't you?"

"Ata!"

"No, we'll have none of that. I might not know
precisely how to do it, I'm sorry to admit, but I did
spy Rosamunde and Luc in an intimate embrace
once and I would suggest you—"

"Stop!"

"Well, if you're going to do this, it had better be
done well, or what is the point?"

"I know how to kiss." Heat tinged her cheeks.

"I see." There was a long pause as Ata searched
her face as knowingly as a mother glances at the
tart-smeared cheeks of a penitent child. "Well
then, perhaps *you* could tell me what precisely
happens when a man takes you in his arms and
puts his—"

"Absolutely not! Ata, we are not having this
discussion."

"When I formed my little secret society, it was
my hope that it would become an intimate circle
of friends who would take comfort in confiding
in each other and finding happiness together."

She looked down. "But no one has *ever* confided in me. I think everyone thinks I'm too old to care about romantic love. But it's just the opposite, you see. When you've never experienced it, you crave it."

"Oh, all right. What do you want to know?"

A huge smile broke out on her tiny face. "What does it feel like to kiss a man you love with all your heart?"

Georgiana coughed discreetly. "But surely you and Mr. Brown—" She stopped. "Or the late duke?"

"No. Never. At the tender age of sixteen my parents never allowed me alone with any gentleman. And Lucifer—well, no . . . I've never experienced any of it." The older lady looked at her expectantly.

Georgiana pondered the question and said softly, "If you've ever dreamed you were flying, that's what it feels like the most." She gazed at the darkening light from the window. "Imagine a nestling perched on the edge of a precipice looking out at the world for the first time—just a step away from deathly danger or heaven in the clouds. Looking into the eyes of the man you love and reaching for him takes the same amount of courage a chick uses, I imagine, to leap off that cliff."

"And then?"

"And then you jump and suddenly realize you are not alone. You're flying with someone who is cradling you in his arms, protecting you from the rocks below and carrying you to the clouds above." She grasped Ata's hands. "And you never, ever, ever want to let go. You want him to hold you forever. And you want to cleave to him and protect him from falling too. And carry him beyond the clouds to feel the warmth of the sun."

There was a long silence before Georgiana raised her eyes to Ata's. Tears streamed down the older lady's face.

"Georgiana, *go to him.* Go to him now, before it's too late. Don't make my mistake. *Please* don't. Fly away with him."

"Scotland?" Quinn said with shock upon his return to the great house. *Georgiana was gone to Scotland?*

"Yes, my lord. Her ladyship was very clear. I was to inform you she was gone to the north country. She said she would have left a note but there wasn't time to waste as the gentleman was waiting for her and it was growing dark."

"What?" A cold tentacle of fear reached out and gripped his spine almost as harshly as he gripped the new footman's forearm as they stood in the front hall. "What else did she say?"

"That she would send a note as soon as they crossed the border—as soon as they reached Gretna Green."

Gretna Green. He closed his mind against the pain and vaguely remembered Miles Langdon saying something during the gathering at Trehallow about taking Georgiana to Gretna Green. *Bloody hell.* She would *not* be so reckless.

He heard a noise and turned to find Ata carefully negotiating the wide staircase in her danger-ously high heels, book in hand. In three long steps he was before her, gripping her small arms. "How could you have let Georgiana go?"

"You know, Quinn," Ata said in an annoy-ingly all-knowing manner much like her devil-ish grandson's, "I've always liked you. And I've always thought you quite clever. But despite your intelligence, you are about as perceptive as every other man I know. Which means you're about as insightful as a brick."

He ignored her. "When did they leave? Perhaps I can catch them." The chick snuggled against his breast in his coat peeped.

"What was that noise? And why is your coat ripped to ribbons?"

"Nothing. Answer my questions," he urged. "Please. Ata, I beg you."

"If I do, will you promise me that you will not muck this up any further? Will you promise to listen to her? Will you promise to make her happy? Will you promise to have the courage to jump off that cliff for her, and protect her and carry her into the clouds, and—"

Suddenly the chick scrambled inside his pocket and poked its head out.

Ata's eyes became as big and dark as a worn ha'penny. "Tell me that's not a falcon chick." And she began to laugh, her eyes watering and crin-kling in the corners.

He shook her, all the while horrified that he might hurt this tiny paragon. He didn't have time for her ridiculous form of humor.

"All right, all right. I'll tell you. It's *Grace* who has left, not Georgiana. Mr. Brown has taken Grace to Scotland with him."

His chest sagged in relief and he could finally breathe again for the first time in many minutes. He loosed his grip on Ata. "I'm sorry, I hope I didn't hurt you. You see—"

"I see very well, young man. I see a man who had better have the diplomatic muscle required to fix this."

"The sooner you tell me where Georgiana is, the sooner I can go after Grace."

"No. You are not to go after the countess. Grace has changed her mind and will not have you. She has decided the two of you will not suit. She is crying off."

"I would still go after her, Ata. I won't see her hurt."

Ata tilted her head. "We shall see, Quinn. For now, I think distance is the answer. And time. But only a little. And then you and I will decide what is best."

"We'll take the phaeton."

"Will I be permitted to drive?" Ata asked without missing a beat.

"If you'll agree to leave sooner versus later."

"If you insist."

She smiled radiantly and then reached for the downy head of the chick. "How adorable."

The nestling pecked her.

"Ouch! I can't afford to lose the use of another hand, silly creature. And here I was hoping you'd make friends with my canary."

"I rather think he'd prefer to eat your canary."
He stopped. "Ata, where is she?"

Ata sucked her digit, a mischievous light in her
old eyes. "I was just reading this lovely poem by
Herbert Trench. I think it might help. You see, I
made a promise not to tell you where Georgiana
is, for she wants to be alone. She is so hardheaded,
that one." She stopped and cleared her throat
guiltily. "Lucky for you I didn't promise not to
hint."

He grasped the book she offered and opened it
to the marked page.

She comes not when Noon is on the roses—
Too bright is the Day.
She comes not to the Soul till it reposes
From work and play.
But when Night is on the hills, and the great
   Voices
Roll in from Sea,
By starlight and candle-light and dreamlight
She comes to me.

Georgiana rose up from the soft pallet in the
glass house in the middle of Loe Pool and pushed
aside the blanket. She'd hoped she would find
a measure of peace here. It had been too late to
return to Trehallow when she'd left Ata. At least
he would not find her here. She would not have to
face further humiliation.

She stood up and walked to one of the myriad
panes around her to watch the fog unfurl across
the dark lake waters. On the edge of the cool night

with the stars glittering all around her above, the creeping mist promised a hoarfrost on the morn. It would be the first of the season and Georgiana was grateful she would witness it. This place of her heart would become transformed into a tiny, white, mystical kingdom.

She wrapped her arms around herself and for the last time imagined him coming toward her. It had been her favorite dream—the image of him rowing a boat toward her had sustained her through the years. But she realized now it had been such a silly, far-fetched fantasy.

She no longer needed dreams to make her happy. Trehallow made her happy. The last two weeks had proven that. She had a beautiful place to live, which she would rebuild and make prosperous once more. And she would repay him. And when she was done she would throw away all those endless lists.

She was going to live life, not plan it.

She leaned forward.

There was something moving in the swirling mist. She opened the door and squinted into the night.

God, it was he.

Her reaction to the reality of her dream was nothing like anything she had imagined in the past. There was no warm, dreamy excitement enveloping her. There was no feeling of unbearable joy.

There was simply sheer panic, while her heart raced within her.

She just couldn't trust herself to hold back any

more. She wasn't sure she could be noble. She feared she'd be unable to rely on sensible platitudes when he was before her in the flesh.

She tried to remind herself of the certain misery she would face being with a man who did not love her passionately. She had been in the exact reverse situation when she married Anthony—and it had been next to impossible, the single evening they had shared.

If she gave in to her dreams, they would both have to pretend for the rest of their lives. She would have to pretend she was less in love than she was and Quinn would have to pretend he loved her more than he did. It would be intolerable.

The full moon glittered a path on the wavelets. Long moments later the boat hit the tiny island and Quinn secured his boat next to hers.

Her heart in her throat, Georgiana quickly seated herself on the bench, the only other piece of furniture in the tiny house other than the pallet and a small table.

The shadow of his giant hawkish form fell across the doorway. She could hear his labored breath and then she breathed in that evocative scent—rosemary and sage and cedar and *him*.

She spread her fingers wide, gripped her knees, and stared at her hands.

"Georgiana . . ."

She heard the sound of the door closing softly, his footfalls coming toward her. And all at once he was crouched in front of her and she saw his hands covering hers and she closed her eyes against the sensations it caused.

"Georgiana, won't you look at me?"

She could not.

He sighed. "For so long people have suggested I have a certain talent for negotiation, of easily finessing difficult situations to the best resolution." He stroked her work-worn hands. "But, in this case, I'll admit that I'm terrified of making a mistake, of not expressing myself clearly, of not convincing you. And so, I've made a list . . ."

"A list?" She concentrated on keeping her voice even. "A list of what?"

"A list of all the reasons why you must marry me."

"No, please," she said, her voice raw. She closed her eyes. "I beg you."

"Georgiana, I must tell you. I only wish I'd had more time to fashion a more eloquent list. But I feared I wouldn't find you and I was very worried. And I couldn't stand the thought of you not knowing these things right away."

"Not knowing what?" She finally raised her head and looked at him. He was as achingly handsome as always. There was nothing remarkable to any one of his features, but it was the arrangement of them—the broad forehead with the even hairline, the high cheekbones with gaunt cheeks below, the straight nose, noble profile, and the hint of a cleft in his chin—that created such an unforgettable face.

"All the reasons I need you." He reached up and moved a lock of her hair from her eyes. "Actually, that's not what I meant to say. It's a list of all the reasons I *want* you."

Her breath hitched as he extracted a wrinkled paper from his greatcoat pocket and a rose fell to the ground.

She picked it up.

"Oh, that's for you, although I know it won't do much for my cause. You never seemed overly impressed by all the others I left at your door."

Her breath caught. "It was you?"

"At first I thought I was bringing them to bring you some joy. But now I realize there was something more to it. I kept arriving later and later in the day, hoping you would catch me and it would endear me to you." He stopped and looked back down at the list.

A lump formed in her throat.

"Well, then, first." He cleared his throat. "I've always admired your character above everyone else's. You are honest, hardworking, extraordinarily gifted with animals and children. You're courageous, generous, kindhearted, and you try to find goodness in everyone and everything."

He gazed at her for a moment and then continued. "Second, you are *beautiful*." He held up a staying hand when she tried to speak. "No, you are more than that. If I could only describe what I saw, what I felt, when I saw you standing in this lake, water dripping off your shoulders, and off the ends of your braids and eyelashes, and well, everywhere else. I cannot imagine anyone ever tempting me as you did at that moment and every moment after."

"Quinn, I appreciate your kindness in telling

me all this, but I know why you're here and I would really prefer that you stop now."

"And why do you think I'm here other than the fact that I am trying my very hardest to convince you to marry me?"

She rubbed her eyes in weariness. "Because Grace has left and Ata has probably shown you that nonsensical letter. And now you think I expect a proposal and you don't want to disappoint me. But Grace was wrong and I am perfectly happy. How could I not be, at Trehallow? And you provided it all for me. I know it. And it is more than was ever expected in my wildest dreams. I shall be content there for the rest of my life."

"Just listen, please?" When she did not respond, he pursed his lips and lowered his gaze to the page, which appeared to tremble slightly before he slowly crumpled it and threw it across the room and gripped his forehead with his hands.

"I told you it isn't necessary."

He grasped her arms and pulled her up to stand in front of him. He dragged his fingertips up her arms, past her shoulders and neck to cup her face. "Georgiana . . . I love you. I'm in love with you."

"No," she whispered. "Don't lie to me. Oh, please don't."

"I love you. And I don't care if Anthony is first in your heart. I don't care if you only dream of him at night. It will be enough to hold you in my arms during the day and each night before you fall asleep."

Something made a *cheep-cheep* sound, but he kept talking without pause. "I know that you at least care for me—that you love me—even if it is not the same sort of passion you reserve in your heart for him. I know I sound like a wretched sod, but you see, Georgiana, I just don't care anymore. All I know is that I don't want to live my life without you by my side. I don't want to wake up each morning without your exquisite face on the pillow beside mine."

She exhaled when she realized the pain in her side was a hitch she'd gained by not breathing.

"And I shall promise to never say an unkind word about the man you've so faithfully loved."

"You know," she said finally, "you didn't have to say all that."

"I don't underst—"

"When I saw you coming across the pool I tried to tell myself I could refuse you. But in my heart I knew I would be too tempted and I wouldn't be able to turn you away again. All you had to do was simply insist that you would not take no for an answer. You didn't have to add all the trimmings. My heart has always been yours. I told you my feelings in the dell."

"Your loyal friendship has been something I've cherished my whole life."

"Damn you, Quinn," she whispered. "This has absolutely nothing to do with friendship."

He paled. And she saw for the first time the raw vulnerability of the great man before her.

She gazed into his haunted eyes. "I've been in love with you since the very first time I saw you. I was herding sheep and you came over a hill and smiled and suddenly I couldn't feel the rain that had started to fall. And . . . and after that it just got worse. A lot worse."

He pulled her roughly into his arms and rested his cheek on her head. "Tell me," he pleaded. "Please, tell me. I need to hear it all."

She felt him take a shuddering breath. "As every year passed a little bit of hope died—the hope that you would one day come to love me. The more I tried to impress you, the more I fell in love with you. I knew you would only ever look at me as a silly young girl—that my feelings were futile. And then when we became older I realized that what I felt for you, Anthony felt for me. And he saw how much I loved you. It tortured him to know that my heart was yours, not his. I finally understood it all the day of the accident, when I told him I wanted to retrieve a falcon nestling for a birthday gift for you since you didn't have one of your own and you loved them."

"What are you saying?" His voice was hoarse and he had pulled back to stare at her.

"The bird was for *you*. Anthony admitted to me later that you warned him the tree was unsafe but he had planned to save me if I fell. He was right beneath me. He had thought it would endear him to me. I know," she said. "The ridiculous machinations of a besotted fourteen-year-old mind at work. But you see, I was just as besotted by you, so I understood. And I forgave him."

He had a pained expression and she stroked his roughened face. "What is it?"

"I was not as generous as you. I never forgave him for telling his father it was my fault."

Pain flooded her. "No. Please tell me he did not—"

"It is over and done with, Georgiana," he interrupted and shook his head sadly. "I only tell you this because there should be no more secrets between us. And I understand now why he did it. If he felt half the anxiety I feel right now, I can understand his desperation to have you for himself."

They were inches apart and he cradled her head with reverence and rained kisses on her until she couldn't speak with the emotions roiling inside. She closed her eyes and tilted her head until warm lips covered her own. A storm of emotion gathered and almost broke until a vague sound intruded.

Cheep-cheep-CHEEEEP.

She drew away abruptly. "What *is* that?"

He eased open one side of his greatcoat. A small bundle of white down was revealed and a tiny black beady eye stared at her. Hungrily.

"Oh my Lord," she breathed. "Where did you find him?"

"He's yours." He slipped off his greatcoat, revealing a dark blue coat, which was slashed in numerous places. "I retrieved him from the cliffs as a peace offering. I'm so sorry for everything I accused you of, Georgiana."

The baby raptor peeped again.

"He's hungry," Georgiana murmured.

"No, he's not. I fed him almost an entire horse before coming." He smiled, a look of intense love spreading across his features as he gazed at her, and Georgiana felt herself being swept away by a current of desire. She longed to rush back into his arms.

But he lowered himself to the bench to make a nest of his greatcoat and placed the bird in the middle. And watching his care of this helpless bird, she realized it wasn't his scent or his voice that had always mesmerized her. It was his generous spirit.

"He's just impatient," he said, straightening.

"For what?" Georgiana asked shyly.

"He wants to fly," he whispered, then nuzzled Georgiana's neck lovingly. "And I know just how he feels. *Come to me, Georgiana. Please.*"

Those words . . . the ones she had wished for, for so long. They caressed her senses.

He kissed her then, not bothering to wait for an answer. And she was swept into a maelstrom of pure yearning. His mouth toyed with her lips, drawing long kisses from her, one after another, until she wasn't sure when one kiss ended and the next began.

She reveled in loosing all the fierce love she had hidden from him over the years, and he accepted it from her like a starving man and returned it measure for measure. The taste, the touch, the scent of him called forth a great roaring within her to answer his demands.

He drew his mouth over the column of her neck down to the edges of her simple gray gown, stroking his hands down her slender frame as if to reassure himself that she was there for him. It was as if he wanted to imprint her form in his mind while she twined her fingers in his hair.

He tugged at her gown and all the trimmings underneath until everything lay in a pool at her feet so he could lay claim to the sensitive skin he couldn't seem to stop tasting. And all the while, his warm hands touched her, stroked her, petted her, with an almost desperate need to give her pleasure.

All of a sudden he stilled. "What was that?"

A loud mewling came from across the lake.

With the last of her rational thought, she leaned forward to help him ease off the rest of his clothing. "Your cat."

"My what?"

"You heard me. She's been bawling at every corner of Trehallow ever since you disappeared. No one can sleep for all the noise." She delighted in caressing him freely and stroking his hair. "So I brought her here to be with you."

"Well at least one of us is not afraid to tell everyone how we feel." He leaned back and smiled at her. The kind of smile she had loved in their youth. He then grasped her hand from his head and brought it to his lips. "Georgiana, you must promise me you'll never hide your feelings, your wants, your needs from me ever again."

"All right." She paused. "I want you to kiss me."

"Of course, my darling."

"And I need you to love me as I do you."

"There's no question."

"And finally, I want us both to make things right for Grace. I don't know how, and I don't know—"

"I'm leaving with Ata much sooner than I can bear the idea of being parted from you."

"You know you're becoming remarkably skilled at interruption."

"And this is my favorite method . . ." He trailed more kisses down her shoulder and nipped her. "Oh God, I can't stop. You're like springtime and rain and a rose garden at night—and I don't ever want to let go of you ever again."

"Then don't, my love. Come to me."

And with that he lifted her as if she were a feather in the summer breeze and drew her down onto the narrow pallet with him above her. His hands, his mouth, his touch were everywhere and he groaned each time she urged him closer.

It seemed an eternity since they had last touched and she was dizzy from wanting. He was driving her wild with his patient, slow seduction.

He stared at her breasts reverently and then teased them to heightened sensitivity by his touch and his lips.

Finally when she couldn't bear another moment, he hooked a hand under one knee, nudged her thighs farther apart and drove his hard thickness deep, deep inside of her with one long, bold movement. His length kissed her womb—as if he were trying to imprint himself on her forevermore. The pleasure raged inside of her. As he began the ancient push-pull of passion, she felt such overwhelming joy rush through her that she thought she might burst from it.

Suddenly he withdrew, breathless with passion, and rested his forehead against hers.

"Georgiana . . . I had meant to wait. Had meant to tell you again and again what was in my heart until you promised. I can't go on until I know for certain. You will marry me, won't you? You never promised." He wore such a look of desperate love and uncertainty on his face. A look she had seen so many times on her own face in her tiny mirror in her room.

She smiled. "Well, how can I not marry you? You wanted a marriage of convenience and I can't think of anything more convenient than discovering we both love each other."

He breathed a sigh of relief and kissed her forehead. "My love, my dearest, dearest love. How I love thee." He appeared years younger at this moment in time—more like the boy she had known but with the seriousness of the man he had become.

She kissed his temple, insanely happy to be able to unleash her love for him. "I've waited so long to hear those words. And all the days, months, and years make them all the sweeter."

He brushed one last potent kiss upon her lips and gave himself fully to her again when Georgiana arched heavenward.

She stared into the inky night sky and gazed at the stars all around them as rapture overtook them both, flinging them into the thready clouds above to soar with the wind.

Epilogue

Ata's list

November 15—to do
- _Discuss menus with Mrs. Killen_
- _Casually find out if Mr. Grayson Wilde is in want of a wife. Very casually._
- _Arrange to go driving with Sarah and Elizabeth_
- _Visit Luc & Rosamunde—don't forget presents for babies_
- _Write a letter to Mr. Brown. Read it many, many times before posting_

Dear Mr. Brown,

You shall write to me at once and tell me precisely where you have taken my darling girl. How could you take her away? Grace Sheffey has always been much like a very special goddaughter to me.

I'm not certain I can forgive you for this. And I was just starting to think, mind you, only a particle of a smidgeon of a thought, that I might consider in a more favorable light what you told me in the phaeton.

But I won't do so unless you bring her back. Grace needs me right now—much more so than ever before. I fear if I'm not with her, she might simply give up on securing happiness altogether or, heaven forbid, do something very rash. What could you possibly have been thinking to take her to Scotland? And at winter's onset?

You are to keep an eye on her every moment of every day. And if I hear anything about someone getting lost in one of those deathly bogs or freezing fogs, I will string you up using Grace's strands of pearls.

You must bring her back to me. I can't stand it a moment longer.

If I don't receive an express from you shortly, Quinn and I have agreed to take his phaeton, which is fully repaired—quite nicely by the by—and we will drive to Scotland to find you both.

I put my faith in you once, long ago, to my everlasting detriment. I might be willing to put my faith in you again. Please, please don't disappoint me. I'm too old for disappointments.

From your lass,
Ata

P.S. Georgiana and Quinn are to be married by Special License. It is all very convenient as Sarah, Elizabeth and I are to reside at Penrose indefinitely while Quinn and Georgiana oversee the renovations at Trehallow. Grayson Wilde is proving an *exceptional steward. But John . . . he is not the same as you.*

The old lady flitted the feathered edge of her quill against her pursed lips and smiled. That should do the trick quite nicely.

Flying. That's what Georgiana had said. *Kissing was like flying.* She just hoped these old wings could stand the strain.

But they were willing. They were *very* willing.

AVON

978-0-06-052513-2

978-0-06-087137-6

978-0-06-084798-2

978-0-06-124110-9

978-0-06-089251-7

978-0-06-137321-3

Visit www.AuthorTracker.com for exclusive
information on your favorite HarperCollins authors.

Available wherever books are sold, or call 1-800-331-3761 to order.

ATP 0308